Deadly Affair

LUCINDA BRANT BOOKS

— *Alec Halsey Mysteries* —

Deadly Engagement

Deadly Affair

Deadly Peril

Deadly Kin

— *Salt Hendon Books* —

Salt Bride

Salt Redux

—*The Roxton Family Saga* —

Noble Satyr

Midnight Marriage

Autumn Duchess

Dair Devil

Proud Mary

Satyr's Son

Eternally Yours

Forever Remain

'Quizzing glass and quill, into my sedan chair and away — the 1700s rock!'

Lucinda Brant is a *New York Times*, *USA Today*, and *Audible* best-selling author of award-winning Georgian historical romances and mysteries. Her books are renowned for wit, drama and a happily ever-after. She has a degree in history and political science from the Australian National University and a post-graduate degree in education from Bond University, where she was awarded the Frank Surman Medal.

Noble Satyr, Lucinda's first novel, was awarded the $10,000 Random House/Woman's Day Romantic Fiction Prize, and she has twice been a finalist for the Romance Writers' of Australia Romantic Book of the Year. All her novels have garnered multiple awards and become worldwide bestsellers.

Lucinda lives in the middle of a koala reserve, in a writing cave that is wall-to-wall books on all aspects of the Eighteenth Century, collected over 40 years—Heaven. She loves to hear from her readers (and she'll write back!).

lucindabrant@gmail.com

A GEORGIAN HISTORICAL MYSTERY

Alec Halsey Mysteries Book Two

Lucinda Brant

A Sprigleaf Book
Published by Sprigleaf Pty Ltd

Deadly Affair: A Georgian Historical Mystery

Editing & proofing: Martha Stites & Rob Van De Laak
Cover art and photography: Larry Rostant
Design, and formatting: Sprigleaf
Cover model: Dan Cook

Typeset in Adobe Garamond Pro.

Also in ebook, audiobook, and other languages.

ISBN 978-0-9872430-6-5

10 9 8 7 6 5 4 3 2 (i) I

for

Pete

ONE

LONDON, AUTUMN 1763

ALEC HALSEY HAD ACCEPTED SIR CHARLES WEIR'S DINNER invitation on the assumption he was the only guest. Now, standing in the politician's drawing room surrounded by a dozen unfamiliar faces, he found himself in the midst of a party political dinner. The other guests were all in some way connected to the government, come together to celebrate the fifth anniversary of Sir Charles's election to Parliament, not career diplomats in the Foreign Department like Alec. The guest of honor, the Duke of Cleveley, twice First Lord of the Treasury and the present Foreign Secretary, had yet to descend among them, and Alec supposed this was why the double doors to the dining room remained closed.

Wine glass in hand, Alec sidled to the sash window that overlooked Arlington Street, and turned his back on the crowded and noisy room. He disliked gatherings of this sort. Too intimate. In a faceless crowd, one could remain anonymous and still enjoy the evening's entertainment. Here everyone knew his family's history, had devoured every scandalous detail in the London newssheets about the macabre circumstances surrounding the murder of his estranged brother. Despite the coroner's open verdict, it was Alec whom society blamed for his brother's death, thus condemning the newly-elevated Marquess Halsey to a lifetime of suspicion.

Why had he returned to the city? He should have remained in Kent, where he had spent the seven months since his brother's death resurrecting the family estate. He should be visiting his tenants and seeing to their needs, not wasting time rubbing shoulders with overfed, opinionated politicians, and their parasitic hangers-on, all of whom avoided his eye. There was so much for him to do and learn about his unwanted inheritance that he hardly knew where to begin.

He sipped at the wine and stared down at a sedan chair come to rest on the steps of Horace Walpole's townhouse, and ruminated on fate. He had spent most of his adult life on the periphery of Polite Society, a diplomat on the Continent speaking in foreign tongues. His estranged brother's untimely death changed his well-ordered life forever. Did he want to run an estate and take his seat in the Lords? He knew so little about either that a winter posting to St. Petersburg held more appeal. What was he supposed to do with a Marquessate he did not in the least want and one his peers considered he did not deserve? Yet he had been compelled to accept with good grace the newly-created title. As if his elevation from the family earldom of Delvin to the Marquessate Halsey would somehow miraculously expunge from the collective memory of Polite Society his connection to a murdered brother who had hated him with a passion bordering on mania. To Alec's way of thinking, thrusting a Marquessate on him considerably complicated his life, and merely heightened suspicion.

Perhaps he would request a second posting to Constantinople?

He was roused from these musings at the mention of his name in loud whispered conversation over his left shoulder. Overhearing the rest was unavoidable.

"I don't know why Weir in*vit*ed him," whined a weak male voice. "He's not one of us. And when one considers what he did to poor Ned—well!"

"Sir Charles has a motive for everything," mused his female companion. "I wonder…"

"Obviously Charlie fails to see the matter as we do, my lady."

"He's rather handsome in an angular sort of way. Big bony nose and *large*—"

"What? No powder and a scrap of l*ace* makes him handsome?"

"—blue eyes," Lady Cobham finished with a crooked smile, appraising Alec from well-muscled calf to coal black curls.

"You're blind! He could very well be mist*aken for an Ame*rican savage."

"Yes. That old ru*mor a*bout—"

"Rumor?"

"—his real papa being a black lackey who took my lady Delvin's fancy has stuck, hasn't it?"

"It's stuck, Caro, because the swar*thy devil'*s a-a half-breed. One only has to look at him to see that!"

The woman sighed deeply. "Yes, just look at him. Common report says he's as virile as a savage…"

There was a snort of contempt. "You're *for* Bedlam, Caro! Egad! The man's unco*uth*, uncivilized, and disrespectful. The Duke won't like him being here tonight, not one bit!"

"I dare say your father won't like it, George, but given the Duke's continued mourning for the Duchess I doubt Cleveley will care who Sir Charles has invited to dine. Can savages have blue eyes?"

"Be reasonable, Caro." Lord George Stanton tucked his chins in his stock and said gravely, "Father is thinking of stepping down from the leadership."

The lady gasped. "You can't be serious? He said so in jest!"

"The Duke, my dear *Lady* Cobham, does not jest. Neither do I. And don't think Father's grief has made him blind to the world. He will certainly have a word with Weir for his lack of moral decency for inviting a man everyone knows but cannot prove murdered his own bro—"

"Oh, look! He's finally here!" burst out Lady Cobham. She gave a nervous titter behind her fluttering fan when Alec stared straight at her. But when Lord George faced the doorway she lowered the fan of carved ivory to underscore her thrust-up breasts before turning to admire the full-length portrait dividing the windows. "I wonder if that's a Reynolds…?" she mused to no one in particular, a sly sidelong glance of open invitation at Alec.

A commotion in the doorway had everybody looking that way. The Duke of Cleveley had arrived. It said much about the man's formidable political and social influence that his mere entrance caused the room to hush. He was soon surrounded by the party faithful, all wanting to be noticed, and Alec had the *satisfaction* of seeing the great man snub his stepson, Lord George Stanton, in favor of a clergyman in tattered collar and cuffs. At least the Duke was not about to allow an arrogant nature to dictate to sense, he thought with a wry smile.

The meal itself was not the ordeal Alec had anticipated. In amongst the twelve courses there was much political discussion and many an impromptu speech praising Sir Charles's five years as Member of Parliament for the rotten borough seat of Bratton Dene. And as Alec was seated between the scruffy clergyman, who ignored him in favor of conversation with the gentleman to his right, and Sir Charles, who sat at the head of the table, he began to feel more at ease. And with the comings and goings of the two footmen with the various courses on offer, he took the time to glance about at the other guests.

The Duke of Cleveley sat directly opposite, looking supremely bored. His Grace said little throughout the discussions, ate sparsely from the many dishes put before him, and continued to drink steadily, although this fact did not affect in any way his political acumen. Alec observed that whenever the Duke tired of the conversation he fiddled with his snuffbox, and that his fellows took this as a sign that they could lower their guard, but no s*ooner did they* do so than the great man would offer up some scathing criticism guaranteed to send the diners into a spin of counter-arguments. Alec would never agree with the Duke's politics, but this did not stop him admiring the great politician at work. Now he knew why his uncle Plantagenet found the Duke such a worthy and infuriating opponent, and it made him smile, contemplating what that old gentleman would have to say at breakfast the next morning when he learned just who had been at Sir Charles Weir's dinner party.

Sir Charles leaned in to Alec.

"It's all rather a bore for you, I'm afraid. Don't worry, with the ladies gone to the drawing room, we fellows can have a good port and a rest." He patted Alec's upturned velvet cuff. "I'm glad you came up to town."

"I should've remembered. At school you had a way of getting what you wanted by fair means or foul."

Sir Charles raised his glass. "That's what makes me such an effective politician, my lord Halsey."

Alec flinched. Seven months was not time enough to be comfortable being addressed as "my lord". Annoyed with himself for letting such a social trifle get the better of him, he downed the rest of his wine in one swig. Looking up, he encountered the Duke's penetrating gaze. He stared back at him and the heat in his face said it all, because the Duke set down his glass, took up his snuffbox, and offered it across the table.

Alec shook his head. "Thank you, Your Grace, but I don't dip."

The Duke inclined his powdered head and put the little gold box back on the table. "One of your uncle's many eccentricities is a hatred of tobacco. I read his pamphlet on the subject with great interest. You were raised by him, were you not?"

"Yes, Your Grace. Raised by him to form my own opinions," Alec replied, surprised the Duke had bothered to read anything his uncle had written. "I simply don't find snuff to my liking."

"Ah," said the Duke, dismissing the topic with a long sniff, as if suddenly bored by it. Alec found the mannerism annoying. "Tell me your opinion of the Midanich question."

"Is there a question, Your Grace?" asked Alec. He knew the rest of the diners had broken off their conversations and were listening intently. "I presumed that little corner of northern Europe now put to rest. England ended French occupation of the principality and invasion of Hanover was avoided, which was your government's prime objective. Thus a successful campaign for you, Your Grace..."

The Duke tapped the lid of his snuffbox and flicked open the filigree lid with one finger. His gaze remained on Alec, weighing up his remark, deciding if it contained any hostile insinuation. After all, his government's decision to drive out the French and occupy Midanich had been met with hostility on both sides of Parliament. Alec Halsey's uncle Plantagenet was its most vocal critic. But Midanich shared a border with Hanover, English sovereign territory, and thus keeping the French out was imperative. The strategic move proved successful and helped England win the Seven Years' War.

"I will allow that remark to stand, Halsey."

"As was intended, Your Grace," Alec answered politely.

There was a long silence broken only by the sound of the Duke taking snuff. It was left to Sir Charles to interpret the mood, and he pushed back his chair and gave the nod to his butler, a sign for the ladies to take their leave to the drawing room. The rest of the gentlemen stood, still silent, waiting a cue from the Duke who was oblivious to the tension hanging about him.

With the door firmly closed on the ladies' backs, Lord George Stanton made his way to the sideboard at the far end of the long room where Sir Charles was refilling his snuffbox, and those belonging to guests who required replenishment, from one of a number of ornamental jars kept on the top shelf of an ornate mahogany cabinet. The rest of the gentlemen had undone the last button of their waistcoats and were settling down to the good drop of port the butler had placed on the table in large crystal decanters.

Alec stretched his long legs by the windows opposite the sideboard, escaping the intense gaze of several gentlemen who were diverted when the scruffy clergyman invited himself to sit beside the Duke. The cleric's familiar behavior annoyed these men who had awaited this oppor*tunity to mak*e themselves better known to the great man. Alec noted that it also annoyed the Duke's stepson, who could not hide his contempt for the old cleric. And two bottles of claret had loosened his tongue.

"Listen, Charlie," Lord George hissed loudly and hiccupped. "I th*oug*ht you were going to do something about him."

"What do you suggest I do with a cleric, my lord?" Sir Charles an*swer*ed with heavy sarcasm.

"What's he doing here?" came the arrogant demand.

"It wasn't my idea to invite him. I thought that obvious, even to you," Sir Charles answered cuttingly, replacing the stopper to the porcelain snuff jar. He returned this and its companion to the cabinet shelves. "And do, please, lower your voice."

"I'm not drunk, y'know," said Lord George, taking a pinch of snuff from the box *off*ered him. "Thanks. The old badger's come to stay. Can you believe it? *Fa*ther allowing that dirty piece of filth to stay at St. James's Square? He's got his own room, for God's sake!"

"Perhaps his grief—"

"Oh, come on, Charlie!" scoffed Lord George and hiccupped again. "*I* miss Mamma just as much but it hasn't unhinged me. It's been a twelvemonth and I call that long enough to grieve. After all, it's not as if mamma was a well woman. She'd been confined to her rooms for the better part of a year before her death. So don't give me that rot about blind grief!"

"My lord, I—"

Lord George leaned a large arm on the sideboard, his round face close up to Sir Charles. "Know what I think, Charlie."

"*N*o, I don't th—"

"He's got something over him."

"What?"

"Blackmail."

"That's absurd," Sir Charles replied with a hollow laugh. "What could that old vicar possib*ly have over*—"

"You think because you were secretary to the great man for ten years you know everything there is to know about him? Then tell me why Father gives that caterpillar the time of day. Only yest*erday they* were closeted in the library for three hours. Three hours, Charlie."

Sir Charles took Lord George by the elbow and pulled him about so that his back was to the room. "Have you thought that His Grace may merely be carrying out your mother's dying wish?"

Lord George belched. "Eh?"

Sir Charles smiled thinly. "If you recall, my lord, it was the Duchess who requested to see Mr. Blackwell. Just before she went into her final decline she summonsed the cleric t*o he*r bedside. It was he who administered the last rites."

"What? That threadbare nobody presided over Mamma's deathbed?" It was news to Lord George, and he turned and looked down the room at the clergyman who was very much at home with the noblemen about him, joining in the laughter at their bon mots. "Why did she do that, I wonder?"

Sir Charles sighed. "We shall never know now, and I suggest you not bother the Duke with it." He pocketed his snuffbox, closed the sideboard door, and turned the little silver key *in the lock.* "If His Grace sees fit to rub shoulders with a threadbare nobody it's not for us to question."

Lord George Stanton gave a snort and slapped Weir's back. "Ever the faithful secretary, Charlie!"

He sauntered off to join the others. Sir Charles grimaced his displeasure and came up to Alec with a smile full of resignation. "You mustn't mind Lord George," he apologized. "He's young, and lamentably, he can't hold his liquor like the rest of us. Makes him say things he doesn't mean. Blackwell's not so bad."

Alec's non-committal reply and the fact he immediately went over to introduce himself to the clergyman had Sir Charles wondering. If he'd not been claimed to settle a dispute on a point of law, he would have followed to hear what his old school friend had to say to a threadbare nobody.

"Mr. Blackwell," said Alec. "I owe you an apology."

The Reverend Blackwell smiled and offered Alec the vacant chair beside him. "Do you, my lord?"

"Yes. I feel rather foolish for not knowing you at dinner, but we have met before, some months back, when on my uncle's invitation the board of governors of the Belsay Orphanage convened at my house."

"Yes, that's right. Forgive me for smiling, but I do know who you are and I am well aware of our previous meeting. I thought it best to allow you the opportunity to acknowledge me or not, as you saw fit."

Alec was surprised. "How could you think I wouldn't want to know you? I admit I've got out of the way of socializing since… I don't come to town often, preferring to spend my time in Kent, yet I enjoyed that nuncheon immensely—all the more because talk centered on the Belsay Orphanage."

"My fellow board members and I are honored to have been appointed, but it is your uncle who is grease to the axle, my lord."

The clergyman caught Alec's frown and spread his fat hands in a gesture of sympathy. "The past seven months have not been easy for you. I am sorry for it. A lesser man couldn't have carried it off. Yet, I have every faith in you making the most of a circumstance that was not of your making."

Alec looked up from the heavy gold signet ring on the pinkie of his left hand, harsh lines either side of his mouth. "Thank you for your support, Blackwell."

The vicar nodded and leaned across the table to grab the nearest snuffbox. It was gold and identical in design to the box carried by the Duke. "Pretty, isn't it?" he said, changing the subject. "A gift. I'd never truly enjoyed snuff until given a good blend." He snorted a generous half-pinch up one nostril. "Always smoked a pipe. But this is more agreeable in company." He then snorted the rest up the other nostril and dusted off his fingers on the sleeve of his frock coat.

Alec politely waited, although he had so much he wanted to ask the clergyman. Not least, how he came to be taking snuff from a gold box in an elegant drawing room full of high-ranking politicians, when less than a year ago he had been ministering to the wretched poor in the parish of St. Jude's. He glanced at the Duke surrounded by the party faithful, intrigued by the possible connection between a nobleman of the highest rank and a poor, ill-dressed cleric of no family. The Duke could not be called benevolent. His disdain for those socially beneath him was well known. He was the epitome of what Alec most despised about his own order. Blackwell was a mild-mannered, honest man without pretense and ambition; a person of little worth to a consummate politician such as the Duke. Strange bedfellows indeed.

"My lord, oblige me by refilling my glass," the clergyman said in a thin hoarse whisper, tugging at his frayed neckcloth as if for air.

Alec did as he was requested but one look at Blackwell told him the man had taken ill. His face had changed color and he looked suddenly uncomfortably hot. Sweat had begun to bead on his forehead. Alec felt for the man's pulse and was surprised by the rapid, pulsating beat in his wrist. He loosened the clergyman's cravat, sitting him back in his chair as he did so. This only seemed to aggravate the old man. Blackwell let his head drop back as he sucked in air through a slackened mouth. Alec had the neckcloth unraveled and the man's waistcoat undone, but still Blackwell gasped, his wheezing so loud that the other guests were alerted to his condition, and conversation and laughter ceased.

Sir Charles rushed to Alec's side, calling for his butler to bring a pitcher of water. He turned to his old school friend for guidance, not knowing what to do with the gasping bulk now convulsing in his chair. "What's to do?"

"Fetch a physician!" Alec commanded, his arm feeling as if it was about to break under the cleric's writhing weight.

Just as he said this, Blackwell pitched forward and vomited. A great stinking mass of undigested food splashed Alec's stockinged leg and fell in lumps to the carpet. It was enough to send the onlookers staggering backwards. One gentleman heaved, stuck his head in the chamber pot beneath the table, and followed the cleric's example. Alec held back his own nausea and maneuvered the cleric to his knees where he vomited once more. The great guttural shudders were the last straw for even the most hardened stomach, and the circle of gentlemen surrounding him broke and scattered. Lord George Stanton made the mistake of peering over Sir Charles's shoulder. The stench hit him before the sight, and he reeled back, almost losing his balance had not the Duke caught his stepson by the elbow and thrust him onto the nearest chair.

Alec was at a loss to know how to alleviate the man's suffering. Until a physician could be found, there was not much anyone could do but shuffle about, helpless and uncomfortable. Sir Charles tried to put a tumbler of water to the vicar's parched lips, but it was to no avail. Blackwell, his once sallow complexion now bright pink, continued to gasp, unaware of his surroundings and unable to ask for help.

Then all at once, the convulsions ceased as suddenly as they had begun. There came a collective sigh from around the room. Blackwell was perfectly still, his bald head now minus its brown-haired bob wig, bent forward as if in prayer. He gave one last great shuddering breath and promptly collapsed, face down, into the mess he had created.

He was dead.

"What a wretched end to the evening," complained Lord George Stanton, refilling his port glass.

No one spoke. No one had spoken for five minutes. This fatuous remark did little to endear the Duke's stepson to his fellow guests. Sir Charles looked pained. He wished the physician would hurry along so his servants could clean up.

The Turkey rugs would have to be replaced.

Sir Charles was reminded of his duties as host when Viscount St. Edmunds summonsed up the courage to excuse himself; he would join the ladies in the drawing room. Sir Charles suggested that the rest of the gentlemen do likewise. There was no reason why they should remain in the dining room, and the ladies would be wondering at their prolonged absence. There was not a man who cared to disagree and they bolted through the open doorway, greatly relieved, if still in shock. A good hanging was one thing, but to witness a dinner guest dropping dead over the port… Well! It was unspeakably distasteful and downright bad-mannered.

The butler took the initiative and sent a footman with a bowl of clean water and cloth to wipe the vomit from the leg of Alec's black satin knee breeches and white clocked stockings. Soft-footed servants quietly cleaned away the glasses and decanters, and the two strongest amongst their number were ready to assist in removing the body once the physician had confirmed the clergyman was indeed dead. Though why this was necessary now, with the man going cold on the rug, the butler was left to wonder at.

Sir Charles seemed unaware he was not the only one left watching over the corpse, until the physician was ushered into the room and began his examination by directing questions to Alec. Sir Charles was quite content to let his friend recount events. Apart from finding the process repugnant, he lacked the energy to do anything but repine on the disastrous end to a dinner party that had held the promise of furthering his political ambitions.

If only he could somehow hush up the whole ghastly business! He knew this for wishful thinking. For one thing, Lord George Stanton had the biggest mouth in town. By morning, not only would the news have gone right through his club in St. James's Street, but also in Parliament he would bear the brunt of the opposition's twisted sense of humor. Just the sort of thing guaranteed to pour scorn on the many years spent carefully building up the vision of a trusted and worthy member of the government. He wondered in what light the Duke would view the whole sordid business.

His mentor leaned out in an opened window, unnoticed and silent. He seemed disinterested in the proceedings until the physician gave the nod for the servants to carry the corpse away, saying,

"The poor fellow suffered a massive heart attack. Could've happened at any time." He looked at Sir Charles, apologetically. "A pity it had to happen at one of your dinners, Sir Charles."

The Duke turned at this, and Alec noted that the nobleman's lined face had blanched as white as the froth of lace at his wrists.

"It is your opinion that the Reverend Blackwell died of heart failure?" asked the Duke.

The physician remained unmoved. "Yes, Your Grace. That is my opinion."

The Duke was unconvinced. "After everything Lord Halsey has told you of the man's final moments, you can state without reservation that it was a heart attack?"

Sir Charles gave a nervous laugh. "Your Grace, what else could it be?" He looked to Alec and then at the physician. "Food poisoning, perhaps?"

"No. No. No," dismissed the physician. "Not enough time for that. Besides, the vicar would not be the only one affected. There'd be signs of distress in the others. And as Lord Halsey has assured me no one else suffered similarly, I very much doubt there was anything in the food to cause the man distress."

"No one has asked the ladies—" began Alec, only to be cut short by the Duke's sniggering.

"Ever the pedantic need for the truth, Halsey?" the Duke sneered. "Then again," he drawled, a significant glance at the place where the clergyman had dropped dead, "this sort of thing isn't new to you, is it?"

Sir Charles's mouth swung open at this bald reference to the suspicious shooting death of his friend's elder brother. He didn't know where to look. And however ludicrous the suggestion, he couldn't bring himself to defend Alec at the expense of incurring the displeasure of his mentor. The physician was left wondering.

Alec bit back a retort, preferring to ignore the inferen*ce. Ins*tead he said calmly to the physician, "His Grace is in shock and perhaps requires—"

"I require nothing," spat out the Duke of Cleveley, not taking his gaze from his opened snuffbox. Unable to control the tremble in his hand, he fumbled to close the lid, and the little gold box clattered to the floor, its precious powdery contents spilling across the polished floorboards.

Alec stared at the snuffbox, which had come to rest at the pointed toe of his polished shoe, and within a blink of an eye, Sir Charles was groveling on his knees before him, eager to be the one to return the little gold box to his former employer. It saddened Alec to see his old school friend prostrating himself in such a demeaning way. The Duke barely noticed this act of sublime subjugation and he certainly did not thank Sir Charles. In fact, he snatched the snuffbox from his hand and without so much as a goodnight strode from the room. For Alec it was not a moment too soon. He hoped tonight would be the first and last time he would ever be in the company of such an arrogant ugly man.

A week later he had the misfortune to encounter the Duke at an art exhibition in Oxford Street.

TWO

Plantagenet Halsey MP considered himself fighting fit for a man entering his sixtieth year, and what he most wanted to do was fight the latest bill put before the Commons. A bill that, if passed, would see an increase in the number of ships leaving Bristol harbor in search of African slave labor for the sugar plantations of the West Indies and the cotton plantations of the American colonies. A bill proposed by the government, and championed by the Duke of Cleveley, as the only means of ensuring the kingdom's supremacy over its European counterparts. Plantagenet Halsey loathed the Duke with a passion, almost as much as he hated the very idea of human enslavement.

Thoughts of the Duke put a bitter taste in his mouth and intruded on what his nephew was saying. The last time he'd confronted the Duke he'd made a fool of himself. He should've heeded the advice of colleagues and left the debate on the floor of the House. Two hours of listening to Sir Charles Weir drone on and on about the urgent need to increase not only the number of ships, but the permissible number of slaves taken on board such vessels, to ensure England's mercantile advantage was not compromised, was all the old man needed to set his blood to boil.

Everyone knew Sir Charles was the Duke's puppet in the

Commons. The man had been Cleveley's secretary for ten years before being rewarded for his loyalty with a rotten borough seat in the Duke's keeping. And for the past five years he had repaid the Duke by being his eyes and ears in the Commons. He never missed a vote, never opposed a government-endorsed bill, and at every opportunity championed the integrity of the Duke's character and political motives on the numerous occasions a Member of Parliament took it upon himself to question such matters. In Plantagenet Halsey's opinion the worst kind of sycophant: Unthinkingly loyal and doggedly determined.

How insane of him, then, to confront the man and his idol in the pavilion at Ranelagh Gardens. It was the first appearance of the Duke at a public gathering since the death of his good Duchess. The orchestra had just finished playing a selection of Handel's favored water music in honor of the Duke's presence. The audience not only applauded the musicians but one of their number took it upon themselves to offer three cheers in support of the Duke. The man himself had appeared nobly self-effacing. His puppet, Sir Charles, was not so humble and grinned from ear to ear at such public enthusiasm for his benefactor.

It was a rare occurrence for a member of the English aristocracy to receive such praise. Plantagenet Halsey considered such affected displays best left to the French who worshipped their nobles with unthinking zeal. That the Duke should be given such an honor, all because his stirring speeches about the expanding British Empire appealed to the swelling moneybags of the merchant class at the expense of those poor African natives, herded up like cattle and loaded into British frigates for slave labor in distant lands, was enough to turn the old man's stomach. His response was immediate and instinctive.

He had marched straight up to the Duke, poked him in the chest with the Malacca head of his walking stick, and called him a murderer of nations, or some such provocative thing which he could not now recall. He had then spat on the sparkling diamond-encrusted buckles of His Grace's well-polished shoes. The outraged Sir Charles quickly stepped in front of the Duke, and the rest of their party closed protectively about *the great man*, leaving the crowd that swelled forward to wonder at all the fuss.

The Duke did not give him the satisfaction of responding to this violation of his immaculate person. He merely turned on his heel and walked away, leaving Plantagenet Halsey to the mercy of his followers, who dragged him outside by the collar of his plain woollen frock coat and tossed him into the cold water of the nearest pond. His walking stick, a gift from his nephew, was snapped in two and thrown in after him.

The old man sneezed—a reminder that he was not fully recovered from this watery ordeal. It served to bring him back to the present. Alec was looking at him as if he required an answer.

"Vomited, you say?" questioned Plantagenet Halsey, recalling the thread of their conversation. "I'm no expert in such matters but that don't seem consistent with a heart attack. Or is it?"

"I've no idea," said Alec. "All I know is the man was perfectly healthy throughout dinner. He was not in any discomfort. No shortness of breath, or flush to his face. And he certainly wasn't in pain. No sign at all of what was to come." He laid aside his gold-rimmed spectacles atop a stack of unopened correspondence. "Blackwell's death came as a complete shock."

"I'll miss the old badger, but I'm not sorry he up and died at one of Weir's dinners."

Alec smiled thinly. He knew very well what had happened at Ranelagh Gardens. His valet, Tam, had inadvertently told him in explaining why he was late in drawing his bath—that he'd been busy preparing an elixir for the old man's sore throat, a consequence of ending up in a fishpond. The whole story had come out, and Tam had begged him not to reveal his breach of confidence. It was not Alec's intention to remind his uncle of his embarrassing impetuosity. He might agree with his uncle's sentiments, but he certainly did not approve of his methods.

"When I accepted Charles's invitation to dine," Alec said patiently, "I did so as an old school friend, and because I owed him a favor. If it makes you feel any better, I found the evening rather dull."

"A diplomatic understatement," grumbled the old man, "given the end to the evenin'."

"As I said, the vicar's death was a complete shock."

"Obviously not to everyone, my boy."

"Meaning?"

Plantagenet Halsey's gray bushy brows lifted in surprise. "Come now. Don't tell me *you* think he suffered a *natural* death?"

Alec frowned. "I've no evidence to suggest otherwise, which means I should dismiss any suspicions as absurd."

"Aha! So you do have suspicions. Got to wonderin' who would want to be rid of a harmless old vicar?" Plantagenet Halsey asked shrewdly.

"Yes. Particularly when just as the port was being put on the table I overheard Lord George Stanton telling Weir he suspected Blackwell of blackmailing Cleveley."

"*Blackmail*? That don't sound like the Blackwell I knew."

"No. But it's Stanton's belief that only blackmail could induce the Duke to let Blackwell live under his roof."

"*What*? *Blackwell* was livin' in that nobleman's *house*?"

"Furthermore, Charles was of the opinion that perhaps it was the Duchess of Cleveley's dying wish that Blackwell be given a home, because it was he who had performed the last rites on the Duchess."

The old man was so agog at this that he leaned forward on the ribbon back chair. "Are you sure we're talkin' about the same vicar?"

"I can't imagine the Reverend Blackwell we knew, the penniless helper of the poor and forgotten of our society, having an enemy in the world. Yet, if he was on friendly terms with the Duchess, whose son accuses him of blackmail, and he'd recently taken to living at the Duke of Cleveley's social and economic expense, then the vicar may well have had enemies, and under the very roof where he was staying." Alec looked pensive. "He showed me a gold snuffbox, a gift. The poor parish vicar we knew would've shunned such luxuries, or at the very least have sold it for medicinals, food, anything to help his ragged flock."

"The man must've been drunk. Or drugged."

Alec grinned. "Perhaps you think I was by the look on your face. When was the last time you saw Blackwell?"

"It's only been about a month since he sent for Tam to—About a month."

Alec ignored the slip for the moment. "If we take the approach that this other Blackwell had enemies—Stanton, for one, was not pleased he'd moved into the Cleveley mansion—and ask if there was opportunity for *murder*, then yes, I think he could've been poisoned; something slipped into his food, or his drink. The servants were coming and going all the time with dishes and bottles. And more than once Blackwell had to get up from the table to relieve himself behind the screen. And I spent more time talking to Charles than I did the good vicar." Alec shrugged. "And that is assuming he was poisoned at dinner. He may have been poisoned before he arrived at Weir's dinner party."

The old man stood with the aid of his old splintered Malacca cane. "Perhaps… Perhaps he did have a heart attack. Perhaps the vomitin' was just a consequence of too much rich food, and a mere coincidence that both happened at the same time? The fact you were sittin' beside him is neither here nor there."

"Is that what you'll be saying to the doubters, Uncle?"

"What y'mean?"

Alec sighed. "If you and I think there was an opportunity for foul play, who's to say others don't think the same? In fact, that's what's being whispered about already, isn't it?" When the old man pretended ignorance by lifting his thin shoulders, Alec said impatiently, "I may have spent the past seven months rusticating in Kent, but that hasn't made me blind, deaf or a simpleton. I know what's being said behind my back. I need only walk into my club, ride in the Park, or take up a foil at Anton's, for there to be an awkward exchange of whispered asides between men who wouldn't normally know me from Adam. I was sitting next to Blackwell. I was the one on whom he vomited. And I was the only one at that dinner party ever accused and acquitted of a man's murder—my brother's murder. There's no need to look into a witch's cauldron to know whom everyone suspects!"

Plantagenet Halsey leaned heavily on his cane and met his

nephew's gaze unblinkingly. "Your brother's greed and contempt for his fellows got him shot. But you blame yourself for his death, for not being able to prevent what was to come. You're still blamin' yourself. The very fact you're uncomfortable with your elevation is proof enough of that. Let me finish! I've been wantin' to say this for some time and it's time I did, before you sink further into that vat of self pity—"

"Uncle, I—"

"No. You'll hear me out. While you continue to let your shiny new coronet sit awkwardly, continue to wince when addressed as *my lord*, continue to put off takin' your seat in the Lords, continue to dress like a man of trade with your natural hair unpowdered—"

"Ha! And this from a man who taught me that to live by the dictates of fashion was to be a slave to vanit—"

"—there will *always* be doubters. *You are* the Marquess Halsey, whether you wish it to damnation or not. There ain't a thing you can do about it now! So you may as well wear the title comfortably."

"Can I?" Alec asked with a skeptical lift of his black brows. "How comfortable can I be when we both know—when it is openly discussed behind fluttering fans and quizzing glasses—that I did not inherit my brother's earldom, but was elevated to a Marquessate in my own right to put to rest the persistent talk that I was not entitled to the family earldom, because nine months prior to my birth, my mother and her footman were lovers. A circumstance you stubbornly refuse to confirm or deny."

The old man did not blink. "The sooner you are comfortable," he said quietly, "the sooner those malicious scandal-mongering whoresons will turn their attention elsewhere. I'm tired," he added abruptly and blew his nose. "By the by, how did the lad take the news about Blackwell?"

"Tam? Better than expected," Alec replied evenly, pleased to take the focus off himself. He wished he hadn't flung his mother's affair in his uncle's face. The old man's love for the Countess had been unrequited; her affair with her footman, a social inferior and a mulatto, was considered abhorrent barbarism by her peers. It remained unspoken between them, but uncle and nephew knew that even if

Alec did redeem himself in the eyes of Society, doubt over his paternity would forever remain. "That is to say, Tam didn't let on to me how much Blackwell's death has affected him."

"He's become a regular close-faced servant since you took him on as valet. And from what I hear about your antics abroad, he'd have to pretend to deafness as well. I don't know why you bothered taking him with you to Paris when you spent the entire week cavorting between the sheets. *His* time would've been better served here." He broke off, embarrassed at saying more than he intended, and mumbled under his nephew's steady gaze, "The boy has a gift for healin'. The poor deserve access to the same medicinal treatments that are provided to the rich, and if—"

"Save me the customary lecture on rich and poor. I know it well enough," Alec answered flatly. "And don't think just because I've been caught up in estate business in Kent, or, as you so plainly put it, romping in a Parisian bed, I don't know what you've been up to. Sending Tam to help Blackwell in St. Jude's, the most dangerous parish in the city, is trying my patience that bit too far. I don't object to the boy using his apothecary's skills to dispense medicines to the poor at my garden gate. I'm even prepared to defend him should questions be raised by the beadles. But exposing a youth who has barely made his mark on the world, and worse, yourself, an infirm old man, to the treacherous underworld of cutthroats, murderers and disease-ridden hags, was reckless, irresponsible and utterly foolish!"

Plantagenet Halsey looked sheepish. "The vicar asked for m'help. As I said, the boy has a gift for healin'. It shouldn't be wasted."

"I don't disagree with what you're trying to do but—Damn it, Uncle! There are other ways of offering help. As it happens, I was about to put a stop to such nocturnal visits when Blackwell's death saved me the necessity."

"It was that snaky-eyed butler who tattled on us," the old man muttered rhetorically. "Interfering old buzzard."

"Then it's settled. You'll take my advice and have a holiday."

Plantagenet Halsey eyed his nephew with loving resentment. "At Bath?" He shrugged, the fight gone out of him. "I'll go at the end of session. Not before. I want my day in the Commons. Then you can send your old uncle to any watering-hole you damn well please!"

TAM SAT HUNCHED AT HIS WORKBENCH, HEAD IN HIS HANDS, A finger absently wrapping a carrot-colored curl about itself. Concentration was impossible. He'd spent an hour flicking through the pages of the English pharmacopoeia, trying to decide the main ingredients for a poultice to apply to weeping ulcers of the legs. He should've known the answer without the need to consult his texts. After all, he had less than a sennight until his examination before the Worshipful Society of Apothecaries. But the voices across the hall disturbed his concentration.

There went the old man's voice again, rising above that of his nephew's measured tone, as if by shouting him down he could win his point. Tam smiled. It wasn't that easy. That tactic might work for the old man in the House of Commons, but Lord Halsey had a way of getting what he wanted without the need to raise his voice.

If I can't study, then it's best to keep occupied.

He decided to tidy his workroom. There was plenty to do to ensure his thoughts did not wander to the death of the Reverend Blackwell. Then he would start crying again. Imagine! Turned nineteen and blubbering like a girl. What would the servants make of his red eyes?

From the lattice-fronted cabinet he took out the specialist apparatus needed in the preparation of his growing collection of prescribed medicines. He hoped to have at least a third of the labeled bottles restocked that evening, when his valeting services were no longer required. And there were the new clippings to sort through, gathered earlier from the herb garden at the back of the kitchen. Several piles of sorted roots, tubers, stems and stalks from various plants were drying on racks by the window; some had been purchased at the Chelsea Physic Garden.

Who would want to harm an old vicar? And why?

The attending physician had diagnosed heart failure, but his lordship's questions hinted at the possibility of foul play. An apothecary worth his fee knew any number of substances could kill man or beast and look for all the world as if death was by natural causes. But the Reverend Blackwell? A harmless old man from the poorest parish in London. It was inconceivable to Tam. Blackwell was a gentle man, a sweet and loving man who cared for the unwanted, nameless children cast on the parish by desperate mothers and faceless fathers.

Common Plantain: *Plantago major*. A weed found by the roadside and in meadowland. As a poultice, fresh whole leaves were applied directly to the ulcerated leg.

Tam smiled. Perhaps the examination wouldn't be so bad after all?

If time allowed, he would unpack the new ceramic jars that had arrived only that morning, another generous gift from his lordship, as was the dispensary and all its contents.

Lord Halsey had given Tam the use of the small room beside the butler's pantry as a preparation room. It was the sort of room every student of pharmacy dreamed of having at the end of a seven-year apprenticeship. It was fitted out with shelves, cabinets, a worktable and a small stove for the brewing kettles, and it was next to the kitchen and the herb garden beyond. It was Tam's alone. He had the only key to the door leading onto the passage; the back door he could bolt from the inside. Not even the butler was permitted to trespass.

Tam fingered the key and its chain which was attached to a button inside his plain cloth waistcoat pocket and grinned. He considered himself the luckiest lad alive and daily thanked God for his good fortune. Valet to a wealthy nobleman, who was not only the best master a youth could hope for, but one who encouraged his servants to better themselves.

Unlike his lordship's butler, who was forever looking over his shoulder, trying to catch Tam out for attending on the poor wretches who often called at the garden gate in search of free medicinals and advice. And making house calls on Blackwell's sick and miserable parishioners was, in the butler's opinion, the height of wastefulness.

The butler's familiar short, sharp rap on the outer door interrupted Tam's thoughts and he reluctantly went in answer to it, wiping his eyes on the back of a sleeve.

Wantage stood in the doorway, scowling. He disapproved of Tam and he certainly did not approve of his hocus-pocus. He considered it beneath the dignity of a Marquess's valet to get his hands soiled with garden filth. He tried to take a look into the room but Tam stood firmly in the doorway. All that study of botanical mumbo jumbo had made the boy's eyes red.

Tam pulled the door closed behind him and made a point of taking his time to turn the key in the latch. The butler stood so close Tam could smell the cheroots on his breath.

"You're wanted," Wantage sniffed, itching to snatch the key that dangled from its long chain in the boy's hand. "No. Not upstairs. In there," he said, a jerk of his thumb over his shoulder at the library door. "Tie your hair back, Thomas Fisher."

Tam abruptly stopped swinging the key and shot a hand to his red curls. Where was that damn riband? He turned out his pockets, found the scrap of black silk, scraped back his hair, and carelessly tied it up under the reproachful gaze of the butler, who took it upon himself to inspect Tam's handiwork before allowing him to pass.

Tam gritted his teeth and let the butler have his moment. It didn't do to upset Wantage. He had a way of making those he disliked pay, regardless of their closeness to the master.

He slipped into the library and waited, only coming out of the shadows when Plantagenet Halsey slowly crossed the room leaning on his nephew's arm. He could tell the old man's arthritis was bothering him, particularly this cold day, and offered to help him to his room. His offer was greeted with a grunt but was not rejected. When Tam returned he found Lord Halsey had put on his eyeglasses and was seated at his desk, writing. Tam smiled. There was a time when his master had refused to acknowledge his failing eyesight. Finally, necessity had conquered vanity.

Alec looked over his gold rims. "Were you by the door while Mr. Halsey was with me?"

"Long enough, sir," Tam answered honestly.

"Then I won't need to repeat myself about your nocturnal wanderings. Do I make myself understood?"

Tam nodded.

"Very well. I should like to know if you think Blackwell had any enemies."

"None, sir," Tam answered without hesitation. "He was liked by all. No one had a bad word to say about him. Why should they? He was a very decent gentleman."

"The times you were with him, visiting his parishioners, did he ever mention anything you thought an odd circumstance or out of character?"

Tam's brow furrowed. "Mr. Blackwell's conversation was always full of questions for me. What I was doing. What I thought of going abroad. He was always urging me to keep on with my studies. He wanted me to finish my apprenticeship. He didn't like the idea of me being a servant. No offence to you, sir."

"None taken. Did you know Mr. Blackwell had quit Old St. Jude's lane?"

"Yes, sir. He sent a note about two months ago, just after Mr. Halsey and I went on our last visit to one of his parishioners, a wain-wright with two broken fingers. Mr. Blackwell wrote he was going to *greener pastures.* I don't know what he meant by that." Tam screwed up his freckled nose. "Come to think on it, sir, he didn't give a forwarding direction."

"Did you hear from him again?"

"No, sir. Perhaps he wrote again while we were in Paris? But we weren't in Paris long enough for letters to cross on account of—" Tam faltered under his master's unblinking blue eyes and lowered his gaze to the Oriental rug. *On account of you having a falling-out with Mrs. Jamison-Lewis,* was what Tam had been about to say. But it wasn't his place to mention his master's titian-haired mistress. Just as it wasn't his place to remember how every night for a week he'd been kept awake by their torrid lovemaking in the next room.

"You may write your memoirs when I'm dead and buried. Not before," Alec said sternly and was pleased the boy had sense enough to remain po-faced. "Tell me: Is it within the realms of possibility that Blackwell was poisoned?"

"But who—?"

"That is something to think about *if* and only if you think it possible."

"It wouldn't be an easy thing, sir."

"To poison him, or to make it look as if he'd had a heart attack?"

"Let me explain, sir. It would be an easy thing to poison him. Something slipped into his wine, or sprinkled on his food, or his handkerchief could've been soaked in Oleander water. When Mr. Blackwell came to use it during the evening, the poison would be absorbed through his nose and go straight to work on his brain. He would almost certainly have died within minutes. But..."

Alec came round from behind the heavy mahogany desk and propped himself on a corner while Tam paced the rug thinking aloud. "But?" he prompted.

"It's got to be the right poison in the right form to produce the right effect. Mr. Blackwell died of a heart attack, so says the physician. So we need to be looking for a poison whose effect imitates that of a heart attack. We need to know the form of that poison to know how it was administered." Tam looked up at his master. "It wouldn't be easy, sir."

"I realize that, Tam. But look into it for me, would you?"

Tam swallowed something in his throat. "Yes, sir. It's just that... It's just that if it wasn't Mr. Blackwell I'd feel better about it. I'd probably even enjoy the challenge, but..."

"Of course," Alec said with an understanding smile. "It is not easy when the victim is someone you know—someone you care about."

Although Tam nodded his agreement, Alec's reassurances didn't make him feel any better. "I still don't understand why anyone would want to poison Mr. Blackwell."

"Nor do I. Yet, if Blackwell's death wasn't from natural causes, I mean to make it my business to find out why someone would want dead a seemingly good and harmless man of God." And to Alec's reckoning, if he hoped to learn more about the Reverend Blackwell, he would have to know more about the Duke of Cleveley. But how to get close to a man whose very nature precluded closeness?

"Sir," said Tam, a glance at the mantel clock, "I'd best see to your clothes if you still intend visiting that picture exhibition."

"Ah, yes," Alec sighed. "Must needs support new talent. Oh, Tam, before you scurry off... What would you say to taking a holiday at Bath after your examinations?"

"To keep an eye on Mr. Halsey, sir?"

"Let's just say, to keep him company."

"What shall you do, sir?"

"Without you?" Alec tried not to smile at the boy's look of deep concern. "I'll manage. I have thus far. Oh, don't look worried. It's more important you pass your examinations. Valets are easy to come by, not so, good apothecaries."

Tam wasn't reassured. In fact he wondered if this was the first step in easing him out of his position. After all, he'd hardly done a full day's work as a valet in months. He tried not to look hurt. "Mr. Halsey might not want my company, sir."

"It's you or a strong-armed nurse. In all seriousness, he'll be only too grateful to have you, and I won't leave the two of you alone for long. I'll join you at the end of a fortnight."

With a sluggish step and a heavy heart, Tam went away to prepare his master's change of clothes. He passed Wantage in the passageway, and such was the look of smug triumph on the butler's long face that Tam was sure it was no mere coincidence he felt his position as a gentleman's gentleman was under threat. He was sure of it when Wantage winked at him and continued on his way with a decided spring in his step.

THREE

"I DO NOT SEE WHAT'S SO INTERESTING ABOUT A RECIPE FOR Mrs. Rumble's Strawberry Relish," Selina Jamison-Lewis commented, not bothering to look up from the heavy oak library table where she sat surrounded by a toppling mountain of ledgers and correspondence. She re-dipped her quill in ink. "Although… It is a particularly good relish. Shall I copy it out for you?"

"Don't be silly, Lina!" retorted her sister-in-law, Lady Cobham, smoothing a crease in her satin sleeve to hide her embarrassment at being caught out reading a letter Selina had been careless enough to let fall off the table onto the Turkey rug. She shut her fan, tossed it and Selina's letter onto a little walnut stand, and selected another sweetmeat from the silver bowl at her elbow. Her teeth worried her constantly. "M… Maria? Mary? Margaret? Miriam? Maude?"

"Miranda."

Lady Cobham's thinly-plucked eyebrows shot up. "Oh? The little orphan with the bastard daughter… Sophie, isn't it?"

"I detest your memory, Caro."

Lady Cobham smiled and chose another sweetmeat. "She forms beautiful letters, if that's any reflection on her character. It's almost time for your yearly pilgrimage to that squalid little farm where you've given her sanctuary, isn't it?"

Selina put the quill in the ornate silver standish and proceeded to sprinkle the page of neatly tallied figures with pounce to dry the ink. "I don't care to discuss Miranda."

"Discuss her? You've not told me more than two sentences about her!" complained Lady Cobham. "You've put a roof over the girl's head; visit her every year; take *her* child gifts. *And*, now I learn you correspond. I sense intrigue and mystery. The very fact you refuse to discuss her with me, your dearest and only sister-in-law, is proof enough of that."

Selina bit her lip. Why couldn't she be left to her monthly bills in peace? But she didn't have the cold heartedness to turn her sister-in-law out; the woman was married to her priggish brother, after all, and that in itself engendered Selina's sympathy.

"You have no reason to be jealous of my friendship with an ill-used girl who lives a blameless life in the wilds of Somerset," she said as she sorted through the smaller pile of bills and extracted the one she was looking for. She absently tidied the others back into formation. When Lady Cobham remained silent, she looked up and saw the pout. "The child came to my door when she had nowhere else to go," she added patiently. "She and her infant had been abandoned by her lover. She had just turned fifteen. What would you have done?"

Lady Cobham shrugged as she tried to dislodge a chewed sweetmeat from an aching tooth. "Directed her to the nearest workhouse. Helping the poor to help themselves is one thing, Lina, but aiding and abetting a girl who is foolish enough to get herself and her bastard abandoned, well! That's just asking to be taken advantage of. The lower orders need to be put in their place, their actions not condoned."

"Thank you for your advice, Caro," Selina answered quietly, her only sign of anger the flash of her large dark eyes. "I must remember that for the next meeting of the Belsay Orphanage Board of Governors."

Lady Cobham shifted uneasily amongst the tapestry cushions on the chaise longue. "Oh dear, I've offended you." She took the last sweetmeat from the silver dish. "The trouble with you, my dear, is that you haven't hardened your heart to the many miseries that surround us. You think you can make a difference with this absurd orphanage of yours. But you can't. No one can. Misery will always be there."

Selina cast her eye over an exorbitant bill for Parisian embroidered silks and delicate lacework. Four more months, and then she could discard her dreary mourning for color and fashionable whims. She was counting the days. "Now *that* is my brother talking," she replied absently.

Lady Cobham eyed her beautiful sister-in-law speculatively. Such delicate features framed by an overabundance of flaming apricot curls gave Selina the appearance of an ethereal being, deserving of being put atop a pedestal, or at the very least surrounded by a diffuse golden halo, like those worn by the angels woven into mediaeval tapestries. But appearances could be deceptive, and none more so than with Selina. There was a saying, something about still waters running deep. Lady Cobham thought this very apt for her sister-in-law. She could well believe the rumor that Selina was having a passionate affair with the notorious and handsomely dark Lord Halsey. Still, it would be gratifying to have the whispers confirmed…

"I hadn't finished telling you about Sir Charles Weir's dinner party," said Lady Cobham lightly, hoping to draw Selina out.

"I've heard all I want to know about the death of that poor cleric."

"If you recall, I was just about to tell you who was seated next to the scruffy cleric when we were interrupted with the tea things."

"Is that important?"

"Oh, I think you'll be vastly interested, my dear, for the man happens to have the suspicion of murder on his own head. Cobham says that must make him the prime suspect in the cleric's death. Though why he would want to murder such a nobody is anyone's guess."

Selina sighed. She really did not have time for Caroline's scandal mongering. Her man of business was arriving at any moment for the purpose of discussing suitable tenants for this monolith of a house in Hanover Square. She couldn't continue to live under this roof. It had been her husband's home and contained too many painful memories of an arranged marriage that had been a disaster from day one.

"A murderer at Sir Charles's dinner party?" she heard herself say as she sorted through a pile of correspondence. "A pity Cobham was out of town. He'd have enjoyed pointing the finger."

Lady Cobham looked about the vast room with its furniture still under covers, strategically avoiding Selina's dark eyes for fear she would give herself away. "I should think most of London is pointing the finger at him, Lina. Cobham says there was talk of reinstating him at White's since His Majesty saw fit to bestow a Marquessate upon him, but not after this latest little drama he's become embroiled in. And as he was seated next to the cleric, that can only make matters worse for Halsey—"

"*Halsey*?" Suddenly, Lady Cobham had Selina's undivided attention. "Why was Al—Lord Halsey at one of Sir Charles Weir's party political dinners?"

"He and Sir Charles were at Harrow together," Lady Cobham replied blandly, though her pulse was up under her sister-in-law's hard stare. "As I said, Halsey was seated next to the cleric throughout dinner and was again beside him when the men sat over their port, and that's when the cleric up and died."

Selina left the desk to stand by the undraped sash windows with their view of the expansive Square, hoping to hide the heat in her throat. "How dreadful," she murmured. "What did the attending physician say caused the vicar's death?"

"*Officially* he died of a heart attack. Of course no one *believes* that. How can we, when the cleric dropped dead at the feet of a man accused of murdering his own brother to get an earldom for himself?"

"That's a lie!" Selina exclaimed, rounding angrily on her sister-in-law. "I won't have you repeating such malicious gossip, Caro!"

Lady Cobham sat up and slowly drew on her lavender kid gloves. "I don't begrudge you your Parisian dalliance with Halsey," she said silkily, a sly glance at her red-faced sister-in-law. "No sane woman could be immune to such potent masculinity. It matters not a whit if he did kill a penniless vicar, or his own brother, for that matter. What Cobham and I find particularly abhorrent is the persistent rumor he's the base-born product of his mother's affair with her mulatto footman. Marquessate aside, one shudders at the likely shade of the offspring from marriage to a man with such muddied blood. But what particularly offends Cobham is not so much the man's black heritage—that could be swept aside had he been a prince of the subcontinent—but that the Countess of Delvin chose to lower herself to couple with her footman—*a menial.* You, Lina, are a Vesey, descended from an unbroken line since the Plantagenets, with no one in the family tree related to anyone below the rank of Viscount. There is most definitely no servant blood of any sort. Our interests must and will be guarded. Do I make myself understood?"

Selina remained stubbornly mute, face averted, a long hand to her burning throat. Lady Cobham glanced at the ornate clock on the mantel and made motions to leave, yet waited for her sister-in-law's assent. Finally Selina nodded, hating herself for being weak-willed enough to appear to acquiesce to family pressure. But she wasn't about to reveal to her sister-in-law the very personal and heartbreaking reason why she could never marry Alec, not when she had yet to tell the man himself.

"Cobham has no need to fear for the Vesey name," she stated dully. "Alec and I… Matters between us… I have no intention of marrying Lord Halsey."

"Your brother will be pleased," Lady Cobham replied sweetly and kissed Selina's flushed cheek. "I'll be at the exhibition. Cobham won't lower himself to attend. But one must support family. I might not approve of Talgarth, but he is your brother and a Vesey, so one must do one's duty. I know *you* say Talgarth is very talented, but…" She shrugged realizing Selina was not listening. "Adieu, my dear."

Selina watched Lady Cobham maneuver her hooped petticoats along the passageway and down the stairs to the waiting sedan chair, then turned back into the library. Damn Caro's love of gossip! How was she to front-up with carefree enthusiasm to an exhibition of her younger brother's pictures (his first, too), when all she could think about was the effect of the unfortunate cleric's death on the love of her life? She resolved to write to him at once. They might have parted acrimoniously but that did not stop her giving him her total support. She wondered how he would receive such a letter.

She worried herself needlessly.

In the exhibition rooms they came face-to-face.

He was not pleased to see her.

THE SHOW ROOMS IN OXFORD STREET WERE CROWDED, THE AIR hot and heavy with perfume. And it was noisy—too much harsh laughter competing with the chinking of wine glasses. Tables strained under the weight of prepared food, punch in silver urns, and elaborate arrangements of fruit and flowers in season. Given the animated conversations and the high spirits, the uninvited would hardly have guessed that they had stumbled across a select preview to honor fresh new talent to the art world.

Those members of the aristocracy who considered themselves of the artistic demimonde had turned out in their best silks and powder; the ladies in wide-hooped petticoats moving sideways through the crush of bodies, and the gentlemen in outrageously tall toupees, powdered blue and threaded with ribbons. Most had not even bothered to venture into the next room to view the pictures. That chore was left to the critical eye of the newssheet hacks, who were expected to provide a succinct review for their readership before the exhibition covering the four walls was formally opened to the public the following day.

Into this frothy soirée sauntered His Grace the Duke of Cleveley, escorting the beautiful widow Mrs. Jamison-Lewis, her long fingers resting in the crook of the Duke's satin sleeve and dressed in a low-cut, pearl-seeded bodice that left little to the imagination. More than one strategically placed mouche quivered with surprise to see the Duke of Cleveley at such a function. It was difficult to imagine *the great man* having an interest in the patronage of new artistic talent. He was too much in favor of the old school. Raphael, Titian, and at a stretch, Lely were more his style. Even more eyebrow-raising was his choice of partner.

The whisper circulating many an elegant drawing room said the apricot-blond widow had left the bed of a Parisian lover to fall immediately into the waiting arms of Cleveley. That Mrs. Jamison-Lewis and the Duke were exchanging witticisms at an art exhibition seemed to bear this out. It changed the entire focus of the evening. Where now was the interest in a collection of pictures by local artists of no reputation, when there was gossip to report? Gossip made all the more tantalizing because it involved the Duke of Cleveley, chief architect of the country's foreign policy. That he, a widower himself, chose to have on his arm a woman in the last months of her mourning sent the reporters into a frenzy of scribbles, backs turned on the art world.

Talgarth Vesey, one of the painters of the moment, did not seem at all concerned by this scene-stealing. Whereas several of his colleagues, who had spent the evening mingling with guests or answering questions about their work put to them by the journalists, were infuriated to be so easily abandoned because a politician had arrived with his latest whore, Talgarth Vesey was content to sit in a corner of the room, broodingly chewing the quick of a ragged fingernail. His gaze was on a canvas draped in black cloth and set on an easel. The cloth was the idea of his majordomo, Nico. As his master's finest work at the exhibition, Nico said the painting deserved to be unveiled with ceremony, when all the guests were assembled and hushed. It would set the work apart from that of the other painters. Talgarth wondered if the Duke of Cleveley would condescend to perform the unveiling. Now that would be a coup!

The painter did not immediately rise when approached by the exhibition's most illustrious guest. A tall gentleman in somber frock coat with no powder in his coal-black curls had diverted his attention. The stranger hovered on the edge of the pastel-shaded crowd and stood so close to the works of art that it was obvious he needed spectacles. Talgarth decided there and then that he must paint this gentleman and was about to cross the room when he was stopped by a beloved voice before he had taken a step.

"The least you could do is appear as if you're enjoying the evening," Selina quipped. "It might get you one or two lucrative commissions."

With a frown of preoccupation, the painter looked away from the dark-haired gentleman. Seeing his sister, he jumped to his feet, smiling broadly and pulled her to him to kiss her cheek. "Lina! You came! I can't wait for all this fuss to be over with, can you?"

Selina smiled reassuringly, pressed her brother's hand, and made the necessary introductions, pleased Talgarth had the good sense to bow respectfully. But when he stared hard at the Duke she wanted to kick him for his lack of manners; the urge became a necessity when he addressed the Duke with one of his blunt questions.

"Where have we met, Your Grace?" he enquired, his mind's eye wondering how the Duke appeared without his magnificent powdered wig, which served only to accentuate a prominent beaked nose.

The Duke took snuff and stared straight ahead. "We have never been introduced before today."

"Are you sure? Venice? Florence? Bath, perhaps?"

"The Duchess frequently took the waters at Bath."

"Not the Italian States. Bath," Talgarth Vesey stated, adding without apology, "You see, I never forget a face. Do I, Lina?"

"Or perhaps it was somewhere close to Ellick Farm? It's on the Duke's estate, Tal. Remember?" Selina said with a smile at her brother's continuing frown, a wary eye on the Duke, who was not pleased at having questions put to him, least of all in so blunt a fashion. She drew the Duke's arm around her own. "Come, let me show you what I consider Talgarth's best work, Your Grace," and walked off with him, blowing her brother a kiss over her bare shoulder. "You must forgive Talgarth," she said at her chatty best. "He is young and quite the eccentric for a Vesey. We are all rather staid creatures except for Talgarth. Cobham inherited the title but no imagination; I am useless at most things except that I have a mathematical brain; Talgarth is a major artistic talent, although devoid of all the social graces. Needless to say Cobham has filled the ancestral pile with hideous works of art, while Talgarth is forced to compromise his great talent by painting yappy little dogs and their hideous fat female owners. So, Your Grace, I am relying on you to provide my little brother with the respectability he deserves," and she directed the Duke's attention to the nearest canvas.

It was Alec whom Talgarth Vesey had spotted in the crowd and whose likeness he decided he must paint. Alec had arrived behind the Duke. In the commotion that followed that nobleman's entrance he was able to slip away to the second room to look at the pictures in relative peace. He had almost come full circle uninterrupted when he was rudely tapped on the shoulder.

A glass of champagne was pressed into his hand.

It was Lord George Stanton who recklessly flung out an arm toward the four walls covered floor to ceiling with paintings. "What do you think of this lot by these new fellows?"

Alec pocketed his eyeglasses. "I like them. Less formal than Reynolds and Lely." He motioned to the painting to his right. It was one of Talgarth Vesey's works. "Take this picture here. The style is particularly refreshing. The expanse of sky, threatening a thunderstorm, and the sun, filtering muted light onto the valley floor below, is in direct contrast to the child's innocence. She seems oblivious to the storm at her back; her future is all before her…"

Lord George gave him a nudge, eyes sweeping over Alec from toe to wavy black hair pulled into a long plait. He hadn't heard a word. "The black velvet suits. So does the lack of powder. A magpie amongst peacocks," he said and stifled a belch. "But don't get me wrong. It won't see you rise to ambassadorial rank. Father says you can't have an ambassador who don't look the part."

Alec decided Lord George was drunk, very drunk. And by the way he was throwing back the champagne, had every intention of staying that way. And it explained why he was talking to Alec. He doubted Cleveley's stepson, if sober, would have come within ten feet of him. That had been proven at Weir's dinner party.

"This hardly seems your sort of gathering, my lord," Alec said conversationally, turning his back on the painting of the beautiful child.

Lord George pulled a face. "It ain't." He leaned closer. It didn't stop him talking loudly. "Can't stand any of 'em. Painters. Pah! Good-for-nothin' bunch of bird-witted parasites. Take this Vesey character for instance. You tell me why the son of our most decorated General is eking a living from paints when he could've made a respectable career following in his father's footsteps. Mad. Has to be. No other explanation. Pictures and letters and such nonsense won't see the kingdom rise to greatness. How can it? Who will care in a hundred years whether Mr. Reynolds or that fellow Gainsborough is the better painter? Who cares *now*?"

"But a far more palatable and enduring legacy of what our great nation is capable of than say—a society built on the ill-gotten gains of slavery...?"

Alec said this with such a nice smile that Lord George didn't know whether to be angered by his insolence or consider it a quip and laugh. He decided the latter and gave Alec a friendly push with his elbow.

"You're not so bad, Halsey. Not so bad at all. Thought you a bit queer in the attic. What with that iffy business over your brother's death, and keeping to yourself. Not one of the lads, if you know what I mean. But I was wrong. You're quite a Trusty Trojan underneath."

Alec gave him a wry smile. "Thank you, my lord. I'm much gratified by your reappraisal. I may now hold my head up in society knowing that I have your approval."

The heavy sarcasm by-passed Lord George. "That's the spirit," he slurred and loudly called out to a passing waiter to bring a bottle and be quick about it. "Do you like pictures? Not this pap—the Italian school and all that?"

Alec was saved a reply when Lady Cobham swept up and claimed Lord George, who showed little resistance at being dragged away and introduced to a group of giggling dilettantes lounging in front of a full-length portrait of an admiral with four faithful hounds at his boot heels. Relieved to be left alone, Alec took out his eyeglasses only to find himself confronted by a tall, slightly emaciated and lanky young gentleman with dark circles under his eyes who wore an over-large flowered frock coat and disheveled neckcloth. He was stared at from head to foot, the gaze lingering a little longer than was polite on his face. He sighed. Another drunkard...

"I must paint you," the young man announced.

Alec moved off to look at a portrait of a little girl seated on a swing. She was no more than three or four years of age and at her bare feet was an overturned basket of strawberries. He was surprised to discover it was the same beautiful child as that in the thunderstorm picture. Talgarth followed him. With great reluctance Alec put away his spectacles. "Thank you for the offer—"

Talgarth Vesey shook his head. "No. No. It's not an *offer.* I *must* paint you. I have an unfinished work, an allegory, which must be completed by Christmastime or I won't receive the balance of my commission. You're precisely the Apollo I've been looking for." He stuck out his thin, white hand. "Talgarth Vesey."

Alec's self-conscious frown was instantly replaced with a bright smile, realizing he was being accosted by Selina's favorite brother. "Forgive me. I should've known. You have your sister's eyes."

They shook hands.

Talgarth Vesey grinned. "Not your fault. Mine. Put down my lack of manners to eagerness. It's not every day I meet someone I want to paint. You will sit to me, won't you?"

Despite a natural embarrassment at the calculated scrutiny of his person, Alec liked the painter's straight-forwardness. "I've never—"

"You must come and see me tomorrow. I'll do a few preliminary sketches. I'm staying with Lina." When Alec looked puzzled he apologized. "We—the family—have always called her Lina. My sister Selina, Mrs. Jamison-Lewis."

"Sorry to disoblige, but I'm going out of town tomorrow afternoon, into Kent and then on to Bath," Alec said without disappointment.

"Come in the morning then. Even better, you'll be in Bath. My studio's in Milsom Street." The painter smiled self-consciously. "I make a living from portraiture mainly: Ambitious mammas with lovely daughters, and stout, little old ladies with ugly pooches."

"I can't promise I'll sit to you, but I will look you up."

Talgarth Vesey nodded, handed Alec a card engraved with his name and Bath studio direction, and disappeared into the crowd to be accosted by an overenthusiastic mamma with her tall daughter in tow.

Not a moment after the painter's departure Alec found himself nudged in the ribs. Lord George had sidled up to him again.

"Looks right at home beside the Duke, don't she?" he sneered. "Thinks she's in with a chance now Mamma's dead. Ha! Not if I have any say in the matter. Father can open her legs as wide as he pleases but as to marriage—*never*."

Alec hid his complete surprise at such a crude speech and followed the direction of Lord George's sneer to where the Duke of Cleveley and Selina Jamison-Lewis stood talking with Talgarth Vesey and Lady Cobham. Alec's gaze held on Selina. He had resisted the temptation to go to her since sliding into the room and disappearing behind a wall of silks and perfume. More than once he had glanced over at her and wished he had not. She was completely at ease with the Duke, and the way she occasionally touched his silk sleeve with a smile and he responded in kind indicated they were old friends. She looked for all the world as if she belonged at *the great man*'s side. Less than a month ago she had belonged to Alec.

"There is the small problem of the Viscountess's husband," Alec pointed out, finally tearing his gaze from the object of his love and desire to look up at a canvas, its subject an inconsequential blur of color and light.

"Not Caro, man!" Lord George said with a snort of laughter, thinking Alec's mistake a great joke. He nudged Alec again (who wished he would stop doing that), and said with another snort, "The widow. I'm talking about the *widow*: Mrs. J-L." He lowered his voice and breathed stale wine in Alec's ear. "Rumor has it she's opened her legs more times in the months since her husband's death than in all her six years of marriage. But if she thinks lettin' the Duke spread 'em wide will end in a proposal of marriage, she's got feathers in her pretty head." He slurped at the wine in his glass, saying as a drop dribbled down his fleshy chin, glazed eyes riveted to Selina's narrow back, "That bitch'd be worth a dose of the pox."

Before Alec could demand that Lord George step outside to repeat such outrageous slander, he was ruthlessly pulled backwards into a windowless alcove and a glass of claret forced between his fingers.

"Sorry. Couldn't allow you to strike him," Sir Charles Weir said on a quick breath, a glance over his shoulder to ensure Lady Cobham had Lord George in hand. She was coaxing him into the next room. Satisfied, Sir Charles turned to Alec with a deprecating smile. "Don't want to see an old friend end up in Green Park at dawn. Besides," he said with a nervous laugh, "you'd have killed him."

Alec drank the claret. "I don't thank you for this, Charles."

"Perhaps not now, but you will. Calling Stanton out would've been the ruin of your career. His Grace'd see to that."

Alec stared at him, still in a white-hot temper. "I wonder, Charles: Did you intervene on my behalf or to save Cleveley the embarrassment of seeing his drunkard stepson worsted in a one-sided duel? You really must cut the leading strings."

Sir Charles glanced down at the claret in his glass. "Surely she isn't worth your career?"

Alec thrust his empty glass at Sir Charles and went to leave but Sir Charles detained him, a hand firmly on the upturned cuff of his frock coat. Alec frowned down at that restraining hand and Sir Charles instantly removed it.

"We need to talk," Sir Charles stated, and when Alec merely raised his eyebrows, reminiscent of his mentor's haughty treatment of him when he was displeased, he stumbled on, feeling slightly foolish. "To talk about the other night. Blackwell's—what happened to him."

"Blackwell's death?"

Sir Charles nodded. "There's been much gossip—*whisperings*—about it."

"Not surprising, is it, given he up and died in the middle of your dinner party."

"The gossip concerns you." Sir Charles looked up then and was secretly pleased his friend was disconcerted. "Yes. Unrelenting, aren't they? People can't leave the past buried. Your brother's unfortunate *accident...*"

Alec hoped his voice held a note of detachment. "I won't discuss that here or anywhere."

"Of course not," Sir Charles said sympathetically. "You and I know, *your friends know*, that you couldn't possibly have had a hand in Blackwell's death, but that's not what others think—what's being whispered behind your back."

"Indeed? You seem to have made it your business to know what others think, Charles."

"And you seem to forget that it was in *my* house that the wretched man up and died!"

"I doubt anyone will forget that circumstance. Now, you must excuse me…"

"No!"

Alec turned and looked down at him.

Sir Charles went on in an under-voice; too many powdered heads had turned in their direction for his liking. "We need to talk and soon. There are certain particulars, certain matters concerning Blackwell that I *must* discuss with you."

Alec, too, saw the interest they were attracting.

"Not here. Not now," he said impatiently, and shouldered his way into the crowd awaiting the unveiling of the draped canvas. He soon found himself just a few wide-hooped petticoats from the canvas itself.

The patroness of the exhibition was addressing the gathering. Talgarth Vesey, Gavin Hamilton and the two other painters whose works were displayed were standing at her side. Just to the right of them stood the small cluster of journalists, pencils at the ready, and the Duke of Cleveley with Selina Jamison-Lewis beside him. There was much laughter and applause, but Alec heard none of it. He was forcing himself to remain calm, but he could not stop himself from looking at Selina.

WHILE CHATTING WITH HER BROTHER AND INTRODUCING THE Duke to him, out of the corner of her eye Selina saw Alec turn away and merge into the crowd. Later she watched as he put on his gold-rimmed spectacles to better view one of the many portraits in the assembled collection. The portrait just happened to be of herself, leaning a silk-clad shoulder against the trunk of an elm, a broad-brimmed straw hat in her hand, its wide blue ribbon caught by the breeze. It had been painted a year ago.

She must have flinched because the Duke glanced at her, saying as soon as he could break conversation, "Do I sense a certain tense expectation, my dear? Rest easy. Your brother is a considerable talent. His first exhibition will be a resounding success. My being here will see to that."

"I doubt Talgarth has a notion as to your social consequence, Your Grace," Selina said truthfully, which had the Duke's fawning cronies gulping for air at her bluntness. "The shape of your face, yes; the length of your hands, that too; but as to your name and title, they are of supreme indifference to my little brother. I warned you, he hasn't an ounce of social grace. But he does paint wonderful pictures, doesn't he?"

Far from finding offense, the Duke smiled. "That is why I came. You promised me wonderful pictures, and wonderful pictures they are." He saw her gaze wander longingly across the room. "Shall I introduce you? Ah! But I forget. You are already *known* to Lord Halsey, are you not?"

Selina feigned disinterest and flicked open her gouache fan, not daring to raise her chin for fear the Duke would see the desolation in her dark eyes. Yet, the Duke was uncannily attuned to her feelings for he guided her to a quiet corner, where a couple seated on an over-stuffed sofa obliged them by going off to find refreshments. He sat her down and took up his quizzing glass to better observe the crowd, all the while speaking to Selina in a low voice.

"May I offer you a word of advice, my dear? Maintain distance from your friend. There has been talk… Questions are being asked about his activities."

Selina blanched. "Surely not to do with the death of that vicar?"

"Reason enough for you to distance yourself."

"You can't think he had anything to do with that man's death? It's absurd!"

The Duke laughed softly. "Matters did not go at all well in Paris, did they?"

Points of color appeared in Selina's high cheekbones, but she bit her lip and fanned herself with an agitated motion. "I do not appreciate being spied upon by Your Grace's toad-eating secretary!"

"Charles is no longer my secretary, and he does not spy; he has others to do the gutter work for him," the Duke replied calmly, continuing to scrutinize the crowd through his eyepiece. "Believe me, my dear. You have chosen the wisest course."

Selina glanced Alec's way. He was talking with Sir Charles, a good head height taller than the Duke's henchman, his blue eyes not once glancing her way.

"Whatever you privately think of him, Your Grace, he is a man of honor and would never do anything to jeopardize my happiness."

"You are misguided, my dear," the Duke apologized, offering her his lace ruffle covered hand. "It is for *his* sake, not yours, that I ask you to maintain a discreet distance," and directed his quizzing glass to a corner of the room. "Now this draped canvas intrigues me..."

Talgarth Vesey was grinning. The crowd assumed it was because his moment of glory had arrived. The Duke of Cleveley was persuaded to unveil the draped canvas. But Talgarth was pleased with himself because he had finally remembered where he had seen the Duke before. It wasn't at Bath but, as his sister suggested, in the wilds of Somerset. It had been several months ago, perhaps a year, just after Talgarth's return from Florence. He was on his way to visit Ellick Farm and the Duke had passed him on the narrow tree-lined road, riding away from the direction of the farm toward his mansion atop the ridge that overlooked the valley in which nestled Ellick Farm.

Here at the exhibition, it was the Duke's magnificent powdered wig that had made it difficult for Talgarth to place *the great man* immediately. When Talgarth had last seen him, Cleveley was without a wig. His wide-brimmed country hat had blown off just as they passed each other on horseback, revealing the Duke's head of natural brown hair, short-cropped above the ears like that worn by a medieval prince. He was rusticated: Dressed in a shabby riding frock and a pair of dusty jockey boots in need of polish, and as far removed in appearance from the unapproachable great statesman as was possible.

A series of small tugs and the cloth finally came away from the large canvas.

There was a collective gasp from the crowd which brought Talgarth Vesey back to the immediate moment. He stepped forward to receive due praise for his full-length portrait of a young woman and her daughter. He knew it to be his best work, and structured in such a way as to gain maximum benefit from the majestic scenery of cliffs and sky and the pale innocence of the subjects. But he was not such an egotist that he failed to recognize the crowd's appreciation of the woman's stunning beauty. That was what made the painting so much more important than a mere portrait. The sitter's beauty was exceptional. No one in London but his sister knew who she was. She lived a reclusive life at Ellick Farm. Talgarth would not have been at all surprised had he been accused of conjury. He could not wait to refute the doubters. His sister would support him, for it was she who had given Miranda Bourdon a home.

He scanned the faces in the crowd, eagerly awaiting their praise, yet none was forthcoming. Their expressions confused him. They looked dismayed, some were angry, someone at the back of the room wanted to know what the painter meant by such barbarity. Another shouted abuse. Talgarth looked to his fellow painters but all three had turned away, and in so doing had disassociated themselves from him and his wonderful painting.

Selina took Talgarth's hand, wide-hooped petticoats a protective barrier between her brother and the outraged crowd. "How could this have happened, Tal?" she whispered, eyes brimming with tears. "It's *monstrous*!"

Talgarth Vesey wondered at his sister's distress. "I don't understand. Why don't you like it, Lina? You *must* like it!"

As he said this he turned. What he saw was incomprehensible. It was his canvas. It was his portrait. But there was nothing beautiful about it. Nothing to show for the long loving hours spent mixing just the right hue of flesh-toned paints and the blues of the stormy sky, each stroke of his brush carefully pondered. Thick red paint—or was it blood?—had been splashed across the canvas from gilt-edged corner to gilt-edged corner, smeared with hand or fist over blue sky and silken gown in what looked to be a frenzied, hate-filled attack. More horrifying, the face of the reclusive beauty had been slashed out of existence. Where once radiated from the canvas the exceptional youthful beauty and kindness in a perfect oval face, now remained only the shredded remnants of painted canvas. Her young daughter too had suffered a similar fate, perhaps even more savagely treated than the mother, for her entire image had been hacked out from the picture. Only her small bare toes remained as visible evidence that she had once existed. The defacement was so viciously wrought that it would have been no worse had mother and daughter been murdered before the shocked eyes of mute onlookers.

The painter dropped to his knees and wept.

FOUR

Alec was in no mood to see Sir Charles Weir. He had just spent an hour in strenuous fencing practice, leaving him hot, sweaty and craving the scented waters of his bath. His house was in a state of upheaval, preparing for his uncle's departure for Bath; portmanteaux were stacked in the hall, to be loaded into the traveling chaise the following morning. He had a hundred matters to attend to and a mountain of correspondence to read before the arrival of his man of business from his estate in Kent.

He was about to give his excuses to the waiting footman when his butler appeared, deftly side-stepping the servant mopping up the sweat from the Gallery floorboards. Alec tossed aside the bath sheet he was using to wipe his face, neck and bare forearms and looked at Wantage with annoyance. The butler picked up his master's frock coat and offered it to him, saying that Sir Charles had stressed it was most important he have five minutes of his lordship's time.

When Alec rejected the frock coat, Wantage said meekly, as he carefully laid the coat over the back of a ribbon-back chair, "Sir Charles was most imploring, my lord."

"Five minutes," Alec stated as he sat on one of the window seats with its view of the Green Park and rolled down his shirtsleeves.

The butler refilled the tankard with the last of the ale and placed the empty carafe and tankard left by the fencing master on a tray, and hovered.

Alec met his butler's gaze with stony silence and waited.

After what seemed an inward struggle as to whether he should speak or not, Wantage said, "Shall I have Jeffries assist with your morning toilette, my lord?"

"I am capable of dressing myself."

The butler bowed. "Very good, my lord. I thought perhaps with Master Thomas—*otherwise engaged*—you would need Jeffries to—"

"That will be all," Alec said firmly and turned to the window.

The butler bowed again and went about his business, leaving his master to contemplate the view of dairy cows grazing on dew-covered grass.

Alec was well aware Wantage was alluding to the fact Tam had leave from his valeting duties to study for his apothecary's examinations, and that he did not approve. Alec was sick and tired of the below-stairs jealousy directed at his valet and knew Wantage took every opportunity to make life difficult for Tam. So he had decided to do something about it. Besides he had "made-do" long enough and had every intention of employing a gentleman's gentleman. The newspaper advertisement was written and merely needed delivery. But how best to handle the situation without offending Tam and disrupting his household? He did not want the boy upset, nor did he want Wantage to think he was victorious, however petty the victory. So the advertisement could wait until after Tam's examinations, perhaps until his return from Bath.

But there was one awkward state of affairs he could not postpone, and that was visiting Selina at her Hanover Square mansion. He had received her note as he was stepping out of the house to go to the exhibition and slipped it into a pocket, assuming it had come from some Continental town where she was staying. Imagine then his shock to see her returned to London, when she should have been half-way to Berne to join her cousin Sir Cosmo Mahon.

The shock had been compounded witnessing Talgarth Vesey's utter despair at the mutilation of his most prized portrait. Alec had attempted to go to him in the aftermath of such a public humiliation, but the crowd had surged forward to better view the painter's personal agony. By the time Alec had shouldered his way to the front of the gawking spectators, Selina and her brother had been bundled through a servant door by the Duke and his cronies, Sir Charles Weir leading a rear guard action to prevent journalists and others from following.

Alec wondered what role His Grace played in Selina's life that he did not know about, as whispered by that drunkard Lord George Stanton. He'd never had cause to be jealous or suspicious, nor had he a moment's doubt that Selina loved him, but seeing her clinging to the Duke's silk sleeve he again felt that growing sense of unease experienced in Paris when they had parted: That a future with Selina as his wife had been taken wholly out of his control.

"Damn it!" he growled and finished the last of the ale in his tankard without tasting it. Sensing someone behind him he turned to find Sir Charles Weir peering at him in a half embarrassed, half smiling way that prompted him to say, "I beg your pardon."

"I've interrupted your morning's recreation," said Sir Charles, an eye on Alec's damp and ruffled appearance. Gingerly he touched the ornate handle of a sheathed fencing sword lying across the padded seat of a mahogany chair. "I'm out of practice myself. But I trust I'll never have need of it." He smiled, patting the ornate handle of his own sword. The fact that he had not unbuckled the sash indicated he did not intend to stay long. "I fear I would fail dismally against robber or potential duelist."

"What may I do for you, Charles?"

"I see that I am not forgiven."

Alec frowned. "I don't waste my time storing past petty spats."

"When you speak in that tone you remind me of your uncle," Sir Charles commented with a weak smile. "Not a day goes by in the Commons that Plantagenet Halsey isn't on his feet condemning some such action put forward by the government. Even my most reasonable requests are greeted with suspicion."

"No doubt you give a more than adequate performance in defense of your government's actions," Alec replied, though it was obvious to

Sir Charles that no compliment was intended. "But what has my uncle's oratorical skills to do with this visit?"

Sir Charles looked uneasy. "Firstly, I want you to know that the Bristol Bill will pass into law with or without your uncle's vote. He can rant and rave all he likes, but when it comes to the vote, morality is the last thing on the minds of parliamentarians. Session is about to close. All anyone cares about is getting the bill up to the Lords before break. No one wants to be held over."

"God forbid the business of government should take precedence," Alec quipped, but added in a more sobering tone as he stood, "What my uncle says and does is his affair. I have no influence over his opinions, nor should I. So, if you mean by coming here to have me dissuade him from attempting to hold parliament over a week or two, then I am sorry. I can't, and even if I could, I wouldn't interfere. So, if you don't mind, Charles, I'm in need of my bath."

"Your uncle's speech on the rights of *all* men, be they savages or statesmen, stirred the consciences of a few of our members. There is a whisper, nothing more, that the vote could hang on the *ayes* of one or two of our most northern gentlemen."

Alec looked pleased. "All power to them."

"This bill *must* and *will* pass!" Sir Charles blurted out, dropping his guard. "Its passage will be a vindication of all the Duke has worked for over the years. Those opposing us will not be able to argue differently. You see, we can't afford to fail. Not now. Not when there are rumors—rumors that His Grace will step down as Foreign Secretary if the vote does not go as anticipated." He gripped the chair back to bring himself under control. This did not stop the tremble in his voice. "Have you any notion what it would do to us to have the Duke resign? You must know the extent to which people rely on him, not only for their posts but for their very existence. If he falls, we all fall."

Sir Charles's tone smacked of the melodramatic, but Alec conceded the man had a right to his angry desperation. His political clout, indeed his very political existence, he owed to the Duke of Cleveley. Without him he had no future. But Alec was not wholly ignorant of the latest goings-on in Parliament. He was in no doubt that the bill would pass, whether his uncle spoke against it or not. A quick read of yesterday's newssheets put the numbers in favor of the Bristol Bill well ahead of those likely to dissent. The government had nothing to fear. And as Cleveley's mouthpiece in the Commons, Sir Charles had to be aware of this, and the fact there was no credible reason for the Duke to resign his offices of state. Then why did Sir Charles have the air of a desperate man?

"I don't know much about behind-the-scenes Parliamentary machinations," Alec said calmly. "But I do know all about the insidious use of patronage. I do not have influence over my uncle's thoughts and deeds, but having been raised by him I do carry some of his opinions as my own. No doubt you have had to sit through his speeches on the corrupting influence the system of patronage has on the governing of the kingdom; how patronage serves those least likely to do a decent day's work. I concede that in a minority of cases it can be beneficial in helping a talented and dedicated man, such as yourself, rise to a position where he is of use to his country. Sadly, you are in the minority. Patronage leaves a man at the whim of his patron. Never is he permitted to forget to whom he owes his allegiance; his own feelings and conscience become subordinate."

"You think me such a man?" Sir Charles was clearly offended.

"I have no idea."

"It is commonly reported that I am Cleveley's puppet," Sir Charles replied sullenly. "That the speeches I make on the floor are nothing more than parrot-fashion diatribes of Cleveley's making. Ha! It is conveniently forgotten that I was secretary to *the great man* for ten years. Who do you think wrote those stirring speeches on the need for England to gain its objectives from the recent peace with France? Who spent hour upon hour until the wax melted onto the table, drafting the policies he put before Cabinet? I have no qualms, no regrets. For His Grace, I would do it all again, willingly. Many do not care for his politics, for the single-minded determination he employs to achieve his ends, or for his cold arrogant manner, but above all else, Cleveley is a man of deep principle and sense of duty. He believes what he is doing is for the betterment of the kingdom. I share his belief. You may think of me what you like, but *puppet* I am not."

The bullish determination in his friend's flushed face warned Alec that to answer in anything but the most sincere terms would be taken with offense, so he said politely, "Naturally no one could accuse Cleveley of being ungrateful. Your many exertions on his behalf have not gone unrewarded: A knighthood; a rotten borough seat. But if he should resign his posts, you stand to lose several wealthy sinecures, sinecures you rely on for your livelihood."

Sir Charles smiled but it was obvious he was far from amused. "It was a great privilege to be the Duke's secretary, and an even greater one to have earned his confidence. I am grateful for whatever rewards I received for my loyalty and trust, but I'd have gladly continued in his service without them." He suddenly looked embarrassed and glanced down at the lace ruffles covering his hands. "Alec, it is not the loss of a couple of sinecures which concerns me. I harbor expectations of becoming engaged to the Lady Henrietta Russell. But Lord Russell won't be much inclined to give his consent to our marriage when Cleveley resigns and I lose those sinecures, will he?"

"But this is wonderful news, Charles. Congratulations," said Alec and offered his hand.

It was reluctantly taken at first, then Sir Charles brightened, seeing the sincerity in which the handshake was offered.

"You're the first to know," he admitted awkwardly. "And thank you for your support. Many would think me aiming too high, given my humble background, but I am confident that his lordship will look on my proposal in a favorable light." Sir Charles smiled weakly. "My sources tell me that despite my unsavory connection, Earl Russell will not hold it against me."

Alec knew that the Russell family was not only one of the foremost political families in the kingdom, it was also extremely wealthy. Lady Henrietta's dowry would be substantial, large enough for Sir Charles not to worry about the loss of income from the sinecures bestowed upon him by his mentor. What interested Alec more was the fact that if Sir Charles did indeed secure the hand of Lady Henrietta, it would be seen as a very public crossing-over into an enemy's camp. It was no secret the Earl Russell and the Duke of Cleveley were bitter political rivals; both headed the opposing factions within the government. The wonder of it was that the Duke had consented to such a match. Then again, if Cleveley were on the point of resigning, perhaps Sir Charles had not felt compelled to tell him?

Alec was left with a nagging doubt about Cleveley's intentions.

"You say *when Cleveley resigns*, as if you know it is a certainty," he said. "I don't see the Duke resigning over passage of the Bristol Bill. You and I know that he has the numbers to push it through both houses. So why should he threaten to resign? Or is that rumor merely a ploy to bring the dissenters back into line? Though I think not." Alec glanced shrewdly at his friend. "Charles, you really do believe Cleveley means to resign, don't you? Why?"

Sir Charles looked his old school friend straight in the eye. "Blackmail."

"Blackmail?" Alec pushed a hand through his thick damp hair and gave an unsteady laugh. "*Cleveley*? Come on, Charles! That arctic piece of walking marble submit to a blackmailer's threats?"

"It seems fantastical," admitted Sir Charles, "and I'd not have given it a second thought myself except—except..." He hesitated, seemed to weigh matters up in his mind, an eye on Alec, then said matter-of-factly, "To be honest, Cleveley's resignation won't come at the hands of a defeated bill. The Bristol bill will be passed. It's Stanton. Lord George. Cleveley's stepson. He'll be the Duke's downfall unless I, with your help, act before it's too late."

"Stanton is blackmailing his stepfather?"

"Stanton isn't blackmailing the Duke. It's Stanton who is being blackmailed."

"By whom?"

"Stanton thought it was Blackwell. That is, until the vicar up and died. Then yesterday Stanton received another threatening letter, and in the same hand, so it couldn't have been Blackwell, could it?"

"What on earth would prompt Stanton to think he was being blackmailed by a poor old cleric?"

Sir Charles sighed. "It's all rather complicated. Stanton was receiving threatening letters before Blackwell came to stay with the Duke. Then they stopped. It was something Blackwell said to Stanton in an offhand way that had him wondering if the blackmailer was the vicar, and that by threatening the Duke with Stanton's secret he had managed to weasel his way into the Duke's pocket."

"Blackwell is the last person I'd suspect a blackmailer, and the Duke is the last person who would be party to blackmail. Are you certain this business isn't something conjured up in one of Stanton's befuddled drunken states?"

"It does sound rather far-fetched, doesn't it? Except, I was shown one of the threatening letters and..." Sir Charles sighed again. "Stanton did perpetrate the crime for which he is being blackmailed."

"Let me understand you," Alec enunciated. "It is because of this crime committed by his stepson that Cleveley will take the dramatic step of resigning?"

"If it should become public, yes."

Alec was astonished. "And if the crime remains secret?"

"Then there is no reason for the Duke to step down from his posts. We can all remain as we are."

"Has it not occurred to you that if Stanton did commit the crime for which he is being blackmailed, then he is answerable for that crime, whatever the consequences to the Duke and others?"

Sir Charles pulled a face. "It is infinitely more important for the good of the country that the Duke remain as Foreign Secretary. Those who owe him their livelihoods may then keep their places on the Government benches. One man's youthful indiscretion should not cause a government's downfall."

Alec was revolted. "And justice...?"

Sir Charles rolled his eyes. "My dear Alec, what a romantic you are! Another fault instilled by your eccentric uncle, no doubt. *Justice*? Do you call it *justice* when a man of Cleveley's abilities is forced out of office for a crime *he* didn't commit? Where is the justice in that?"

"Can't Cleveley ride out the storm, distance himself from his stepson's youthful indiscretion?"

"Easier said than done."

"You're not going to tell me Cleveley will do all in his power to avert a family scandal, to the point of risking reputation and position, just to save face? Are—you—Charles?" When this was met with silence, Alec threw up a hand impatiently and stared out the window.

"I thought Cleveley a cold-blooded, calculating manipulator, but I never expected his judgment would be clouded by hubris!"

"My dear fellow, if only it was that simple. His Grace cannot distance himself even if he desired it."

"Ah," Alec said with dawning realization. "He's known about Stanton's transgression from the beginning and sought to cover it up. He hoped to get away with it, but now his stepson is being blackmailed. Cleveley, too, could be blackmailed. After all, he has aided and abetted, hasn't he?"

Sir Charles reluctantly agreed and came to stand by Alec at the window. "That's why I—*he*—needs your help."

"What gives Cleveley the grand presumption I'd help save his neck?"

Sir Charles stared into the middle-distance. "It would get you an ambassadorship…"

Alec's laugh was harsh. "My God, he thinks he can *bribe* me to help him?"

"I would not call it *bribery* but a *return* on the favor done you."

"I beg your pardon?"

Sir Charles turned and faced Alec in the window embrasure. "The whisper around town is that it was your godmother, the Duchess of Romney-St. Neots, who had the accusation of murder against you quashed. That it was through her efforts that you were elevated to the Marquessate Halsey, because there are those in the Lords who were, and still are, against you inheriting your brother's earldom. And before you ask it, I was not one of those who believed you capable of shooting your own brother in cold blood, not without good reason. Your brother was a repellent being. The Duke added his voice to your godmother's efforts." Sir Charles couldn't help a smug smile. "It was through his efforts, not hers, that His Majesty was finally swayed to grant you letters patent."

Alec scowled at his school friend with a mixture of disgust and disbelief. "You think I should be *grateful* to *the great man*? You think by telling me this I will be sympathetic to his predicament—*to yours*? How very wrong you are!" He snatched up his frock coat. "Tell your master to bestow his ambassadorship elsewhere!"

Sir Charles was so taken aback that for a moment he just stood there, stunned. But in the next breath he came alive and hurried after Alec, tripping over his feet along the length of the Gallery as he tried to match Alec's angry strides. He caught him up as he opened the door, and shuddering in breath said, "Listen—Alec!" He swallowed, chest heaving. "I'll grant you… You—you do not care for the Duke's politics… And you—you care even less for the man, but I know you do care—you care very deeply for-for—Mrs. Jamison-Lewis…" He leaned his shoulders against the paneled wall, swallowed in air and breathed deeply. "Do you want to see her family disgraced? Do you want harm to come to her brother; to *her*, the center of scandal? Well? *Do you*?"

Alec slowly closed over the door. "What has Mrs. Jamison-Lewis to do with Stanton?"

Sir Charles's breathing became more regular. "It's her brother; not Cobham, her younger brother, Talgarth Vesey. He's the blackmailer."

"You seem certain."

"I am. The letters are in his fist."

"Why would Talgarth Vesey, a painter of portraits, blackmail Lord George Stanton?"

"Do you know why the Duke bundled brother and sister from that exhibition in such a hurry?"

"I imagine the embarrassment at having unveiled a mutilated portrait, and Vesey's subsequent breakdown in full view of a hundred people, was all too much for His Grace's delicate sensibilities."

"Because he realized at once who had mutilated that portrait and why."

"So you think?"

Sir Charles ignored the heavy sarcasm. "Lord George did it. He did it in a drunken rage."

"I suppose he told you that?"

"He has confessed all to the Duke, although His Grace had already guessed."

Alec was suddenly weary. "Would you get to the point, Charles."

"My friend, the point is this: If you cannot or will not put a stop to Vesey exposing Lord George's indiscretion, then I'm afraid steps will be taken to make certain Vesey can never voice his threats."

"Is that what happened to Blackwell? Did he discover Stanton's sordid little secret while staying in the Cleveley household, and for that he was murdered?"

"I'm sure I don't know what you're talking about. But we are not discussing the demise of one poor old vicar, are we?"

"How brave are little men when protected by the hand of power and privilege," Alec enunciated coldly.

"I do not apologize," Sir Charles replied, "Lord George cannot be allowed to bring down our Foreign Secretary and all those who nestle within his velvet glove." He took out his pocket watch. "Good Lord! I've a meeting with the party whips in an hour. I can inform His Grace you will see what you can do to help…?"

"May I know Lord George's crime?"

Sir Charles couldn't help a smile of embarrassment. "About five years ago he—er—*forced his attentions* on a young lady of good family: The female in Vesey's portrait that was subsequently mutilated. Unfortunately she was impregnated—"

"*Jesu…*"

"—and gave birth, most unfortunately, to a healthy female child. Her family was *persuaded* not to press charges, and the female was bundled off to an undisclosed direction. No more was thought of her until letters of a threatening nature arrived on Lord George's doorstep. It is not known how he found out, but Talgarth Vesey is now championing the woman's cause for monetary compensation from the Duke or he will expose Lord George's folly to the world."

Alec was skeptical. "What trump could Vesey possibly have in his possession that could outmaneuver the likes of Cleveley?"

Sir Charles followed Alec out onto the landing where they were met by the butler coming up the stairs.

"In a moment of guilt-ridden drunken weakness, that fool Lord George replied to one of those letters and wrote the girl a sniveling apology; Vesey now holds this damming piece as evidence."

"Wantage," said Alec, suppressing the urge to rearrange the politician's neckcloth, "show Sir Charles the street door."

"I should think, given your—um—*influence* with the sister, persuading the brother to give up such a trifling letter will be a simple task," Sir Charles concluded with a condescending smile, and passed the butler to walk down the stairs before him.

Wantage remained fixed on the top step.

"Wantage," Alec said through his teeth, "*get rid of him.*"

The butler bowed. "Certainly, my lord. I shall do so immediately. It's just that, it's Mr. Halsey, my lord. He's up in his rooms with a nasty knock to his head. The physician says it's a concussion and wants to bleed him…" His voice trailed off.

His master had turned and was running along the passageway to his uncle's rooms.

FIVE

EARLIER THAT SAME MORNING, WHILE ALEC WAS GOING through his paces with the fencing master, Tam was visiting the *Stock and Buckle*, a crowded coffee house in St. James's on the corner of Berry and King Streets. The *Stock and Buckle*, like most coffee houses in London, was identified by its regular clientele, who spent their few idle hours drinking coffee, tea, or chocolate, playing at cards, and enjoying the freedom of speech within its comfortable surroundings. If one were not inclined to conversation, then newspapers could be rented and read on the premises.

Tam often enjoyed an hour within the cozy rooms of this establishment amongst his fellow upper servants. Being valet to a Marquess afforded him the respect due his master's rank, begrudgingly so because of his youth, and with suspicion because he was well-versed in the secret arts of the apothecary and was known to dispense medicines to the needy.

It was in his role as apothecary that he shouldered past a group of valets gathered in the foyer, making noisy preparations for their departure, and slid onto the chair at the table in the bay window. He ordered a coffee. He should have been studying for his exams. He felt a great sense of guilt wasting the valuable time so generously given to him by his lordship, but the summons had come from 'the Duke' himself and so could not be ignored. Besides, there were a number of questions he wished to put to 'the Duke,' and if the answers were not forthcoming, he planned to withhold the small glass bottle of oil he carried in a deep pocket of his frock coat.

Since his first visit to the *Stock and Buckle*, Tam had been warned that the table in the bay window with its view of the street was reserved exclusively for Robert Molyneux, valet to the Duke of Cleveley. Known as 'the Duke', a term used with derision because he carried himself as if he were indeed of that rank and even spoke with the same arrogant inflection peculiar to his master, Molyneux had been valet to the Duke of Cleveley for twenty-two years. He always drank his coffee while perusing the latest newssheets, coldly oblivious to those about him. Most of his fellows avoided him, not only because he was insufferably arrogant, but also because his face and neck were hideously scarred from the smallpox.

The coffee came, and Tam waited.

Molyneux continued to read the *London Gazette*, hidden from view behind its upheld pages. Ordinarily such rudeness would not have bothered Tam, who was used to 'the Duke's' ways, but he did not have the leisure to wait to be acknowledged. He sipped his coffee and put the little blue glass jar on the table, careful to keep his fingers curled about its stem.

"I've brought the oil, as you requested, Mr. Molyneux. Bathe your knee with it at night before you retire and you should have some relief by morning. If not, I suggest—"

"What's it made of?" came the blunt question from behind the spread-out newssheets.

"An ounce each of Friar's balsam and tincture of myrrh; two ounces of spirits of turpentine—"

The newssheet came down and was folded away. "I didn't ask for the recipe, Thomas Fisher." Molyneux put out a hand to take the bottle, but slowly withdrew it when Tam kept his fingers closed around it. He was so taken aback that at first he did not know what to say. He was not used to being denied. "Is it payment you want, *boy*?" he spat out in a whisper.

Tam shook his head. His intestines churned with nervousness, yet his eyes did not waver from the man's face. "No, Mr. Molyneux. I don't take payment. You know that. What I want is the answers to a few questions."

"*Questions*? *Answers*? You presume a damn lot."

Tam swallowed. Now was not the time to be tongue-tied. "Yes, sir, I do," he said politely. "But only you can answer them for me."

Molyneux stared at the freckled-faced youth with his mop of carrot-red hair and clear green eyes, weighing up whether he was being deliberately insolent or stupidly naive. He decided the latter. He threw several pennies on the table and made to rise. But Tam's next sentence put his stiff knees back under the table.

"It's about the death of the Reverend Blackwell, Mr. Molyneux. Thank you, sir," he said when the man resumed his chair. "I appreciate you taking the time to speak with me."

Molyneux leaned across the table. "If you think we have anything to say to you about a scruffy man of God, you're much mistaken!"

"His Grace didn't like him, sir?" Tam asked innocently. He knew he was treading on hallowed ground; it was an unwritten rule that one's employer was never discussed within the walls of the *Stock and Buckle*. So it was no surprise when Molyneux visibly stiffened. "Then again, sir, he must've had some consideration for him. After all, it was at his invitation that Mr. Blackwell came to stay in St. James's Square, wasn't it, sir?"

"What do you know about that?"

So it was true. The Duke had invited the cleric to his house. Why? Tam looked at the liquid in the blue bottle. "Mr. Blackwell was my friend, Mr. Molyneux."

Molyneux sniffed contemptuously. "A pity then that he didn't come begging at *your* master's door. It would've saved us a great deal of trouble!"

"When he died so unexpectedly, Mr. Molyneux?" asked Tam, all wide-eyed innocence. "Or was it expected?"

"Listen, boy. I don't care for your insolent tone. How could we have known the old fool would up and die like that? He had a heart attack. And very inconvenient it was for us, too."

"I know the physician said it was a heart attack," Tam said calmly. "I also know what is being whispered around town, Mr. Molyneux."

"Whispered?" The valet looked confused. "Why would anyone be interested in the death of a nobody vicar?"

Tam sipped the last of his coffee. It was cold and very bitter. "Servant gossip, Mr. Molyneux."

Molyneux drew himself to sit up. "Not in our house," he enunciated.

Tam took a gamble. "Sir Charles Weir's servants don't possess the same loyalty, Mr. Molyneux," he said with apology.

This hit the mark.

Molyneux frowned. To hide the fact he was rattled, he gestured for a waiter. The waiter knew what to bring without asking.

"You know not to listen to servant gossip, lad." Molyneux said, focusing on Tam with something of a sneering smile. "If I listened to servant gossip I'd say you needed the wind taken out of your sails. Too cocky by half, that's what's said about you. Valet to a pretty-faced Marquess, and you such an infant. Whoever heard of the like. What did you do to earn it, eh? I'll tell you what they say around here: That you're his catamite."

Tam felt the heat rise in his face and cursed himself, but he wasn't about to let 'the Duke' get the better of him. "You know that isn't true, sir," he said quietly. "And I'm not half as cocky as people make out. Every day I count my good fortune." He leaned toward the valet. "You and I have something in common, don't we, sir? I mean, people are just as jealous of you, what with you taking care of such a powerful nobleman and for so long. They say you're a papist plotter for the Jacobites, and that His Grace hasn't a clue. What do they know? I don't believe for a moment you're a traitor to King and country; not being as devoted to His Grace as you are. And I don't care in the least if you're a papist. When all's said and done we're all Englishman, one and all, aren't we, sir?"

Molyneux pushed a coffee toward Tam and waved the waiter away. For what seemed like minutes he merely sipped at the bittersweet brew, regarding Tam over the rim of the mug. Then he winked and said very quietly, "Stick to your instincts, boy."

Tam permitted himself a small smile. He felt a huge relief, as if he had been permitted to cross over to Molyneux's side of the river. They drank their coffee in silence for a moment, conscious that the coffee house was filling up and that they had been sitting together long enough to cause more than one head to turn in their direction. Fortunately, there was enough noisy chatter to cover their conversation.

"Sir. Do *you* think Mr. Blackwell was poisoned?"

This time Molyneux did not sneer. "Why would anyone want to poison an old vicar who spent his days helping the poorest wretches in the City?"

Tam sighed. "Precisely, sir. It does seem fantastical. But don't you think it strange he should up and have a heart attack just like that at a dinner party?"

"Why? If a king can collapse while sitting on his *pot de chambre*, I don't see why a vicar can't keel over in the middle of dinner."

Tam was not convinced. "I suppose that's true, but it don't seem at all right, sir. I have this awful feeling he was poisoned."

"Only you might know if that is so," reasoned Molyneux. "You tell me if he had any enemies. You were his friend."

"Friends or enemies, sir, I doubt they'd have earned a place at Sir Charles Weir's table."

"Listen to me, Master Fisher: Take care what you're about. If anyone can have the finger pointed at him, it's *your* master. Think about it. Seven months ago he was accused of murdering his own brother. That the charge was dropped don't mean a groat to anyone wanting to apportion blame. Nor does the fact His Majesty saw fit to elevate your pretty-boy master to a Marquessate. As if a title can somehow make us forget his brother had his brains blown out! It don't. We think it only makes it worse for him. And you don't make it any easier either."

"*Me*, sir?" Tam was surprised.

Molyneux laughed softly. "You really are a greenhorn! You were an apothecary's apprentice before your master took you in, *and* he's let you continue on making up your lotions and potions. You prepare and dispense medicines. You have access to all sorts of drugs and poisons and you know how to use them. Who's to say you didn't supply your master with the poison that killed old Blackwell?"

Tam was horrified. "But Mr. Blackwell was Lord Halsey's friend too."

Molyneux shrugged. "No one knows that, do they?"

"Why would his lordship want to murder him?"

"Same reason as anyone else at that dinner party, although we don't know the reason, do we?"

"Does *your* master think—"

"We have no idea," Molyneux answered curtly, and looked out the window.

"I understand, sir," Tam said quietly. "I didn't expect you to break any confidences. I just need to know where to go from here. Whatever you thought of Mr. Blackwell, I knew him to be a kind and caring man who meant no harm. To think someone poisoned him makes me sick in the gut. Here," he said and placed the blue glass bottle before Molyneux and stood. "Remember, just a few drops in warm water." He gave a quaint little bow of the head. "Thank you for the coffee, sir."

He turned to go, but the valet grabbed his wrist and jerked him back. "Don't get mixed up in this, lad. Your Reverend Blackwell wasn't all he seemed. He tried to right his wrongs, but some wrongs just can't be undone. That's all I can tell you. And you didn't hear that from me. Understand, lad?" He squeezed Tam's wrist. "*Understand*?"

Tam nodded and his wrist was released. "Yes, Mr. Molyneux. Upon my honor."

"FISHER? THOMAS *FISHER*? WHERE'S THOMAS FISHER?"

Several men crowded the entrance to the coffee house and a great deal of arguing was going on amongst them. A waiter tried to stop two men from coming further into the establishment, but they pressed on regardless. Between them they carried a gentleman above the elbows who looked for the all the world to be dead drunk. They propped him up against the nearest wall and slid him down to sit on the floorboards, upsetting the leg of a table where three men were playing at whist.

Playing cards fluttered everywhere.

As soon as he was let go, the gentleman slumped forward so his chin came to rest on his chest. From this angle, the semi-circle of onlookers had a good view of his bare head. In the candlelight, blood glistened wet in the gray grizzled hair above his left ear. There was speculation as to the reason why an old man had been attacked. One of the waiters called out to his fellows to bring hot water and rags. Another volunteered to run up to the local tavern for some brandy, knowing full well there was a bottle under the counter, but could not say so because coffee houses were, by law, not permitted to have alcohol on the premises. An astute customer was quick to point out the expensive cloth on the old man's back. Perhaps he'd been set upon for his purse? said another. What an old man of means was doing in a filthy laneway was anyone's guess. Another wondered if he had gone into the laneway to relieve himself. Perhaps he had been propositioning a whore? At this there was general laughter.

"*Fisher*? Thomas Fisher!"

"He's with 'the Duke'!" came a shout by the fireplace.

A waiter grabbed Tam's elbow and hurriedly led him across the room, saying, "There's been a scuffle in the lane, lad. A couple of thugs set-to on an old gent. Got a great gash to his head. Can you do anything for him? Come on, you fellows! Give way! Give way, before the blood ruins the floorboards!"

The crowd shouldered apart and began to disperse. Now that the young lad had everything in order, there was no need to stand about gawking. Besides, the coffee was getting cold.

The old man lifted his head with an effort and blinked as Tam knelt beside him.

"Damn glad it's you, m'boy," Plantagenet Halsey mumbled and promptly fainted.

ALEC THREW OPEN THE DOOR TO HIS UNCLE'S BEDCHAMBER with such violence that the door handle punctured the Chinese wallpaper. Plantagenet Halsey was lying in his four-poster bed, propped up on a mountain of pillows, head swathed in bandages and arms lifeless at his sides. A physician and his assistant were conferring by the bedside. The assistant took from a large black leather medical bag a jar swimming with leeches. Plantagenet Halsey's valet and Tam stood grim-faced and silent at the foot of the bed.

"Well? How is he?" Alec demanded, sitting on the edge of the mattress and taking his uncle's limp cold hand in his. He looked around at all four men. "What happened? Did he take a fall? Will he be all right?"

"My lord, if Mr. Halsey would only be bled and take the medicinal—"

"I've lost enough blood already, so don't you be worryin' his lordship," the old man interrupted with a grumble. He turned his bandaged head slowly on the pillow. "But I'll take your foul-tastin' brew if you'll just get out of m'sight. The lad here can give me what I need."

The physician sucked in his fat cheeks, a glance of disapproval at Tam, and waved away his assistant, who meekly replaced the jar in the black bag, before pointedly handing the measured dose of laudanum, not to Tam but to the old man's valet.

"I need hardly remind your lordship that it is unlawful for anyone but a qualified physician to prescribe medicinals, and that I have previously warned Mr. Halsey on *several* occasions that should it come to my attention that Thomas Fisher is practicing his unqualified apothecary skills on the populace of my parish, I will be forced to report such a grievous matter to the proper authorit—"

"You *dare*, you miserable painmerchant," Plantagenet Halsey growled through his teeth and half rose off the pillows.

"Yes, I am well aware of your threats, Miller. Thank you," Alec said curtly and turned his shoulder in dismissal, the physician and his assistant bowing silently to his back before departing. Alec squeezed his uncle's hand. "I see a knock to the head hasn't dulled your senses," he said with a lopsided grin, greatly relieved knowing the old man wasn't seriously hurt. He pretended not to see the grimace of pain that crossed his uncle's lined face as he lay back amongst the pillows, adding quietly, "All the same, for my sake, and I'm sure Tam will agree, take the laudanum merely as a precautionary measure."

The old man opened his eyes. "Not yet. Got somethin' to show you first. Thomas, those papers Barlow found in my frock coat pocket, give 'em to his lordship. By the way, I did thank you for patchin' me up, didn't I, lad?"

"Yes, sir. You did. Twice," said Tam as he handed Alec a dog-eared, yellowed pamphlet. He then retreated, as requested, with the old man's valet to the dressing room; the valet with the dose of laudanum held covetously to his chest.

"Just before I was knocked on the head, a ridiculous fellow in canary yellow silks who'd been followin' me since I left me meetin', shoved his hand in m'waistcoat pocket," Plantagenet Halsey explained. "I thought he was tryin' to steal m'watch, but when he ran off just as everythin' around me went black, I put m'hand in m'pocket and realized the fellow had put somethin' in there, not taken somethin' out."

Alec nodded absently as he put on his gold-rimmed spectacles and flicked through the closely-printed yellowed pages of a weathered pamphlet denouncing slavery. There were arithmetic jottings in a number of the margins. There was also a dark circular stain, such as that left by a chocolate or coffee mug. But what really caught Alec's interest were two thin sheets of parchment, folded neatly in half and slipped between the pages of the pamphlet. "Did you know these were here?" he asked over his gold rims as he unfolded the thin pages. "Have you read them?"

"Took a quick look while the lad was bandagin' m'head," replied the old man. "You'll find it plain and to the point, like the man himself."

The pages proved to be the last will and testament of the Reverend Kenneth Blackwell Dempsey-Weir, late of the parish of St. Jude's in the City of London; second son of the late Viscount Dempsey-Weir of Hawkhurst in Kent. It was signed, witnessed, sealed and dated the day before Blackwell's death. The will had been witnessed by Justinian, Duke of Cleveley, and signed off by Thaddeus Fanshawe Esq., lawyer. The main beneficiary was one Catherine

Sophia Elizabeth Bourdon of Ellick Farm in Somerset, bequeathed Blackwell's entire estate, consisting of two sugar plantations in Barbados, a townhouse in Mount Street leased to the Cornwallis family for a further ten years, and ten thousand pounds plus accrued interest, deposited in the Bank of England over twenty years ago. A further five thousand pounds was bequeathed to Sir Charles Weir, past private secretary to His Grace the Most Noble Duke of Cleveley. Blackwell's Bible, gold pocket watch and a thousand pounds were willed to Thomas Fisher, apothecary and valet to Lord Halsey; a gold snuffbox and a small miniature of the Duchess of Cleveley in a gold frame were to go to Lord George Stanton. Blackwell asked that he be laid to rest in the family vault at Hawkhurst.

From amongst the down-filled pillows, Plantagenet Halsey regarded his nephew with a smile of satisfaction, the relentless throbbing pain in his head momentarily forgotten. "Makes you sit up and wonder, don't it? I mean, here we were thinkin' Blackwell eked out an existence in the poorest parish of the City because he was a penniless vicar, and one who couldn't possibly have an enemy in the world, yet the man who made out that will was wealthy and well-connected. So who's to say he didn't have enemies? You've got to admit, it's a damned intriguin' business."

"Very," agreed Alec and returned the will between the pages of the pamphlet. "Two plantations in Barbados and ten thousand with the Bank of England… And yet he devoted his life to those less fortunate than himself. What a remarkable gentleman."

"But somethin' or someone in his past must've come back to haunt him, because the man was murdered at Weir's dinner party."

"But why was he murdered? For his money? No one at the dinner party except Cleveley knew Blackwell was a wealthy man. And who amongst the diners stood to gain from his death? Charles? I doubt he poisoned Blackwell for five thousand pounds. Charles's sinecures from Cleveley alone must be worth that per annum. As for George Stanton, he is a drunk and a parasitic dullard, but even he wouldn't stoop to murdering a vicar for a gold snuffbox and a miniature of his mother." Alec removed his spectacles. "It's Catherine Bourdon we need to find out about, and by virtue of being signatories to the will, Cleveley and the lawyer Fanshawe must know this woman and her whereabouts."

"Blackwell's death has made her a rich woman," stated the old man, closing his eyes and secretly wishing he had taken the laudanum when it was first offered. The pain in his head was becoming unbearable. "And you said it yourself, Cleveley knew Blackwell was wealthy..."

"And he was signatory to Blackwell's will. But he didn't need to poison him for his money," reasoned Alec. "If you're going to accuse Cleveley, you'll have to come up with another explanation for why he wanted the vicar dead." He signaled for his uncle's valet to take his place beside the bed, saying to Tam as he crossed into the dressing room," Where did my uncle come by that knock to his head?"

"In the lane beside the *Stock and Buckle*, sir."

"*Stock and Buckle*? That isn't far from here, is it?"

"Just up King Street, sir."

"He should've taken his chair. He knows he isn't steady on his feet. Will he be all right?"

"Yes, sir. Mr. Halsey is remarkably healthy for a gentleman of his age. He'll heal in no time. His skull isn't fractured, so there's no reason to think his brain is bruised. And so I told Dr. Miller, but he didn't believe me and had his assistant remove the bandages so he could make a proper *informed* diagnosis."

"I would've been most disappointed had Miller not done so, Tam," Alec stated, and watched the boy drop his gaze with a frown. "Miller means well, but he's prejudiced like all his kind against the growing expertise of the apothecaries. The physicians feel their unique position in the world is under threat." He smiled. "And no small wonder is it, when a lad of nineteen is just as expert as our good doctor at making a diagnosis. Now tell me: Do you know what induced my uncle to stroll into a laneway to be accosted by some fool dressed in canary yellow?"

Tam thinned his lips. "Well, sir, I don't think he meant to go into the laneway."

"Meaning?"

"He went to the aid of the gentleman dressed in canary yellow, who'd been following him since he left a meeting of the anti-slavery league," explained Tam. "The gentleman in yellow was dragged into the laneway by two thugs and Mr. Halsey heard his cry for help. And from what the lads who brought Mr. Halsey into the *Stock and Buckle* could tell me, the gentleman in yellow managed to escape and run off up Berry Street when the thugs set-to on Mr. Halsey…"

"And?" prompted Alec, seeing Tam hesitate.

"Just an odd circumstance, sir. And I don't know what to make of it, but the thugs were wearing livery."

"Livery?" Alec was incredulous. "The thugs were *liveried* servants? Your friends were certain?"

"Yes, sir," said Tam, glancing through the open doorway at the old man who was meekly sipping the laudanum from the cup his valet held to his mouth.

"If this unknown gentleman was set upon by men in livery, then it seems highly unlikely that stealing was their motive. Was anyone able to give a description of the gentleman wearing the absurd colored clothing?"

"Not much of a physical description I'm afraid, sir. But the lads reckon a gentleman wearing a canary yellow silk frock coat and matching breeches, which you'd usually see on a dandy at a rout or a ball, shouldn't be difficult to run to ground." Tam smiled in spite of himself. "Definitely not daytime attire here in St. James's, sir."

Alec put up his brows. "How a man in his sixtieth year could delude himself into thinking he could play hero, and to a dandy in canary yellow being set upon by liveried servants, defies the imagination. But you're right, such a fellow shouldn't be hard to find, not least of all after we have a proper description from my uncle." He glanced at the now-dozing figure lying still in the huge bed and beckoned Plantagenet Halsey's valet. "Let me know the moment Mr. Halsey wakes." And taking one last look at his uncle, as if to convince himself that the old man was indeed resting comfortably, patted Tam's shoulder as he made to depart. "Thank you for taking care of him, Tam."

Tam smiled and, noting that his master still wore the clothes he'd dressed in early that morning, said, "Shall I see to your bath, sir?"

"No. Take yourself off to clean up. Jeffries can see to what I need."

"But—sir!" Tam blurted out rudely as he followed Alec out into the passageway, feeling more unsettled than ever that he was losing control over his valeting duties. Hadrian Jeffries, a haughty upper footman, had been attending on his lordship from time to time when Tam was preoccupied with his studies. "Jeffries insists on rearranging what I've just arranged in the closet, and he refolds *all* your neckcloths sayin' I don't know how to—"

"That will do," Alec said firmly.

When Tam threw him a petulant look, shoved a hand deep in his frock coat pocket and hung his head, Alec was about to get angry. But the boy took out a handkerchief, carefully unfolded it and held it out to him. In its depressed center nestled a silver button.

"One of the gentlemen who helped Mr. Halsey said this must've come off in the scuffle. He found it in Mr. Halsey's grip." He waited for Alec to put on his spectacles. "It's unusual, isn't it, sir?"

Alec peered at the shiny, silver-domed button with its intricate pattern. "The engraving appears to be that of a bumblebee?"

"Yes, sir. Apparently it's quite unusual for livery to have engraved buttons, so the lads down at the *Stock and Buckle* tell me." Tam smiled in spite of himself. "One of the regulars knew it straight off."

Alec looked over his gold rims with a raised eyebrow.

"That button can belong to only one nobleman's livery, sir," Tam said with satisfaction. "His Grace the Duke of Cleveley."

SIX

The porter of a particular townhouse in Cavendish Square opened wide the front door with a bored yawn and blinked into the darkness. On the top step stood a magnificently dressed gentleman. He wore a splendid powdered wig and carried a pair of velvet gloves with brocade cuffs. The porter had no idea who he was, but knew from the gentleman's richly-embroidered frock coat, the large diamond-encrusted shoe buckles, and the ornate and bejeweled hilt of his sword that he was someone very important indeed. The porter wondered if he were dreaming; the butler knew he was not. With a deft elbow, the butler shoved aside the sleepy and ignorant porter, and with a bow worthy of a vassal of the Turkish sultan bid the visitor welcome.

The Duke of Cleveley had come calling on his bitter political rival, the Earl Russell.

Lord Russell was expecting His Grace and greeted him in his library.

In this book-lined room these two politically-powerful noblemen, who between them owned much of England's green rolling hills, remained closeted until late into the night. It boggled the butler's mind to speculate on just what was being discussed.

He wished himself a flea in his master's wig.

The Duchess of Romney-St. Neots peered out of her box seat at the King's Theatre, Haymarket, and pretended to be as captivated as the rest of the audience by the soprano's enchanting voice. She wasn't particularly fond of opera. She knew she must be one of the few people who did not appreciate "high-pitched shouting matches", as she was wont to call them. The theater was more to her taste, but her youngest daughter, the Lady Sybilla, preferred the opera; it made her cry. God only knew why, wondered the Duchess, pleased her godson had accepted the invitation to join them, thus saving her from an evening of her daughter's morbid weeping. She was well aware Sybilla harbored an infatuation for Alec Halsey, despite her wifely devotion to her husband, the dear Admiral. She hoped Alec's presence would provide the distraction needed to stop the woman's constant tears, no doubt a consequence of her advancing pregnancy.

The Duchess would have preferred to be at home, propped up in a warmed bed, writing a letter to her granddaughter Emily, who was on her way to Venice, or was it Copenhagen? She missed Emily's company. It showed on her features as the prompter's bell tolled on the second act, bringing with it a general crescendo of noise and movement amongst the audience.

Those seated in the double horseshoe boxes sent servants off for refreshments, conversation hardly lagging throughout the performance under the yellow glow from the wall sconces, while the more adventurous made the dash to relieve themselves in the chamber pots hidden behind ornate screens.

The Duchess unfurled her fan of painted chicken skin and resettled herself more comfortably against the tasseled cushion at her back. She failed to notice her daughter standing dutifully beside her chair, ready to assist should she wish to stand for a few moments. The Lady Sybilla coughed politely into a gloved hand, and when this did not distract her mother, she turned to the other occupant of the box with a pleading look.

"Your frown has turned into a smile, Olivia, and I know you loathe the opera," Alec commented near the Duchess's ear. "What has taken your fancy? I trust it's not Lord Rutherglen's appalling wig *à la Mariner*? He appears to have swum the Channel in it."

"Horrid boy," complained the Duchess with a laugh, and poked her daughter's wide hooped petticoats with the sticks of her fan. "Sit down, Sybilla! How am I expected to *see*? Standing in your condition. What would the Admiral say to it?"

"Mamma, I thought, if you wished to take a walk about the box…?"

The Duchess scoffed. "So Rutherglen's ferret-faced wife can see me limp about? Don't be absurd!"

Lady Sybilla dutifully curtsied and disappeared once more into a corner at the back of the box, Alec's reassuring smile enough to make her blush and retreat behind her fluttering fan.

"He does look a fool, doesn't he?" the Duchess commented behind her unfurled fan, a glance at the group seated in the third box along the row. "Poor Jasper. It's a wonder his wife hasn't killed him by now. You needn't look surprised. I don't mean in the literal sense. Though…" She rested the opened fan on her ample bosom and regarded the woman in question through narrowed eyes. "I believe Frances Rutherglen capable of anything she put her mind to. She's a cold-blooded serpent."

"Until Rutherglen was kicked up to the Lords, he was the only MP Uncle Plant saw fit not to ridicule," Alec commented. "I'd no idea it was out of pity because the man's wife is a murderous reptile."

The Duchess's eyes twinkled. "You are better than any tonic, my boy. It's a shame your uncle couldn't join us. How is he faring?"

"He was still sleeping when I left the house," said Alec, a curt nod in the direction of a lady who, by the subtle movements of her ivory fan, was trying to engage him in flirtation. "I dare say he will awaken in the morning with a thumping great headache."

He avoided the eye of a painted temptress two boxes along the row and looked out across the void that separated the somber-clothed merchants in the pit from the silk-clad nobility above, to the box occupied by the Duke of Cleveley. His Grace sat resplendent in rich blue satin, glittering decorations and orders pinned to his breast, with half a dozen bewigged and high-heeled grinning cronies lounging about him, ready to jump to attention with just one softly-spoken word. This nobleman and his pampered, powdered and patched friends oozed arrogant self-confidence from every pore of their soft white skin.

The Duchess followed Alec's gaze. "You still aren't seriously entertaining the idea that Cleveley had a hand in your uncle's assault?"

Alec turned his angular profile to look directly at his godmother. "It is mere coincidence then, that the button found in my uncle's fist belongs to the Cleveley livery?"

The Duchess shrugged. "I have known Cleveley since he was in leading-strings. He has too much pride to use bully-boy tactics."

Alec was unconvinced. "He has only to express the desire and his lackeys would be more than willing to oblige him. But you think *the great man* would not stoop…?"

The Duchess dropped her gaze to the pointed toes of her purple and gold silk mules that rested on a padded footstool. "As much as I would love to support you in this, my dear boy, I cannot. Cleveley would not, *could* not, resort to such craven tactics. It's not in his nature." When Alec remained unmoved she added, "One little button; it cannot condemn a man."

"No, but it can cast suspicion in his direction."

"Certainly," agreed the Duchess. "Suspicion, not *conviction*."

Alec again turned his attention to the Duke's box. It was Cleveley's first appearance at the King's Theatre since the death of his Duchess, and as had happened at Ranelagh Gardens, he was attracting more than his fair share of notice. And, as always, the Duke seemed oblivious to all the fuss. He continued to sit, unmoved by the noise of conversation and music and the toll of the bell, with a slight inclination of his left ear to the conversation at his back between Sir Charles Weir and the Viscount St. Edmunds. Alec noted that the Duke's stepson was not playing shadow tonight. He wondered if Charles had got up the nerve to tell his mentor of his plans to marry Lady Henrietta Russell, and guessed he had not. The Lady Henrietta and her mother were seated in the box next to that occupied by the Duke, and Charles had neither looked in their direction nor made an effort to lean over the divider to engage them in conversation.

Alec finally looked away from the Duke and his party saying casually, "Olivia, tell me about Cleveley."

The Duchess wrinkled her little nose. "What about him? I must confess to knowing very little about his politics, although I have followed his career. His mother and mine were cousins and Romney showed an interest in him when he first took his seat in the Lords. He was very young when he came into the dukedom—only seventeen. Romney thought the political wolves would have him for supper, but the boy soon proved him wrong. It was not quite a year later when he married Ellen. Ellen had been Duchess of Stanton less than four months when she was widowed, pregnant with George, and married off to Cleveley before old Stanton was cold in his coffin! A most unseemly business.

"Of course, like her first marriage, this too was an arranged union, and a very astute financial transaction: Cleveley's titles, her wealth. It consolidated Cleveley's position as the pre-eminent peer in the realm. Romney and I often dined at Cleveley House when Ellen played hostess, but I never went to any of the party political dinners. I left all that to Romney. Why do you ask, my boy? I thought you despised the Duke's politics."

"My interest is in the man. I want to know what sort of man is capable of pushing through a bill that permits men to be stuffed into the stinking hold of one of His Majesty's frigates like animals—"

"My dear Alec," the Duchess scoffed, "they are but savages after all."

"All men have a right to their dignity, to—"

"Your uncle's radical ideas won't wash with me," the Duchess said haughtily, waving a bejeweled hand in dismissal. "And I won't have either of you force Cleveley to shoulder the blame for what occurs on His Majesty's frigates. Unlike your uncle, I, indeed the majority, believe the Duke has the country's best interests at heart. He is one politician who prides himself on working within the framework of what is legally possible *for the good of the Kingdom*. He is not one of these self-serving placemen who will stoop to any means to gain a political advantage." She struggled to sit up, restless, and looked at Alec critically. "To suggest that he had his liveried servants attack a ridiculous personage dressed in canary yellow to seize the last will and testament of a nobody vicar is fanciful nonsense!"

"Your Grace, I—"

"After all, what does Cleveley gain by employing such spineless tactics? He can't rise any higher."

"There is always the prospect of a fall..." Alec suggested lightly, pretending to brush lint from a crossed-legged, satin-covered knee, an oblique eye on his godmother.

"I suppose there is that," the Duchess grudgingly conceded. "Though—you will think this strange and your uncle would certainly scoff—I don't believe Cleveley has ever contemplated such an eventuality. Call it sublime arrogance, if you will, though I prefer to think it merely an overabundance of self-confidence. You laugh! But there is a distinction."

Alec kissed her frail hand. "I missed you while I was in Paris."

"Liar," she chided playfully, yet turning pink with pleasure. "I have it on good authority you spent your entire visit in a Parisian bed."

"Shame on you, Olivia," Alec murmured at her ear. "There are some remarkable Da Vinci etchings in the Louvre..."

"Devil you cared," the Duchess replied with a girlish giggle, a glance at the adjoining boxes, gratified their flirtatious antics were attracting attention. "You knew of course that Selina stayed behind in Paris while Emily and Cosmo ventured on without her?" she added, fluttering her fan across her bosom, a smug smile directed at Frances Rutherglen, who was glaring at her in disapproval.

Alec was surprised. "But I presumed you knew—that Mrs. Jamison-Lewis had told you—I went to Paris at her invitation."

The Duchess's head snapped round. "Her invitation?" She removed her hand from his silken knee and shifted uncomfortably against the tapestry cushion. Cavorting with an unnamed Parisian whore was all well and good for her rakish godson's reputation, but resuming a passionate affair with her niece, a wealthy English widow still in mourning, was not only detrimental to her efforts at rehabilitating her godson's character, but was likely to have devastating consequences on Selina's fragile emotional well-being. "No. I did not know," she stated with annoyance. "I suppose she failed to tell you why she remained in Paris?" His look of total confusion answered the question for her. She took a deep breath. "She appeared—well?"

Alec was still frowning. "Selina's never been ill a day in her life."

The Duchess merely nodded in a preoccupied fashion. "She's not one to complain, is she?" and abruptly changed the topic. "I wish you'd do something about Letitia Strangways. The pathetic, doe-eyed creature has done everything imaginable but shown you what she has on offer under her petticoats, and you continue to ignore her."

Alec wondered to what the Duchess was alluding regarding Selina, but did not feel the theater the place to seek enlightenment, so kept his questions for later and returned to the subject of the Duke of Cleveley, a shoulder turned away from the overtly-eager Lady Letitia Strangways. "Tell me about Cleveley the man, not the politician."

"Why this sudden interest in Cleveley?" asked the Duchess, relieved Alec had the good manners not to question her further about Selina. She would never break her niece's confidence, not even for her godson. But it bruised her heart that he was to be left ignorant of the truth.

"I value your counsel, and frankly, there is no one else I can ask without stirring up a hornet's nest, which is the last thing I want so early in my enquiries—"

"Enquiries? Surely not to do with the death of that vicar at Weir's dinner party?"

"One can only hope the physician got it right."

"You're not suggesting *Cleveley* had anything to do with that? Your uncle may believe Cleveley capable of poisoning the entire clergy, but that's sheer prejudice!"

"There is more to this than my uncle's bias," Alec said seriously.

The Duchess thinned her painted lips. "Am I to give you this picture here and now?"

"If you would be so kind."

The prompter's bells were vigorously ringing, signaling the performance was about to resume, but the Duchess of Romney-St. Neots ignored the jarring jingle, saying impatiently as she smoothed out her voluminous silk petticoats with an agitated hand,

"I suppose that's why you accepted this old lady's invitation to the opera," she grumbled, but was somewhat mollified by his engaging smile—she never was able to resist a handsome rogue, particularly when that handsome rogue happened to be her favorite godson. "If I'm to give you Cleveley's history then let us sit further back with a good claret, if such a thing exists in this chatterbox of a theater. Sybilla? Sybilla!" She made to rise and Alec had taken her elbow before Lady Sybilla was on her feet. "Damn! I wish I'd never taken a fall on that wretched horse. Pass me my stick, dear boy. Sybilla?" When her daughter emerged from her quiet corner she said, "Send Peeble to the carriage for a bottle of claret and two glasses. Oh! And my bourdaloue. You will have need of it, in your condition. Then you can pay your respects to your sister-in-law. Frances has been staring daggers at me these past fifteen minutes."

"But—*Mamma*."

"Tell her you're breeding again. She'll be delighted to know her brother's wife is with child. It will give her a legitimate excuse to be miserable. Not that Frances Rutherglen ever needs one."

Lady Sybilla glanced at Alec, cheeks inflamed. Her mother could never be made to understand how uncomfortable she felt at having her pregnancy openly discussed, and before a gentleman who was so swooningly virile that it was no surprise he had spent an entire week cavorting under the sheets with her cousin Selina. Oh, to open her knees to such a man…

"Yes, Mamma, of course," Sybilla managed to whisper, averting her gaze, face burning bright with shame at having such lascivious thoughts and at the opera! "I shall tell her how happy I am."

"Yes! Yes! How happy we *all* are. Now run along."

LADY SYBILLA WAS ADMITTED TO THE PRIVATE BOX OCCUPIED BY the Rutherglens and found it overflowing with callers. She wondered what had induced four young gentlemen of marriageable age to bother calling at interval on an old couple without any daughters. She then spied the Countess Russell and her pretty but exceedingly silly daughter, Lady Henrietta, an heiress with a dowry exceeding thirty thousand pounds, seated with the Rutherglens. This discovery made her sigh with relief. Her sister-in-law Frances Rutherglen frightened her and Lord Rutherglen was quite deaf and senile, so the presence of the Russells, with whom she was well acquainted, made her feel more at ease with the task she had been sent to perform.

The four gentlemen surrounding Lady Henrietta and her mother politely shifted along the bench to allow Lady Sybilla's wide petticoats unhindered passage to their hosts. A fop in apple green silk breeches and a purple flowered waistcoat was obliging enough to fetch her a glass of Madeira, he having all but given up on his chances with the heiress. She who had giggled incessantly at his witticisms at the Talbot turnout was this night as responsive as a doorknob, and even that, being brass, had more shine. Lady Henrietta looked miserable. Whatever pains her mamma and lady's maid had taken to apply cosmetic over the circles under her exquisite brown eyes, it was obvious to anyone with even partial sight in one eye that the girl had spent the previous evening crying into her down pillows.

Lady Rutherglen took one look at Lady Sybilla standing in the middle of the box and shooed her aside. She was blocking her view of the performance. The green curtain had risen to a thundering crescendo of noise from orchestra and chorus. The voices in the pit were drowned down and conversations in the boxes lowered to an inaudible hush for the smallest of pauses while they took in the scenery, before conversations started up again, regardless of the performers and their vocal abilities. There was nothing for Lady Sybilla to do but retreat to sit beside the Countess Russell and wait her opportunity to speak to the Rutherglens.

The four beaux made good their exit, deflated at not having made an impression on the gloomy-faced Lady Henrietta. As for their ordeal in making polite conversation with Lady Rutherglen, the young gentlemen were incapable of putting into words their relief at what could only be described as having survived a spider in her sticky web. It was beyond their comprehension how such a vile old woman could be sister to an Admiral of the Fleet, who was not only a war hero, but also the most amiable and good-natured fellow of their acquaintance.

The Countess Russell seemed oblivious to her daughter's distress and the distress suffered by the young gentlemen at the spidery hands of Frances Rutherglen. In fact, she smiled serenely on everyone, even on her hostess when that woman condemned her towering headdress of feathers, bows and strategically placed miniature ship with sail as resembling refuse clogging the gutters.

Nothing could shake Lady Russell's smile. After all, her youngest daughter, who was plumply pretty but not very bright, had just made the match of the season, and this despite compromising her virtue. She had despaired of ever marrying off her youngest daughter after she had confessed to drinking to excess at the Cavendish turnout and waking up to find her petticoats up over her navel, her hindquarters exposed to the cold night air and Lord George Stanton buttoning his breeches. That horror was now extinguished knowing Henrietta was to marry, and marry far beyond her mother's wildest expectations.

Lady Sybilla, who was breathing a sigh of relief that her sister-in-law had shooed her away, which meant she could postpone the inevitable for at least another half an hour, suddenly had her lace flounce tugged by Lady Russell.

"Tell me: What is *he* like?" she whispered hurriedly from behind her stiff lace fan, a fervent glance down the row of boxes to her left, disappointed the Duchess of Romney-St. Neots and Lord Halsey had disappeared out of her line of sight.

Lady Sybilla followed the direction of Lady Russell's veiled glance and her eyes widened, but she remained mute.

"*Halsey*," Lady Russell enunciated with annoyance, thinking Lady Sybilla's mind impenetrable. "It's been confirmed in more than one boudoir that he is *most* considerate to a lady's *needs* as to be worth breaking the seventh commandment."

"But he's not—not a *libertine*," Lady Sybilla protested, cheeks burning scarlet under her white lead cosmetic. "I mean… Naturally, I have no idea about his—about *that*, but he—he is—he is everything a-a *gentleman* should be."

"Precisely," purred Her Ladyship, and shivered, entirely forgetting in whose box she sat. She pulled Sybilla closer. "I saw him in Paris, at the Louvre, in company with Selina Jamison-Lewis. God knows what wiles your cousin used, but it was obvious from her vulgar displays of affection that he'd been rutting her senseless. But when one considers why she fled to Paris in the first place I'm surprised she allowed any man between her thighs so soon. Then again, for Halsey I'd have risked it."

"Fled to Paris?" Lady Sybilla repeated with a blink.

Maria Russell's eyes widened and she pursed her painted lips. "Come now, Sybilla. You're her confidante. I need not elaborate for you, surely?"

Lady Sybilla frowned down at the sticks of her ivory fan. "I don't know what you mean…"

Lady Russell pulled a face and whispered in Sybilla's red ear. "You never were a good liar. I shan't blather about Selina ridding herself of the brat. Truth be told, it must be a huge relief not to bring it to term. Farming out a bastard of indeterminate color and lineage would be a fatiguing business. Now let me tell you my news. You'll never guess who called on Russell very late last night…"

Lady Sybilla placed a comforting hand on her sizeable belly and schooled her features to remain stoic. But her mind was reeling. She wondered how Maria Russell had come to find out about Selina's miscarriage. It had never occurred to her that the baby had not been wanted, and for the reasons alluded to by Maria Russell. She did not believe for one moment the persistent rumor that Alec was the product of his mother's affair with a mulatto servant, and yet from where had those blue-black curls and olive skin originated? Lord Halsey's brother had been sandy-haired; his mother a pale blonde. And why had Selina not told Alec about the baby, for surely he was the father, if she did not harbor reservations about giving birth to a colored child? Sybilla mentally shook herself; shocked by her own fickleness about a man who had always been kind and considerate and deserved only her loyalty. Of course she had no idea who had called on Lord Russell.

"*Cleveley*," was Lady Russell's breathless answer, and mistook Lady Sybilla's silent preoccupation for astonishment that the Duke of Cleveley had graced the Russell household with his presence. She added that the two great political rivals had spent several congenial hours in Lord Russell's library and then hinted she was in hourly expectation of her dear Henrietta receiving an offer from His Grace of Cleveley. She then had the satisfaction of watching Lady Sybilla's eyes grow very round.

Lady Sybilla could only peer anew over the pleated rim of her fan at the Duke of Cleveley and inwardly shudder for poor Henrietta. No wonder the girl looked wretched. A great match it certainly was, a great honor done Henrietta, too, but the girl was barely twenty, and despite the rumor she was soiled goods, an indiscretion or two while drunk at a ball, the Duke was far enough on the other side of forty as to be considered a cradle snatcher. Besides, Sybilla was inclined to forgive Henrietta her drunken mistakes for she was not mentally acute and thus was easily led, and she was warm-hearted and kind; the Duke had about as much warmth as the bleakest of January days.

"Naturally, I've not mentioned any of this to Frances," the Countess Russell was saying, a sidelong glance at Frances Rutherglen. "It will break her heart. Not that she won't be happy for Henrietta; she will, given time. But one must not forget the tragic loss of her little Mimi."

Lady Sybilla had not forgotten about Lady Rutherglen's only child. After all, the girl had been Sybilla's niece and a great beauty from a young age. She had died less than five years ago, and in the same week that Sybilla had given birth to the Admiral's second son. Her death had indeed been heartbreaking.

Lady Russell was all too eager to relive the tragedy.

"You remember Mimi. The poor child died of pneumonia just days short of her fifteenth birthday. Her constitution was never strong. Reason she rarely if ever left the schoolroom. Frances was so afraid for her health. The malicious gossips would have you believe it was jealousy of her daughter that kept Mimi shut away; that after one of Frances's parental rages Mimi bolted, only to catch her death for her truancy."

Lady Sybilla could well believe it. Her sister-in-law Frances possessed a heart with the temperature of an icicle and was as plain as a bowl of cold custard; Lady Rutherglen's sister, Ellen, Duchess of Cleveley was prettier but not considered a great beauty. What beauty there was in the family had gone to the sisters' younger brother the Admiral, Sybilla's husband. And as much as Sybilla loved her dear Admiral she was not blind to his physical imperfections; he was no Adonis, no Alec Halsey by any stretch.

"What nonsense," Lady Russell continued scornfully. "Mimi did not bolt. It was all the fault of her country cousin, a wafer-headed creature who had as much sense as a bee in a bottle! She led Mimi astray and what should have been a quiet stroll up the Mall ended in both girls missing for hours, improperly dressed for the inclement weather, and the poor Rutherglens out of their minds with worry fearing Mimi had been abducted. Then their relief at the news Mimi had been found safe only to be told she had collapsed and died. Poor Rutherglen had a stroke at the news and what you see before you is the result!"

Lady Sybilla glanced at Mimi's elderly papa; spittle bubbled at the corner of his slackened mouth. She quickly returned her attention to Lady Russell.

"I seem to recall that the cousin, she did not—"

"—return? How could she? Why would she? It was her fault Mimi died. Wretched *evil* creature. No, Sybilla, you must not believe the gossipmongers. Frances was devoted to her only child. There was a pact between the sisters that Ellen's son George and Frances's Mimi would wed; that one day Mimi would be the next Duchess of Cleveley. Then she passed away and so their dream came to nothing."

This was a revelation to Lady Sybilla, but she thought it typical of her sister-in-law to scheme for such an outcome. Her eyes widened as her glance took in the stocky figure of the Duke of Cleveley. Marriage to the Duke was enough of a repellent notion, but being wed to the Duke's errant corpulent stepson Lord George would be much worse. She would not have been at all surprised had poor Mimi up and died just to get out of such an atrocious arrangement; the country cousin may have done her a favor after all.

"So you see my dilemma," Lady Russell was rattling on. "Henrietta is to gain what Mimi did not live to take." She smiled her delight and satisfaction, gloved hands flexing about the handle of her fan. "I wish Ellen were alive to see the day."

Lady Sybilla wanted to point out that had Ellen, Duchess of Cleveley, been alive it would be impossible for the Lady Henrietta to marry the Duke of Cleveley. She was of the opinion that poor Mimi's fate was infinitely preferable to wedding such a cold fish as *the great man*. These sympathetic musings were cut short, not by the Countess Russell, but by the rasping voice of poor dead Mimi's mamma. Lady Sybilla found herself clutching at Lady Russell's hand for moral support, and realized the Countess was just as terrified of the old woman as she was herself and had caught up her hand first.

"I know why you've come calling, sister," Lady Rutherglen hissed, annoyed the two women were sharing confidences out of her earshot. She leaned sideways on the arm of the chair, the loose flesh about her neck folding into the hollow of her shoulder. "I know all about your expected brat, Sybilla. D'you think the Admiral don't write letters to his own dear sister? He may be your husband, but he's a most dutiful brother. Give him another son. He don't need daughters. Waste of time and expense, daughters. Daughters cause *trouble*. Daughters *disappoint*. Daughters cause *mischief*." She fell back against the upholstery in a fit of coughing, for the final word was spat out with such venomous wrath that it dried her throat. Her watery eyes remained fixed on her open-mouthed sister-in-law.

Lady Sybilla did not know what to say. She had never been so insulted and yet she could not bring herself to make even the mildest of protests. She hated herself for being so ineffectual. She was grateful her mother and Alec Halsey had not witnessed her cowardice. Fortunately, she was spared further anxiety.

The Lady Henrietta was suddenly on her feet and swaying, a gloved hand clutching at the folds of her silk petticoats and her brown eyes swimming with tears. She was staring at the occupants of the next box. To her amazement and that of every powdered head in attendance, the Duke of Cleveley and Lord Russell, the bitterest of political rivals, were bowing to one another with a flourish of lace worthy of any stage-managed performance. All semblance of interest in the baritone's performance evaporated amongst the silk-clad audience. A hushed whisper of expectation of an even greater entertainment gathered momentum until it became a babble of noise that drowned out the recital on stage and set heads turning in the pit with vulgar shouts of complaint to the audience above.

The Duke and Lord Russell exchanged pleasantries. They smiled on one another. They shared a private joke! More than one jaw swung open at that. An astute journalist took out his pad and scribbled away, aware that he was witness to an historic moment that would be the talk in every drawing room by supper.

What this very public display of friendship meant for the government could only be wondered at. Those in opposition were not so speculative. Padded shoulders slumped amongst their number as it was realized that an alliance between the Duke of Cleveley and the Earl Russell posed an unbeatable force, with no expectation of a future factional split in the cabinet's ranks to topple the government and force an early election.

But the uppermost thought occupying the nobles was what could have happened to bring about this unlikely alliance. The answer was soon apparent. The two noblemen raised their glasses in a toast to the adjoining box. Quizzing glasses and false eyelashes flashed wildly in that direction, to see whom the toast honored. The answer brought a collective smile and sigh. Of course! Why had no one predicted such an outcome earlier?

With a jab of her fan, Lady Russell urged her daughter to curtsy prettily in response. After all, it was not every day a girl was so honored in such a public and demonstrative way with an engagement announcement to the most eligible widower in the kingdom.

"Oh, Papa... Not that one..." Lady Henrietta muttered on a shattering sob and promptly fainted at her mother's satin-heeled feet in a billow of ballooning petticoats.

"GIVEN THE CHOICE, I SUSPECT CLEVELEY WOULD HAVE preferred the life of gentleman-squire," the Duchess of Romney-St. Neots was saying as she sipped claret from a crystal glass. "But of course he was never given the choice. His mother had his life chartered before he was out of leading strings. Great things are expected of an only son of a Lord High Chancellor. Spending one's life counting sheep and tilling soil don't figure into the equation. Of course, Cleveley was brought up to believe he had a divine right to a place in the great scheme of things, and acted accordingly. He was, *still is*, an immensely proud man. When his father died and he inherited the illustrious title and grand pile of stone, he set about making his mark in politics. As for his marriage… What can I tell you? He accepted an arranged marriage with Ellen because the Conqueror's blood ran in her veins too. Oh, I thought that would impress you," she quipped when Alec rolled his eyes. "Ellen was pregnant to the old Duke of Stanton when she married Cleveley, a mere boy of eighteen. A messy business."

"Odd that there was not the required period of mourning," Alec commented dryly, thinking of his own predicament; that Selina was intent on waiting out the requisite twelve months. "Especially when she was pregnant to Stanton. Wouldn't marriage to Cleveley before she gave birth transfer her unborn child's legitimacy to her new husband?"

"Ellen was Stanton's second wife; he had three grown sons by his first Duchess. But you are quite right. It was a highly unusual circumstance. As it was, she had only been married to Stanton four months when he up and died of heart failure. Too much romping in bed with a much younger wife was said to be the cause of that! Then, within two months, she was married off to Cleveley, she six months pregnant. In vulgar haste, if you ask me. A clause in the Cleveley marriage contract stated that if Ellen did not give Cleveley children, that if he had no legitimate children, *sons*, in his lifetime, should Ellen predecease him, then the child she was carrying and which would be born after marriage to Cleveley, would become the Duke's nominated heir."

Alec frowned into his glass of claret. "Doesn't that strike you as rather remarkable, given the bride was patently fertile and Cleveley a young man? Such an arrangement would suggest the parties who drew up the marriage contract were not in expectation of the newly-married couple producing offspring of their own."

"You are very astute. It does, doesn't it?"

"And?" prompted Alec.

"And what, dear boy?"

"Why would such a clause be considered necessary unless... unless it was thought Cleveley was incapable of fathering children? Or have I pressed on too far? Don't tell me: *The great man* is *impotent*?"

"He is a fully functioning male, as many a bordello beauty can attest," the Duchess answered with an abruptness that told Alec she was not pleased with his levity. "But around the time of his marriage to Ellen there was a very real concern he was impotent. Their marriage remained unconsummated for over two years. Then a physician performed a simple and effective, but quite painful, procedure that corrected the difficulty. I am told the Jews barbarize all their sons in this way when they come of age."

"Circumcision? Cleveley was circumcised to correct an erectile problem? But that doesn't explain why their marriage remained childless."

"No, it doesn't. And as Ellen gave birth to George, then one must suppose the fault lies with Cleveley." The Duchess sighed. "I know one should not speak ill of the dead, but I could never embrace Ellen. She wasn't *suited* to being a duke's wife, though she loved the trappings of title and wealth. She certainly was no helpmate to Cleveley's career."

Alec refilled their glasses. The singing below intruded on his thoughts and he glanced toward the stage in annoyance. On this particular occasion he was inclined to agree with the Duchess's assessment of opera. He did not much care for Gluck's work. "I assumed the Duchess of Cleveley was universally liked."

"Yes, she was. My feelings are tainted by the fact she had a brief affair with Romney."

"Surely a momentary lapse on his part," Alec replied politely.

The Duchess gave a hollow laugh, amusement in her pale eyes. "One of many, my dear boy. But one doesn't expect the girl one presented at court to sleep with one's husband. It's in such bad taste, and what's worse, she had the bad manners to get herself pregnant by him."

"By Romney?" Alec was surprised. "Are you certain?"

"My dear boy, Romney only had to put a foot across the threshold of my bedchamber and I was with child. I was pregnant more times than I care to remember and had *sixteen* lying-ins. The man was a modern-day Ramses. Too fertile for any female's good. I was only too pleased he went a'roamin."

Alec stifled a laugh on a mouthful of claret.

"But what I did not appreciate was being told."

"She told you?" Alec was surprised. "To what purpose? I assumed she would rid herself of such ill-gotten offspring, or at the very least hide the fruits of her adultery, if only to spare Cleveley the indignity of his glaring inadequacy?"

The Duchess gave a shrug of indifference, but Alec detected a wisp of emotion in her reply. "I imagine she wanted to confide her predicament in someone, and who better than the wife of her lover; the one person who was unlikely to bleat it about drawing rooms. But I did have some sympathy for Ellen…"

"Your forgiveness is boundless, my dear Olivia."

"Stop funning! Her marriage was barren. And she was desperate to have a child and here she was pregnant with my husband's bastard and couldn't tell a living soul. And then she miscarried, which was a far better outcome than had she brought a bastard to term, not that I told *her* that, because she had made me her confidant! *Me*."

Alec looked down at his long fingers. "A difficult time for you both."

"Difficult? That doesn't begin to describe it. Not three months after her miscarriage she came to me with the most astounding news. She was *in love*. Can you believe it? *In love*, and by all accounts for the first time, too! Silly goose of a woman. And at her age."

"Age is no barrier to falling in love, Olivia."

The Duchess shrugged, as if made uncomfortable by this simple truth and said flatly, "Well, age was no barrier to Ellen falling with child either! *Again*, Ellen found herself pregnant, and *again* not by her husband, and *again* I found myself not only her confidant but colluding with her to hide the fruits of her adultery from Cleveley."

"She never thought of passing the child off as Cleveley's?"

"Couldn't. He would know. The timing was all wrong."

"So she did think about duping her husband."

The Duchess eyed him resentfully. "We both thought about it."

Alec kept his opinion of such conniving and betrayal to himself and said calmly, "I presume then that she managed to keep this pregnancy a secret from him. How did she manage it?"

The Duchess smoothed out an imaginary crease in her petticoats. "Ellen's unwanted pregnancy isn't the first to ever make it to term without anyone, including a husband, being any the wiser. Women go into the country to visit relatives; come down with all sorts of imaginary illnesses that require complete bed rest and solitary recuperation. The fact is she had the brat, farmed it out in the depths of the country, to God knows what impoverished couple only too willing to take on an extra mouth to feed, in return for a guaranteed annual income, and returned to London, Society, and Cleveley oblivious."

"Except to you."

"Yes. Except to me." The Duchess sighed. "I don't think Ellen ever recovered from giving up that child. Her loss was made worse by the fact her sister the serpent had just given birth to a daughter. Ellen wasn't able to sufficiently harden her heart. Her marriage remained barren. The myth is she was devoted to Cleveley, and yet she got herself pregnant twice and one of her lovers was my husband." She tapped Alec's silken sleeve with her fan. "Do you know, I really think *he* was devoted to her for the first half of their marriage. Sad. She spent her final three years bedridden and bitter, goading him at every opportunity about his inability to beget a child, even out of wedlock. I witnessed several of her outbursts. Is it any wonder he was not at her bedside when she died?"

Alec pulled a face. "Dear me. Pride poked and prodded but surely not deflated?"

The Duchess's face tightened. "You have no idea."

"Forgive me. That was uncalled for."

"Their barren marriage was a living hell for a proud man like Cleveley, particularly when he has a genuine fondness for children. He was a very caring uncle to Mimi, Frances Rutherglen's only child. A surprisingly beautiful girl, no *astonishingly* is a better word given her lineage, and with such poise for one so young. I saw her only the once. It was not many months before her tragic death. She was brought down from the schoolroom to play at the pianoforte at one of Frances' excruciatingly dull afternoon teas. Cleveley turned the sheets of music for her while she played. The child's death was a great blow to him. I will always remember Cleveley's expression when he told me that, at the Rutherglens' request, he identified Mimi's body. He looked so ill I thought he'd stop breathing..." The Duchess mentally shook herself and squeezed Alec's silken sleeve. "I knew that sliver of Cleveley's humanity would surprise you. Makes him less the uncaring brute, doesn't it? And any man who is willing to own that drunken buffoon George Stanton as his son must have a strong paternal instinct."

"Strong enough to want to protect Stanton from the folly of a youthful indiscretion?"

"What is a youthful indiscretion in the scheme of things? And what father wouldn't protect his child? The Duke will not allow anything or anyone to stand in the way of George inheriting the Cleveley dukedom."

"And count no cost?"

The Duchess of Romney-St. Neots did not hesitate. "And count no cost."

SEVEN

ALEC HAD NEVER SET A BUCKLED SHOE INSIDE THE HANOVER Square mansion Selina had shared with her loathsome husband. He hoped never to do so, and wondered why she continued to reside in a house that held so many painful memories of an abusive marriage. Alec wanted her to sell it, not merely lease it out, so there would be no lingering ties, material or otherwise, with her deceased madman of a husband. His townhouse in St. James's Place was more than adequate for their needs. It at least was a comfortable warm place to call home, unlike this monolith of cold marble and opulence that resembled its dead master: A façade of wealth and privilege that lacked a heart and soul.

He glanced at the pearl face of his gold pocket watch a second time, reading the numerals at half an arm's length. The footman who showed him to the anteroom off the library said the mistress had visitors but that it would not be many minutes before she would be free, as the Duke's traveling coach was waiting in the street. Alec had already been kept waiting fifteen minutes.

When the butler emerged from the library with a footman in tow, they left wide the door giving Alec a clear view into a long book-lined room with its central massive mahogany desk. Here sat two men of business surrounded by parchments and papers. Selina, hair brushed up off her nape and dressed in her customary black velvet, was pacing the space between the desk and the warmth of the fireplace with her slender arms folded behind her back. She was listening intently to the conversation between the two men of business and the Duke. His Grace of Cleveley appeared at home, propped on an edge of the desk. He was swinging a stockinged leg, with his ever-present gold snuffbox at the ready.

It was to the Duke Selina spoke and it was he to whom she listened. When she stopped and faced him, clearly agitated by a comment made by one of the men of business, Cleveley pulled her to him and lightly held her by the upper arms as he spoke. When she finally dropped her chin and nodded, he kissed her forehead and slowly let her go, hands running down the length of her arms to briefly squeeze her hands. At that familiar action, Alec retreated to stare out of the window, annoyed that a simple light kiss and caress given by a man old enough to be her father should arouse feelings of unease. But in spite of a pleasurable week spent together in Paris, matters with Selina had not gone to plan and he did not know why, and so he felt he had every right to his apprehension.

When there was movement at his back, he pretended an interest in the Duke's magnificent traveling coach standing idle in the square below, the Cleveley coat of arms emblazoned in gold leaf on the black door. Two pompous-looking footmen in livery stood up on the box, another waited patiently between the horses' heads while the driver sat back in his duffle coat holding the reins in his gloved hands. Four armed outriders remained mounted, walking their horses up and down the street and circling their master's coach, impatient to be off. By the mountain of luggage strapped to the roof, it was to be a considerable journey. When he finally turned into the room he found the Duke watching him.

"I wonder who has disturbed whom?" quipped Cleveley as he drew on his kid gloves. "Unfortunately, I can't stay to find out. So, you will excuse me—"

"Do you make a habit of disturbing this widow, Your Grace?"

The Duke raised his graying black brows. "May one ask what prompts such an unexpected question?"

The muscles about Alec's mouth set hard at the smirk that accompanied the Duke's remark. "Mrs. Jamison-Lewis and I are betrothed."

"Indeed?" said the Duke with no hint of surprise. "I received the strongest impression from Mrs. Jamison-Lewis that she was in two minds. Now, you must excuse me. The horses…"

In a rash move prompted by a moment of intense jealousy, Alec thrust the silver button belonging to the Cleveley livery at the Duke. "This, I believe, is yours, Duke."

His Grace held the small button between gloved thumb and forefinger to the light of a branch of candles on the mantelshelf. "It is?"

"That button is part of your livery, is it not?"

The Duke blinked. "I beg your pardon?"

"I thought perhaps you could tell me how two of your liveried servants came to be involved in a scuffle in a laneway beside the *Stock and Buckle* Coffeehouse."

The Duke remained blank-faced.

"It never occurred to you to wonder why my uncle was not at the Commons' vote yesterday?"

"I don't make a habit of concerning myself with Plantagenet Halsey's whereabouts," the Duke said coldly, all urbanity at an end.

"Had my uncle made his speech condemning the Bristol Bill, he might possibly have persuaded more than one member to vote it down. As it happened there were a surprising number of abstentions. The bill passed by the narrowest of margins."

The Duke was incredulous. "Plantagenet Halsey's emotive ravings wouldn't have made one tester of difference to the outcome of that vote." He frowned his distaste. "His speech would only have held up proceedings—an annoying habit he has claimed all his own."

"My uncle was bashed unconscious. His head is wrapped in bandages."

The Duke frowned. He stared again at the button in the palm of his gloved hand and then at Alec. He seemed to require further explanation.

"He went to the aid of a gentleman who had been set upon by two of your liveried servants, and for that he, too, was assaulted."

The Duke looked very hard at Alec. "Who was this fellow?"

"Perhaps you should ask your servants that question, Duke."

"You think *I* would enlist my servants to use such tactics?"

"I would not have thought so," Alec answered with remarkable composure. "However, if it comes to protecting one's pride of place at the expense of decency and honesty—"

"How dare you," hissed the Duke, taking a step forward, face livid with indignation. "You—*you*—have the effrontery to—to... Are you *drunk*?"

"You deny sending Weir to enlist my help on your behalf?"

The Duke's anger melted into bewilderment. "On my behalf? *Weir*?"

"A small matter of your stepson's deplorable past, Your Grace," Alec stated with dangerous politeness.

"Weir visited you about *George's* conduct?" The Duke's bewilderment turned to impatience when his valet slipped into the room unannounced and motioned to the window with a jerk of his head. "I have no notion of what you're blathering about." He gave a sealed parchment to Molyneux. "See this is given to Mrs. Jamison-Lewis."

Alec decided to change tack because he was beginning to wonder if the Duke did indeed know of his servants' violent behavior, or for that matter, about Weir's visit. Either that or the man was a consummate performer. "Perhaps Your Grace would care to comment on the possibility that the Reverend Blackwell was poisoned?"

There was the slightest of pauses before the Duke answered, but it was not his hesitation that convinced Alec that Cleveley considered it a very real possibility—it was the way in which the valet, Molyneux, flinched and looked swiftly at his master, as if to say, *I told you so.*

"Blackwell suffered a heart attack—"

"—leaving his considerable fortune to one Catherine Bourdon," Alec interrupted him. "Your Grace was a signatory to his will."

The Duke did not try to deny this and it was evident he was momentarily startled that Alec should know the contents of the dead vicar's will. He made a swift recover, however, saying with icy composure, "A man may make as many wills as he pleases."

"Wills?" Alec repeated. "He had another, earlier will?"

The Duke stiffened. "That is not an unusual circumstance in itself."

"Indeed not. What is unusual is the fact Blackwell died the day after making this, his last will. This will was in the possession of the gentleman who was accosted by two of your liveried servants. My uncle went to the gentleman's aid, and in the *mêlée*, Blackwell's will was shoved into my uncle's pocket. That will is now in my possession and I intend to see that it is put into the hands of Blackwell's lawyer, Thaddeus Fanshawe. You look surprised, Your Grace..."

Alec let the sentence hang, and the Duke seemed about to speak until the heavy silence was prematurely broken by Molyneux, who continued to hover at his master's elbow.

"The horses, Your Grace..."

At that, the Duke turned on a heel, saying, "As you can appreciate, Halsey, I cannot afford to let my horses stand in the street a moment longer. I am obliged to leave for Somerset at once."

Alec, who had let his eyes drop from the valet's disfigured face to the letter in his hand, itching to know its contents, looked up swiftly. He had a flash of insight. "Somerset?" He followed master and servant out onto the landing where, at the bottom of the curved staircase, the butler and a footman waited patiently with the Duke's greatcoat and sword. "Going to take care of Catherine Bourdon yourself, Duke?" he asked with casual insolence. "A wise decision. Lord Russell would be an unnatural parent if he permitted his daughter to marry into a family that condoned the ruin and abandonment of a young girl of good family."

If Alec had hoped to goad Cleveley into making an unguarded reply he got more than he bargained for when the Duke staggered and half-turned; he looked as if he were about to faint, such was his unhealthy pallor. There was a tightening in jaw and throat, and a gloved hand was clenched so hard about the banister rail that each knuckle was clearly outlined through the taut black leather. The consummate cold-blooded statesman, through sheer force of personality, was holding tight rein on the distraught and exasperated parent. It was not difficult for Alec to sympathize with a parent who called Lord George son.

Molyneux bounded down the stairs two at a time and snatched his master's sword, sash and greatcoat from the wide-eyed butler and held these out. The Duke came slowly down the stairs after his manservant, still holding the polished banister rail and was helped into his greatcoat with all the care and solicitude of Molyneux's twenty years of devoted service, but with a sense of urgency to be out from under the prying eyes of strangers. It did not stop the valet glancing up at Alec with such utter contempt that it was evident he was aware of the situation to which Alec alluded, even if his master could not bring himself to speak of it. But speak of it he must, Alec decided, and he followed master and servant into the wide expanse of the black and white marble entrance foyer and tried once more to rouse the Duke to confession.

"If a terrible injustice has been committed, how could you turn your back—?"

The Duke cleared his throat loudly. "Whatever you've been told," he said hoarsely, "you've been singularly misinformed."

"Have I, Your Grace?" Alec answered with skepticism and lowered his voice so that he would not be overheard by the opened-eared servants who had retreated to the back of the foyer, leaving only the porter holding wide the heavy front door. "A supposedly penniless vicar may have been murdered. As it turns out he was the son of a viscount. He left a considerable fortune, bequeathed to one Catherine Bourdon of Ellick Farm in Somerset. Would it be presumptuous of me then to assume that this female is one and the same as the girl who was seduced, impregnated and abandoned five years ago—"

"This matter is no concern of yours! Do not involve yourself!"

"A terrible injustice was confided in me, and thus I am now involved. I cannot so easily dismiss it; not without good reason; not if it is true."

The Duke looked out through the open front door to his waiting carriage and stretched his neck in its fine white lace cravat. His features wore a hollow expression. His eyes were blank. "Do not interfere in a matter you know nothing about, Halsey." And in a whispered aside close to Alec's ear, "The future of the Cleveley name depends upon it."

"Avoiding his lordship won't help matters," Evans lectured, a bundle of freshly-laundered silk stockings clutched to her thin chest as she followed Selina Jamison-Lewis from the warmth of the cozy sitting room through to the expansive bedchamber. She placed the stockings in an opened wooden trunk that was neatly packed with clothes and stood in the middle of the floor and waved forward two hovering footmen. The brawny servants closed and bolted the lid, and between them carried the trunk down to the traveling carriage. "You should tell him the truth," she added as she continued on through to the cluttered dressing room. She scooped up a pair of Selina's discarded silk mules. "Mr. Halsey—I mean, *Lord Halsey*—I will never get used to calling him that—His lordship would understand."

"He is not used to the title himself," murmured Selina as Evans unpinned her embroidered stomacher and unfastened the silk ribbons holding up her petticoats. She stepped out of the heavy velvet petticoats and sat before the gilt dressing table in her stays and linen chemise to strip off her garters and white silk stockings. "Have Mr. Vesey's trunks been loaded onto the carriage?"

"Yes, m'lady." And before she could help herself, as she scooped up the discarded petticoats and stockings, "His lordship has a *right* to the truth."

At that forward pronouncement Selina glared at her lady's maid, momentarily mute with anger. "If you feel you cannot live with my decision then you are free to g—"

"No! I could never leave you," Evans answered swiftly. "How could you think it, at a time like this—at *any* time?"

"Then keep your puritan principles to yourself, Mary," Selina ordered, although she was ill with despair every time she thought about what she had forced upon herself during her detestable marriage and how the consequences of her actions then would now haunt her for the rest of her life. "Help me dress and then you can get on with the packing," she added quietly as she rolled clean white stockings over her knees and fastened them in place with silk garters. "I want to be gone from here before nuncheon."

Evans nodded and looked away before Selina saw the tears of sorrow in her eyes. Pouring warm fragrant water into a large patterned porcelain bowl on the dressing table she asked lightly, "May I ask if your—your meeting with His Grace went well…?"

"Yes, better than expected. I have leased this marble monstrosity to a very wealthy mill owner from Lancashire. He and his wife have six daughters and three sons."

"Praise be." Evans sighed with relief, helping Selina step into a fresh petticoat before she tied the ribbon with two pockets attached around her mistress's small waist. A scratching on the outer door saw her quietly go in answer, as if on a cushion of air, knowing their days within these wretched walls were numbered. She hated this mansion. It had been ruled over by a monster who had made her darling Selina's life a misery for six long years. Perhaps now they could put the terrible memories behind them forever…

Selina disappeared behind the ornate dressing screen to finish dressing.

Draped over the upholstered back of a frail-legged chair was a traveling gown in deepest blue silk and a matching delicately-embroidered stomacher with sprays of flowers in the Chinese manner, the colors so deep they could easily pass for mourning black; matching silk shoes complemented the gown. She was looking forward to her month in Somerset with Miranda and Sophie. If only her brother's painting had not been vandalized… Who would want to be so hideously destructive to a harmless picture? And by a harmless painter. There wasn't a wicked bone in Talgarth's body.

They had returned home from the exhibition in silence, her brother cradled in her arms, neither speaking of the wanton destruction to his beautiful painting, she unable to find adequate words of comfort. He had looked so ill she wanted to call a physician, but he refused and went straight up to his rooms, to be left alone with his devastation, and had locked himself in. She knew he would deal with the pain in his own way; in the same way he had dealt with the mental and physical abuse meted out by their overbearingly rigid father.

A much-decorated General, their father had never understood his youngest son's artistic inclinations, and had had him beaten senseless every week since the age of seven in the belief physical punishment would force Talgarth to conform. Talgarth had not conformed. Nor had he become an army officer as was the family expectation. The years of abuse had turned him into an opium addict, opium secretly supplied to him by the General's batman, an infantryman who had served in the Far East and was himself an opium eater. The irony was not lost on Selina.

The door to the dressing room opened with a squeak, bringing Selina out of her abstraction and to the realization Evans wasn't there to help her complete her toilette. How was she expected to shrug herself into her gown alone, least of all pin the stomacher into place? The soft measured tread across the polished floorboards and then the Oriental carpet did not belong to her maid, nor did the equally measured and deeply masculine voice.

"How does your brother fare?"

The question was simple enough. But it made Selina stand still, and her heart to thud hard against her ribs. After what seemed the passing of minutes, and fearing her ears had deceived her, she poked her fair head around the ornate screen. And there was Alec, propped on the window seat, his handsome angular profile with its strong narrow nose to the daylight, and he seemingly interested in the traffic loudly tumbling along the cobblestones in the square below. She disappeared again and hurriedly shrugged herself into the gown, cursing her romantically-minded lady's maid.

"He is dealing with it in his own way," she called out calmly, though she wanted to throw herself in his arms and tell him how much he was missed since their acrimonious parting in Paris. She smoothed out the tight satin sleeves down the length of her arms to her elbows and did her best to fluff out the lace ruffles that cascaded from elbow to wrist. But there was no means by which she would be able to pin the stomacher onto the front of her stays without assistance. She swore under her breath that Evans had dared to abandon her, and that Alec's presence had the power to turn her fingers all to thumbs.

"Have you spoken to him?" Alec enquired.

"No. But there'll be plenty of opportunity shut up together in my carriage. The journey west is tedious in the extreme."

Alec smiled, knowing her to be an indifferent traveler.

"Do you have any idea who would want to vandalize one of your brother's pictures and in such a public place?"

"Not in the least." Where was Evans? Her maid's presence was sorely needed and would preclude intimate conversation, although that notion appeared absurd, given the run of Alec's conversation. It was as if their Paris disagreement were quite forgotten. But had he forgiven her? "Although, I must admit that there have been several occasions, one episode in particular, when he has displayed a most unpleasant temper."

"During self-inflicted episodes of withdrawal, perhaps?"

There was an extended silence, and then Selina reluctantly answered from behind the ornate dressing screen, voice barely audible. "Yes. But he has never succeeded and such episodes are mercifully short-lived."

Alec came away from the window. "It's been suggested that the portrait was vandalized as a warning to your brother."

Selina's head showed itself again, hair a little more mussed than before. "Warning? Why?"

"To stop Talgarth's threats of exposing a crime committed against the sitter."

This brought Selina out from behind the screen. She tiptoed across the carpet in her stockinged feet, mass of bright apricot hair without hairpins falling freely about her bare white shoulders. She was doing her best to hold the gaping front edges of her satin gown across her low-cut stays while she held in her left hand the embroidered stomacher, pressed against the space where it needed to be attached, yet failing miserably at both.

Alec smiled to himself, watching her struggle to keep the stomacher of chinoiserie black—or was it blue?—silk pressed against her full breasts. She was useless at dressing herself, but what female of the nobility wasn't? Female clothing was not designed for ease of wear, or movement for that matter, and was dictated by the whims of fashion; as much about self-protection as anything else: Difficult to take off as well as put on.

Selina still frowned. "Crime? Against the *sitter*?"

"May I know who sat to your brother for that portrait?" he asked, coming to her assistance. He turned her to face him squarely, took the stomacher from her, and proceeded to fasten this delicately-embroidered piece of stiffened material, pinning the tabs at the sides of the stomacher to the stays.

"I don't see why—"

"You will. All in good time," he said mildly, a glance up from the task at hand. "The portrait was a full-length of a woman with a small child, wasn't it?"

Selina shrugged and tried to appear disinterested. "Miranda. Her name is Miranda. She sat to Tal on his return from the Continent, which was about a year ago."

He was silent a moment, inspecting the sit of the silk stomacher across her breasts and if it sat flat against the yards of silk gathered at her waist. His long fingers lightly touched her bare left shoulder and then her breast as he gently tucked the pretty lace edging of her chemise out of sight under the square neckline of the stays' embroidered hem. Blotches of color appeared on Selina's throat. There was something very intimate in his propinquity and the feel of his fingers on her skin, despite his no-nonsense approach. It made her lift her dark eyes from the intricate folds of his plain white stock up to his smooth-shaven chin, then dared to go higher and look at his blue eyes, but as expected, he was focused on the task at hand. This did not stop the spread of heat up her throat where it deepened into color in her cheeks.

"Miranda?" he repeated as he proceeded to gently push the tabs of the stomacher out of sight into the silk pleats. "The child's name?"

"Sophie: Miranda's daughter." Selina looked up at him through her lashes. "Should I give Evans her marching orders?" she asked saucily.

Alec gave a hint of a smile as he stepped away before her fingers could caress his cheek. “The real expertise is in the *un*dressing, m’lady. How old was Miranda when she gave birth to Sophie?”

“Fifteen or thereabouts,” Selina answered mechanically, wondering why he chose to put distance between them by returning to the window seat. She retreated to her dressing table and caught Alec’s frown of distaste in the reflection of her looking glass. “It’s not uncommon for girls to be married off to the highest bidder at a young age,” she said matter-of-factly. “Especially the daughters of rank. After all, we are but commodities to our parents, floated on the marriage market as soon as possible after our first bloody rag to ensure we catch a husband of wealth and title.”

Alec smiled away his discomfort, knowing it was precisely what had happened to her. “Yet… I don’t think Miranda was auctioned off to the highest bidder in the marriage mart, do you? Little Sophie is the product of something more vulgar than a contrived marriage for parental advantage.”

Selina could not deny this. “Miranda wasn’t *auctioned.* She ran away from home, denying her parents the satisfaction of parading her about society.”

“Do you know why she ran away?”

“She could hardly remain, given her condition,” Selina explained with asperity. “I’m surprised she managed to hide her pregnancy for as long as she did because she is a slight little thing; but with hooped petticoats and a good corset—”

“She was impregnated while still in the schoolroom?” Alec interrupted, incredulous. “I presumed governesses to be better keepers than any Newgate jailer. She told you this?”

“I worked it out for myself. Miranda doesn’t readily volunteer information about her previous life. For one so young she is very cautious.”

“She’s never mentioned her family or friends?”

“No. That is, I’ve never enquired after them. I assumed she wished to put the past behind her and start afresh.”

“If she wished to put the past behind her then she could very easily have changed her name to suit her new life, couldn’t she?”

“Perhaps…”

"Where did she go after she fled her home? To Ellick Farm? Is that where she gave birth to Sophie?"

"No. She disappeared into the slums here in the city and arrived on my doorstep when Sophie was just weeks old, and with a letter of introduction from her parish priest—"

"Parish priest? Do you still have the letter? Do you remember the name of the priest?"

Selina regarded Alec's reflection with a thoughtful frown. "The letter could still possibly be amongst my things at Ellick Farm. As to the name of the priest or the parish… It was almost five years ago… I've no recollection… It didn't seem important at the time. What I do remember is my great surprise that this beautiful child and her baby should come to me and from such a wretched place. There was no need to ask the obvious question why she was living in the slums, nor did it matter a jot to me. I was just glad her vicar had the sense to send her and the baby to the country." Her dark eyes widened as she saw Alec's brows lift. "Good God! You think that poor man who died at Sir Charles Weir's dinner party and Miranda's vicar are one and the same, don't you? But isn't that just too coincidental?"

"Not if you consider that the Reverend Blackwell was in truth a very wealthy man who left his entire fortune to one Catherine Bourdon, whom I believe is in all probability your Miranda."

"Did he? How intriguing! Then the vicar and Miranda are related?"

"Quite possibly." Alec came away from the window. "Have you ever wondered why mother and child were sent to Ellick Farm?"

"Yes, of course. But my yearly visits to Ellick Farm have always been a time for me to forget my—concerns… I presumed also that Miranda had no wish for me to pry into her past. That she too wanted to forget…"

"And the identity of Sophie's father?" When Selina shook her head and began to brush her long hair free of tangles, lips firmly pressed together, Alec added patiently, "I ask in the hope that the information confided in me might prove false."

"Information?"

Alec looked down at his black leather shoe with its large silver buckle. "Do you think it at all possible Miranda was seduced—possibly raped—in her own home? That she ran away for fear the rape would be disbelieved?"

"*Raped*?" Selina paused in mid brush stroke and stared at Alec, who held her gaze with an understanding small smile. It was a painful subject for both of them. Selina's husband had raped her repeatedly over the course of their six-year marriage. But within marriage it was not called or even considered rape when a husband took from a reluctant wife what was his by right. "I thought—I *presumed* an illicit liaison."

"What were you to think when she fled her home pregnant? And she has not helped her cause by remaining silent on the subject."

"Who would've believed her?" Selina answered quietly, flushed cheeks blanched white. "That poor child. *Raped.* Impregnated by her tormentor… To give birth to such monstrous offspring…" She shuddered, staring at her reflection without really seeing herself. "*Impossible.*" When she came out of her abstraction it was to find Alec staring at her acutely. It made her say sharply, "Who confided this in you?"

"Sir Charles Weir."

Selina's dark eyes narrowed. "Weir? How could that toad know such intimate details about a girl he has never met?"

Alec smiled crookedly. "How do you know they have not met? The information Charles imparted to me leads me to suppose that he does indeed know her and her family. You see, Charles confided in me that the adopted son of his illustrious mentor is being blackmailed because it was he who raped and impregnated Miranda."

"*George Stanton*?" The prospect so revolted Selina that her shoulders hunched with disgust. Yet she had to concede there must be some truth to the allegation. After all, as the Duke's secretary, Weir had been party to a whole host of confidences. He not only cultivated the Duke but had been intimate with the Duchess, and as a consequence, her good-for-nothing son. "But why would Weir enlist *your* help?"

Alec took a turn about the room. "In the misguided belief I can somehow put a stop to the blackmail. He wants me to retrieve a letter

Lord George wrote to Miranda in which he admits to being the father of her child."

"Why would Weir think you'd help Stanton out of his difficulties?"

"Charles hopes I can influence *you* to put a stop to the blackmail."

"Me? Why? Who is blackmailing Lord George?"

"According to Weir: Talgarth."

Selina paused in mid brush-stroke. "*Talgarth*? Blackmailing *Lord George Stanton*? But what proof has he to make such a contemptible accusation against my brother?"

"Charles says Talgarth threatens to reveal Lord George's rape to the world if Miranda isn't adequately compensated for her suffering," Alec explained as he gently took the brush from her and laid it aside, a hand in her soft curls. "He says Stanton has in his possession threatening letters written in your brother's fist."

"Letters? Written by *Tal*?" Selina said with considerable surprise but was remarkably calm given the seriousness of the allegation. "Were you shown these letters?"

"No. Weir told me of their existence."

"Has Weir seen these letters?"

"I presume so, or he wouldn't have approached me with such confidence. Do you think it possible Miranda has confided her past to your brother and he's taken it upon himself to champion her cause?"

"Oh, it's just the sort of thing Tal would do, especially for Miranda," she replied, trying to sound offhand as Alec's long fingers tangled in her curls, pad of his thumb caressing the bare skin at her nape. "He's been in love with her since he first saw her at Ellick Farm."

"And when was that?"

"Twelve months ago, on his return from Florence."

"He lives at the farm with Miranda?"

"No. She and Sophie live there alone. Tal has a studio in Bath, but from Miranda's letters I know he has taken to paying her regular visits."

"Then perhaps on one of these visits she confided in him."

"I don't know… What I do know is that Tal isn't capable of writing letters, threatening or otherwise…"

"Is that so…?" he murmured, distracted by the pleasing, ever-present scent of lilies in her hair. He brushed aside the weight of long curls from her bare shoulder and stooped to kiss her there. "Four wretched months of abstinence," he murmured. "Is that what you want?"

Want? Barely a month had passed since they had made love. Yet, that final night of unrestrained passion which had started on the dining room table, progressed to the chaise longue in the sitting room, climaxed on the hearth rug in the bedchamber, and roused the long-suffering landlord to pound his fist against the thin apartment walls in Gallic protest, was, to Selina, a lifetime ago now. *Of course* it wasn't what she *wanted.*

She turned on the dressing stool to face him, arms up about his neck, lips parted in anticipation of his kisses progressing to her mouth. She knew she did not possess the god-like willpower to resist this man whom she loved above all others. And yet the tiny, nagging voice of conscience castigated her for lacking the moral fortitude to deny herself earthly gratification (after all it was she who had demanded they end their affair until her mourning was over), and for possessing a gross conceit.

She was acutely aware that after a past littered with a succession of lovers, his deep physical need was now singularly devoted to her; that he loved only her, and wanted her to be his wife. Yet this only made her miserable, because she had no right to her triumph when it meant living a lie and ruining his future. She must deny herself and him any further physical expression of their feelings and commitment until she found the resolve to tell him the truth. And so she pulled free of his embrace before passionate need got the better of them both.

"Forgive me," she whispered, dropping back onto the dressing stool, a hand to her trembling mouth. She lowered her gaze to the clutter of crystal cosmetic jars and trinkets littering the surface of the dressing table. "I didn't mean for that to happen…"

There was a long, awkward silence between them. Then Alec spoke, and in such an altered voice that Selina gave an involuntary shudder. She stole a look at his reflection and wished she had not. His handsome face was taut and the confused anger in his blue eyes starkly evident.

"Am I making a fool of myself, Madam?" he enunciated coldly, the acute unbearable ache of frustrated longing giving his normally placid deep voice an edge. When she remained mute, he gritted his teeth and let out a great huff of anger. "Christ, Selina, I was willing to remain a monk for an entire twelvemonth if it meant at the end of your mourning we would be married. Then, without warning, you send word from Paris. It didn't need a second thought from me to be in your arms, glad to dispense with this ridiculous charade, believing we could finally get on with our lives. A week of mutual pleasure and you decide *my* interests are better served if we remain apart?" He stopped to breathe deeply, blue eyes never wavering from her pale reflection. "What was that week all about? If I was sent for to satisfy your *itch*, better you had found a Parisian cicisbeo! Or perhaps you think me incapable of constancy, and summoned me before I went mad from wanting you and headed off to the nearest brothel to slake my lust?"

"You hold my thoughts very cheap, sir," Selina said in a low voice.

"Oh, I'm not really complaining," he said with a flippancy that belied an angry confusion. "Our week of love-making was well worth the preceding months of celibacy." He took a turn about the room and something on the mantel caught his eye. It was an opened letter propped in front of a Sèvres vase. Instinctively he knew it for Cleveley's note. The Duke's presumptive kiss and smug assurance of knowing Selina's mind stung enough for him to retort, "But perhaps it is your dear friend the Duke who now avails himself of your considerable allure?"

At such a totally outrageous and unjustified suggestion, Selina was stone no more and she stood before him, hands angrily bunching up the yards of her silk petticoats. "Has my character sunk so low in your estimation that you believe me capable of making love to *any* man, all because I so readily give myself to you?"

He was instantly contrite.

"Selina, I—"

"There has never been another man—I never shared my husband's bed *willingly*, and well you know it—only you."

He looked away from her then and stared unseeing across the cluttered room. "That was unforgivable of me. Yes. I do know that." Yet he could not help voicing a niggling doubt as he brought his gaze back to her flushed face. "But I wonder what influence His Grace of Cleveley does have over you?"

Damn Cleveley's wise counsel, Selina thought angrily. "I value his opinion," she stated coolly, bravely looking up at him.

He lifted a mobile eyebrow.

"You mean you're prepared to be influenced by him to the detriment of our future happiness?" And when she looked away, crookedly biting her lower lip, he knew it to be so. Well, at least he knew who he was up against. It was now a matter of finding out the Duke's persuasive line of argument, and it must be a damn good one to influence Selina, for she was nobody's fool. "As you know him better than I, perhaps you can tell me to what lengths Cleveley would go to ensure his stepson's future isn't ruined by a past act of lustful madness."

"Cleveley? Cover up for Lord George?" And although Selina sounded unconvinced, privately she had to concede that as Lord George was Cleveley's nominated heir, the Duke would do all in his power to protect him. It was a depressing thought and one she did not voice.

Alec took her silence for stubborn disbelief.

"Whatever your faith in him, I cannot rule out Cleveley's involvement in concealing his stepson's despicable behavior. When I offered His Grace the opportunity to deny the rape, impregnation and abandonment of Catherine Bourdon, he gave me the satisfaction of telling me he was off to Somerset—"

"His estate is in Somerset," Selina interrupted defensively.

"—and any interference on my part would jeopardize the Cleveley name."

"He said that?" Selina asked rhetorically, knowing Alec would never lie to her, whatever imagined jealousies prejudiced him against the Duke. "Then it's just as well Tal and I are not half a day behind him. We leave for Ellick Farm today. Miranda will need our support more than ever if indeed what Weir has told you is true. Although…" A thoughtful expression came into her dark eyes and she plucked the Duke's note off the mantel. "This is my annual invitation to the Michaelmas ball at Bratton Dene, the Duke's estate. All the local landowners are invited. Ellick Farm, the farm where Miranda and Sophie live, is on the Duke's estate, in fact it's visible from Bratton Dene's east turret, and this year I've been specifically requested to bring Tal. He's been commissioned to paint an official portrait of the Duke. Why would he give Tal such a lucrative and honored commission if he thought my little brother was blackmailing Lord George?"

"You are Cleveley's tenant?" Alec asked, his annoyed surprise overshadowing her pertinent question and the fact he had been about to voice the same thought.

"Yes. He gave me the farm for my lifetime. A retreat, he said; a place where I could get away from—from J-L."

Alec smiled crookedly. "A clever ploy. Your husband would never have dared trespass on *the great man*'s lands."

She sank onto the window seat, silk petticoats billowing out around her, and clasped her hands in her lap. "You have no right to mock him for providing me with the only sanctuary I had from that fiend." She made to rise at a persistent scratching on the outer door, but Alec sat beside her and took hold of her hands. "The door…" she began, and faltered when he gently planted his lips to one wrist then the other.

"Forgive me," he said gently. "It is I who am acting the fiend. I'm jealous of Cleveley because he was able to offer you some respite from that madman, when I could not. I am forever grateful to the Duke for sheltering you." He brushed a wisp of apricot curl from her cheek. "I meant every word I said to you in Paris. In and out of your bed. I repeat the question I put to you then, and I want an answer now, before you run off to the wilds of Somerset and the company of others: Will you do me the honor of becoming my wife?"

She kept her head bowed, unable to meet the expectation in his blue eyes, and withdrew her hands from his. She wanted to marry him more than anything she had ever wanted in her life, but Cleveley was the voice of reason. Marriage was out of the question. As a wife she could not give Alec what he deserved and had a right to expect. The past was unalterable. She had no right to ruin his future.

With all the courage she could muster she met his unblinking gaze.

"Alec... Darling, I love you with all my heart... I just... I just can't marry you." His silence made her stumble on to say what she had not said in Paris, anxious her nerve would not fail her a second time. "I thought perhaps we could come to some—some *arrangement.* It's a common enough practice, particularly amongst our kind, as you know. Of course I would have to be discreet, for Cobham's sake, but Tal would understand, in fact I don't think he would much care one way or t'other. I've given the notion plenty of thought and the more I think about it the more I'm certain such an arrangement would suit us both."

Alec's eyebrows drew sharply together. "You're willing to be my mistress in preference to becoming my wife?"

Selina smiled hopefully. "Yes, that's it."

He could hardly believe his ears. The hope in her dark eyes and the accompanying anxious smile made him feel hollow.

"You want me to visit you under cover of darkness, via the tradesmen's entrance and skulk up the back stairs, so you can play the whore for me behind the closed doors of your boudoir? And if we are discreet you can remain the respectable wealthy widow, accepted in all the best drawing rooms, your elder brother none the wiser?" He swallowed. "You would be satisfied with such a beggarly arrangement?"

"When you put it in such terms—"

"For God's sake, Selina, what other terms are there? You've no idea what it is to be a man's whore!"

Selina blushed. "Of course I do. I'm not so naïve."

"Indeed? Then do you think so little of *my* character that you believe I look upon you as nothing more than a desirable means of satisfying my lust? That I may avail myself of your body and your carnal talents where and when it suits me with little or no thought to your needs? That is a whore."

"Many a nobleman has loved his mistress more than his wife."

Alec sighed his exasperation. "Selina, I *love* you. I want you to be my wife, not my whore or my beloved mistress," he said patiently, again taking hold of her hands. "You mean so much more to me. I couldn't conceive of you in such an undignified role. I want to wake up each morning with my wife, not catch a few hours of temporary satisfaction whenever the urge strikes. I want you as my life's companion, for you to take your rightful place beside me as Marchioness Halsey; for us to share our lives as one, for us to have children—"

"No! Please—*Please* don't ask that of me," she pleaded croakily and snatched back her hands. "I must answer the door. It could be Tal..."

Alec roughly caught her to him.

"Up until a month ago, until I came to you in Paris, you gave no indication that you'd had a change of heart—"

"Not of heart. *Never* of heart." She struggled against his arms encircling her waist. "I must answer the door. *Please*. You know—I can't—I can't *bear* to be—to be *trapped*."

Her plea of desperation brought him to his senses and he released her, instantly ashamed of having caused her a moment's distress. For all her outward serenity, the emotional scars of an abusive marriage had yet to fully heal. He had hoped their marriage would help that healing process—indeed, bring closure to that abhorrent chapter in her life, but marriage did not now seem probable. Why had she suddenly decided against marrying him? Why had she turned to Cleveley for support? Why did he feel as if she were withholding something fundamental to their happiness? Why couldn't she confide in him? Bewildered and feeling as if their future were out of his control, he wrenched open the door.

Selina's maid fell into the dressing room and dropped a curtsy, saying without preamble, eyes lowered to the floorboards, "My lady, it's Mr. Vesey. He's awaiting you in the carriage."

Evans was ignored as Selina pursued Alec into the passageway. He bowed to her in farewell, saying with a coolness that was much more hurtful than any angry outburst,

"I need you in my life. Wife or mistress, you decide. But in either *rôle*, I enter by the front door or not at all. Good day, Madam."

EIGHT

When Alec returned to St. James's Place, his butler greeted him in the hall, eager with the news Plantagenet Halsey had come downstairs and was partaking of a very late breakfast in the dining room. In fact the old man was sharing his kippers with an absurd-looking gentleman with overlarge teeth and dressed in a canary yellow frock coat that had seen better days. But Alec was so grim-faced and preoccupied that Wantage kept his mouth shut. He watched two footmen divest Lord Halsey of greatcoat and sword, before his lordship took himself and his black mood off to the billiard room.

Alec hoped that by knocking a few billiard balls about before nuncheon his anger and frustration with Selina would burn itself out before he went up to see how his uncle was faring. His grim solitude lasted all of ten minutes.

There was a perfunctory knock on the door which he ignored, but Tam bounded into the room anyway, carrot hair falling into his green eyes and hugging a leather-bound text to his chest. The heavy curtains had been pulled back to allow light to stream across the green baize surface of the billiard table where the three balls had been scattered. The rest of the paneled room was in shadow, and it was in the shadows that Alec stood chalking the tip of his cue while absentmindedly pondering his next shot. Tam saw him nonetheless and went straight up to him, and such was his anxiety that he spoke without first being addressed.

"Mr. Wantage said I'd find you here, sir. Sir, the rumor circulating town is that because I dispense medicines to the poor and because you were at the dinner party at which Mr. Blackwell died, that you—that we had a hand—Sir, just because you were falsely accused of mur-murder once don't mean—Well, it ain't fair!"

"Yes, I've heard that rumor, too. I hope you didn't give the doubters the benefit of argument?"

"I wouldn't give them the satisfaction of speech!"

"After all, Blackwell may indeed have had a heart attack. He wasn't exactly the picture of health," Alec answered in a clipped voice, and more for the benefit of relieving the boy's anxiety than his belief in such a statement. He went to the table and sized up his shot. "You have more important matters with which to concern yourself. Tomorrow is your exam—"

"But, sir, the more I think on it the more I'm convinced Mr. Blackwell could've been poisoned. I didn't get the opportunity to tell you earlier, on account of Mr. Halsey's injury, but while I was at the *Stock and Buckle* I had a most interesting conversation with Mr. Molyneux and he said—"

"Mr.—er—Molyneux?"

Tam dropped the heavy leather-bound text on the sideboard and returned to the table, absently scraping back the mop of hair falling into his eyes.

"Mr. Molyneux is the Duke of Cleveley's valet. He doesn't usually speak to us—the other valets and upper footmen—just sits in his corner and reads the newssheets. He thinks we're beneath his touch on account of his grand position with such an important nobleman. We all refer to him as 'the Duke' and that's the way he likes it too, sir."

"This conversation?" Alec prompted, and racked his cue after a particularly dismal attempt at potting the red.

"He only spoke to me because he owed me a favor. He suffers with an arthritic knee and I supply him with an oil preparation that helps relieve the pain. The thing is, sir," Tam continued as he followed Alec around the table, completely oblivious to his master's brooding preoccupation, "I managed to turn the conversation to Mr. Blackwell. Mr. Molyneux was reluctant to speak about Mr. Blackwell's stay at St. James's Square. All he would say was that Mr. Blackwell *was not all he seemed* and that *some wrongs just can't be undone*. But what wrongs could Mr. Blackwell cause a duke? It just don't seem possible."

"Do you believe Mr. Molyneux spoke with sincerity?"

Tam nodded. "Yes, sir. He was quite upset about it. It was as if *he* had been ill-used by Mr. Blackwell."

Alec leaned against the table and crossed his arms, the boy's enthusiastic questioning bringing him sufficiently out of his angry abstraction to ask, "Mr. Molyneux's feelings aside for the moment, why do you now suspect Mr. Blackwell may have been poisoned?"

Tam took a moment to collect his thoughts.

"You asked me if poisoning was a possibility and I've thought about it. To begin with I tried to rule it out, that it was an impossibility for Mr. Blackwell to have been poisoned at dinner, or just before, so that the effects of whatever substance was administered took effect while he was at the dinner party. The more I tried to rule out poisoning, the more possible it became, until I was forced to admit that he could've been poisoned so that it *appeared* as if he had suffered a heart attack."

"Poison administered before or during dinner?"

"The fact he was ill so soon after eating would suggest the poison was administered during the meal."

"I see. As I recall, you said that it was an easy thing to poison a man at a dinner party, but what we need to be looking for is a poison which reproduces the symptoms of a heart attack, and the form of that poison to know how it was administered...?"

"That's right, sir! And in this instance we need to establish how such a poison could have been given to one man without his fellows being poisoned into the bargain."

"A very deliberate and premeditated action with no room for error... And do you know of a poison which can reproduce the symptoms of a heart attack?"

Tam could not control his enthusiasm. His freckled face broke into a grin. "Yes, sir. It came to me while I was reading up on the preparation of abortifacients." His smile dropped into an embarrassed frown and he looked uncomfortable. "Not that I'm in the habit of making up such preparations, sir. I just thought the examiners might ask, if—"

"It is quite unnecessary for you to offer me an explanation," Alec said placidly. "I have every confidence in your judgment. The poison…?"

"Thank you, sir. I have two in mind: *Taxus baccata* and *Aconitum napellus*. That's Yew and Monkshood, sir," Tam explained. "I can't decide which was used. Both are equally toxic and readily available. Both produce symptoms experienced by a victim of a heart attack. Yew leaves can be made into a tea which, when swallowed by a female, will bring on her infant before its time. More often than not both mother and infant die in the attempt. Monkshood, or more correctly, aconite, is used in tinctures and as an ingredient of liniment, which, if applied *externally*, is not fatal. However, if *ingested*, and often this is in a powdered form added to other ingredients, then death can occur within minutes."

"Powder?" Alec enunciated, blue-eyed gaze fixed on Tam. "Blended powder? Snuff. The poison could've been mixed into Blackwell's snuff. Is that possible?"

"Certainly, sir. As I said, aconite is readily available as a powder. In fact, to blend a lethal dose of poison into a man's snuff would be a simple and effective way of committing murder with least suspicion."

"Precisely! Especially if the victim appears to all the world as if he's had a heart attack," Alec said as he took another turn around the table. "A man's snuff is his personal domain, especially to a man such as Blackwell who was not used to the etiquette of communal dipping. He mentioned that snuff taking was new to him; that he had recently been given a superior blend. He showed me an ornate gold snuffbox. A gift, he said…" Alec stopped his pacing, leaned his palms on the billiard table's polished mahogany frame and looked at his valet. "Blackwell's snuffbox was an identical twin to that carried by the Duke of Cleveley."

Tam's eyes widened and he let out a low whistle. "Perhaps the snuff Mr. Blackwell snorted was intended for the Duke? Perhaps, in the course of the evening, their boxes got switched and Mr. Blackwell dipped into the Duke's snuffbox by mistake? Seems likely, don't it, sir? After all, Mr. Blackwell had no enemies, well not the Blackwell we knew, whereas the Duke must have plenty. Stands to reason someone might want to do away with him."

"I don't doubt *the great man*'s political actions have made him enemies over the years, but to want him dead because of them? That's the wish of a madman."

"Poisoning is the act of a madman, sir."

"Poisoning," said Alec as he thrust Tam's leather-bound textbook back at him when the butler trod into the room to announce nuncheon, "is the act of a coward."

WHEN ALEC ENTERED THE DINING ROOM HE WAS PLEASANTLY surprised to discover his uncle partaking of a hearty late breakfast, grizzled head still swathed in bandages, a little lopsided from a restless night's sleep, and a richly embroidered banyan thrown negligently over his crumpled nightshirt. Yet it was the visitor sitting across from the old man who brought Alec up short. A fresh-faced young man with a receding chin and overlarge front teeth was enjoying a plate of egg and kippers and a tankard of ale. He was wearing a frock coat of canary yellow damask. This garment of dandified fashion was so ill-fittingly tight that it rounded the young man's shoulders, excessive and ill-advised movement having split the seams of the watered damask in several places along both arms where the sleeves were attached.

Plantagenet Halsey hailed his nephew with a friendly wave of his fork and mischievously announced him to the visitor as the Marquess Halsey, whereupon the young man dropped his knife and fork onto his plate with a clatter and shot up off his chair. He swallowed whole a mouth full of egg as he hastily doubled over in a bow befitting a foreign potentate, the dirty lace ruffles at his wrists trailing in coddled egg.

"Thaddeus Fanshawe, Esquire, attorney-at-law and your most obedient, my lord," the young man announced grandiloquently, and when politely asked to resume his seat, did so with another series of small bows that threatened to overset his wig *a la pigeon*. "I'm most grateful to Mr. Halsey for obligingly offering to share his breakfast, my lord," he said by way of an apology for picking up his knife and fork and savagely slicing a kipper in two. "And I beg your lordship's understanding when I tell you I've not eaten since breakfast yesterday. I must own that there is nothing more soothing to troubled nerves than a large plate of warm egg."

"Sharing his breakfast is the least my uncle could do given, and correct me if I am wrong, he took a direct hit to the head in your defense, Mr. Fanshawe?"

"I offer my humble apologies to your lordship, as I have to Mr. Halsey, for causing him to suffer at the hands of those two brutes who accosted me in the laneway," the lawyer replied seriously, oblivious to Alec's heavy irony. "I would not for the world have followed Mr. Halsey from the anti-slavery meeting had I realized I myself was being followed, and by two such fiends. I feared for my life, I may tell you, my lord, and still do!" He licked his rabbit-like front teeth, dropped his voice to a whisper, and lifted his gaze from Alec's elaborately-tied linen cravat to his unblinking blue eyes. "I have not dared to venture home for fear of those thugs doing violence to my family, and thus you find me at your table in such a deplorably bad-mannered state of dress."

"You don't suppose the men who followed you know your name and your direction and may go to your home in spite of your absence from it?" Alec asked lightly, spreading a linen napkin across his lap.

"I did have such a wild thought, my lord," Thaddeus Fanshawe agreed earnestly, eyes very round, "and so I sent a linkboy with a message for my father to keep the front door bolted and on no account open the door to strangers—"

"—particularly strangers dressed in the Cleveley livery?" prompted Alec.

Thaddeus Fanshawe blinked and looked to the old man for confirmation. "My lord? Cleveley livery? Indeed! Those fiends were in the pay of the Duke of Cleveley? I did not know." He smiled deprecatingly. "It is my great misfortune to be blind to many colors, my lord, and so one Duke's livery is as much the shade of another's."

Hence the canary-yellow frock coat, thought Alec, smiling to himself and exchanging a glance and the same thought with his uncle as he picked up his wine glass. No doubt an underpaid tailor's prank, or a gift from a prankster brother. "And have the beneficial effects of warm egg reduced the bump and pain to your head, Uncle?"

"Egg and Fanshawe's company have done me wonders," Plantagenet Halsey replied briskly, though he did not in the least feel hearty. He should have had a breakfast tray sent up to his room, the thump to his head was still that bad, but the opportunity to interrogate the buck-toothed lawyer was not to be missed. Thus, he ignored his nephew's note of censure and smiled encouragingly at the visitor. "Fanshawe, be good enough to explain to his lordship what you were doin' followin' me from me meetin'."

"Yes, sir. Of course, sir," said Thaddeus Fanshawe and addressed himself exclusively to Alec. "Mr. Blackwell asked that I seek out Mr. Halsey at a meeting of the anti-slavery league because, he said, it was the only place Mr. Halsey and myself could converse without the circumstance being reported to certain persons within the Cleveley House, by which I took him to mean he did not wish His Grace to know of my mission on Mr. Blackwell's behalf. And now I discover that the thugs who accosted me were in the Duke's employ!" He licked his wet lips free of ale. "I may tell your lordship I was never more terrified for my life than when those fiends loomed large over me, demanding that I hand over Mr. Blackwell's will. Had it not been for Mr. Halsey's timely intervention I shudder to think of the consequences to my person of such an encounter!"

Alec glanced at his uncle's bandaged head but refrained from commenting.

"Do you have any idea why the Duke's liveried servants would demand Blackwell's will when surely, as signatory, the Duke of Cleveley was well aware of the vicars wishes?"

"I wish I knew, my lord. For it makes no sense. As you say, His Grace knew only too well the contents of Mr. Blackwell's will. Indeed, if he feared I was in possession of a copy of the earlier will, then I understand his wish to retrieve it. For he made me assure him on no less than two occasions that there was but one copy of Mr. Blackwell's original will, and this I had placed in his hands under Mr. Blackwell's instruction. As we all then witnessed the burning of that particular document in the grate of his fireplace, His Grace must surely have been satisfied as to its destruction. Indeed, he was most insistent that we all remain in the room until the parchment had turned to ash."

"What was in Blackwell's original will that Cleveley would want it turned to ash?" asked Plantagenet Halsey. "Can you tell us that, Fanshawe?"

"Most certainly, sir, for the second will was just like the first. All beneficiaries and their legacies remained unchanged. Reference to certain inconsequential particulars regarding the beneficiaries were removed, as was reference to the main beneficiary's mother. I can only say that the removal of such wordage made the second will a much more succinct and unsentimental document, and perhaps that was His Grace's object? There was one other change, and one that was insisted upon by His Grace to which Blackwell most reluctantly acquiesced. That was the removal of one of the two executors, leaving the Duke as sole executor of Blackwell's estate."

"As my uncle and I have read the will you placed in my uncle's pocket during the scuffle, there can be little harm in you elaborating on the contents of the original."

Alec said this with such a nice smile as he put down his knife and fork to take up his wine glass that the lawyer smiled back, thinking he had been asked rather than told, and so did not hesitate, saying in a confidential tone, as two soft-footed footmen removed and replaced dishes from the table,

"Not at all, my lord, for Mr. Blackwell requested of me most strongly that his last will and testament be given to his good friend Mr. Plantagenet Halsey, for it was he who had been named one of the executors of the first will and whom His Grace was most insistent must be removed—"

"*What*? The Devil!" exclaimed Plantagenet Halsey, half out of his chair. His fist came down so hard upon the table that the wine glasses rattled. "The lousy livid cur! Of all the mean despicable acts! To bully a meek-mannered man like Blackwell into removin' me from carryin' out his last wishes! Ha!" He sat down again and adjusted the slide of his bandages from his left eye. "But it don't surprise me that leech would stoop to such craven tactics all to get an advantage for himself, for I'd not have let him get away with a penny more than was due to him!"

"But, sir, the Duke of Cleveley did not stand to gain from Mr. Blackwell's will," Thaddeus Fanshawe correctly pointed out. He gave a little jump and an involuntary squeak when the old man's fist again thudded upon the table.

"Then what was he tryin' to hide by havin' me removed, eh? Tell me that!"

"Precisely, Uncle," agreed Alec and focused on the lawyer. "You mentioned that certain *inconsequential particulars* about the beneficiaries were omitted from the second will, as was reference to Catherine Bourdon's mamma…?"

"Oh, yes! I remember the omissions most clearly." The lawyer smiled smugly. "I am frequently complimented for my exceptional capacity for remembering the mundane… As you'll recall, Blackwell bequeathed his Bible, gold pocket watch and the sum of one thousand pounds to one Thomas Fisher, who just so happens to be your valet, my lord. The words omitted being: *For putting to good use his apothecary skills in providing medical assistance free of charge to the parish poor of St. Jude's.*"

"Hardly inconsequential particulars," Plantagenet Halsey grumbled, a guilty sidelong glance at his nephew as he downed knife and fork and pushed his plate away.

"But best removed from a legal document if Tam hopes one day to be accepted into the Worshipful Company of Apothecaries," Alec calmly pointed out. "And Sir Charles Weir, Fanshawe? The fact Sir Charles and Blackwell, or more correctly Kenneth Blackwell Dempsey-Weir, as is his proper name, share a common surname has not gone unnoticed."

"Egad! I'd not thought about that," announced the old man.

"Just so, my lord. As you will recall, Sir Charles Weir was

bequeathed the sum of five thousand pounds, *my nephew having made his own mark in the world without my assistance* being omitted—"

"*Nephew*? That mealy-mouthed sycophant is Blackwell's *nephew*? It beggars belief!" declared Plantagenet Halsey, astonished. "You have a strange sense of the inconsequential, Fanshawe. Blackwell's life becomes more complicated with every sentence you utter. Next you'll be tellin' us that Catherine Bourdon was the vicar's long-lost mistress or his long-sufferin' wife and Charles Weir's mamma, no less!"

"That is impossible, sir," the lawyer answered respectfully, ignoring the old man's levity, "for Mr. Blackwell confided in me that Catherine Bourdon is a precocious child only four years of age, with her mother's black ringlets and her grandmother's gray eyes."

"A-a *child*—of—*four*?" Plantagenet Halsey blurted out.

"Not his child, Fanshawe?" Alec asked rhetorically.

"No, my lord."

Alec tried to sound disinterested. "But a child of his parish perhaps…?"

It was the lawyer's turn to be amazed. "I do believe you are correct, my lord, for Mr. Blackwell mentioned with no small amount of pride that Miss Catherine was one of his flock."

The old man sat bolt upright. "Eh? From St. Jude's? He left his fortune to a *beggar's* brat?"

"Can you think of a more deserving beneficiary, Uncle?"

"No! Of course not!" Plantagenet Halsey blustered.

"Fanshawe, you said the original will mentioned Catherine Bourdon's mamma?"

"Yes, my lord. The first will stated that Catherine Sophia Elizabeth Bourdon is the *natural daughter of Miranda Ann Miriam Bourdon*."

"You are certain that was the name of the child's mother, Fanshawe?"

"More certain than I am that this frock coat is the color of puce, my lord," the lawyer declared emphatically.

"Did the Duke make any comment as to why he wished mention of Catherine Bourdon's mamma removed from the will?" Alec asked with a thoughtful frown. "Aside from the obvious desire to erase reference to the child's bastardy."

"His Grace made no specific comment, but it was quite clear, even to me, a functionary, that the mere mention of the name Miranda Bourdon was enough to make His Grace exceedingly uncomfortable. Indeed, he made no secret of the fact that he found the whole interview repellent in the extreme."

"Aha! There you have it!" declared the old man, though he said this with little conviction, and was not exactly certain what he meant by such an outburst, adding belligerently when Alec and the lawyer looked at him expectantly, "Don't tell me there ain't some sinister intent behind Cleveley's actions, because I'll not believe it. He don't squat without purpose. Who's to say he wasn't coverin' up for his secretary's abominable behavior in gettin' this Miranda with child and then abandonin' her. Just the sort of sordid behavior right up His Grace's noble alley!"

"I don't disagree with you, Uncle, and I believe you may be closer to the mark than you realize, but the connection between Blackwell and Miranda Bourdon may be more tenuous than you imply. If, for argument's sake, Charles Weir had fathered her child, then I believe Blackwell would have stated that fact, or at the very least the connection between his nephew and Catherine Bourdon, in his will. That he did not leads me to believe Weir is not the child's father."

"Then why leave a fortune to a stranger?"

"If Miranda Bourdon gave birth to her child in the parish of St. Jude's, then she and her child were hardly strangers to their vicar. Perhaps her tragic circumstances pricked at Blackwell's conscience? Perhaps he wanted to give her child an inheritance that she would not otherwise have been entitled had she been the legitimate offspring of her father…?"

The old man's eyes narrowed. "There's more to this than you're lettin' on. You got an idea as to the identity of this child's father, my boy?"

Alec shot a warning glance at the lawyer, which closed his uncle's mouth, and said calmly, "Other than removing mention of Catherine Bourdon's illegitimacy and the name of her mamma, did Cleveley make any attempt to influence Blackwell to change his will in favor of his nephew Charles, rather than leave his estate to a child of his parish?"

"Indeed he did not, my lord!' replied Thaddeus Fanshawe in shocked accents. "His Grace may not have agreed with Mr. Blackwell, but he certainly did not attempt to influence his wishes beyond removal of the aforementioned references."

"Then as much as I hate to admit it, Cleveley may have been acting purely in his role as executor to protect the privacy of the beneficiaries, by having a second will drawn up with such sensitive and potentially damaging information omitted," Alec concluded. "As I pointed out earlier, Tam would not have been accepted into the Worshipful Company of Apothecaries had they come to hear that one of their apprentices was practicing his skills outside of their guidance, and without charging a fee for services rendered. And Charles was raised by his mother in the belief that his uncle, his father's elder brother, had died a hero at sea. Imagine then if Charles were to discover through the reading of a will that in actuality the deceased was this same uncle; not a great seafaring hero at all, but an ill-dressed cleric administering to the poor, who cared not a fig for wealth and even less for title. And to heap insult upon insult, this uncle preferred to bequeath his entire fortune to a precocious four-year-old girl of indeterminate lineage. How utterly humiliating for Charles."

"But nothin' less than what that leech deserves," muttered Plantagenet Halsey.

"Even you must admit, Uncle, that Cleveley did Tam and his long-suffering secretary a service by persuading Blackwell to keep his bequests short and to the point."

"Well, no, I can't argue with that," grumbled the old man. "But I wish I could! I just can't bring m'self to believe that an arrogant puff-adder like Cleveley, who hasn't an ounce of feelin' for the unparalleled human misery and sufferin' those poor black wretches endure on His Majesty's frigates, can have an ounce of feelin' in his marrow for anythin' or anyone else!"

"*They are but savages after all*," Alec quoted, and when his uncle gave a questioning start, added, "An opinion expressed to me at the opera, and one I fear the majority of our fellows sincerely believe. You and I know that even decent-minded men prefer not to know what goes on aboard His Majesty's frigates, just as they turn a blind eye to the deprivation that occurs here on our doorsteps." He looked to the lawyer, saying casually as he helped himself to a heaped spoonful of ragout of mushrooms, "You failed to mention the fourth and final beneficiary, Lord George Stanton, who was willed a gold snuffbox and a small miniature portrait."

"Odd choice of bequest," opined Plantagenet Halsey, taking up his mug of ale. "And to a man so opposite in every way to the good vicar as to be bafflin'. Wouldn't you say, Fanshawe?"

"I did wonder at it myself, sir," agreed the lawyer without looking up, preoccupied with rummaging in a deep, frayed pocket of his frock coat. He pulled out and dumped on the table by his dirty plate a crumpled handkerchief with torn lace, a tarnished etui, a large key, and a handful of folded papers, before finding the object of his search, a rolled, crushed parchment tied up with a frayed black ribbon. "Particularly when there was no elaboration for such a bequest in the first will."

"Pshaw! There's more to this than that will, damme!" Plantagenet Halsey interrupted, frowning at the assortment of odds and ends from the lawyer's pocket now littering the table. "Come on, man, *think*. Blackwell named me as executor for a damned good reason, and then he permitted that pompous windbag Cleveley to remove m'name, just like that? It don't wash. By your own admission, Blackwell wanted me to be aware of his will, even after I'd been removed as executor, so there's somethin' about this business that smells as putrid as a cod's head rottin' in the summer sun!"

"I don't disagree with you, sir," the lawyer replied respectfully, talking into his deep pocket as he thrust back the odd assortment just produced. But the parchment tied up with ribbon he passed to Alec. "As I was about to add, while neither the first or second wills provide illumination as to the small bequest to Lord George Stanton, this document, written as a codicil to the first will, and one Mr. Blackwell did not wish to make known to the Duke, undoubtedly offers an explanation. I'm sure you'll agree, once you have digested the information contained within it, that it is a most startling piece of prose."

"*Codicil*? Why in Hades didn't you slap it down when you first put your knees under the table?" wondered Plantagenet Halsey.

The lawyer looked baffled. "Sir, you questioned me about Mr. Blackwell's will and I obliged you."

The old man was too flabbergasted to offer a reply, and a long silence followed while Alec read the unrolled parchment. When he had finished he looked over the rims of his gold spectacles, considerable surprise in his deep voice as he handed his uncle the codicil. "You had best read this for yourself. You are unlikely to believe me otherwise."

NINE

In his eagerness, the old man snatched the document from his nephew.

I, Kenneth Blackwell… this, that and the other, Plantagenet Halsey read to himself, skimming over the sloping handwriting, then slowing as he absorbed words that required more careful consideration,

…wish it to be known that I secretly married Ellen Sophia Dewalter at Hawkhurst Church in Kent on Sept 6th 1738, three days prior to my departure for Barbados, where I was sent to manage my father's sugar plantations. It was agreed with my bride that once established in the colony, I would send for her. Tragically, fate conspired against us.

Through a series of misfortunes, I was shipwrecked, marooned and ultimately imprisoned on a Portuguese colonial outpost, accused of being a spy for my country. After a year of wretched confinement, I was permitted to make my way to my original destination, whereupon I obtained news of home. Upon discov-

ering my wife was now Her Grace the Duchess of Cleveley, I preferred to be "given up for dead" by my family.

Whilst living in Barbados, indeed while still a prisoner, I began studying for my true vocation, that of a priest in the Church of England. This worthy profession I had always aspired to but was denied me by my father. Deciding to dedicate my life to the poor, I returned to England in the spring of 1742 as the Reverend Blackwell, of no particular family or connections, and became the parish priest of St. Jude's in the City.

Not many months after my return to England, I reunited with my dearest wife in the utmost secrecy, and we passionately reaffirmed our love, but agreed, most reluctantly, that due to the passage of years, our disparate circumstances and the ardent wish not to inflict pain and embarrassment on others, we would remain forever apart in this life, to be reunited, with God's good grace, in Heaven.

No blame is to be attached to my good wife for the sorry state of affairs which unfolded after I set sail at my father's behest. The fault lies entirely with her parents, who bullied and badgered her into accepting an offer of marriage from His Grace the noble Duke of Stanton two months after my departure, for what they deemed their daughter's wanton malicious conduct in falling pregnant to the impecunious second son of a lowly Viscount. Although our union was lawful, my young wife, with no friends to confide in and parents who threatened to disown her and cast her adrift on the world should she disobey them, was persuaded in her distracted, sorry state to forsake me.

When His Grace of Stanton died only three months into this bigamous union, my wife was again threatened and abused by her parents until she agreed to form a bigamous attachment with His Grace the most noble Duke of Cleveley, all to secure the future of her unborn child. Thus the nobleman known as Lord

George Lucius Stanton, believed to be fathered by one duke and born to another, is in truth my son and heir.

The marriage between myself and Ellen, Duchess of Cleveley, as she was known in her lifetime, remained, until her last breath, lawful under the laws of Church and State. It is my earnest desire that this unalterable truth be set down in ink so that one day, long into the future, when those living cannot be hurt by such a revelation, the truth will out. I cannot, in clear conscience, as God is my witness, allow my marriage to a woman I loved and cherished all my life remain unacknowledged.

Therefore, I entrust this codicil to my good and honest friend Plantagenet Alec Halsey Esq. of St. James's Place, and express the wish that he never divulge its contents to a living soul except to my son, so that he may understand why he was bequeathed a small gift of gold snuffbox and a miniature of his mother as a young woman that was in the possession of a poor old vicar, who was called to his mother's deathbed in her eleventh hour, so it seemed, without reason or explanation.

Should I predecease His Grace of Cleveley, and His Grace expire without legal male issue, I request most humbly that Plantagenet Halsey, in the presence of Mr. Thaddeus Fanshawe and such legal representations as my son seeks to employ, make George Lucius Stanton aware of his true paternity and the tragic set of circumstances that led to his mother's bigamous acts. I believe Plantagenet Halsey, whatever his prejudices, justified or otherwise, against His Grace of Cleveley and Lord George Stanton; and Mr. Thaddeus Fanshawe, a young lawyer of unimpeachable character who came to my aid, are both gentlemen beyond reproach who will respect my last wishes without question, and I thank them. Words cannot express my gratitude.

Signed this day in the year of our Lord this, that and the other etc., your humble servant etc., Kenneth Blackwell Dempsey-Weir.

The old man's mouth had dropped open with the reading of the first paragraph. He placed the parchment on the table and watched it curl in on itself, as if it had a life of its own. He was without words.

The lawyer took it upon himself to correctly roll up the parchment and secure it with the ribbon.

"Would I be correct in assuming this document is the only one in existence?" asked Alec.

"Most certainly, my lord," Fanshawe confirmed. "Mr. Blackwell wrote it in some haste and gave it to me with the ink not quite dry, as you can see by the slight smudging to his handwriting on the final line. He desired that I be present to witness his signature, in the event that the codicil and its contents should be called into question. I then immediately took possession of the document, some half an hour before the commencement of our meeting with His Grace."

"To redraft the first will?"

"That is so, my lord."

Alec removed his spectacles and met the lawyer's open gaze squarely. "Did the Duke have any idea of Blackwell's intention to write a codicil?"

"I do not believe so, my lord."

"But you cannot be certain," argued Alec. "That you were attacked by two men in the Duke's livery may suggest otherwise…"

The young lawyer licked his buck teeth, pondering this statement. "You may very well be correct, my lord. You believe the two thugs were after the codicil and not the will?"

"The thought did cross my mind," Alec said dryly. "As did the notion that obtaining the codicil was not their only object."

The lawyer's eyes widened, but it was the old man who spoke first. "They were to silence Fanshawe by whatever means necessary?"

"Yes."

The lawyer's gulp was audible.

"Did His Grace make comment about Blackwell's bequest to Lord George?" Alec asked Fanshawe

Fanshawe shook his powdered head. "His Grace made very little comment about Mr. Blackwell's bequests, merely the omission of certain particulars, as we have already discussed."

"But it makes no sense! George Stanton can't be Blackwell's son and heir, can he?" Plantagenet Halsey argued. Absently, he scratched his bandages. "If that good-for-nothin' lout was the progeny of Blackwell but was born after his mamma married Cleveley, then doesn't that make him legally Cleveley's son?"

Alec smiled thinly. "Fanshawe can correct me if I am wrong, but if Blackwell and Ellen Dewalter were legally married, then her subsequent marriages to Stanton and then to Cleveley would both be deemed bigamous. She was never legally married to either duke. George Stanton is the offspring of her first and only husband, Kenneth Blackwell, and thus the vicar's legitimate son and heir."

"That is indeed correct, my lord," the lawyer beamed.

"Well, I'm flabbergasted!" announced Plantagenet Halsey. "The more I learn about the good vicar, the less I know about him. He waits until the end of his life to acknowledge his marriage to a woman who paraded about society as a duchess, and whose son was believed to be sired by one old duke and heir to another! And what does the good vicar leave of his fortune to this estranged son? A trinket of a snuffbox and a small miniature. Now ain't that marvelous!"

"Iniquitous is the word that springs to mind," Alec replied as he pushed back his chair. He nodded to his butler to have the footmen clear the table of the remainder of the dishes and glasses. "I believe your good friend the vicar had no intention of exposing Lord George Stanton for a fraud. You were to inform Lord George of his true lineage only *after* the Duke's death, and that assumes with Lord George safely elevated to the Dukedom of Cleveley. I should think *that* bequest made by Blackwell far outweighs any other, not forgetting a fortune willed to a small child of four into the bargain, don't you?"

Plantagenet Halsey and the lawyer exchanged a wide-eyed look before both stared at Alec with dawning realization.

Alec regarded both his uncle and the buck-toothed lawyer with a crooked smile. "Question is: Would you have allowed Blackwell to get away with fraud, and see Lord George elevated to a dukedom to which he has no legal entitlement?"

The old man's brows drew together over the bridge of his long nose. "Blackwell knew me for a man of my word," he said darkly, squaring his shoulders. "I'd be bound by his wishes. You know that."

"Yes, he knew that also. That was selfish of him, and an inexcusable abuse of friendship." Alec showed the lawyer to the door. "I have one final question, Fanshawe: In the course of finalizing Blackwell's second will, was mention made of the whereabouts of Catherine Bourdon and her mother?"

"Somerset, my lord. A farm on the Duke of Cleveley's estate," Thaddeus Fanshawe replied without hesitation as he straightened the front of his canary-yellow frock coat.

"Eh? Not St. Jude's, then?" asked Plantagenet Halsey in bewilderment as he shuffled across the room after them.

"No, not St. Jude's," Alec said with satisfaction, "but a farm in Somerset, as I suspected. Do you know the name of the farm, Fanshawe?"

"Unfortunately not, my lord, as such correspondence as I franked on Mr. Blackwell's behalf was sent to a hotel in Bath. Barr's of Trim Street; a rather select establishment, so I am told."

"Did Mr. Blackwell give you an explanation why correspondence for Miranda Bourdon was sent to Barr's rather than to the farm?" asked Alec.

The lawyer was confused. "I presumed he did so because the letters were addressed to a Mr. Ninian Bourdon at that direction, my lord."

Uncle and nephew glanced at one another.

"Mr. Ninian Bourdon?"

"Miranda Bourdon's husband, my lord," replied the lawyer as if the connection was self-evident. When nephew and uncle exchanged a look of surprise, Thaddeus Fanshawe blinked and added, "Mr. Blackwell conducted the ceremony himself, a little under a year ago. He was particularly pleased for the little girl to finally have a father."

"Naturally," Alec responded with a faint smile, as if nothing was amiss. He stepped aside to allow Wantage to escort the lawyer from his house. "Thank you for coming here today, Fanshawe. Your visit has been most invaluable. I will have my carriage take you home."

"The codicil, my lord—"

"—will remain safely lodged here until this imbroglio is set to rights. If you should receive any further visits from the Duke's servants, I would be obliged if you would refer them to me. I doubt they will bother you after that. But, if it will make you feel more at ease, I offer two of my most burly servants to post at your door for a week or two."

"Thank you, my lord," the lawyer bowed gratefully, and bowed again as he backed out into the passageway. "I am most grateful to your lordship. Thank you, my lord."

"Who's this Ninian Bourdon fellow?" Plantagenet Halsey asked as the butler closed the door on the lawyer's continued bowing and scraping. "Perhaps he poisoned Blackwell so his wife's child could get her inheritance?"

"No one of that name was a dinner guest."

"So he used another name!" the old man threw out recklessly.

Alec grinned. "Invert that thought and you may be closer to the mark." When his uncle looked puzzled he added, "Mayhap one of the gentlemen who attended Charles's dinner party uses the name Ninian Bourdon as a *nom de guerre*? Yes, I thought that would open your eyes. It's an avenue worth exploring. But we'll talk about this later," he added gruffly, putting a supportive arm across the old man's stooped back. "Now it's back to bed with you, and a dose of laudanum. We've a long journey ahead of us tomorrow."

Plantagenet Halsey was tired and his head hurt. He did not have the strength to argue. Laudanum and sleep would be welcome. Still, he voiced a last niggling doubt, "Neat how Miranda Bourdon and her daughter happen to live on a farm on the Duke's estate…"

Alec smiled grimly at his uncle's astuteness. He wondered at the parts played by Talgarth and Selina Vesey in Miranda Bourdon's enigmatic life, and was of the opinion that in truth Selina knew very little about her orphaned charge, and even less about the depth of her brother's involvement with the woman and her daughter. As for the Duke's part in Blackwell's demise just days after the vicar's writing a most extraordinary codicil…? The revelations contained in that document threatened the very future of the Cleveley dukedom, and made a mockery of the Duke's marriage to Ellen Dewalter. George Stanton was not what he claimed to be, whether he knew it or not, and Charles Weir was just the kind of sycophant who would do anything in his power to have the Duke and his nominated heir beholden to him. All had reason and motivation enough to want the good vicar dead.

"Neat?" Alec responded with a huff. "A sinister contrivance, belike."

"Ha! I knew it," the old man said with relish, looking up with satisfaction into his nephew's hard-set features, "Cleveley's up to his neck in dirty dishwater and drownin' fast!"

Alec didn't doubt it.

SIR CHARLES WEIR FOUND LORD GEORGE STANTON FACE DOWN in a pool of his own vomit. The servants dared not move him. His lordship's manservant had departed for a post befitting a gentleman's gentleman. This last drinking bout had been the breaking of him. He could not, *would* not, stay in the employ of such a drunken lout, whatever his nobility of name; the man was in every other way fit only to inhabit Gin Alley.

Sir Charles's first action was to send for a pail of cold water. He then removed his frock coat, took off his lace ruffles, rolled up his shirtsleeves, and with some effort, managed to turn Lord George onto his back. The young man gave a series of snorts that unclogged his nostrils, then went back to sleep. Sir Charles felt himself heave, rushed to the window, forced up the sash and gulped in fresh air.

When the servant returned with the pail of water, he was ordered to dash its contents over his sleeping master. This the servant did with a horrified thrill, threw aside the bucket, and ran out of the room on the nobleman's blasphemous yelp.

At first, Lord George was inclined to continue to lie sprawled on the floor, the thudding in his head was that bad. But he was cold and wet and his dry tongue felt twice its normal size. He struggled up, cursing his servants, and wiped spittle from his face with his wig. It was then that he saw Sir Charles Weir's reflection in the long looking glass and he wondered if he were in the middle of a nightmare—a weekly occurrence since the death of his mother. Sir Charles soon put paid to his doubts.

"I'll wait for you in the dining room," he said curtly. "I suggest you wash. Your person reeks."

When an unshaven Lord George reappeared, leaning in the doorway, he wore an open-necked shirt without ruffles and a pair of brown buff breeches in need of pressing. On his shaved head sat a turban of red and gold silk thread that not only appeared ridiculous in itself, but had the effect of making its owner appear egg-headed. Sir Charles couldn't help smiling into his ale, despite the fact he was furiously angry with the Duke's stepson.

Lord George slumped down at the table and covered his face with his fat hands. "Christ, I feel ill. Why did you wake me, Charlie? Did I ask you to wake me? I don't recall—"

"Do be quiet," Sir Charles complained and pushed a tankard toward his lordship. "Drink up. You'll feel better for it."

"I don't want—"

"Do it!"

Lord George stared resentfully at Sir Charles through splayed fingers. "I don't care for your tone, Charlie."

Sir Charles smiled unpleasantly. "Then behave yourself."

Lord George dropped his forehead onto the table and groaned. "Go away; there's a good little *secretary*."

"You haven't an ounce of gratitude, have you?" Sir Charles said bitterly.

Lord George shrugged his indifference.

"Listen to me. If you don't sober up and see what's going on around you, you stand to lose everything, *everything* that is rightfully yours. Do you understand?"

"What is rightfully mine?" Lord George moaned. "All I dreamed of having died with Mamma."

"What self-pitying twiddle-twaddle!"

Lord George's head snapped up and he shook Sir Charles's arm. "Apologize, *secretary*! Apologize! Apologize, damn you!"

Sir Charles sighed. Why must he be bothered with this simpleton? But he knew the answer to that, and although he wanted nothing better than to tell this big bloated oaf what he really thought of him, he controlled the urge and said in a voice dripping with false sincerity, "Of course I apologize, George. You know I am only interested in what is best for you. So was the Duchess. It is because of her I am here today."

"Because of Mamma?"

"Yes. It was her wish, was it not, that you succeed Cleveley?"

"What does that matter now?" whined Lord George, dropping his chins onto his sleeve. "You saw what happened at the opera. So much for Mamma's wishes! Dearest Papa has gone and gotten himself engaged to be married to Hatty Russell. *My* Hatty Russell! *Mine*." He pushed away the ale and covered his face with his hands. "How could he do that to me?"

Sir Charles rolled his eyes heavenward and prayed for patience. He patted Lord George's arm. "There. There. *Dearest* George. One cannot always predict the actions of others. I, too, was just as devastated by that display. It never occurred to me. This time His Grace's political astuteness has surprised even me. But one must learn to adjust and turn to one's advantage what could be a potential disaster. He may have the upper hand for the moment, but that will soon change..."

Lord George shrugged him off. "What are you blathering about, Charlie? Who gives a damn if it caught you off your guard? Thing is, what are *you* going to do about it?"

Sir Charles raised his eyebrows. "I? About what?"

Lord George pulled a face. "Come on, Charlie! Don't play close-faced with me. You'll put a stop to this engagement, won't you?"

"Why should I?"

A rare flash of insight made Lord George momentarily forget his headache. "You've invested too much in me to see it all go to waste on any brat Father might have with Hatty." When Sir Charles laughed, Lord George knew it to be forced and he couldn't help twisting the knife a further turn. "For a man who practically wore Father's wig for him, you're in a bit of a quandary as to what to do about this engagement, aren't you, Charlie? And I'll wager you can sign his fist better than he can himself. So what are you going to do to stop him marrying Hatty?"

Sir Charles took snuff. He didn't think Lord George amusing and it showed.

"And if Cleveley discovers to what lengths you've already gone to *lay claim* to *your* Hatty?"

"Now Charlie, don't go threatening me!" Lord George growled and sank his head into his hands again. "Oh God, I feel ill," he moaned. "I wish you'd blow away…"

"You and I must decide what's to be our next move."

Lord George sighed impatiently. "You're such a bore. But I'll listen. I've no ideas of my own."

"Just so," murmured Sir Charles.

Lord George had a sudden thought.

"Mayhap I don't need to worry. After all, it's not as if it were Mamma's fault the marriage was barren. We all know what's whispered about the clubs: Father can't even get a whore with child. And God knows he's had his fair share of them over the years." He snorted a lop-sided grin and gave Sir Charles a nudge. "Who's to say he'll fare any better with Hatty? Ha! No need to panic at all!"

"Think on it a moment, George. If Lady Henrietta marries your father then she'll be in *his* bed, not yours."

Lord George frowned and chewed on a fingernail gloomily

"Although… There has been no *official* announcement of the engagement…"

Lord George bit off a piece of quick and flicked it away.

"Meaning?"

"Meaning, that until a notice appears in the newssheets announcing the engagement between His Grace and Lady Henrietta Russell, you have as much hope as I do of becoming Lady Henrietta's husband."

Lord George's mouth dropped open and then he burst out laughing as he shuffled to a walnut sideboard that concealed a chamber pot in its lower drawer. He proceeded to urinate into the opened drawer. "*You*? *Hatty's* husband?" he said over his shoulder. "That's priceless, Charlie!" Turning back to adjust himself he discovered the chamber pot missing. A servant had removed it to empty, and not bothered to put it back. Undaunted, Lord George buttoned his breeches and kicked closed the now dripping drawer.

Sir Charles regarded him with barely concealed loathing. It nauseated him to think this turbaned buffoon had even placed a paw on the Lady Henrietta Russell. As for succeeding to a dukedom… Yet, while he could overcome his bitter disappointment should the Duke marry Earl Russell's daughter, the thought of that marriage producing an heir and Lord George not being the next duke, did not bear thinking about. Such an outcome left no room for Sir Charles to exercise any political influence. He had spent the better part of his formative political career cultivating the Duke's family, the Duchess, and her son in particular, and he wasn't about to let his efforts come to nothing. Up until the Duchess's demise, he had been supremely confident of enjoying many more years bathing in the golden glow of the Cleveley patronage. With her death had come uncertainty of its continuance; the impending engagement of the Duke a severe jolt that his political career was at an end, unless, that is, he could rally Lord George into action.

"Be a good fellow, Charlie, and have a lackey fetch a physician."

Sir Charles ignored the request.

"His Grace has gone posthaste into Somerset. I presume he means to pay a visit to the Bath studio of a particular painter, to ascertain by what divine right he took it upon himself to immortalize a bastard brat and her whore of a mother. It was the devil's own luck that his most prized painting was mutilated beyond recognition. That may yet save you."

This had a profound effect on his ailing lordship. He looked at Sir Charles with a sense of overwhelming panic. His eyes went very round. "She's Vesey's whore? And Father has gone to find her?" He slumped onto a chair again. The ale did not look so bad after all. He drank it down in one breath and belched. "You told me she'd run away!" He pouted at Sir Charles and shook his arm. "You *promised* on oath to Mamma she was as good as dead to us. Ha! And now you tell me she's got a brat, too? You *lied* to me, Charlie!"

Sir Charles freed himself. "I did no such thing," he answered haughtily. "Against my better judgment, but in deference to the Duchess, I implicated myself irrevocably in your sordid business. I did what was asked of me. Nothing more and nothing less. That the whore is being championed by an emaciated boy-painter and has come back to haunt you after all these years is hardly my affair."

Lord George chewed on a non-existent thumbnail. "But you will do something about it, won't you?"

Sir Charles balked. "I? Why should I further incriminate myself? Unlike you, I can explain away my involvement as a loyal secretary merely looking after his noble employer's best interests."

"Damn it, Charles!" Lord George whined. "You're just as much a part of this!"

Sir Charles sniffed contemptuously but was secretly pleased Lord George had the honesty to be frightened. He sensed the tide had once more turned in his favor. "Oh, don't look so forlorn, George," he said with a bright smile. "I am willing to offer you my assistance." He propelled Lord George into the bedchamber. "Get dressed. We're off to Somerset as soon as you're packed."

Lord George visibly froze in the doorway. "You won't get me to confess a syllable to father! Not after all these years. *Never.*"

"No one is asking you to do that," Sir Charles said with forced patience, his accompanying smile tight. "Those pictures were a mightily unpleasant reminder for you, George, but I am of the opinion that the dead should stay dead. The only person who can ensure this matter is dealt with once and for all time and before the Duke becomes involved is your aunt Lady Rutherglen. She is the person we are to visit. I have it on good authority she's at Bath taking the waters."

Lord George tossed his turban onto the tumble of bedclothes and scratched the back of his matted head. "Aunt Rutherglen?" he grumbled. "What can that old serpent do for me?"

Sir Charles deliberately bit his tongue. Lady Rutherglen had done more to save her ungrateful nephew's fat neck than any other person living. In many ways she had paid the ultimate price for her devotion to her sister's offspring, and she was going to be called upon one last time to make certain that Lord George Stanton succeeded to the Cleveley dukedom. Too many people's livelihoods depended on that outcome, her ladyship's included. But Sir Charles knew that Lord George did not care in the least what sacrifices had been made on his behalf, or by whom, because all of his life what George wanted George received, regardless of the consequences to others. Hence their present predicament. But Sir Charles didn't have the energy or inclination to lecture on the obvious, so he said simply,

"Trust me, my lord. All will become clear once we reach Bath."

His lordship did trust him. He had every confidence in Sir Charles being able to right matters. After all, he had managed it five years ago, and with the blessings of his mother and his aunt. He expected nothing less than absolute loyalty from his stepfather's henchman. Suddenly he did not feel so ill.

"So what's your plan, Charlie?"

"That, my lord, has already been set in motion. We must now put our trust in my raven-locked school friend's pathetic desire for truth and justice." He took out his pocket watch to view the time and grinned. "I should think by now he is on the road into Somerset to confront the Duke."

"*What?*" thundered Lord George. "You've roped *Halsey* into this? Why, in Bedlam's name? If anyone's capable of raising the dead, it's that cursed principled troublemaker."

Sir Charles smiled unpleasantly. "Precisely. And what better way to get a self-righteous duke to keep the dead in their graves than to have a crusader of righting wrongs on his back?"

Lord George was not as dull-witted as Sir Charles supposed, for in response he broke into such unrestrained laughter that the former secretary was quite prepared to ignore the stench of stale vomit and urine about his lordship's large person.

TEN

SELINA SAT IN A CORNER OF HER TRAVELING COACH BEING bumped about on uneven roads as she tried to read the morning edition of the *Gazette*. She loathed travel, being constantly jostled, bounced and swayed this way and that on narrow, rutted and muddied roads; the tedium of miles and miles of countryside; and the smell of horse sweat and manure in the crowded stable yards of the inns along the way. It was not that she disliked the country or country life. It was the getting there she found irksome.

And her two traveling companions weren't providing her with any diversion to help the passing of the hours.

Evans sat beside her, back rigid as ever but fast asleep, with her head forever falling forward so that her pointy chin bounced on her emaciated chest. Talgarth was huddled in a corner diagonally opposite, wide awake and ignoring the open fields. He stared vacantly at the padded velvet upholstery between the two women. Despite being rugged up under three blankets, and with a hot brick under his feet, his forehead was beaded with perspiration and he continued to shiver, arms folded tightly across his chest in brooding silence.

He had not spoken since their overnight stay at Marlborough, where he had been violently ill in the stable yard, the third such vomiting episode since leaving London. Selina was well aware his suffering was self-inflicted. Nausea, chills and sweating always accompanied her brother's periodic episodes of opium withdrawal. He was punishing himself for what he saw as his failure as an artist. It was an act of self-loathing, and although Selina hated to see him in such distress, she knew no amount of cajolery on her part would make him feel any better, and it certainly wouldn't get him to speak. He must be allowed to initiate conversation in his own good time.

So she returned to the pages of the *Gazette* and finished reading an article on the successful passage of the Bristol Bill, her interest only momentarily piqued by a quote from Sir Charles Weir, praising the Commons vote and giving *verbatim* his long-winded explanation of what it would mean for the mercantile greatness of the kingdom.

"Whatever did Cleveley see in that man?" she asked herself aloud and tossed the folded newssheet to one side to pick up the *Public Advertiser*.

"I'm a damned failure!" Talgarth announced, momentarily forcing his thin body to stop its involuntary shudders.

Selina pretended a moment of distraction. She did not look up from the newsprint. "I beg your pardon, dear… What did you say?"

"I'm a failure."

"Failure…?"

"The exhibition was a failure. No one will care to commission a portrait from a failure. God damn it! I allowed myself to fall all to pieces in full view of the *world*."

Selina folded the *Public Advertiser*, a sidelong glance at the dozing Evans.

"Tal, you are being too harsh on yourself. Anyone with proper feelings couldn't but be affected by such hideous vandalism. Who could think less of you for showing your emotion? In fact, I would be surprised if you didn't receive a flood of commissions because of it." She held up the newssheet. "Why, in here there is an article on the exhibition that gives you three paragraphs to Hamilton's one."

What she did not add was that there was just as much ink devoted to speculation, as to the identity of the vandal or vandals of Talgarth's portrait, and to the identity of the figures in the portrait. One reviewer proudly stated that he had inspected the damaged canvas and was of the opinion the mystery lady was none other than French Louis' latest mistress, Jeanne du Barry. Selina had no idea how this startling conclusion had been reached given that the portrait had been so badly defaced with red paint that it was impossible to discern even the hair color of the sitter.

"Lina," Talgarth said in an agonized whisper, "it was my *best* work. My *very best.*"

Selina had not viewed the portrait before its ruin but she was sure he was right. She wanted to gather him up in her arms and hug away his hurt. She wasn't given the opportunity to agree with him. Talgarth suddenly slammed the side of his fist against the door paneling, rage welling up within him.

"Cobham will think *I* did it, just to get attention. He thinks I'm mad." He met his sister's open look. "Am I? Am I *mad*, Lina?"

"Not at all," she answered calmly, which she truly believed.

What Cobham thought was entirely different. But then their elder brother lacked all imagination. So had their parents, who, unable to deal with Talgarth's scholastic ineptitude, had had him strapped to a chair for hours on end, with a tutor standing over him reciting Latin and Greek verse. As if their recalcitrant son could breathe in his education by simply being in the presence of an Oxford don!

"The fact you ask the question shows you are as sane as I am," Selina added with an understanding smile. "Besides, what do you care for Cobham's good opinion? I certainly don't."

Talgarth was not completely convinced. He pulled the blankets closer about his thin frame, shivering uncontrollably. "Then why did you side with him and have me sent away?" he complained. "You said Continental travel would do me good. You said it was best I get away from England. And when I returned, where did you and Cobham send me, but to Bath?! A declining waterhole best suited to hypochondriacs and invalided soldiers! He considers me an embarrassment to the family name. Do you? Is that why you sided with him?"

"An embarrassment? Good God, Tal. Your black moods are nothing to Cobham when compared to my *independence of spirit.* His euphemism for the fact I refused to share the marital bed with a husband who was a misogynistic lunatic. He detests having a plain-spoken sister. Besides," she added with a sad smile, glancing down at her gloved hand, "once I was married off, it was best you were away—away from all that—*unpleasantness*."

Talgarth's self-loathing increased tenfold and he snuffled into the blanket. "God, Lina, I'm a callous *fiend*. Forgive me. What's the loss of one canvas compared to the years of torment you endured at the hands of that monster… I hope Apollo is deserving of you."

Selina dipped her head, an ache in her throat, thinking it apt her brother should refer to Alec as the Greek God of manly beauty and reason. But with her feelings still painfully raw after Alec's abrupt and angry departure from her house, she felt unequal to speaking about him. Indeed, he was still angry with her. At Marlborough their carriages had crossed. He was preparing to leave when her carriage had pulled into the busy stable yard.

Talgarth voiced what she was thinking. "He didn't say more than two words to you at Marlborough."

"You saw him?"

"Apollo's handsome features are hard to miss even when this painter was retching into the straw. What did you do to upset him?"

Selina's jaw dropped in indignation. "Why presume I'm the one at fault?"

"Because you're like me," Talgarth said with a rare smile. "Damned mulish."

Selina had to concede this was true, but added in a small voice in her defense, "I made the best decision for both of us."

When Talgarth shrugged and looked unconvinced and stared out the window as if losing interest, she deftly turned the subject, hoping he was still receptive enough to answer a few of the questions Alec had put to her.

"Do you know who would want to vandalize one of your pictures, Tal?" she asked gently.

"You know me, Lina," he answered with a sigh of resignation, gaze on the windowpane and not the scenery beyond. "I've offended more people than I've made friends. I don't suffer fools. Bath is populated by fools and old women. I'll paint anyone's portrait for the right fee, but I won't be treated like an ignorant lackey!"

"Oh, I agree. It's your method of dealing with fools that perhaps needs refinement. There was that *incident* with Mrs. Sudgemoor and her three little pooches, remember?"

Talgarth ground his perfect teeth. "Oversized furry rats! They would've destroyed my favorite Turkey rug had I not hurled the chamber pot at them."

"But, my dear," Selina pointed out, biting the corner of her lower lip to stifle a smile, "Mrs. Sudgemoor was the one who suffered the contents of that chamber pot."

"Foolish woman got in the way," he grumbled, illness and a persistent headache making him oblivious to the humorous side of the incident. "Her fault, not mine."

"And you publicly humiliated Lady Russell in the Assembly Rooms, telling her, in a voice that could wake the dead, that if she was not pleased with the portrait of her two youngest daughters it was entirely of her own making, *they being so ugly that only a beheading would see them suitably married off.*"

"Did I? Well, I did my best. They *are* ugly, Lina. The finest silks and pomading don't make an ounce of difference. *And*, I omitted the warts."

"A similar incident occurred involving Cleveley's sister-in-law, Lady Rutherglen. You said that when she came to your studio to view the portrait of her and Lord Rutherglen she was so outraged as to demand you paint another, refusing to pay your fee until the second canvas was completed… And you said to her that only a portrait of her—her—*buttocks* would produce an improvement on the original!"

"Did I?" Talgarth said, momentarily pleased with himself. He shifted restlessly on the upholstered bench. "I could paint a hundred portraits of that woman and it wouldn't change the fact you can't dress a swine up in silk and expect it still not to stink of pig."

"I know you do try your best, Tal," Selina sympathized. "It is a sad trial to have to paint these people just to earn a place amongst the painters of the day. But you don't dislike living at Bath altogether, do you?" she asked, a gloved hand clutching at the strap above her head when the carriage lurched to the left as it slowed to negotiate a fork in the road. "And Ellick Farm is less than half a day's ride away. Miranda and Sophie so look forward to your visits. You've made a difference to their lonely lives."

Talgarth gave a huff, not at all convinced, but he swallowed his sister's leading question by blurting out, "*Lonely*? Much you know about life down on the farm! On one particular visit, I rode out there to see if there were any errands Mrs. Bourdon wanted running, and I found her and Sophie in the midst of unwrapping a cartload of gifts from some old London gent who'd come a-calling."

"Old London gent?"

"Felt an intruder, I can tell you, Lina," Talgarth grumbled. "Though they did their best to make me welcome, I could tell I wasn't wanted."

Selina sat up, a frown between her fair brows. "Who was this gentleman?"

"You needn't look concerned he was wooing her. He was old and portly enough to be her grandfather. And he was at pains to tell me he wasn't staying at the farm but up at the big house on the hill—"

"Bratton Dene?"

Talgarth nodded. "Friendly fellow. Full of chat. Retired vicar. Shabby clothes. Strange, that. By the gifts he'd brought with him, skeins of Spitalfields silks and velvets, silk stockings and the like, I'd have thought he'd have dressed himself better. Still, he seems the sort who prefers to give rather than receive, which I guess is why he's a vicar. He certainly doted on your Miranda and Sophie."

"Did he tell you his name?" Selina asked, though a sense of foreboding told her she knew already.

"Blackburn? Blackbird?" Talgarth pulled a face. "Black-something-or-other—"

"Black—*well*? Was his name Blackwell?"

"Blackwell? Yes. I dare say that was it."

"Did he say what had brought him to the farm?" Selina persisted. "Do you know if this was his first visit or if he'd been to the farm before?" She let go of the leather strap above her fair head, the carriage now rumbling along on a more even road, and chewed on her lower lip in thought. "Tal? Did he tell you anything about himself? Obviously he was well known to Miranda, but… Tal?"

Her brother had snuggled back into the corner of the carriage and closed his eyes. The throb at his temple had become so bad it was affecting the vision in his left eye. He'd talked too much. At the next inn, he would smoke opium from his bamboo pipe and the pain would be more bearable. He had just enough *chandu* to last him until he reached his Bath studio.

When would this wretched journey come to an end?

"Tal, I need to know what he—"

"Enough, Lina. That's enough for now," Talgarth muttered without opening his eyes, and turned his head away from her into the velvet corner.

Selina closed her mouth on a sigh and sat back beside her still-sleeping maid, knowing it was pointless to continue. She would have to be patient and await the next opportunity for Talgarth to feel open to confidences. She stared out the window unseeing, ruminating on the connection between a shabby vicar and a young woman and her illegitimate daughter, and had to concede that Alec's supposition seemed even more plausible now—that the Reverend Blackwell was the parish priest who had sent Miranda to her all those years ago.

But why send the girl to her? And why to Ellick Farm? Did the vicar often visit Miranda at the farm? And if he did, it begged the question: If he had kept regular contact with Miranda, then perhaps she had confided the circumstances of Sophie's conception, and thus it was he who had blackmailed George Stanton after all, seeking retribution for Miranda and her daughter for Stanton's appalling crime. Had Stanton known the identity of his blackmailer all along and taken matters into his own hands at Weir's dinner party? But Blackwell didn't seem the sort of man who would be party to blackmail. And George Stanton was a coward. He would get someone else to do his dirty work for him; someone with brains… Sir Charles Weir immediately came to mind.

But the Duke had also been at that dinner party. And Talgarth did say Blackwell was staying up at the Duke's mansion… Did Cleveley know the vicar had visited Miranda at the farm? Had Blackwell confronted the Duke with the knowledge that the woman raped by his adopted son lived practically on his doorstep? Had Cleveley decided to take matters into his own hands and shut the vicar up before the truth would out?

Such postulating and being bounced over bad roads for hours on end had definitely contributed to a travel-induced sick headache, so that Selina audibly sighed with relief when the carriage pulled up outside the George Inn in the High Street of Norton St. Philip. Here they were to put up for the night and go on to Ellick Farm at first light. And when a postilion handed her down to firm ground, Selina was just as eager as Talgarth to seek the relative peace and quiet of the George's best bedchambers.

The flaggings were strewn with straw to conceal the mud and filth trampled in by weary travelers and wool merchants come to meet and enjoy this thirteenth century inn's hospitality. It was crowded and noisy, but Selina hardly noticed men or chatter as she made her way under the archway of the porch to the warmth indoors with Evans in tow. But just inside the doorway, Selina did notice the slight figure of the tall, thin boy with a pronounced limp, because in his haste to get outside, his shoulder knocked her sideways, and she looked hard at him as she fell back into the arms of a fellow traveler.

The traveler hurled abuse at the boy's clumsiness and half the room turned and stared. The boy froze and mumbled an incoherent apology as he glanced fleetingly up at the lady he'd unwittingly collided with, then fled into the cold afternoon air.

Selina's astonishment was visible, and her fellow traveler, thinking her shock was due to the uncouth behavior of a local bumpkin, offered to go after the runt and whip some manners into him. This Selina declined, but she would seek out the boy as soon she had secured their rooms for the night. She knew him.

It was Billy Rumble, nephew of her cook at Ellick Farm. He had one leg shorter than the other and a clubfoot, and cared for Selina's horses when she came to stay. At other times he did odd jobs around the farm, and at harvest time worked on the Duke of Cleveley's estate. What was he doing here, miles from home and alone? Miranda had confided to her that the boy dreamed of going to sea. Had he finally run away?

ꝟ

BILLY HOBBLED AS FAST AS HIS UNEVEN LEGS WOULD TAKE HIM to the furthest, darkest and quietest corner of a narrow laneway that separated the inn's kitchens from the stables. Stopping to catch his breath, he unbuttoned his old woolen coat, roughly pulled his shirt out of his breeches, and extracted a bundle of letters stuffed in a worn stocking that he'd kept next to his skin since leaving the farm. He then thrust his shirt back into his breeches, roughly rebuttoned his coat and shoved the bundle in a deep pocket.

He'd stolen jewelry and letters from Mrs. Bourdon for the promise of the princely sum of five guineas. The guineas were Billy's freedom. His new wealth would allow him to escape the drudgery of his pitiful existence. He hated working the land. He wanted to go to sea. He wanted to be a smuggler like his Uncle Nate.

And then fortune had smiled upon him further.

While in Mrs. Bourdon's bedchamber ferreting amongst her personal belongings, he'd discovered a lace handkerchief tied in a bow hiding jewelry worth a king's ransom. The fine linen handkerchief with its delicate lace border had been tucked in a far corner of the bottom drawer of the small carved mahogany writing desk by the window. Three gold bracelets, an engraved silver button, a pair of diamond drop earrings, and an engraved gold band sized to fit a lady's dainty finger. And there was also a bundle of letters tied up with ribbon.

The promise of a few guineas didn't matter all that much now he had gold in his pocket.

Still, Billy wanted the guineas. He'd promised his sister Annie a crown for helping him spirit Miss Sophie away from the farm. He had increased it to two crowns when Annie was reluctant to hand the child over to some London gent *we knows nothin' 'bout*. But Billy had lied to her, telling her the gentleman was in truth Sophie's pa come to fetch her away to live a better life with him in a big London house.

What Billy planned to do was offer little Sophie to the London gentleman, for a price. His Uncle Nate told him that kidnapping paid better coin than smuggling, depending on the hostage. Billy figured that little Sophie must be worth at least ten guineas, maybe twelve.

Half a guinea had sealed Annie's cooperation.

Annie and the London gentleman need never know about the diamond drop earrings or the gold bangles. Mayhap he'd offer the gold band fit for a lady's slender finger. If the London gentleman didn't want Sophie, he'd be on his way, leaving Annie to deal with the brat, especially now he'd been seen by the fine London lady who came to the farm once a year. Of all the tricks to serve, for her to be at this very inn on this very night! He hoped Annie had the sense to remain out of sight until he returned from his meeting with the London gentleman. He'd stow the letters up in the rafters of the third stall along on the right, just as the London gentleman had ordered, collect his guineas from under the saddle in that very stable, and make good his escape.

He'd buy an inside seat on the Bristol mail coach…

Annie wouldn't see her money until he was good and ready to send it to her. That way he was assured of her silence and cooperation. Billy smiled at his own cleverness. Cripple he may be, but no one could accuse Billy Rumble of being a slow-top!

The stables were alive with the bustle, noise and sweat of exhausted horses coming in for the night, stable boys too busy going about their business of feeding and watering animals and bedding them down before sunset to bother about a cripple who weaved his way amongst the multitudes of sweaty horseflesh and dozens of scuttling lads loaded up with bridle and tack. Billy disappeared into the unoccupied third stable. He stripped out of his woolen coat, and had he not been so anxious to off-load his stolen property and wedge it between two beams out of the line of sight, he might have noticed that in a darkened corner lurked a figure in a greatcoat and jockey boots.

Billy jumped down off one of the crossbeams and stepped back, satisfied the bundle was out of view. He adjusted his shirt and breeches, and was about to pick up his woollen coat to shrug it back on when he felt his pocket for the jewelry, wrapped in the soft lace-edged handkerchief. To reassure himself for the umpteenth time that the jewelry was indeed real and still in his keeping, he dropped his coat and took out the handkerchief. As he did so the silver button and the earrings fell to the straw-strewn floor.

He shoved the handkerchief back in his breeches pocket without bothering to check the rest of its precious contents, and in the fading light scrambled to retrieve the priceless earrings amongst sodden straw and muck. His sigh of relief at finding one of the diamond earrings was audible. He would have kept searching for its twin, but he sensed a presence, and righting himself he found his nose swallowed up by a linen cravat between the high collar of an expensive many-caped greatcoat.

He fell back with surprise, a lump in his throat, knowing who it was without glancing up, and felt something cold and sharp prick the soft underside of his chin. He swallowed and hot tears welled up behind his eyelids. The earring he clutched in a tight fist.

"You're a miserable disappointment, Billy-boy," drawled the insolent voice of the London gentleman. "Up and get those letters."

Billy wanted to duck under the London gentleman's arm and run as fast as he could, but the tip of the sword hovered dangerously close to his reddened ear, and he knew with bitter certainty that his uneven legs wouldn't get him very far. He prayed the handkerchief and diamond earrings had gone unnoticed. So he did as he was told, the earring clutched a little tighter and his legs and arms weaker at the thought of what the London gentleman might do to him if he disobeyed. Knowing the stableboys continued on with their tasks just outside the stable door was small comfort that he was not alone.

Back on firm ground, Billy held out the packet of letters. The London gentleman snatched at them with his gloved hand, sword still trained on Billy, and loosened the silk bow by tugging impatiently on an end with his front teeth. When the letters spilled and scattered he cursed. Billy was ordered to pick them up and show the direction of each letter, one by one, to the London gentleman so that he could peruse the handwriting in the fading light.

Heart thudding against his ribs, Billy did as he was told and waited for the inevitable question he knew would be asked of him as the London gentleman's swearing intensified with each letter presented for his inspection. The sword was waved menacingly.

"Are you certain these are her only correspondence?"

Billy nodded vigorously. He didn't trust himself to speak. Gingerly, he held out the bundle of gathered up letters. They were snatched up and flung to the ground.

"Christ! *Worthless.*" These letters were not what he wanted. They had been written by that Jamison-Lewis trollop—of no use to him whatsoever. There had to be other letters; she'd been secreted away in the country for how long now—three, or was it four years? She must have corresponded with someone in that time; told someone about her predicament.

Movement had his eyes fixed on Billy again. In the light of one burning taper he could see the boy kept his gaze firmly on the ground. What was he hiding? His left hand was shoved deep in his breeches pocket.

"What you got there, Billy-boy, eh?"

"I-I brought you some'in' else!" Billy said eagerly. "I got Miss Sophie. She must be worth somethin' to ye?"

"What? What are you blathering about, boy?"

"Mrs. Bourdon's dau'ter. I got her too. Her ma don't know 'cause she's gone to Bath. Ye can have her too for a price."

"You *stole* a-a *brat* from its *mother*?" The London gentleman was incredulous. "Hell and damnation! Not only a bloody cripple but a flesh-monger!"

"She's healthy and bonny and would fetch a good price. M'sister's keepin' her safe while I negotiate a price for her."

"Negotiate a price?" The London gentleman's shoulders shook with silent mirth. "I'll own you've got ballocks, Billy-boy!"

"Wooder I fetch her for you, sir?" Billy asked eagerly, hoping for an excuse to escape.

The London gentleman viewed him dispassionately. His voice was flat.

"Take your hand from your pocket and open your fist."

Billy hesitated.

He felt the sting before he saw the sword move. The London gentleman had slashed his shirt above the elbow of his left arm and blood began to seep from a long deep scratch. He managed to muffle the scream in his throat and readily extracted his left hand, but his fist remained closed. Again there was pain before the movement of the sword registered, and the boy stared down at his fist in incomprehension as a long thin line of raw flesh peeled back across his knuckles. He blinked up at his tormentor, biting his lip to stop himself from crying, and opened out his grubby fingers.

The London gentleman snatched up the diamond earring and a twisted smile curved his lips. He knew this piece of jewelry. "Where's its twin, Billy-boy?" he asked silkily.

"What, sir? Other earring? I don't have it, sir," he lied. "I just took the-the—*that*. Not'in' else. Honest."

"You had time to rummage amongst that harlot's undergarments, to do a bit of *thieving,* and yet you bring me a worthless packet of letters?" The London gentleman set his teeth. "There's a handkerchief in your pocket, *liar*. Give it to me."

Billy dug into his pocket and had the presence of mind to extract the handkerchief by a lace corner so at the very least one of the gold bracelets might drop deep into his breeches pocket to escape detection. It was the small gold band that slid back into his pocket. As he handed over his bounty, he hung his head at being discovered a liar, disappointed he'd only managed to salvage the small gold band from his treasure. Still, gold was gold and he'd get something for it. From under his lashes he watched the London gentleman feel the handkerchief's contents without opening it out and then shove it in a pocket of his riding frock coat along with the diamond earring.

"You're a liar, Billy-boy," the London gentleman slurred. "A *liar* and a *kidnapper* and a *thief*."

Billy wanted to sob. Blood trickled down his arm and between his knuckles. "Pleaze, sir, I—I brung the letters like you wanted. The jewelry, it waz layin' there amongst her things and I thought you could sell that along with the brat and fetch a good—"

"I didn't offer you payment to think, *cripple*."

"Pleaze, sir, y'must believe—"

"Do you know what happens to thieves and kidnappers, Billy-boy?"

Billy knew. He'd seen three men and a boy, younger than himself, hanged in the village square for stealing a sheep from Squire Hinton. Everyone had turned out in their Sunday best and it was talked about for months afterwards. Still, he thought it better to plead ignorance, and reasoned the London gentleman was just as much at fault for asking him to steal the letters. He said nothing, just shook his head.

The stranger's smile broadened into a grin as shouts outside the stall demanded that the stable boys stop their tomfoolery and get back to work or they'd forfeit their supper.

"No supper for you, Billy-boy," purred the London gentleman, and with one quick deep thrust of his bloodied sword he pierced Billy Rumble's heart.

WITH TALGARTH SAFELY ENSCONCED IN THE BEDCHAMBER NEXT to her own, Selina left Evans to supervise the making of beds with her own clean linen while she went in search of Billy Rumble. She reasoned the boy hadn't gone far because it was almost dark, and no one traveled on a moonless night without good reason, not without a fresh horse and an escort, all of which Billy was too poor to afford.

On the second floor gallery that wrapped around three sides of the inn's internal courtyard, she came face-to-face with a slip of a girl leading a small child by the hand. The narrowness of the passage and Selina's wide petticoats prevented her from passing them, so she patiently waited until they were at the stairwell that led down to the courtyard or up to another level of rooms, wondering which direction they meant to take. The slip of a girl put her foot on the stair leading up, so Selina stepped forward in anticipation of going down the stairs. But the small child hesitated. The little round face framed by a wealth of black ringlets stared up the darkened stairwell as if it were an insurmountable object, and rubbed her eye with a chubby fist. She yawned and blinked and asked the slip of a girl for her mother.

The child spoke French but the girl leading her did not, evident in her clumsy response about no coin for food. The child's French tongue triggered a memory for Selina, but the girl's county dialect froze her in disbelief, for she reasoned the tired child had to be Sophie Bourdon, and the slip of a girl whose hand she held must be none other than Annie Rumble, Billy Rumble's younger sister.

How did they come to be here, at a bustling inn full of weary travelers, miles from home, alone, ill-clothed and unfed? More importantly, wondered Selina, why were they at the inn, Billy and his sister Annie with little Sophie in tow? Where was Sophie's mother Miranda? That the little girl was dressed in nothing more than a white linen nightgown that was grubby and creased, and without benefit of a warm cloak for such a cold night alerted Selina that all was not right. Miranda would never allow her daughter out of doors without proper clothing and she certainly would not leave her in the care of a young scullery maid and a boy stable-hand. So where was Miranda?

Selina inched her way forward, hoping not to startle Annie into making any sudden move with the child. She wanted to get as close to the pair as possible, so in the event that Annie made a dash for the stairwell, she would be able to grab Sophie from her with a minimum of fuss. She was almost upon them when there was the sound of voices from the third landing above.

Annie jumped with fright and hesitated, listening.

Doors creaked open and slammed shut above their heads. There were shouts, too, from the courtyard below. There seemed to be some sort of gathering of men. The sudden flash of light as several flambeaux were lit all at once confirmed this. The light passed on out of the courtyard, towards the stables was Selina guess, but she dared not look over the railing. Her focus remained on Annie and Sophie, and Annie's next move.

Annie had her back up against the wall, as if she did not want to be seen. When Sophie took a few short steps toward the stairs and again asked for her mother, Annie yanked her close, squeezing her tiny wrist hard in the process.

Sophie let out a howl and Annie went down on her haunches to hush her.

Measured footfall in the stairwell coming up from below

distracted Annie for a moment, and she glanced over her shoulder before saying to the little girl, face stuck in hers.

"Stop y'whining! D'y want Billy to fetch the gurt beastie? He will. He will if y'don't shut off that noise! Y'frightened of the gurt beastie ain't ye?"

Sophie shook her ringlets vigorously and tearfully said *no* several times before again asking for her mother.

Selina's heart missed a beat. Annie and Billy had abducted Sophie.

It was time to act.

The footsteps had ceased.

Annie took a tentative peek along the passage, the sobbing Sophie pushed behind her woolen skirts, to see if the stairs were now clear of travelers. Just as she did so, Selina dashed forward, across the mouth of the stairwell, and scooped up the little girl and turned away from Annie so the girl could not make a grab to take the child back. She held the little girl close to the warmth of her own body and spoke soothing words in French about being reunited with her mother and having something warm to eat and drink, all to stop the child's struggles and her frightened sobs.

With Sophie soon quiet and clinging to the perfumed lady's brown velvet cloak, Selina rounded angrily on Annie, a hand covering the child's bare feet which were as cold as blocks of ice.

"Where's Mrs. Bourdon, girl?"

Startled, Annie was too frightened to speak or move. She stared wild-eyed at the splendidly dressed lady, with her translucent skin, dark eyes and flame-colored curls mussed from travel, as if she were staring at an apparition. But in two blinks she knew who she was. She gulped. There was a large painting of this lady over the mantel in the drawing room back at Ellick Farm. Billie told her the London lady's brother had painted it. Annie liked to gaze upon the portrait every time she cleaned soot from the grate, dreaming of herself in such splendid petticoats of sky-blue silk and riding about in a horse-drawn carriage. But Billie hadn't said anything about the London lady being at the inn this night. Perhaps she was a friend of the London gentleman come to collect Miss Sophie?

"Dun rightly know, m'lady. Billy says she's gone to Bath." Annie bobbed a clumsy curtsy for good measure. "M'sister Janie went with her."

"*Bath*?" Selina did not believe her. She held Sophie closer. "Why have you and Billy brought Sophie to this place?"

So the London lady didn't know about the London gentleman. Annie hoped Billie would be back very soon. He could explain matters much better than she ever could. But Billy had been gone a long time now and that's why Annie had ventured out of their hiding place to find him. She didn't think Billy would want her to mention the London gentleman to this London lady. He might not give her the promised half guinea if she did. But now the London lady had Sophie, what were her chances of receiving anything?

Annie glanced at the stairwell, wondering if she could make good her escape, and her eyes widened at the sight of a tall stranger in a many-caped greatcoat and jockey boots, standing in shadow and blocking the entrance. Maybe she could turn tail and flee back along the gallery? The London lady wouldn't be able to follow her with Sophie tight in her arms. For now, best to remain ignorant. It was all Billy's fault anyway.

So Annie shrugged, a sullen pull to her mouth, in response to Selina's question and retreated a few paces along the passage, a fearful glance at the stranger in shadow.

Selina saw the glance and looked over her shoulder. As she did so Annie picked up the hem of her Sunday-best gown and fled back along the passage. She was caught around the neck in two strides.

Annie squawked and struggled and tried to break free but there was no chance of escape from the stranger, and so he told her in a measured tone as he brought her back to stand once more before the London lady.

"What are you doing here?" Selina demanded, astonished, though she felt a huge relief and strangely uplifted all at the same time.

"I took pity on you," Alec commented, a firm gloved hand about a terrified Annie's upper arm, though there was amusement in his blue eyes at Selina's wide-eyed shock. "I'd no idea Talgarth also suffered the family trait of poor traveler." He glanced at Sophie cuddled into the crook of Selina's neck. "Best get the child indoors. I'll return shortly."

Selina blinked. "Where are you taking her?"

The amusement went out of his eyes. He was grim-faced. "To identify a body."

ELEVEN

By the time Alec returned, Evans had the little girl scrubbed, fed and tucked up asleep in Selina's bed, a hot brick wrapped in cloth between the sheets to keep her warm. Selina had tidied her hair but her dinner remained uneaten on the sitting room table, a glass of wine half consumed. Each time there was footfall on the landing she was at the window thinking it was Alec, only to return to pace in front of the warmth of the fireplace. Evans had retreated to the bedchamber, to sit by the bed to watch over the little girl lest she stir, though she purposely left the door to the sitting room ajar in anticipation of Lord Halsey's arrival.

Two short raps and Selina wrenched open the door, saying without preamble, "Where's Annie Rumble?"

"May I come in, Mrs. Jamison-Lewis?" Alec asked, though his smile was at odds with the formality in his deep voice. He stepped off the landing into the cozy sitting room and dumped a small calfskin portmanteau just inside the door. "I hope you didn't wait your dinner for me?"

"Did she run off? Where's her brother Billy?"

"Ah, I see you couldn't stomach the inn's fare," he continued, spying the untouched plate of cold roast lamb and an indefinable mass covered in white sauce which he presumed to be an assortment of vegetables. Through the connecting doorway he saw Selina's long-suffering lady's maid sitting by the bed. "Mrs. Jamison-Lewis, you really should have eaten something while it was hot."

"There's only an audience of one, y'know," she enunciated in a loud whisper, following him to the hearth. "You didn't explain about the body. Whose body? Why did you need Annie Rumble?"

"Yes, Mrs. Jamison-Lewis, I am rather cold and tired. Hungry too," Alec continued loudly, stripping off his gloves. He spread his long fingers to the warmth radiating from the small fireplace. "But coffee would suffice if it isn't too much of an inconvenience…?"

"Stop it, Alec," Selina hissed at his back as she helped him shrug out of his greatcoat. She dumped this and his gloves over the arm of the sofa. "And stop repeating my horrid name! There's only Evans here—the audience of one."

Alec looked over his shoulder, an eyebrow raised in question. "But the walls, my dear, are thin, so we must observe the formalities. There is your reputation to think about. Oh, and speaking of formalities, it's *my lord* when in company."

Selina pouted and looked mutinous. "You're being difficult to prove a point!"

"Yes."

She put up her chin. "I won't call you *my lord*."

"Won't you?" he threatened, turning back to the fire, but not before Selina caught his smirk. "Indeed, a bedchamber is the perfect place for a mistress to call her lover *my lord*."

"*Ballocks*!" Selina said rudely and threw her arms about his neck to be gathered up in his embrace. She smiled up into his handsome face. "Between the sheets, mayhap I will condescend to call you my lord. But… only if you please me. Now kiss me so I know you are not angry. Evans has been most upset since you stormed out of my dressing room."

"Evans and I both," he murmured and stooped to kiss her passionately. When he came up for air he said seriously, "This doesn't mean I'm at all happy with the arrangement you've imposed upon me. But because I want us to be together, I'm willing to put up with it—for now." He pinched her chin. "It isn't final. Understand me?"

"Yes," she answered with a trembling smile, staring up into his searching blue eyes from the circle of his embrace. "But in time, you'll come to understand why this is our only recourse."

Alec wondered how much time she needed before she confided in him why they could not now marry and why she felt able to tell the Duke of Cleveley, yet could not share the reason for her change of mind with him. He just hoped he had the patience to bide his time until she was ready. He smiled reassuringly, though he felt anything but pleased, and gently kissed her forehead.

"Now send for food and coffee. I haven't eaten since breakfast and that was at Marlborough."

"But your arrival in Bath with your uncle was uneventful?" she asked anxiously, disengaging herself from his arms to fuss unnecessarily with the pinning of a stray curl, aware that Evans had risen from her chair by the bed. With a look Selina sent her in search of food.

"I left him in Tam's capable hands, finding fault with Barr's excellent bill of fare."

"You should've stayed to nuncheon," Selina admonished him, seeing the tiredness in his eyes. "You needn't have ridden all the way back here. I was managing."

Alec gave a bark of laughter. "Yes, so I saw at the Marlborough Arms. My poor darling, it's been a frightful journey from London, hasn't it?"

"Surprisingly, the time went by faster than usual," she confessed reluctantly. "What with Talgarth's bouts of ill-health and my preoccupation with a certain lordship's displeasure..." She touched his stubbled cheek. "I'm pleased you came. I've been wretched since we parted in Hanover Square."

"Likewise," he answered, and kissed her wrist.

She led him to the sofa and they sat, her hand in his.

"Shall you tell me about Annie and Billy?" she asked as casually as she could manage, "Or shall you dine first?"

He grinned, knowing her curiosity would be at bursting point if he made her wait, but the thought of what had confronted him in the stables removed his smile. "The news isn't pleasant," he said soberly. "A boy was found dead in the stables…"

Selina sat up very straight. "Billy?"

"Yes. A sword thrust to the heart."

"My God… That poor boy…" Selina put a hand to her mouth, swallowed and then took a deep breath before saying quietly, "*Why*?"

"That has yet to be determined."

"Who then? Who would want to kill Billy Rumble? The boy is harmless and a cripple. I saw him only a few hours ago leaving the inn. Did he get in some sort of fight? But with a sword… I don't understand."

"No. I don't think it was a fight. He has a slash to the upper arm and another across the knuckles of his left hand, but there was no real sign of struggle. A local physician should bear this out, but such minor injuries and the single thrust to his heart suggests the boy knew his assailant.

Selina was still nonplussed. "Knew his assailant? Billy know someone who carried a sword, who could do that to a boy? It doesn't seem possible!"

"It doesn't, but his sister confirmed that Billy was here to meet a gentleman from London.

"Gentleman from London?"

"Annie said she has no notion of the identity of this gentleman," Alec continued patiently, "as she never met the man in the flesh and Billy always met *the London gentleman*, as Billy called him, alone. That was clever. All Annie knows—"

"You believe her?"

"Yes. The poor wretch had to identify her brother's body. The shock was enough to purge her of any tendency to lie. Mind you, she didn't know much at all."

"What have you done with her?"

"I left her in the care of the landlord's wife—for a price. She'll be given a hot meal and a bed for the night. In the morning I will make arrangements for her to accompany her brother's body back to Ellick, where no doubt she'll have plenty of explaining to do before her—Aunt Rumble, isn't it?"

Selina nodded. "My cook and housekeeper at Ellick Farm. The only family the three Rumble children have. Both parents perished from the sweating sickness some years ago." She touched his hand that lay across the worn back of the sofa. "Thank you for taking care of her—and Billy. Though Annie hardly deserves her hot meal for the mischief she and Billy were about. Poor Mrs. Rumble. Billy's death will be a great shock to her. What were they doing here, and with little Sophie in tow? Did Annie tell you?"

"Yes. From what I gathered from Annie's blubbering confession, Billy brought her along because he couldn't manage the child alone. He offered Annie two crowns. God knows what this London gentleman had promised Billy to snatch little Sophie from her home, but my guess it was in guineas."

"But how did they contrive to lure Sophie away?"

"With the promise of being reunited with her mother who, incidentally, is at Bath."

Selina was surprised. "Why would Miranda travel to Bath and leave Sophie behind in the care of servants? That is most unlike her. The few times she's traveled to Bath, she's taken Sophie with her."

"Whatever her reasons for leaving her daughter at Ellick Farm, there is a Miranda Bourdon registered at Barr's of Trim Street. As luck would have it, I spied her name in the register as I was signing my moniker. I very much doubt there are two Miranda Bourdons. She arrived in Bath two days ago."

"You saw her?"

Alec shook his head. "I barely had time to shuffle my uncle upstairs to his rooms before I turned tail to ride back here in daylight." He smiled. "I've given Uncle the honor of making her acquaintance at the earliest opportunity. He can't wait."

Selina smiled. "He'll be smitten. Not only is she the prettiest creature I've ever set eyes on, but she's all that's good in the world. She could be a slave-trader and I challenge your uncle not to fall under her spell!"

"Hence your brother's infatuation."

"Precisely! But why did Billy and Annie kidnap Sophie for a handful of guineas?"

"It might be pin money to you, darling, but to the likes of a poor farmhand and a scullery maid, a handful of guineas is a small fortune."

Selina smiled crookedly at his misinterpretation of her question and squeezed his hand a little too tightly. "Not all wealthy widows are immune to the plight of the less fortunate, *my lord*, whatever your uncle's prejudices to the contrary. I do know the worth of a guinea. I may have spent on shoes alone a sum that could feed Bristol's poor for a week, but my man of business can't praise enough my meticulous account keeping. In fact," she said with thoughtful frown, "I do believe every time I put my books before Browne he feels his employment is under threat..." She roused herself. "No, not Billy and his guineas, silly. What did Billy's murderer want with Sophie?"

"I really have no idea," Alec answered on a sigh. He was so tired that if Evans did not return with a bowl of broth, at the very least, food would soon be of no interest. "Any number of possibilities come to mind, but given that your brother's painting of Miranda and her daughter was vandalized, my guess is the child was to be used to get at her mother. The vandalized painting was a warning to your brother. Likewise taking Sophie from Miranda, if indeed it is the same man, though I have no reason to think otherwise. It would be too much of a coincidence if Talgarth's vandalized picture and Sophie's attempted abduction were not connected in some way."

"You think Lord George vandalized Talgarth's painting and is also somehow involved in Billy's murder?"

"I have no evidence connecting him to either circumstance, and only Charles Weir's word that Lord George was being blackmailed."

Selina was skeptical. "You think Lord George capable of cold-blooded murder? Vandalizing a painting, yes, I can see a drunken George Stanton performing that cowardly act, but a sword thrust to the heart requires rather more backbone."

"I agree with you, but I suspect Billy was killed out of spite, for not giving our murderer what he wanted, and if so, then piercing the poor boy's heart was done in an impotent rage."

"When you put it like that," Selina conceded, "it's just the sort of act I could believe of Lord George. He may be cowardly, but he has no conscience."

"I'm not convinced Lord George had a personal hand in any of these crimes. Pay someone else to do it, yes. But get his own fine hands dirty?" Alec shrugged. "He isn't the only one under suspicion."

Selina put her hands to her white cheeks in thought and gazed into the darkened bedchamber. "The notion of that buffoon getting his hands on Sophie..." She shuddered, appalled. "The dear little thing was terrified, exhausted, hungry, and on the verge of frostbite. If a harmless farm boy with a limp can be murdered in cold-blood, then his killer wouldn't have a second thought for Sophie's welfare, now would he?"

Alec followed Selina's gaze to the bedchamber where a small hump in the bedclothes indicated the sleeping child. "Don't let her out of your sight. Who's to say Billy's killer isn't still at the inn awaiting an opportunity to pounce?" He looked intently at Selina. "She wasn't harmed in any way, was she?"

"No, not physically. Sophie's a very healthy little girl. But the sooner I can return her to Miranda, the better for the child's peace of mind." Selina smiled wistfully. "Sophie doesn't remember who I am. It's a twelvemonth since I saw her last. But she trusts me because I speak to her in French. Miranda has always conversed with her daughter in that tongue."

"If Miranda Bourdon speaks fluent French, then she certainly received the upbringing of a young lady... But why choose to speak it in a cultural backwater such as Ellick Farm?"

Selina regarded Alec as if the answer were self-evident, but when he continued to look puzzled, she explained with a laugh, "The locals. They can't read or write, so it is perfectly acceptable to write one's letters in English. But they aren't deaf. It's all very well for us to regard servants as if they're part of the furniture, but when one is in the depths of the country, the same approach just doesn't work if one wants to hire good help from the village. Hence, conversing in French is preferable to having the locals eavesdropping on conversations and spreading it about the village by sundown." Selina screwed up her nose on a sudden thought. "Although... by doing so, we are denying them their only form of entertainment, aren't we? It's not as if they can attend the theater or the opera, is it?"

"The minds of females," Alec murmured with a roll of his eyes. He took from his frock coat pocket a bundle of letters. "These were found strewn near Billy's body. They're letters you wrote to Miranda Bourdon. And this," he added after perching his gold-rimmed spectacles on his nose and dropping in Selina's palm a small silver button with the raised engraving of a bumblebee, "was found near Billy's body. Have you seen a similar button before?"

Selina shook her head and handed the button back. "Should I know it? It looks a perfectly ordinary button. Or is it a button of significance? It must be, because you're laughing at me!" she accused him when he regarded her over the rims of his spectacles as a tutor might his pupil. It didn't stop her snuggling into his embroidered waistcoat with a practiced pout. "First you accuse me of being a feckless creature, and now you expect me to know the origins of one tiny silver button! You tell me. You're the Bow Street Runner masquerading as a nobleman."

"I didn't expect you to know," he confessed, holding the button between thumb and forefinger. "I admit I had no idea until Tam enlightened me. But I would wager that if you asked any upper servant in Westminster to identify this button, he could do so in an instant. Livery and unusually engraved buttons and such are very important social minutiae in servant circles."

"I had no idea," Selina said with mock awe. "I must show your button to Evans to see if she can pass inspection. Although, being a Methodist, she will decry such fribbles as useless vanity. Why she remains with this immoral creature I know not."

Alec tweaked one of her loose curls. "Perhaps she desires to see you made an honest woman? Or have you told her of your new vocation? Either way, you will provide her with a surfeit of material to add to her nightly prayer."

"This button. To whom does it belong?" Selina asked, taking the button back and examining it closely to hide the heat in her cheeks.

"The Cleveley livery," Alec responded casually, though he was watching Selina intently over the rims of his spectacles. "That there is no thread attached suggests it wasn't ripped from the killer's frock coat, as would happen in a struggle. Just as there was no thread attached to the button discovered in my uncle's fist. My first thought was that Uncle had pulled off the button in a struggle. That this button was also found near Billy makes me wonder if it was placed there deliberately."

"There you are then!" Selina said with certainty, handing back the button. "They were placed there to incriminate Cleveley."

"Or as a warning from the Duke to stay out of his way, perhaps?"

Selina scowled, yet had to concede Alec had a point. "I don't know why you're so ready to condemn Cleveley over one—*two*—buttons," she argued, the heat intensifying in her throat and cheeks because he was regarding her as if she had something to answer for. "Lord George or Weir could just as easily have hired a ruffian or ruffians to place the buttons there to cast suspicion Cleveley's way."

"True," Alec agreed, pocketing his spectacles. "Charles is the methodical type, but George Stanton…?"

"George is a buffoon and Weir a toad, but Cleveley is neither."

"Your Aunt Olivia defends him too. She has her own reasons for doing so… What are yours?"

"I told you in London…" she faltered, tightly entwining her fingers in the lap of her voluminous petticoats. "He was kind to me during my marriage. He was no friend of J-L's. And when I needed someone… When I needed a shoulder to cry on—he-he was there."

"You were lovers."

It was not a question. He wished it were.

When Selina looked away, desolate, he lifted her chin and turned her face to his.

"It's all right, darling. It doesn't change how I feel about you. I love you. And we are together now. That's all that matters. God, I was no saint during your horrid marriage to Jamison-Lewis. I wanted to expunge all thought of you married to another. That you found comfort in the arms of an understanding lover doesn't surprise me. I just wish I'd been there for you; that I'd been he."

Selina swallowed.

"Once. It happened just the once," she confessed, and voiced her thoughts, because it was better than dealing with silence between them. "I'd been married two years. His Duchess had been told she was dying, and he had just buried his niece. We were both very low and lonely. It's just something that happened. I can't explain how. He was very gentle and understanding." She glanced up at him. "If it's any consolation, the whole time I was with him, I was wishing it was you…"

"Don't be too harsh on yourself," Alec heard himself say in an even tone, though he felt anything but calm. "Sometimes circumstances arise… Situations develop…" His voice trailed off, he didn't know what else to say.

He was thinking that once was once too often. No wonder Cleveley's smile had been smug at Hanover Square. He knew he shouldn't let it bother him that Selina had found comfort in the arms of the Duke, because the Duke had treated Selina with kindness and an understanding of her plight, married to a sadistic misogynistic husband. But it did bother him, not only because they had shared a bed, but because the Duke was still very much part of Selina's life. He knew he was being utterly selfish and vain, possibly unreasonable, but it smarted whichever way he thought about it.

What she confided next sucked the air out of his lungs.

"I fell pregnant, but lost the child early in the pregnancy."

"To Cleveley? You were pregnant to *Cleveley*?"

"Yes. Such things can and do happen."

"Are you sure it was his child and not your husband's?"

Selina scowled, wondering where his questions were heading and not liking his tone. "Yes. Certain. Women know these things."

Alec tempered his tone and said evenly, "I only ask because the rumor, according to Olivia, is that Cleveley is—"

"—barren? Yes, that's the whisper. But it's not true. It's just that he—Justinian—thought it best not to shout my pregnancy from the rooftops; and the Duchess was dying of cancer…"

"His Grace is all consideration," Alec murmured, asking before Selina could launch into another defense of *the great man*, "So you told him?"

"Of course. J-L? Never in a month of Sundays!" Selina suddenly teared up. "He—Justinian—was so joyous at the news. He said my pregnancy was a gift; it gave him *hope* and then—and then I lost the baby..."

When Alec just sat there, a deep furrow between his brows, Selina could not bear with his brooding silence, which was much more difficult to deal with and hurtful than a jealous lover's castigation, so she blurted out, as if by confessing every lurid detail she would be cleansed,

"Cleveley is my *godfather*, which renders the affair and the subsequent pregnancy that much more sordid, doesn't it? Making love with one's godfather isn't far removed from sleeping with one's own father or brother or uncle. After all, he was there at my christening with them. As for falling pregnant by him... It's the stuff of Julio-Claudian melodrama. And to make certain I would loathe myself forever more for what I'd done, while I was imagining he was you, he was imagining I was *her*... At the crucial moment, he cried out for Mimi. He cried out for his fifteen-year-old *niece*."

Evans opened the door on a heavy silence. Following her were four of the inn's waiters. Two carried trays heavy with dinner things, a third had two bottles of the inn's finest claret and two glasses, and the fourth brought extra candles and an ornate candelabra for the center of the table. Alec got off the sofa and went to stoke the dying fire while the table was reset with cutlery, plates, wine glasses and candelabra. Bread, a fancy tureen containing soup *maigre*, a pot of olio, bowls of pickles, parsnips, mushrooms and carrots, and various sauces in small dishes completed the feast. Nothing had been spared for his lordship. Evans had made it clear to Cook that the dinner he was to prepare was for the Marquess Halsey.

When a waiter remained behind the chair at the head of the table, Alec dismissed him, saying they would serve themselves. Evans saw the gaping functionary to the door before she once again retired to the darkness of the bedchamber, a look from one bleak face to the other deciding her that the food could not have arrived at a more inauspicious moment. She silently closed over the door to give the couple further privacy.

Alec was starving. He had eaten his soup and was well into the main course before Selina took her place at the table and decided that whatever her frame of mind, her stomach required sustenance. The silence continued between them until Alec, pouring her out a glass of wine, asked mildly,

"Where's Talgarth?"

"The next room along. He's locked himself in. No doubt, by this hour, he's experiencing some nether world after finally feeding his addiction."

"There goes my plan of bedding down on his floor for the night." When Selina glowered at him he added with a crooked smile, "It's not a new thought, darling. I'd always intended to bunk in with your brother. There's not even a spare square of hay to be had here tonight. And with your maid and little Sophie for company you'll find the bed crowded enough. But I might need to take the sofa, and be up before the sun. Talgarth should be able to drag himself to the door by then and I can wash and shave in his room. Here, try these caramelized onions. They're delicious."

"I shouldn't have told you!"

"Why?" He tried to sound offhand. "If spending one night with your godfather is the worst of it and the reason you can't see your way clear to marrying me then—"

"No! *That* has little to do with my decision."

Alec suspended his fork midway between plate and mouth. "I see. Well, no, I don't see..." He set the fork on his plate. "Correct the grand supposition, but I presumed Cleveley, doing his duty as your godfather, counseled you against aligning yourself with a man who many believe hasn't the right to wear his brother's coronet, least of all be presented with a shiny new Marquessate, and who has the suspicion of murder upon his head—twice now, what with the good vicar dropping dead after eating his meal seated beside me."

Selina fortified herself with a sip of wine. "Yes, he did advise me, as my godfather. But you have it topsy-turvy. He is against your marriage to me. He says your character needs rehabilitating in Society and that takes time. But his most persuasive line of argument can't be faulted."

"His consideration is noted," Alec muttered dryly, and took up his fork again. "But I do believe the decision to marry the woman I love is mine alone, don't you, whatever your godfather's valid arguments?"

"Not tonight," she pleaded, reaching for his long fingers curled about the stem of his wine glass. "*Please.* I don't want to sink any lower tonight."

He stared into her pale face and nodded, and returned to eating what was on his plate, the food less appetizing than before.

Actually he was relieved to drop the discussion. Food had restored his vigor but he was mentally exhausted. She was right, too. Knowing Cleveley had abused his position as her godfather and not only seduced her when a young married woman of twenty and he a middle-aged man, but impregnated her, had given him a severe jolt of disgust. He had always been sensitive to the age difference between him and Selina; not such a great gulf in their ages now, but she had been only eighteen and he in his late-twenties when they'd fallen in love and he had asked her to marry him. But Cleveley didn't love Selina, and he, old enough to be her father and in a position of trust, had taken advantage of her, a young, unhappily married girl; that while making love to his darling Selina the Duke's carnal thoughts were for his even younger niece revolted Alec's every moral fiber.

"Did you manage to speak with Talgarth at any stage during your tedious journey?" he asked casually, breaking the silence with a question he hoped would lighten the mood.

Selina selected a piece of candied fruit and pushed the small bowl away.

"He wasn't very amenable to confidences. And when I pressed him for a name as to who might want to deface one of his portraits, he rattled off a number of previous clients whom he had offended in some way. But I doubt even the likes of Lady Rutherglen would stoop to attacking one of Talgarth's canvases to vent her dissatisfaction, do you?"

"Talgarth would only have to render a true likeness to raise her ladyship's ire."

Selina smiled.

"So you do know Lady Rutherglen. Vile woman. Poor Sybilla lives in terror of her sister-in-law's visits. Despite her nobility, descended from an unbroken line of Dukes of Romney-St. Neots that goes back to Edward the Third, Sybilla will never be good enough in Frances Rutherglen's eyes for her adored brother, the Admiral. Frances absolutely dotes on men. The dear Admiral and her nephew George Stanton can do no wrong. But she has a very Greek view of girl children. Worthless creatures to be put out for the wolves. Her daughter Mimi was doomed at birth for not being the son she so craved." She bit into the candied fruit on a wistful sigh. "Long suffering Mimi and her country cousin were confined to the schoolroom to rot. Poor Mimi left it in a casket."

"And the letters to Lord George?" Alec enquired, breaking her abstraction.

Selina was reaching for another sweetmeat, but at his simple question withdrew her hand and put out her glass to be refilled. "I have a confession. I meant to tell you when you came to Hanover Square but we became distracted and then you went away... I'm sure Talgarth won't care in the least if I tell Apollo—"

"Apollo?"

"You. Talgarth refers to you as Apollo. He has a very good eye for manly beauty..." She tilted her head and smiled at him quizzically. "I wonder if there's ever been a painting of Apollo with evening shadow...?"

Alec flushed in spite of himself and rubbed his stubbled cheek.

"This confession?"

"Talgarth cannot read or write."

"I beg your pardon?"

Selina smiled thinly at his astonishment.

"He never has been able to read and he can barely form the letters to write his name. God knows he tried, just to stop the beatings. The opium helped him cope with the years of abuse, or as my parents liked to think of it, their son's willful conduct."

"The poor fellow," Alec muttered, appalled. "But he paints such wonderfully emotive paintings. Didn't your parents see the value in such enormous talent?"

"My father was a General lord in the army. A man's man who knew how to instill discipline and expected absolute obedience. My mother was a pretty airhead who could barely read and write her own name. What of that? She's female. Talgarth's great talent was considered an abomination by my parents."

"Dear God, what demons must he carry around with him? No wonder he's found solace and oblivion in opium!"

"Just so," was Selina's tight response, gaze focused on the intricate folds of Alec's linen cravat. Talgarth's treatment at the hands of their parents never ceased to bring tears to her eyes. "So, you see, Sir Charles Weir was lying to you when he said my brother was blackmailing George Stanton. Those letters are a fabrication."

"That is one possibility… Or Lord George duped Charles into believing the letters were written by your brother… Or, the letters do exist and Lord George believes, for one reason or another, that they were written by Talgarth."

"How? That's absurd when Talgarth cannot read or write!"

Alec patted his mouth with a corner of his napkin and set it aside. "Absurd that Talgarth wrote them, yes, but not necessarily absurd to *think* they were written by Talgarth. I gather that neither Charles Weir or George Stanton knows your brother is illiterate?"

"Very few people know. So, no, Weir and Lord George would not know that about Talgarth." She wrinkled her nose in thought as she absently twirled a loose curl about one finger. "What you're suggesting is that if there are letters written in Talgarth's name, they were written in someone else's fist? Now that *is* absurd!"

"Is it? Did you receive letters from Talgarth when he was in Florence?"

"Of course. Almost weekly."

"Who wrote those letters?"

"Nico."

"Nico?"

"My brother's valet, major-domo, call him what you will."

Alec raised one mobile eyebrow.

Selina's jaw dropped. "No! Not Nico. He's devoted to Talgarth. Talgarth couldn't survive without Nico."

"Nico is in a position of trust. He must know your brother intimately. He also reads and then writes all your brother's correspondence and looks after his accounts."

"But why would Nico write threatening letters to Stanton purporting to be Talgarth?"

"I never said that. If Talgarth dictated the content and Nico was merely his scribe, then it's as if Talgarth did indeed write those letters to Stanton."

"I don't see Talgarth as a blackmailer. He wouldn't threaten anyone in that way."

"You said yourself he's threatened many of his clients, so what's to say he wouldn't threaten George Stanton?" asked Alec as he pushed out his chair to stretch his long legs so that his dusty jockey boots were to the warmth of the fire, and to better view Selina, who had left the table to pace in front of the same warmth. "Seeking revenge on behalf of the woman he loves is motive enough. Seeking revenge on behalf of his wife and her child is even more reason to blackmail her tormentor."

"You can't be suggesting that Talgarth and Miranda are *married*?" Selina's swaying petticoats came to a swishing halt. She smiled her incredulity. "Now who is being duped! Never. He would never... She would never... Not without speaking to me first."

"Perhaps they didn't have the luxury of time nor want to await your negative response?"

"I don't know why you're laughing! Besides, how do you know they were married?"

Alec told her what Blackwell had confided in Thaddeus Fanshawe about marrying Miranda to a Mr. Ninian Bourdon at Ellick Farm. Selina was unconvinced.

"The word of a flunky lawyer who can't provide proof of this ridiculous notion, because the vicar is dead? And he never mentioned Talgarth by name."

"You only have to ask your brother to find out if the lawyer speaks the truth."

"And you think Talgarth and this Mr. Bourdon are one and the same man?"

"Do you have another candidate for Miranda's husband?"

Selina did not. Miranda lived a solitary existence in the wilds of the Mendips, and aside from the local villagers and her infrequent trips into Bath, she saw no one and went nowhere. Or so Selina had always presumed.

"Tell me, darling, if you think Talgarth isn't the sort of fellow who, when the mood comes upon him, would just up and do something without thought to the consequences?" Alec took out his spectacles from a shallow waistcoat pocket, perched them on the end of his nose then extracted from the same pocket one diamond drop earring and a slim gold wedding band and these he placed on the table. "You don't think your brother has the emotional character that lends itself to chivalrous behavior? Not to mention his affliction, which must make such behavior erratic and spontaneous at the best of times...?"

Selina was shaking her fair head, but then she paused in thought. "Now and again... perhaps," she begrudgingly conceded. Curious, she picked up the gold band. Realizing what it was she quickly put it down again.

"It's not for you," Alec drawled over the rims of his spectacles and held out the ring to her with a lopsided smile. "I wouldn't dare to presume to offer you such a token of my esteem and fidelity until your mourning is over. And when I do offer it, yours will be set with diamonds. This was found in the dead boy's pocket; the earring was in the straw near where his body lay. No doubt stolen along with the letters. Yes, the ring is a wedding band and if you take a closer look you will see engraving."

"Three initials: T or is it a G or a J? It is difficult to make out. The other two letters are better etched. B and an M. All three intertwined, the initial B is the larger of the three."

"Any thoughts on who owns these initials?"

Selina shrugged and returned the gold band to Alec, who slipped it back into his waistcoat pocket. "The obvious answer is Miranda. But now that seems an all too simple response." She scooped up the drop earring and held it close to the branch of candles on the table. The configuration of heavy teardrop diamond surrounded by a gradation of a dozen smaller diamonds sparkled and winked in the candlelight. "How does a girl who lives in the depths of the Mendips come by extravagant earrings better suited to a London ballroom? And who gave them to her?" Her gaze drifted to the darkened bedchamber and the little lump in the bed; Alec's eyes followed hers. "The more I learn about Miranda Bourdon the less I know her. I have more questions than answers."

"And the only person who may have been able to supply those answers is dead."

Hearing the tiredness in his voice she turned back to him and with a cheeky smile deftly slipped the gold hook of the diamond earring through the piercing in her right ear lobe. She laughed at his surprise "Can you think of a safer place for an earring until it is reunited with its twin?" and led him by the hand to the sofa, where she snuggled into the warmth of him, suddenly very tired. "There is someone else who may be able supply the answers…"

Alec nodded, a hand lightly to her hair and gaze on the flickering flames in the grate of the small fireplace.

"Yes. Miranda."

TWELVE

BATH, SOMERSET

Miranda was searching through the wrapped parcels from a shopping excursion of the day before when her maid came silently into the sitting room carrying a tray laden with morning tea things, and set it down on the low table between a striped sofa and overstuffed wingchair.

"Janie, I cannot find the parcel from Bricknell and Moore's. The one containing colored thread. I promised Sophie I would have her apron finished by the time we returned home," said Miranda as she sat on the sofa to take the weight off her aching feet. "You needn't have brought the tray in yourself," she added, watching the girl pouring out tea into a porcelain dish. "There are the hotel servants to do such tasks, even for you."

Janie Rumble recalled the lewd sidelong glances exchanged between two nose-in-the-air maids who had curtseyed to them in the corridor on their return from their shopping expedition. It had decided Janie then and there to forbid the hotel servants access to their rooms.

"Yes, ma'am," Janie answered, handing over the dish of tea and a plate of thinly-sliced bread and butter. "But they wouldn't have made the tea just the way you like it."

Upon their arrival at Barr's of Trim Street, the most exclusive small lodgings establishment in Bath, the haughty proprietor had put up his brows as if openly questioning the correctness of two young females traveling without a male chaperone. Janie had felt her cheeks flame as she stood on the thick Turkey rug at her mistress's shoulder, uncomfortable amongst such luxurious surroundings. The rooms were altogether too grandly furnished, and the persons who came and went in the time they stood in the foyer were all dressed in what she assumed must be the height of fashion. But Miranda showed no signs of embarrassment or irritation at this affront and had calmly signed the register, paying for their suite of rooms in advance. This barely thawed the proprietor's long features as he scrutinized Miranda's signature with a deliberate slowness bordering on insolence.

But this morning, after three days of freezing looks and barely a civil word, to Janie's amazement the proprietor was transformed from ice block to grinning idiot when he had deliberately stopped Miranda in the foyer. The transformation was so great that Janie had blinked and blinked again to recognize him.

It was only when they were halfway up the staircase, following a footman ordered to relieve them of their parcels, that Janie realized the reason for the change in the proprietor. He had handed Miranda a sealed parchment with a little bow, saying his lordship was desirous of a reply at Mrs. Bourdon's earliest convenience.

Janie had never heard of Lord Halsey, and she would stake her Aunt Rumble's life upon it that neither had Mrs. Bourdon.

"Are you certain you wouldn't care for some soup or a slice of pie, ma'am?" Janie asked as she propped a cushion behind Miranda's back and drew up a padded stool to allow the young woman to rest her stockinged feet. "If you don't put up your feet, they'll swell."

"You must stop fussing over me," Miranda said kindly. "My condition doesn't make me an invalid."

Janie looked away, instantly uncomfortable and equally annoyed at herself for this feeling. It wasn't as if she didn't know how matters stood. After all, she was Miranda's personal maid. Besides, she was secretly happy about the baby. But how very differently would everyone view her mistress's pregnancy if there truly were a Mr. Ninian Bourdon.

"I'm pleased you came with me, Janie."

"Let you come to town at such a time without me to look after you?" Janie blustered, unnecessarily repositioning the tea things. "I'd not've slept a wink at the farm. I had to come."

"I wish… I wish I could confide in you. You've been such a support, sometimes my only support." Miranda looked up from the pale liquid in her dish. "Until certain particulars are finalized I'm not at liberty to confide in anyone. You understand, don't you?"

"Yes, ma'am," Janie answered, not understanding at all.

"Thank you, Janie.

Miranda drank the remainder of her tea in silence, while Janie fussed about the room, the attendant sounds of carriage wheels, and town visitors walking along the cobbled pavement under the arch below their windows filling the silence in the prettily furnished sitting room. Janie cleared away the tea things, glancing at her young mistress, and wondered for the thousandth time the true extent of this young woman's sad history.

Sharing a dilapidated and draughty limestone manor house with only her four-year-old daughter and the servants for company was no life for such a beautiful creature. The girl's patrician features, graceful manners and fluency in two languages were a testament to her careful upbringing, but Janie guessed why her family would not own her. Having a child out of wedlock had brought shame on her family, a family that had wealth and connections and thus would not tolerate a daughter's wanton mistake. And now another bastard child was due any day. At first Janie had refused to believe the servant gossip about the mistress, until the inevitable changes in the girl's body confirmed the malicious whisperings. Miranda had managed to keep her swelling belly well corseted for the first six months of the pregnancy but now no amount of lacings could conceal the result of her wickedness.

Gossip said her lover and the father of this child was the gentleman painter, brother of the fashionable and very rich London lady, Mrs. Selina Jamison-Lewis, who made yearly visits to the farm. Returned from the Continent only a twelvemonth, the painter lived in Bath but regularly visited the farm to make drawings and paintings of Mrs. Bourdon and her daughter, the servants and the wild scenery of the Mendip hills. It saddened Janie to think the painter had not taken the honorable course and married the girl before tumbling into bed with her.

Distant shouts brought Janie out of her thoughts and she looked up from the tray to find Miranda peering out the window. "I'll take the tray back to the kitchen," she said brightly, "and then I'll make a start on knitting that shawl I promised you."

Miranda turned away from the view of the street with an uncustomary frown. "Shawl?"

"Yes, ma'am. While you were purchasing thread yesterday I bought woolen yarn for Aunt Rumble's knitting needles."

"Woolen yarn?" Miranda repeated distractedly.

"I'm knitting a shawl for the babe, ma'am. But perhaps you wish to use Miss Sophie's birth shawl?" Janie asked hesitantly.

"Sophie's shawl? No. No," Miranda responded quickly and forced herself to smile. "A shawl would be lovely, Janie. Thank you," and turned away from the girl's questioning look to draw on her soft kid gloves. It made her chest ache to think about Sophie's shawl. It had disappeared the day of her birth. "There is an eleven o'clock service at the Abbey," she managed to say lightly, despite a feeling of panic that threatened to overwhelm her. "While I'm away, you can see to the rest of the parcels."

Janie was surprised. "Shouldn't you rest awhile, ma'am?"

"I'm very well, Janie."

"You don't wish me to accompany you, ma'am?"

"I'll take a chair."

Miranda scooped up her straw bonnet and was out the door before Janie could protest further. Halfway down the main staircase the pressure on her chest lifted enough for her to breathe without effort. Why, after all these years, did the mention of a baby shawl still affect her so deeply? She had painstakingly knitted a shawl in the lonely months of the first confinement. After a long painful labor, in which she had passed out several times, the apothecary had presented Sophie to her, not wrapped in the shawl she had knitted but bundled up in a torn sheet. No one could tell her, not the vicar, the apothecary or his boy-assistant, what had happened to the baby shawl she had knitted.

In those first few weeks after Sophie's birth, when she and the baby were spirited out of the city, it became an obsession to know the whereabouts of that shawl. It almost unbalanced her mind, convinced that the loss of the shawl was the reason her dearest cousin Miriam had died, and that if she had taken better care of the shawl, her dearest dear might have lived. Only after the repeated reassurances of the vicar did she allow herself to realize that there was nothing she could have done to prevent her cousin's death, and that her obsession with the shawl was the result of the traumatic events of the birth and the consequent sleepless nights looking after a newborn. It had taken a long time for her mind to finally settle. But what had happened to the shawl? Four years on, she did not want to think about the lost shawl, or about Sophie's birth and the loss of her dearest most beloved cousin. In losing Miriam she had lost part of herself.

She placed a protective hand on her swollen belly. Soon this baby would be born, and *he* had promised her that the birth of this child would be so very different from Sophie's entrance into the world.

Then why had *he* thought it necessary for her to come to Bath to have the baby? They had agreed the baby would be born at Ellick Farm. He had promised to be there as soon as he could quit London. But she had not had a letter in over a month. Then a week ago a letter had arrived so unlike his previous letters that it made her sick with worry. It contained none of his usual assurances about the future and looked to have been written in haste. He told her to leave Sophie at the farm and come to Bath, to Barr's, where he kept rooms. He would alert the proprietor, a very discreet fellow, of her impending arrival. Under no circumstances was she to tell anyone of her whereabouts and she was to come alone.

She had disobeyed him, but for good reason. She could not give birth without Janie being present. She trusted Janie. Janie was her insurance that her baby would be safe. Janie would look after the baby if she fell into a fever or, worse, died. Janie wouldn't let anyone take the baby from her. She had made Janie swear on the Holy Bible that if anything happened to her, if she died, she was to give the baby to no one but Mrs. Jamison Lewis, with the letter she had sewn into her stays.

Men could be so unthinking.

What if *he* was delayed? How long was she supposed to wait? What if business kept him in London? Was Lord Halsey his friend? His lordship's note was certainly welcoming, and written in such a way that she had to assume that he knew all about her. Was it a mere coincidence that Lord Halsey happened to be staying at Barr's at the same time as she, or had he been asked to keep a watchful eye on her? But *he* had never mentioned his lordship. What if *he* failed to be with her for the birth? Now that was an even sillier notion. Of course *he* would be there. *He* had given his word. She must remember that. She couldn't afford to have doubts. Doubts would weaken her resolve. The birth of this baby was going to be so very different from Sophie's birth—this time she wouldn't be abandoned, alone and so very, very frightened. If only she knew who to trust…

So deep in thought was she, and eager to get out of doors to breathe fresh air, that on the staircase she collided with an elderly gentleman and his youthful companion who were making their way slowly down the carpeted stairs. In the confusion that followed, Miranda knocked the Malacca cane out from under the old man's gloved hand, sending it and her straw bonnet tumbling to the bottom of the stairs. She lost her footing on the carpet covering the steps, but the old gentleman, who had instinctively hard-gripped the banister rail to stop himself pitching forward, caught her to him and steadied them both, assuring her in a kind voice that he was entirely to blame. His companion, a young man with carrot-colored hair, darted down the stairs and retrieved the cane and bonnet from the middle of the passage, where a couple of newly-arrived travelers stood gawping up at the activity on the staircase.

Miranda was shaking so much she continued to grip the old gentleman's coat sleeve as she descended the rest of the stairs and walked slowly across the foyer and out the front door. They were under the brick arch that led to Queen Street before the old gentleman put out a gloved hand for his cane.

"THANK YOU, TAM," PLANTAGENET HALSEY SAID AND TURNED A friendly eye on Miranda. "Your bonnet, Madam." He wasn't surprised when his voice brought the girl to her senses. She had been staring at Tam while still hard-gripping his arm, but quickly disentangled herself and hurriedly tied on the bonnet with a lop-sided bow that brought a smile to his eyes. "Ha! *Madam*: It's a fusty word for such a lovely young butterfly. Now I've made you blush and it wasn't my intention to make you uncomfortable. Is this your first outing to this watering hole?" When the girl glanced up at him and then around at her surroundings, as if to see if their conversation were being overheard, he added, "You must forgive the ravings of an old gent. We've just arrived ourselves. The carriage ride from London must've addled me brain. Ain't that so, my boy?"

Tam grinned but Miranda was so taken aback by the old gentleman's forwardness that she stammered an incoherent reply in French, adding in English that she was late for the Abbey service. She would have walked off, but the old man detained her.

"Just the place we're headin'," he said good-humouredly and bowed, making a mental note of her French tongue and cultivated voice. "The name's Plantagenet Halsey. This here is Thomas Fisher, apothecary. You may have met my nephew, Lord Halsey…?"

"Lord Halsey is your nephew?" Miranda replied and added when the old man nodded and smiled, "I have yet to make his lordship's acquaintance but he wrote me a very civil letter of introduction." She glanced at Tam again, at his freckled face framed by a mop of carrot-colored hair; he looked far too young to be an apothecary. Inexplicably, the knot in her chest returned. There was something about the young man that made her uneasy. She swallowed for breath. "Are—are you all staying at Barr's?" she heard herself say.

"Just so, ma'am. Call it a family holiday of sorts," Plantagenet Halsey said with a laugh, though his keen eyes saw her distress. He offered her the crook of his arm. "May this old gentleman have the pleasure of your company to the Abbey? I've no wish to be roped into a circle of old dowagers or pounced on by wounded relics of the

Seven Years War. When last I frequented this waterin' hole I never met a more lemon-faced bunch of old fusties in m'life!" Her hesitation made him remark, "My dear, there ain't any harm in m'company. I don't bite. I might very well be your grandfather."

At this Miranda did smile and she obliged him by taking his arm. "Forgive me, Mr. Halsey. I would be honored to have your company." She glanced up at his lined face. "And thank you for saving me from a fall on the stairs. I hate to think what might have happened…"

"You're safe. There's no need to think on it, ma'am," Plantagenet Halsey said quickly, indication enough he was aware of her advanced state of pregnancy.

She lowered her long black lashes, grateful for his understanding, and they walked along Queen Street in the mute light of an overcast day, Tam following at a discreet distance. They had crossed Upper Borough Walls when Miranda abruptly stopped in the middle of the cobbled pavement.

"Oh! How rude of me not to have introduced myself." She turned and offered Plantagenet Halsey her gloved hand. "It's Bourdon; Mrs. Bourdon."

Plantagenet Halsey's keen gray eyes blinked but his voice remained level. He knew exactly who she was, knew what rooms she was occupying, and that a young woman servant had accompanied her. The hotel proprietor had obliged his nephew, and they had been on the alert for when just such an opportunity as this would arise. A pity Alec had felt obliged to run back to Marlborough to play knight-errant to his virago ladylove and her sickly brother. Still, the old man was pleased to have the upper hand at something.

"Will you indulge an old man by permitting me to know your Christian name, Mrs. Bourdon?"

"How can I refuse you, sir, after your kindness to me on the stair? It's Miranda."

"Ah! And here was I thinkin' you might be a Catherine. But don't get me wrong. Miranda suits you very well. Very well indeed."

"Catherine? How strange of you to say so, Mr. Halsey," she answered with surprise as they crossed Cheap Street. "My daughter's name is Catherine."

"Is that so?" replied the old man with enthusiasm. "In my day little Catherines were blessed with a string of pretty names. Is that still the fashion, Mrs. Bourdon?"

Tam gaped openly at Plantagenet Halsey's straight back. When had the old man ever been interested in conducting small talk with young mothers about their offspring? He wondered if the hit to his head had done more than leave a dent in his skull.

"I don't know anything about the fashion, Mr. Halsey," Miranda was saying, now completely at ease with her elderly companion. "But she does indeed have a string of pretty names: Catherine Sophia Elisabeth; after my husband's mother. It's rather a mouthful for a four-year-old, isn't it? We've always called her Sophie."

"Sophie? How delightful!" Plantagenet Halsey said with a satisfied smile and a jaunty spring in his step that closed Tam's mouth and narrowed his eyes, wondering at the real meaning behind such seemingly inane questions. There had to be more to this pleasant walk to the Abbey than what met the eye and Tam was going to find out what it was. He was not in the least surprised when the old man abruptly turned the conversation into a lesson on the town's historic past, in particular the Roman occupation of Bath, keeping his young companion enthralled until they reached the imposing West front of the Abbey.

TAM POLITELY DECLINED TO JOIN THE SERVICE WITH Plantagenet Halsey, Miranda Bourdon and the rest of Bath's elite who were filing into the Abbey. He excused himself saying he had errands to run. His decision had little to do with his duties or his religious beliefs and everything to do with knowing his proper place. The old man might disregard, even openly ridicule, the social order, but as son of an earl and uncle to a marquess, he could say and do as he pleased, his radical opinions excused away by his own kind as mere eccentricity. Tam could not afford to step outside the boundaries of what was expected of him as valet to a peer of the realm, and sit shoulder-to-shoulder with the old man and his social equals.

So he went for a stroll along North Parade to the river Avon and sat on the grassy embankment to admire the view. He still had no idea if he had passed his apothecary's examination. He was confident he had provided more than adequate responses to satisfy the detailed questions put to him by the somber-faced examiners in the Great Hall. He had correctly identified, classified and offered uses for any number of plants put in front of him. He had spoken with knowledge on simples, and provided answers, almost word-for-word, from passages in the Pharmacopeia. Not even the last question of the morning had shaken his self-confidence. He knew the answer well enough, could recite the response in his sleep, and he rattled on without thinking very hard about it at all. The preparation and application of tinctures containing Monkshood; more specifically, what would be the most likely outcome should such a preparation be ingested, particularly in its powdered form, was more than satisfactorily answered.

It was only later, waiting in the quiet of the paneled anteroom with several other nervous apprentices, that panic set in and fear chilled his bones. *Monkshood: Its preparation and ingestion.* He'd been so puffed up with his own cleverness that he was blind to the significance of such a question. And it had been put to him by the Chief Examiner, a haughty, gaunt little man who had been apothecary to the previous King George, and knighted for his services.

Surely the question was mere coincidence? Sir Septimus Bott could know nothing of Tam's suspicions regarding the cause of death of the Reverend Blackwell: Asphyxiation and stoppage of the heart brought about by the inhalation of a powdered form of Monkshood blended with his snuff. But the coincidence was enough for Tam to seriously wonder if the question was deliberately put.

As he drifted off to sleep, stretched out on the grassy bank, listening to the flow of the river and the mews of waterfowl amongst the reeds, he wondered if he was being overly sensitive to Bott's pertinent question. But Sir Septimus knew he was valet to Lord Halsey, and like every other educated Londoner, he read the newssheets, and thus knew that his lordship had been present at a dinner party where a vicar had up and died of a heart attack. But surely Sir Septimus could not know his lordship's suspicions regarding the Reverend Blackwell's death? Yet, that was exactly what Tam now believed.

He had been the last of the apprentices to be dismissed and the only one to be informed that as he had a dispensary at his place of employment, which was not presided over by a master apothecary, it would be inspected and appraised before a final decision was made on Tam's suitability for admission as a fellow of the Society. No time or date was given and he was sent on his way.

Tam didn't know how to tell his lordship that not only had he no idea if he had passed or failed the examination, but that Lord Halsey's London residence, No. 1 St. James's Place, was to be visited without invitation by three wardens of the Worshipful Society of Apothecaries.

Dogs barking as they chased waterfowl out of the reeds had Tam scrambling to his feet and brushing grass from the back of his breeches and frock coat before he was fully awake. The sun's position high in the sky told him he had fallen asleep and he ran all the way to the Abbey, only stopping when he reached the churchyard. Bent over from being out of breath, he looked up from his knees and saw that the service was well and truly over, the last of the congregation coming out into the sunshine. Most of the worshippers lingered, making plans for the afternoon, while the more infirm were carried back to their lodgings by sedan chair, their servants and retainers walking behind the burly chairmen.

One private sedan chair remained by the Abbey entrance, its door held wide by a liveried servant and the two long poles on which it was carried allowed to rest easy by its carriers as they awaited its aged occupant. Several of the churchgoers drifted back to this chair as word went round that one of their number had taken ill inside the Abbey. For one dreadful moment Tam thought it was the old man, but as he did not have a chair the thought was quickly dismissed. Then, as he continued to skirt the small gathering looking for Plantagenet Halsey and his companion and not seeing them, he wondered if the young lady had gone into early labor.

He felt anxious for Miranda Bourdon. But it was not only her advanced stage of pregnancy that caused him to be apprehensive. The moment he caught a flash of her face on the hotel's stairwell he had experienced a frisson of recognition, and with it a sense of foreboding. But later, watching her talk with the old man, he convinced himself that there was no circumstance he could think of when he would have come into contact with such a well-bred young lady. Her beauty alone was cause for remembrance. Yet, the feeling he had met her before had stayed with him and again, as he shouldered his way to the open front doors, he racked his mind to think of an occasion or a place where he might have met the young woman.

He would have stepped inside the Abbey but for the tight knot of persons coming out into the muted sunshine. At its center was a grand dowager, kept upright by two men who supported her bulk by holding her limp arms at the elbow. She was incapable of walking unaided and her rich silk petticoats dragged under her feet. Her head, with its elaborate coiffure of powdered curls brushed over padding and bright turban with ostrich plumes, lolled to one side and her eyelids fluttered.

In Tam's opinion, the woman was clearly in no fit state to be moved, but one of the two richly-clad gentlemen following up behind was loudly urging the men carrying her to get her into the chair as quickly as possible. To add to this din, the dowager's maid was sobbing and trying to put salts under her mistress's nose, while another woman patted a limp hand and mouthed soothing platitudes.

Leading the charge was a po-faced churchwarden officiously parting the ways with his outstretched arms, clutching his Bible in one hand, and this he flung left and right as if it were a sword fending off the hordes.

Tam flattened himself against the brickwork to allow the commotion to pass out into the courtyard and slipped inside the cavernous Abbey. He found Plantagenet Halsey standing to one side of a group of chairs, leaning on the head of his Malacca cane, talking with another of the churchwardens. Miranda Bourdon was seated on a chair close by.

"I regret this incident occurred here before you both," apologized the churchwarden, as Tam approached and waited a little way off. "As you will appreciate, particularly at this time of year, Bath has many elderly inhabitants who are not in the best of health. Those with exceptionally delicate constitutions require the utmost care and attention. Her ladyship could just as easily have taken a turn at the Assembly Rooms as here in the Abbey. And it was far better that she did so here than, say, whilst bathing in the King's Bath. I have every confidence that, God willing, she will be herself again in no time at all."

He looked expectantly from the old man to the young lady, as if requiring their confirmation, and was surprised when Miranda continued to stare straight ahead at the great East window. Her delicate profile was deathly pale while a rapid pulse beat in her long slender throat. It was only when she dabbed at her eyes with the corner of a lace handkerchief that he realized she had been crying. She was so lovely to look at that he allowed his gaze to linger longer than was polite. His little eyes wandered from her tear-stained cheeks to her slim arms, over the fullness of her breasts and down to where her hands were clasped under a very round belly. His eyes widened and flashed up at the old man, whose slow lift of bushy eyebrows not only confirmed the warden's immediate thought but made him fire up red with embarrassment in cheeks and bulbous nose.

"If anyone will make a recover it'll be Frances Rutherglen," Plantagenet Halsey stated, aware of his young companion's distress, and more to cover the warden's acute embarrassment than to provide an opening for further discussion. "The woman has the constitution of an ox and as much feelin' as a dead cod. Besides, she ain't as old as she looks. White lead paints and too much snuff have aged her before her time."

"You know Lady Rutherglen, sir?" the warden asked, feeling he should say something, although he had a great desire to crawl under the nearest vacant chair. "She is one of the more, dare I say it, *acerbic* members of our congregation. But a most generous benefactress."

"I don't doubt it. The only way she'll see the gates of Heaven is to buy 'em!"

The warden forced a laugh. "Now, now, sir! I hardly think this the place to jest about her ladyship's—"

"Who's jestin'?" said Plantagenet Halsey to cut him off. He made an upward gesture with his thumb. "He knows only too well what I mean. It's time we got some fresh air, don't you agree, Mrs. Bourdon?"

"Perhaps Mrs.—?—Mrs. Bourdon would care to sit a little while longer?" the warden suggested gently. "Lady Rutherglen's collapse has unsettled her nerves. Most understandable, given the—um—circumstances. Perhaps her ladyship had an unexpected fright? Perhaps a mouse ran out from—"

"Don't be an ass, man! The woman had a fright all right. But it'd take more than a mouse to frighten Frances Rutherglen."

Miranda turned wide, glistening blue eyes up at the old man. "Why do you say so, Mr. Halsey?"

"She looked straight at me, that's why, ma'am."

Miranda blinked and glanced down at the wet, twisted handkerchief on her lap. "At you? Oh… Yes, yes at you… But why, sir?"

"My outspoken—fools would call 'em radical—opinions on particular topics offend the Quality, especially the stiff-necked matriarchs of Frances Rutherglen's ilk. If she had her way I'd be clapped up in the Tower." The old man grinned sheepishly. "I'm sure they think I ain't fit to enter God's Temple."

"Surely not, sir—" began the warden but was interrupted.

"You have a good heart and a clear conscience, Mr. Halsey," Miranda stated. "Lady Rutherglen has neither…" She made a sudden move to stand, and the old man and the churchwarden were quick to assist her. "Thank you. I—I am not quite myself."

"What you need is fresh air," Plantagenet Halsey stated. With a nod to the warden and a signal to Tam to follow, he led Miranda across the wide-open expanse of the Abbey, a hand holding her arm above the elbow, the other resting on his Malacca cane. "And a good dish of black tea back at Barr's will revive us both."

"Yes, I should like that," she answered in a distracted voice, and permitted the old man to lead her out of doors into the openness of the busy church courtyard.

Lady Rutherglen's chair had been taken up and was making a slow progress toward the sycamore trees of the Orange Grove, her retainers keeping step with the chairmen. One gentleman with a lace-covered white hand lightly on the chair door was talking earnestly to its suffering occupant. Plantagenet Halsey's eyes narrowed, taking in this scene but he quickly recovered, remembering his companion, and turned to suggest they continue on their way and found her staring fixedly at the departing chair. A glance at Tam, who shrugged his shoulders in acknowledgement that he, too, was aware of Mrs. Bourdon's preoccupation, and the old man's curiosity about the young lady deepened.

He wondered if Miranda Bourdon had any idea that Blackwell was dead. He wondered what had brought her to Bath when such a journey must be twice as hazardous in her advanced stage of pregnancy. He wondered about Mr. Ninian Bourdon and if that gentleman was the reason she had left Ellick Farm to come to Bath. Not least that she may be in Bath for her lying-in. And then there was her distress just now in the Abbey…

But he was unlikely to find the answers standing in the churchyard and so he was about to suggest they head on their way when a smooth, insolent voice grated on his ear. He knew at once to whom it belonged, and it was no surprise that the man had doubled back to confront him; in fact, he was glad he had.

"Dear me, Halsey! I can't decide what boggles the mind more: Seeing you emerge from a church, or the fact you have on your arm the most beautiful creature I have ever laid eyes on." His brows rose slightly at Miranda's obvious pregnancy but his gaze remained riveted to her face. "May I say how well you're looking, ma'am?"

Before Plantagenet Halsey could unleash a torrent of abuse at the man's forwardness, Miranda put out a gloved hand. "How do you do, Mr.—Weir?"

Sir Charles Weir bowed over her hand, a smug smile at the old man. "How good of you to remember, ma'am. It's Sir Charles now." His gaze again dropped to her belly. "And to see you looking as bonny as the last time we met is a joy to behold…"

"Thank—Thank you, Sir Charles," Miranda replied politely and withdrew her hand, not knowing what else to say.

"May one enquire where you are lodging?" asked Sir Charles.

"At-at Barr's—"

"—in Trim Street? A most respectable establishment and one that offers quite a good dinner…?"

"You are welcome to call upon us there if you so wish, Sir Charles," Miranda answered, well-aware the invitation was being forced from her, yet not feeling up to inventing an excuse to rebuff him. She hoped the old gentleman was keen enough to take the hint at her joint invitation.

Sir Charles inclined his powdered head. "And under what name should I enquire for you, ma'am?"

The old man felt her tremble and lean in against him.

"Name?" Miranda repeated, even more flustered. "Yes, of course. It's Bourdon. Mrs. Bourdon."

"You're not to outstay your welcome, Weir," Plantagenet Halsey lectured, adding as if it was the most natural thing in the world, "My niece needs her rest."

The politician's eyebrows shot up at this piece of interesting information but he made no comment and bowed to Miranda with a crooked smile. "I shall call upon you this evening, Mrs. Bourdon." And wandered off to rejoin the others surrounding Lady Rutherglen's chair as it continued its slow progress to her lodgings.

"Thank you, Mr. Halsey. I am most grateful to you," said Miranda, eyes on Sir Charles Weir's back. She looked up at the old man, a slight flush to her porcelain cheeks. "Forgive me for ill-using you in that way, sir, and if you have no wish to join me for—"

"I'd be honored, ma'am," he answered, patting her hand in a fatherly way. "And my apologies for being so forward as to own you as my niece, but it was the quickest way of being rid of him. You should know that Weir and I are bitter political rivals."

"Oh? I am quite ignorant of the world beyond my little corner of the Mendips; a circumstance Mr. Bourdon assures me he counts as one of my most endearing qualities," Miranda confessed with a shy laugh. "No doubt Sir Charles is somebody very important in the government by now. It was remiss of me not to have congratulated him on his knighthood."

Plantagenet Halsey stopped abruptly on the corner of Trim and

Queen Streets and faced her. "Weir was knighted some five years ago, ma'am."

"Is that so? Yes! It must be so because I have not seen him since before his elevation. How odd he was in the Abbey with Lady Rutherglen..." she mused, then suddenly came to life with a smile and put out her gloved hand to the old man. "If you will excuse me, Mr. Halsey, I have an errand that cannot wait. And I have walked quite enough for one day. I look forward to continuing our acquaintance at dinner."

The old man watched her walk a little way down Queen Street before hailing a sedan chair, which took her up and disappeared from view into Quiet Street. To Tam, who stood at his shoulder, he said softly, "My boy, see where's she's headed. And mind you keep your distance." He then went off to Barr's with a spring in his step, hoping Alec had returned from playing the knight errant, for he could hardly wait to tell him he had spent the morning in the Abbey in company with the elusive Miranda Bourdon.

THIRTEEN

"*HARLOT*!" LADY RUTHERGLEN SPAT OUT, SHOVING ASIDE HER hovering maid who was attempting to put a burnt feather under her nose. "Out, woman! Out!" she screeched. "I've not fainted, you dim-wit!" She struggled to sit up amongst the silk cushions and threw off the tasseled rug covering her voluminous petticoats, ignoring the glass of claret Sir Charles was patiently waiting to hand her. "How *dare* she show herself amongst respectable persons, and in the Abbey of all places! And flaunting the fruits of her wantonness in God's temple. Whore! Harlot! *Witch*!"

"Your wine, my lady," Sir Charles reminded her.

"To think she took the sacrament…!" Lady Rutherglen breathed, lace handkerchief pressed to her cracked pale lips. "Brass-faced. Wanton. *Wicked*!"

"Halsey had the stupidity to own her as his niece."

Lady Rutherglen's jaw swung open and outrage turned to mirth. She let out a loud watery cackle of disbelief, falling back against the silk striped sofa, wheezing. "Did you hear—hear that, George? George! *His* niece? That old fool's *niece*?" She cleared her throat of phlegm and stuck out a hand for the glass of claret that Sir Charles was only too pleased to relinquish. "Well! Two people couldn't be better suited than an old cunny-hunter and a mistress cunny-warren!"

A series of loud laughing snorts issued forth from behind the outspread pages of the *Bath Chronicle* before the newssheet was ruthlessly crushed in Lord George Stanton's crossed-legged lap. "Mistress cunny-warren? Now that's a great joke, Aunt! Cunny-warren! Ha! Ha!"

Sir Charles took a turn about the drawing room; to distance himself from Lady Rutherglen's repellent person; a decaying corpse had more life to it than her husk of wrinkled flabby flesh and brittle bone, and Lord George, who smelled of horseflesh and sweat. He had ill-manneredly gone riding to escape accompanying his aunt to the Abbey, as he had done the day before, in preference to attending a recital in the Assembly rooms, leaving the old serpent in Sir Charles's care. He wouldn't be at all surprised to learn that Stanton was still wearing the riding raiment of the day before, such was the pungent odor pervading his bloated person.

"A pity she isn't Halsey's niece, then we wouldn't be in this predicament, would we, my lady?" Sir Charles commented wryly, looking out the window at the meandering river Avon beyond the Green.

Lady Rutherglen grimaced. "Think she's told him?"

Sir Charles shrugged and took snuff. "No. Or he wouldn't have made such an outrageous claim as to own her as his kinswoman."

"Did you discover her direction?"

"She is staying at Barr's in Trim Street.

"Barr's?" Stanton pulled a face. "How can she afford it?"

"More to the point," mused Sir Charles, "why would such an exclusive lodging house permit one such as she to stay under its roof. I wonder if she's brought her bastard in tow?"

"Egad! I hope not!" Lord George shuddered. "Not sorry I missed the service. Coming face-to-face with her in the Abbey would've been unbearable." He appealed to his aunt in a pleading whine, "She won't try and foist the brat on me, will she, dearest Aunt?"

Lady Rutherglen's watery yellowed eyes narrowed. "With another bastard on the way? She wouldn't *dare*."

"Eh? *Another*?" Lord George asked, as if this information had just penetrated his brain. He stared at Sir Charles. "She's carrying another bastard?"

"I agree with you, my lady," Sir Charles answered, ignoring Stanton's whine. "Her present—er—condition must surely preclude any further attempts to blackmail Lord George; for how can she cast blame in his direction when this second pregnancy must forever damn her as deplorably base? I wonder if the painter will own to being its father?"

"Well this one ain't mine!" Lord George declared with a snort, and retreated behind the crinkled newssheet.

"I invited myself to dine with her this evening," Sir Charles informed them with a self-satisfied smile.

The crumpled newssheet was ruthlessly crushed once more in Lord George's lap.

"*Dine* with her?" Lord George scrambled to sit up straight, his bottom lip stuck out in a sulk of incomprehension. "Dine with a harlot? To what purpose? After what she's put *me* through? Are you mad, Charlie?"

Lady Rutherglen extended a thin hand to her nephew and was pleased when he took it. She tugged at him until he got out of his chair and knelt beside hers. "You're a good boy, Georgie," she whispered, pinching his fleshy cleft chin a little too hard. "If you continue to be a good boy your Aunt Frances will see to it you are the next Duke of Cleveley. But you must leave Charles to do the thinking. Do you understand me, dear boy?"

"Yes, Aunt," he answered docilely, staring into her yellowed eyes with an equal measure of revulsion and fear. He pulled a face at Sir Charles. "You're welcome to the whore, Charlie!" for which he received a severe tug on his thick earlobe. "Ow! What-what did you do that for, Auntie?"

"Insolent boy," Lady Rutherglen hissed at him, cursing the memory of her dead sister who had been a sentimental fool yet managed to produce a son who would one day succeed to a dukedom, when she, Frances, the younger and far more intelligent sister, had produced one sickly insignificant and recalcitrant daughter, who had been nothing but a disappointment and then had the bad manners to die before she could marry her off. She let go of her nephew's reddened ear, saying in a deceptively sweet voice, "Treat Charles well. He has our best interests at heart. Now help me up."

Begrudgingly, Lord George did as he was told. Unable to help himself he glared over his aunt's powdered wig at Sir Charles. "Are you sure he has *my* best interests at heart and not his own?"

Lady Rutherglen regarded Sir Charles from under half-closed lids devoid of eyelashes. "By serving us, he serves himself, George. Is that not so, Charles?"

Sir Charles bowed politely, his face masking his feelings, and ignored Lord George's snort of contempt, as did Lady Rutherglen who said to Sir Charles,

"Maria Russell and her daughter are due in Bath today. I don't want that whore within five miles of town."

"As you wish, my lady," Sir Charles replied obediently, a glance at Stanton. "It would be too bad if Lady Henrietta were to—"

Lord George took an angry stride toward Sir Charles. "Don't say Hatty's name in my presence! Ever," he bellowed. "I know your game, *secretary*."

"—come face-to-face with Mrs. Bourdon," Sir Charles enunciated, ignoring Lord George's tantrum. His brows contracted over his snub nose. "What do you mean *game*, my lord?"

Lord George gripped his aunt's thin arm convulsively. "Auntie told me about your designs on Hatty Russell. As if her father would ever allow you to touch one hair on Hatty's head, least of all *marry* her! Ha!"

"And does his lordship have any notion of what you've touched, my lord?"

"Enough! Enough!" growled Lady Rutherglen, fending off both gentlemen with outstretched arms when they bristled at each other. "I won't have Cheltenham tragedies here!" She gave Lord George's puffed-out chest a contemptuous little push. "Sit down and read your newssheet, Georgie, and let Sir Charles and me do the thinking."

"Any notion why Mrs. Bourdon, as she calls herself, has suddenly decided to pester us from beyond the grave after all these years, my lady?

"I've no idea why the trollop has shown herself in good society at this time, but she is mistaken if she thinks she can outwit me," Lady Rutherglen ruminated, grinding her few remaining teeth, gaze fixed beyond the window on a memory. "She thought herself so very clever, seducing Georgie under my roof, and even cleverer when she got herself with child by him. Pshaw! As if a bastard amounts to anything! Polluted creature! Like begets like. I blame Ellen."

"Blame Mamma?" Lord George blinked, expression suitably vacant as he looked over the spread newssheet at his aunt, then at Sir Charles and back again. "Auntie? Charlie? What's Mamma got to do with this damnable pickle we're in?"

Lady Rutherglen regarded her nephew, not at all surprised. She opened her dry mouth to answer him, then thought better of it and fixed her gaze on Sir Charles.

"I won't allow that ungrateful hedge-whore to jeopardize our future, Charles. Find out if she knows about the vicar's demise. If she's ignorant, tell her. It may yet persuade her to skulk back to the bushes from whence she came. And Charles: By dusk."

Sir Charles bowed. "Have I your permission to use whatever methods of persuasion I deem necessary, my lady?"

Lady Rutherglen waved a dismissive hand. "After the hell she's put George—us all—through? Send her with my good wishes in a box to Hades for all I care!"

❦

Tam followed the sedan chair carrying Miranda all the way to Milsom Street. Here the chair set her down and she began to walk up the street, the chairmen following behind, as if she merely wanted to stretch her legs before climbing back within the confined space of the chair to continue on her way. Tam kept a discreet distance yet was close enough to run to her assistance should she, a young lady without a chaperone, be accosted by an unwelcome stranger. Enough heads turned in her direction, shoppers, ostlers, laborers upon scaffolding, that there had to be more to it than the fact she was heavily pregnant and unattended. It was no surprise her exceptional beauty was attracting attention in the street. Yet she seemed unselfconscious of the effect she had on those around her. Or if she noticed heads turn she ignored them. Tam would have supposed pregnancy an anathema to such waiflike beauty, yet it suited her very well.

She halted abruptly on the opposite side of the street from a narrow townhouse squeezed between the Octagon Chapel and a wide-fronted building whose façade was covered in scaffolding. Outside the townhouse was a horse and cart piled with crates, large flat parcels wrapped up in cloth, and pieces of furniture all a jumble, and held in place by strong rope. Several chairs and an easel remained on the stone pavement waiting to be thrown up to the two strong-armed lads loading the cart; a third man stood by the wide open door. A short, swarthy, dark-haired young man wearing a gaily-colored waistcoat came out of the premises on the heels of a man of business, gesticulating wildly from the townhouse to the laden cart and back again to the man of business, who kept his head down as he called out loudly from a list of chattels to the two lads atop the cart to be heard over the traffic of carriage wheels.

Tam waited patiently for Miranda to continue on up the street or cross the busy road, as if the activity of an eviction (for that's what it looked like to Tam) was a mere distraction to her real purpose. But she remained watching the comings and goings of the bailiff and his henchmen for a full five minutes before her hired sedan chair took her up again, the burly chairmen making an about-face to retrace their steps down Milsom Street to disappear around a corner. Tam watched the sedan's slow progress, then chanced to glance across the street at the narrow-fronted townhouse that had held Miranda's attention to the exclusion of all else going on about her. And there, standing on the pavement, talking to the bailiff and the gesticulating little man in the gaily-colored waistcoat, was Lord Halsey.

By the time there was a break in the traffic of carriages, carts and horsemen, and Tam crossed Milsom Street, Alec had disappeared inside the narrow-fronted townhouse, and the bailiff was directing his men to unload the cart of its confiscated contents and return them within doors. Tam skipped in front of two men juggling a heavy mahogany lowboy and entered the building, taking the stairs to the first landing, where two more men were carefully angling what looked like a table top wrapped in canvas through the open doorway. Giving them directions was the little man in the gaily-colored waistcoat, who waved his hands about and hopped on the balls of his feet. He rattled on in a tongue Tam suspected from his Latin training to be Italian, and thus was no help to the burdened men. Yet it was obvious from his expressions and the pitch of his voice that their cargo was precious.

Once the men had successfully negotiated the doorway, Tam followed the Italian into the room and found his master strolling about a painter's studio. The room ran the entire length of the building, and was half its width. At the furthest end was an ornate screen partitioning a narrow bed from a small kitchen dominated by a large recessed hearth. Above the bed a circular iron staircase led up to a loft with a fireplace, large mahogany four-poster and several pieces of furniture. The rest of the cavernous space belonged to the serious business of painting. The once polished floorboards were thickly speckled with paint, the walls groaned under a large assortment of portraits and landscapes, and a long workbench pushed under two sash windows was littered with an artist's tools of trade. Rolled canvases were stacked higgledy-piggledy beside the workbench and several large finished canvases in ornate gilt frames were neatly displayed along the rest of this same wall. Here the two men, who had unwrapped the canvas, were placing three more framed pictures under the frenetic direction of the Italian.

No sooner had these men departed than two of their fellows arrived with the heavy lowboy, and behind them, another carrying a spindle-legged upholstered chair and a couple of easels. The Italian gestured where to place the furniture and then shooed them out. At the end of these comings and goings, Tam thought it time to make his presence known to his master, but the Italian got to him first.

. . .

Alec had his back to the activity and was casually flicking through a bundle of ink and charcoal sketches stacked on a chair by the workbench. One pencil sketch in particular caught his eye. It looked to be an early outline of the mother and daughter painting hideously attacked at the Oxford Street Exhibition, for he recognized the composition of figures and landscape. Taking up the lower third of the sketch was a larger, more detailed study of the mother's face. That she possessed great beauty was indisputable, but there was something about her expression that reflected a goodness of purpose and heart, and said as much about the artist's exceptional talents as it did about the sitter. He felt suddenly very sad for Talgarth at the loss of his painting, but was shaken out of this momentary melancholy by the little Italian, who fell to his knees at his feet and proceeded to cover his long white hand with kisses.

"*Grazie*, *Signore*! *Grazie*! You save Nico! *Grazie*! *Grazie*!"

"*Fermata*! Stop that at once and get up!" Alec ordered in Italian, disentangling his fingers as the little man's grasp transferred to the embroidered short skirts of Alec's dark blue velvet frock coat. He smiled at Tam who stood in the middle of the vast space. "Good to see you, Tam. Do you understand the Italian tongue?"

"Not fluently, my lord," Tam replied, coming forward with a suspicious glance at the groveling Italian.

"Then Nico will have to do his best with what little English he does speak. *Si*? And do get up. *Subito*!"

"*Si*, *Signore*," Nico replied obediently, getting up off his knees. "Nico cannot thank you enough, *Signore*. I tell *Signore* Vesey about demands for payment but he ignore them always. Always! I tell him he cannot ignore accounts and expect that we eat. But he too proud to seek help from family. So, the bailiff he come."

"How are Mr. Vesey's accounts usually settled?"

"Ah! The bills they are collected every other month by a servant of *Signora* Jamison-Lewis, the beautiful sister of *Signore* Vesey. And accounts she settle. This time, *Signore* Vesey he decide to take accounts with him to London. I said to him you will forget to give to *Signora* Jamison-Lewis. And this, it happens!"

"Mr. Vesey's sister settles his accounts? And you, do you read and write for Mr. Vesey?" Alec asked smoothly, as he flipped through the pile of charcoal sketches. When there was no response he looked up and saw Nico regarding Tam with suspicion. "Tam is my *servitore*—my *valletto*. *Capisce*?" When Nico nodded, he added, "I know Mr. Vesey cannot read and write."

"*Si*, *Monsignore*, but *Signore* Vesey he not like for people to know this. He say only peasants not read and write and he, *Signore* Vesey, he not a peasant. But I say to him, let me, Nico, write the English letters. My writing in the English," he added proudly, "it is better than the speech. When I read the letters to *Signore* Vesey I translate to the Italian. It makes it easier for both of us. *Signore* Vesey he speak my language beautifully."

Alec held up a corner of the parchment he was admiring. "Do you know this lady?" he asked Nico, and when he saw Tam give a start, eyes widening in recognition, looked to him for a response.

"Mrs. Bourdon, sir," Tam replied, just as Nico began to shake his head.

"Yes, of course," Alec answered placidly, and before he could repeat his question to the little Italian Tam added,

"Mr. Halsey and I made her acquaintance on the stairs at Barr's. Mr. Halsey's been invited to dine with her this evening."

"I see that bump to his head hasn't dulled his charm," quipped Alec and repeated his question.

"Nico he never met this *signora*. But men, they want," Nico replied in his broken English. "She very beautiful, so is natural *Signore* Vesey, he sketch her. But *Signore* Vesey, he tell me I never to sell her likeness. *Never*."

"*Signore* Vesey has had offers for her pictures?"

Nico made a face of resignation. "*Signore* Vesey he make her a promise. He sketch her, but he never to paint her. And he never to sell her likeness. *Never*. *Signore* Vesey he keep promise about the selling, but he not able to resist to paint her from sketches. She not know this. But me, I never make her such a promise. *Never*."

"Are *Signore* Vesey and this woman lovers?" Alec asked bluntly in Italian.

The little man grinned and made an exaggerated gesture of

embarrassment with a lift of his shoulders, as if not comprehending his native tongue. When Alec repeated the question, Nico answered him in his native tongue, saying with a little knowing smile, "*Signore* Vesey makes love to her many, many times, but only with his brush. You understand, *Monsignore, si*?"

Alec pretended not to understand.

"Because she repelled his advances, or because your master's addiction to opiates has made him impotent?"

Nico looked momentarily stunned but when Alec held his gaze he turned down his mouth and shrugged. "He is in love with the beautiful *signora*, that is true, but the situation you have hit the nail, *Monsignore.*"

"Did your master have you write letters to a Lord George Stanton on behalf of the beautiful *signora*?"

"Stanton? No. I do not know that name," Nico replied, though Alec noted he could not meet his gaze. "Why should I write letters for her when she can write for herself? I have the letters she wrote from her farm to *Signore* Vesey."

"Did her letters mention a Lord George Stanton?"

"I told you: Nico has never heard that name before. And I tell you this for nothing," he added, pulling a face, "the *Signora's* letters are full of female trivialities about jam and the weather and her little *bambina*. Very boring, I assure you, *Monsignore*. So it is as well she is beautiful because her likenesses they fetch a good price for Nico."

Alec smiled at the Italian's obvious disgust for female matters of importance but asked him seriously, "Why did you sell her likeness?"

"Because *Signore* Vesey and I, we need food and to be warm," Nico responded in angry defense. "My master's mind is on his art or on nothing at all. Food it is not important to him but to Nico, it is very important. One of us must be practical. *Si*?"

"Yes, of course," Alec replied placidly, adding in English for Tam's benefit, "Who bought the sketches?"

"A gentleman; he very persistent. He come here two, three, maybe five times," said Nico in English. "He want all pictures of this beautiful lady. He say very important. I tell him no pictures of her here. I do not tell him about large canvas that *Signore* Vesey he taking to

London for important exhibition. Everything else I say is *immondizia*; not important. Just sketches like this one, on scraps of blotter."

"But this gentleman still wanted them?"

Nico grinned and opened wide his arms. "*Molto*! *Molto*! He want to buy up *all* her likenesses! I think Signore Vesey he not mind when he realize Nico he get enough of your English guineas to pay for food and wine and new coats! This one," he added with a pout, giving the parchment Alec still held a casual flick with his thumb, "I not know it here, or it too I sell."

"Did the gentleman give you a name?" asked Alec, moving away from the bench to inspect the row of framed portraits stacked against the wall, Nico and Tam following, the little Italian rudely shouldering past Tam to be one step behind Alec.

"No, *Monsignore*. He never say and he always come at dusk, when only Nico here." The little Italian pulled a face. "I think he come in darkness because he very, *very* ugly."

"Ugly? In what way?"

Nico lightly tapped both his cheeks with his fingertips "*Vaiolo*. Smallpox. Scars. They very *very* bad."

"Molyneux!" Tam announced.

"He give me the English guineas in advance and I have sketches tied up with string ready for him the day *Signore* Vesey he go up to London. But Nico not speak to him again."

Alec turned away from several realistic and thus unflattering portraits of what appeared to be minor members of the nobility and local Somerset gentry. No doubt still here at the painter's studio and not adorning the revered space above their respective owner's marble mantels because the sitters had refused to face up to the truth. "The gentleman did not return to collect the sketches he had purchased?"

Nico shook his head. "No. He come, but he wait on far side of street. I see when I outside instructing men how to put most important canvas for exhibition onto cart. When we go in to get other canvases, I have other troubles. The *Signora dell'aristocrazia* she is here with her frightened maid and she very angry as usual. She complain. She always complain, but *Signore* Vesey he refuse to alter her portrait." The Italian grinned showing gaps in his otherwise clean white teeth. "*Signore* Vesey he say likeness flattering enough. *Signore* Vesey, he stubborn but right. She want her money returned; she pay half commission now, half on finish. We get half and spend it as always. Nico he only understand one word in five of her ranting so pretend ignorance as usual. It is best with women like that. Especially with one holding a knife."

"*Knife?*"

"*Si, Monsignore.* She take it from workbench and wave it around like a mad woman. Her maid very scared of her with the knife. She stay back. I understand. Only natural she worried. The *Signora dell'aristocrazia* very, *very* angry. She furious. I think maybe she close to having pain of the heart."

"So if the gentleman did not take the sketches, who did? This lady?" Alec asked with infinite patience, an eye on Tam who was unconsciously flexing his fingers in irritation.

"I see from window that the man he still waiting, but he not come inside. I not blame him, with the *Signora dell'aristocrazia* making so much trouble and noise," he replied as he went over to the workbench. "She pick up bundle that belong to the man, thrust at maid and walk out just like that! And still holding the knife! As if she had paid for sketches! *Si.* It is true, I tell you! I follow but stay well back because she still have knife and still very angry. She take them and I *never* see her again. Very strange. Now you please wait, *Monsignore*, and Nico he give you something for your great troubles on his behalf."

"The canvas that was already strapped on the cart, was anyone with it while you were dealing with this *Signora dell'aristocrazia*?"

"No, *Monsignore.* The two men loading the cart were ordered by the angry *Signora dell'aristocrazia* to come up to the studio as witnesses," Nico said in Italian. "Witnesses to what, I ask you, when it was her crazy behavior that was very bad. And of course the men they were so scared of her with the knife and what she might do with it that they waited here for many minutes before I come fetch them to return downstairs to the cart. Me I do not blame them."

"And the canvas of Mrs. Bourdon and her daughter? Was it still safely strapped on the cart?"

Nico shrugged and stuck out his bottom lip. "What can I say? My eyes they stay on the knife held by *Signora dell'aristocrazia*."

"The name of this *Signora dell'aristocrazia*?" Alec asked.

"Yes, yes, I show you, but first I have something for you…" Nico returned holding the sketch Alec had admired, now rolled up and tied with a white ribbon. He made a quaint little bow, and said in halting English, a glance to make certain Tam was watching and listening, "You please accept, *Monsignore*. From Nico. It small token but Nico he very grateful you send away tiresome bailiff."

When Alec took the parchment he clapped his hands and quickly went over to the framed canvases leaning against the wall. With a bit of a struggle he extracted one from a group and propped it against the turned splat of a ribbon-back chair. "This is she. The angry *Signora dell'aristocrazia*. Perhaps you think *Signore* Vesey cruel? But I tell you, she has a very ugly heart. *Signore* Vesey he merely paint it and show the world this. *Si*?"

Alec couldn't agree more. The portrait was of Lady Rutherglen.

Leaving Talgarth Vesey's studio, Tam wondered what his lordship was about when he stepped back to the edge of the pavement to better view the collection of townhouses and shops running the length of this section of Milsom Street. His master's question completely threw him.

"How many red doors do you see, Tam?"

Tam screwed up his freckled nose and joined his master by the side of the road, back to the traffic of carriages and horses.

"Red doors? Two, sir." He pointed. "This one belonging to the painter's studio, although it can hardly be called red, can it? What with the amount of dirt and dust, it looks more brown than red, but that door, the next one along, the one with the scaffolding covering the front, it's a nice bright red, sir."

Alec smiled and patted Tam's shoulder before setting off up the street, the valet scrambling after him. "Yes, Tam, a nice bright *new* red."

FOURTEEN

Alec and Tam walked the rest of Milsom Street towards the town center in silence, despite Alec's desire to ask Tam about Mrs. Bourdon and Tam wanting to know the significance of a bright *new* red door. Instead, Alec politely inquired about Tam's examination before the Worshipful Society of Apothecaries. He knew of Sir Septimus Bott's intention to have three wardens of the society inspect Tam's place of work. While his uncle and his valet had started the journey to Bath in the comfort of Alec's traveling coach, he had elected to go on horseback to allow him a few extra hours to see to estate matters with his steward. Thus he had still been at home when the letter from the estimable Sir Septimus was delivered.

Sir Septimus's note was long-winded and full of verbose rhetoric, informing him of the upcoming visit to No. 1 St. James's Place, and outlining the society's disapproval of Tam's dual roles of valet and apothecary. Sir Septimus made it clear he would not entertain Tam's admittance to the Society while he remained employed as an upper-servant in the house of a nobleman. An apothecary must devote all his energies to his chosen profession. And Tam still had one year of a seven-year apprenticeship to serve, regardless of the results of his examination.

The letter was a thinly veiled snub to Alec and designed to keep

Tam in his place, for how could a youth who had lost his master in unpleasant circumstances (and thus his apprenticeship), and become a valet to put food in his mouth, ever hope to complete his apprenticeship without financial independence? But Sir Septimus's letter was precisely the excuse Alec needed to ensure the boy returned to full-time study. He had already set events in motion by lodging the advertisement for a suitable gentleman's gentleman. And in a civil reply to Sir Septimus, requested the name of a master apothecary willing to take on the added burden of an extra apprentice for the year Tam needed to complete his apprenticeship. All expenses to be met by Lord Halsey, naturally.

By the time Alec entered the elegant surroundings of Barr's of Trim Street, he had managed to assuage Tam's fears about the impending visit of Sir Septimus Bott's cronies, and dismissed as fanciful the notion that there was any sinister intent behind the questions put to him by the examiners. He thought this as good a time as any to broach the subject of Tam returning to full-time study, and then Jeffries appeared as if from nowhere in hushed conversation with one of the hotel's servants and the moment was lost.

Spying the po-faced Hadrian Jeffries, Tam's silent anger was palpable.

Jeffries immediately shooed the servant away and stepped forward with a bow and helped Alec shrug out of his greatcoat, which he placed over an arm, then took Alec's leather riding gloves, not a flicker of recognition at Tam as he said tonelessly to Alec, with a quick raking glance over his lordship's travel-worn riding breeches and dusty jockey boots,

"I managed to secure for your lordship's sole use the hotel's largest bath. It is being positioned as we speak." And as Alec went up the stairs with a nod, he followed close on his master's boot heels so that Tam was left with a view of the obsequious footman's narrow back and perfect braid of hair tied off with a neat black silk bow. "And I ordered the bath to be drawn immediately. Would your lordship prefer to wear the Venetian Verde silk or the Midnight Blue velvet frock coat to dine? Both complement the cream silk waistcoat I have selected. And I think a cream silk riband w—"

"Whichever you prefer, Jeffries," Alec interrupted mildly, thinking a long soak in hot scented water would be just the thing for his aching muscles after a restless night spent on a hard horsehair sofa, Selina curled up beside him for half the night; the other half spent listening to a very confused little girl who had woken sobbing for her mother and being soothed, not very successfully, by Selina, her lady's maid, or both. He smiled to himself. He did not envy Selina's journey to Bath with her somnolent brother and frightened Sophie as traveling companions, and no doubt he would hear all about it when she arrived at Barr's. More than ever did the bath beckon. He sighed. "Let me know the moment the bath is made ready. I must first speak with Mr. Halsey. Thank you, Jeff—"

"Sir! My lord!" It was Tam and he had pushed past Jeffries on the landing to be at Alec's shoulder. "That's my job, not his, and I don't—"

"Not a word," Alec snapped, and shot Jeffries a quick angry look when the footman let out an involuntary snort of disapproval that was instantly swallowed up, as was his supercilious smirk, his gaze lowered to his immaculately polished black leather shoes. "I remind you that this arrangement is temporary, Mr. Jeffries. If you hope to make more of it, you had best make more of yourself. Go."

The footman bowed, not a glance at Tam, his gaze very much to the floor. He quietly stepped back and away as Alec turned to Tam, who had had the good sense to also shut his mouth and lower his eyes, though the fact he rocked on his heels, hands gripped behind his back was enough of a sign that he was finding it difficult to contain his anger.

"Don't crush that wonderful sketch," Alec said quietly. "I wish to show it to Mr. Halsey. Take yourself off to his rooms and I will join you both for afternoon tea directly." At this invitation Tam visibly brightened, but the boy still had a wary look and so he added with a half-smile, "We need to discuss your future in my household. Not leaving it, but where you belong *within* it. After dinner. Sir Charles?" he said with barely concealed surprise, turning from Tam to greet Sir Charles Weir who was coming up the wide staircase behind a hotel porter.

Sir Charles stopped on the stairs and glanced up, just two steps down from where Alec waited. He was so preoccupied with his thoughts that he was at first startled to be addressed, and then seeing who owned the deep measured voice, he became guarded, remembering their previous conversation at Alec's London townhouse. He bowed politely. "My lord Halsey."

"I was unaware the Russells were guests in this establishment," Alec said with a friendly smile, a significant glance at the bouquet of fresh flowers Sir Charles held in his right hand, a profusion of purple and red sage, dahlias, meadow saffron and fuchsias, which he hastily let drop to his side as if not wanting Alec to bear witness to his gift, and yet knowing it was too late to do so. "The Lady Henrietta partial to the color purple?"

"No. Yes. I am not entirely sure, my lord," Sir Charles muttered, clearing his throat. "The Russells always take a house in Queen Square."

"Ah. I see..." Alec replied with a crooked smile. "Forgive my impertinence."

Sir Charles waved a hand, self-composure returned. "No. No. It was only natural you would think... But you were at Drury Lane. You saw the declaration made by His Grace and Lord Russell." He joined Alec on the landing. "Nothing has been said. There is no announcement but it was patently obvious what was meant by their open truce, and what, or should that be *who*, was going to be used to seal their political peace."

"Surely if there has been no announcement..." Alec shrugged. "You know His Grace better than anyone... But I would not despair until the engagement is printed up in the newssheets."

Sir Charles smiled and shook his head. "For a diplomat, you are woefully romantic."

Alec pulled a face. "It is merely a matter of separating the private from the public. Surely even His Grace is capable of the distinction?"

Sir Charles held up a lace-ruffled hand.

"Please. It was a compliment. I did not say so with derision but with genuine goodwill. But as you say, I know His Grace better than anyone, and so you may believe me when I tell you he takes no action, makes no grand gesture in life, without careful deliberation. Every action has a reason. Every decision made with all possible outcomes thought through before it is taken."

"The consummate politician. Yet, what a dull private life..."

Sir Charles was unsure if Alec was being derogatory or merely making an observation, given the smile that accompanied the remark. A devilishly handsome smile used to great diplomatic effect, Sir Charles thought with a twinge of envy. He sighed and made Alec a short bow, the large bouquet now resting along the length of his left arm, conscious of the hotel porter who still hovered, eyes cast down but no doubt with ears wide open.

"You must excuse me, my lord," he said politely, a glance at the hotel porter. "I must not keep my hostess awaiting her afternoon tea."

And with another short bow, he waved the servant onwards down the passageway. Alec looked after him with a slight frown between his brows, for Sir Charles had sighed heavily without knowing it, such was his preoccupation with his thoughts.

That sigh bothered Alec. It was as if his friend from schooldays had a great weight upon his shoulders that could not be lifted. He had meant what he said about the Lady Henrietta's engagement to the Duke of Cleveley not being fixed and for Charles to maintain hope. Yet, it seemed Sir Charles had given up all hope—but so soon to offer another flowers? Alec had not the heart to mention that nestled amongst the profusion of purple and dark red petals he had spied an inert bumblebee. He hoped, for Sir Charles's sake, the insect was shaken loose and remained inert before presentation. A little warmth would wake it and cause his friend more trouble than the gesture of the bouquet was worth.

Sir Charles would have been greatly surprised that his friend was concerned for his welfare, for no sooner had he turned his back on Alec Halsey than he set his mind to the task ahead of him. He knew it was the right course of action; indeed it was the only option open to him if he hoped to maintain any influence, political or otherwise, with the Duke of Cleveley's heir apparent.

Any second thoughts were vanquished when he was shown to the door of the Arch Apartment, the largest and most sumptuously furnished suite of rooms on offer at this exclusive establishment that numbered Dukes, Marquesses, Earls and Foreign Princesses amongst its select clientele. And now occupied, thought Sir Charles as he forced himself not to grind his teeth but to fix a polite smile, by a beautiful heartless harlot whose very existence threatened the downfall of them all.

"You're late!" Plantagenet Halsey grumbled at Tam. But there was no heat or passion in his voice, only concern. "Got to worryin' unnecessarily when Mrs. Bourdon arrived back here in a chair and you weren't two steps behind her." He glanced about as the door opened again and in walked his nephew. "But now I see who kept you. I expected to see you hours ago, my boy. But I should've realized that flame-haired termagant would keep you detained. How is she?" he asked, ignoring his nephew's grin. "And how's her weaklin' brother?"

"Selina is well; her brother less so but faring better, though far from being able to be left to his own devices. They should be in Bath by sunset. There was an incident." Alec told them about Billy and Annie Rumble's abduction of little Sophie, and the death of Billy by a person or persons unknown but assumed to be the London gentleman who had promised Billy a few guineas to take Sophie from her home, adding, "You will appreciate that it is best we not mention any of this to Mrs. Bourdon until she is reunited with her daughter."

"Egad! The poor woman would be beside herself. What d'you have there?"

The old man watched Alec unfurl Talgarth's charcoal sketch of Miranda Bourdon on a table that had been set for afternoon tea with the hotel's best silver and china. Alec placed a silver sugar bowl and a jam pot at opposite corners of the parchment to stop the paper curling in on itself.

"What do you think of her?" asked Alec.

The old man peered over his nephew's shoulder. "It's a creditable likeness."

Alec's laugh held a note of skepticism. "Creditable?"

The old man exchanged a look with Tam and smiled crookedly. "You ain't seen her in the flesh, my boy."

At the sideboard, Alec poured coffee into three cups.

"Smitten, Uncle?"

"So will you be. I've been invited to dine with her, and you'll come with me and judge her for yourself."

When Tam hesitated to take the cup of coffee held out to him, Alec said kindly, "If you are to sit at my table, you must learn to accept with equanimity your new position within my household. Which means I may occasionally pour you out a cup of coffee."

"But, sir—"

"As a young man of means you can no longer be my valet," Alec stated, a glance exchanged with his uncle. "Mr. Blackwell bequeathed you a thousand pounds—"

"*A thousand pounds*?" Tam blurted out, the cup in his hand rattling on its saucer. He looked from Alec to the old man and back again. "Me, sir? A *thousand* pounds?"

"To complete your education, m'boy," Plantagenet Halsey added, taking the cup of coffee Alec offered him. "And by my reckonin', best use of a man's blunt, too."

"Just so, Uncle. And as a young man of means," Alec continued smoothly, sipping at his coffee, "you, Tam, will have all the time you need to finish your apprenticeship while sitting at my table."

"You should have the blunt, sir," Tam suggested. "I owe it to you for all you've done for me—for the dispensary."

Alec smiled and shook his head. "A fine gesture, Tam, thank you, but no. The legacy is yours and you must use it wisely. If you wish to repay me, then do so by finishing your apprenticeship and honoring the memories of Master Apothecary Dodds and Mr. Blackwell. Now, tell me," he asked, changing the subject because Tam was close to tears "what brought you to Milsom Street?"

"I followed Mrs. Bourdon from the Abbey like Mr. Halsey asked, sir, and that's where the chairmen took her. She stood on the opposite side of the street watching the men load up that cart and then she got back in the chair and went down the street again." He smiled sheepishly, taking a slice of seedy cake from the plate Alec held out to him.

"Thank you, sir. I assumed she had the sedan chair bring her straight back here?"

"It did. Don't know what got into her pretty head to go traipsing all over town given her delicate condition."

"*Delicate*?" Alec pulled a face. "She's with child?"

Plantagenet Halsey sucked in his thin cheeks, a glance at Tam. "Heavily with—er—child, my boy."

"I wonder what possessed her to come to Bath at such a time?"

The old man put up his bushy brows. "Mr. Ninian Bourdon, perhaps?"

Alec was skeptical and sipped silently at his coffee, watching Tam consume every last cake crumb on his plate. He offered the boy a second slice, which was taken with another bashful smile.

"Jeffries says the hotel proprietor ain't too pleased to have a woman stayin' under his roof whose pregnancy is so advanced," Plantagenet Halsey explained. "He don't want the child born here, y'see. Bad for business. But Jeffries says the proprietor ain't goin' to say boo to Mrs. Bourdon, not after he presented her with your note and seal upon it. So your elevation has proven useful after all."

"Jeffries has settled himself in well; he could yet prove useful," Alec commented, ignoring his uncle's lopsided grin and Tam's almost inaudible grumble about upstart footmen.

"One of the surly nose-in-the-air waiters told Jeffries that Mrs. Bourdon ain't a Mrs. at all, but a nabob's fancy woman. Damned barefaced cheek!"

"That may be closer to the mark than you think," Alec answered quietly, and was surprised when his uncle's cheeks instantly glowed with embarrassment. "Dear me, you *are* smitten. Selina predicted as much."

The old man ground his teeth. "Did she? Ha! Any excuse to lock horns with dear Mrs. J-L when she arrives!"

Tam felt he should contribute to the conversation, particularly when Hadrian Jeffries was bending himself over backwards to ingratiate himself into his lordship's good graces. Besides which, he needed to voice his frisson of remembrance about Mrs. Bourdon, if only to have his master reassure him that the feeling he had met Mrs.

Bourdon before was absurd, and thus could be dismissed without consideration.

"Sir, you don't think... With Mr. Vesey making all those sketches of Mrs. Bourdon, and she waiting outside his studio today... You don't think they... That he and she... I know his valet says differently, but I can't help thinking, what with her being with child..." He swallowed when Plantagenet Halsey glared at him and his lordship raised an eyebrow at the old man but said nothing. "Perhaps that's why she's come to Bath? To be with him. And she went to his studio today to see if he'd returned from London. I know she calls herself Mrs. Bourdon, but just like the hotel waiter said, and you must forgive my impertinence, sir," he apologized to Plantagenet Halsey, "but I know for a fact that many unmarried women of a certain age do that. Not that Mrs. Bourdon is of an age to do so, but she does have a child and another on the way. And in St. Jude's parish there were plenty of females calling themselves Mrs. This-or-that, but they didn't have husbands as far as I could see. Mr. Blackwell said they called themselves Mrs. to hide their shame and the shame from their brats who had no father who'd own them... You understand, don't you, sir?"

"Yes, Tam," Alec answered evenly. "Your skepticism regarding the excitable valet's assertions that Mr. Vesey and Mrs. Bourdon are not lovers is justifiable. I was inclined to believe Nico when he said that Mr. Vesey saw Mrs. Bourdon in an entirely platonic, somewhat revered light: Diffuse and wearing a halo. But perhaps I need to amend my confidence in the valet's statement, having discovered Mrs. Bourdon is with child?"

"If she's a painter's doxy, or any man's wife in watercolors for that matter, I'll kiss Cleveley's hoary big toe!" the old man spat out, finger jabbing at Talgarth Vesey's sketch. "And I'll have you take care with your low opinion of her when you meet her! *Both* of you."

Tam held his tongue, not as confident as before, regarding his niggling suspicion he had met Mrs. Bourdon before. More coffee and cake were consumed in silence, then a short sharp rap on the outer door was Hadrian Jeffries, come with the welcome news the hot scented waters of the large copper bath awaited him. Alec finally said as he stood to take his leave,

"I had no right to cast aspersions on the character of a woman as yet unknown to me, Uncle. For that I apologize." Thinking of his own circumstances, he added quietly, "One should not make assumptions about a woman's character if, for whatever reasons, she finds herself a man's mistress." He glanced at Tam and saw that the boy had put his cup on its saucer and lowered his gaze to the crumbs on his plate. He wondered if it was from embarrassment or guilt or a bit of both. "Yet, just because Mrs. Bourdon looks and acts the virtuous angel, Uncle, does not necessarily make her one. Tam's remarks, the fact Weir believes she is party to Talgarth's blackmail of Stanton, and when you consider she has already given birth to one bastard child and is pregnant with a second—"

"Well, I don't buy it!" argued the old man stubbornly. "You can think me a smitten old fool, and I don't give tuppence for that, but she just don't come across as the type who'd be party to blackmailin' someone. There's somethin' about her… I wish I could put me finger on it… Most girls in her predicament are either brazen strumpets or overemotional weeping pots, and yet she calmly goes about her affairs without a chaperone, ignoring the snubs of the hotel staff with her head held high, and politely shaking hands with this old gent whom she doesn't know from Adam and yet willingly allows him to escort her to church. To church! Bless her. Now off you go and have a good soak," he added gruffly at his nephew's self-restrained smile; nothing could hide the humor in his blue eyes. "A meditative soapy scrubbing will give you time to mull over what I've said. When you return to take dinner with me and finally meet her you'll see that I am not dribblin' pap about the woman!"

Alec made his uncle a small bow and silently took himself off. Tam was about to follow to discover for himself what havoc Hadrian Jeffries had wrought with his fastidious ways—no doubt he had rearranged to his own exacting standards Tam's careful unpacking of his lordship's portmanteaux—when in through the servant door shuffled a young woman, hands scrunching up the front of her plain muslin petticoats with worry.

Tam and the old man thought her come to clear away the afternoon tea things, but when she hesitated in the doorway, bobbed a quick curtsy, and hovered in expectation of being addressed, Plantagenet ushered her forward. It was her hard stare at Tam that stopped him from leaving the room, and when she turned to address the old man, he waited to hear what she had to say.

"Sir, the hotel porter told me this was the rooms of Mr. Plan—Mr. Plant—of Mr. Halsey. Is that you, sir?" When the old man nodded, the girl bobbed another curtsy. "Very good, sir. Mrs. Bourdon mentioned ye were kind to her. There's no one else, no one else in Bath that knows her... Mr. Vesey ain't at his studio..."

When the old man sat forward on his chair, a worried glance exchanged with Tam, the girl let out a shattering breath.

"She was al'right until her visitor. He upset her, sir. I don't know what he said 'cause I was sent to fetch the tea. But I could tell him just being there was not right. I wanted to stay but Mrs. Bourdon sent me for tea, and I was away such a long time on account of everyone in this place wantin' their tea at the same hour, and the housekeeper not wantin' to bother with searchin' out a vase for the flowers he gave her, and then when a vase was found and I came back up to the rooms, he was gone and she was in a frightful state. Shakin' all over she was and as white as white can be."

"Are you Mrs. Bourdon's maid?"

The girl nodded vigorously.

"Yes, sir. Janie. M'name's Janie. Janie Rumble. I be Mrs. Bourdon's maid these past few years." She bobbed another curtsy and let go of her scrunched up petticoats, looking from Plantagenet Halsey to Tam. "You will come, won't ye?"

Plantagenet Halsey slowly rose to his feet and Tam passed him his Malacca-headed cane. "I'll come," he said firmly.

Janie bobbed another curtsy.

"That's very kind of ye, sir. But it's him she wants," she said with a nod at Tam. When Plantagenet Halsey and Tam exchanged a startled look, adding, "She was *very* particular about it."

"She asked for *Thomas Fisher*?"

"No, sir. She didn'a say a name." Janie looked at Tam. "Is that your name: Thomas Fisher?"

Tam nodded but was still too surprised to speak.

"Are you certain, girl?" the old man asked without heat.

"Yes, sir. She said I was to fetch the red-haired boy who was with Mr. Plant—with you, sir." She looked anxiously at Tam. "You will go to her won't ye, Master Fisher? She needs you. She says only you can help her at a time like this."

Tam found his voice. "Needs me, miss? Time? What time is that?"

Janie stared at him as if it were self-evident.

"The babe. The babe's on his way."

ꟸ

An hour earlier, Sir Charles had the hotel porter rap on the door to the Arch Apartment. There was a moment's hesitation when the hotel porter let it be known to the maid who came in answer to his short sharp rap that Sir Charles Weir had come to call on Mrs. Bourdon. Miranda had told Janie that she would be dining with a Mr. Plantagenet Halsey and a Sir Charles Weir later that evening and to have a couple of the hotel servants set the table at the far end of the sitting room, and as well, see if two could be engaged to wait on the table for the evening. She had then disappeared into her bedchamber to rest. She was still asleep when the unexpected visitor was shown into the parlor and was offered to sit on the silk striped sofa while Janie went to rouse her mistress; Sir Charles apologizing but saying it was necessary for him to speak with Mrs. Bourdon now rather than later. Janie bobbed a curtsy and did as she was told, Sir Charles's commanding tone alerting her to the fact that it was pointless to try and put him off with the genuine excuse her mistress needed her rest at such a time.

Sir Charles continued to wait, holding the bouquet of flowers and feeling awkward, and when five minutes came and went he started to wonder if his ruse was necessary after all. And then Miranda appeared in the doorway, hair mussed and cheeks apple red from sleep, a heavy silk embroidered open robe over her nightgown which did little to hide the fact she was heavily pregnant. For all that, she looked heavenly, reminding Sir Charles of a medieval painting of a pregnant Madonna. All that was missing was the halo. He felt a stab of nostalgia. At that moment he had never hated his association with the illustrious House of Cleveley more, Lord George Stanton in particular. He wished the nobleman had choked on his own vomit years ago; five years ago to be precise.

Miranda recoiled upon seeing the parliamentarian, but quickly masked any feelings of uneasiness by coming across the room with a smile and hand outstretched. He bowed politely and gingerly offered the flowers, Janie quickly coming forward and taking the bouquet.

"What lovely autumn colors, Sir Charles," Miranda said, taking a tentative sniff of the floral arrangement when Janie presented them to her, but drew back at the overpowering smell of sage. "The kitchens will have a vase, Janie. You can find one when you fetch the tea. Tea, Sir Charles?" She invited Sir Charles to sit on the sofa, saying in apology, "I fear if I sit now I shall never get up. Janie? The tea…" she reminded the girl when Janie hovered in indecision by the servant door that opened onto the back stairwell that led down to the kitchen, the flowers propped on the window seat with its view along the length of Trim street.

Sir Charles did not sit and he did not speak until Janie, who reluctantly bobbed a curtsy and departed, had closed the servant door. He then turned to Miranda with an expression she found difficult to interpret. It was as if he were trying to penetrate her skin, or some other layer beneath, known only to her and no other. His scrutiny made her blush and slowly back toward the window seat. She tried her best to make it a natural action and not one that showed she wished to put as much space as possible between her and her uninvited guest, a hand to her rounded belly, as if her child required protection. Her action made him smile crookedly, confident again that he had the upper hand; any feelings of remorse had departed with the maid. He spoke to her in an altogether different voice to the one he had used when Janie was present.

"I shall not take up your time, and neither shall you mine," he said flatly, a step toward her. "You know why I am here and you can no doubt guess who sent me."

Miranda balked at his tone and pretended an interest in the bouquet, lifting it up and then leaning it against the window ledge as

Janie had done. Taking a deep breath, hoping her features did not communicate her sense of uneasiness, she turned to him with an enigmatic smile,

"As to the former, I have no notion, Sir Charles. And as I must guess the latter perhaps you would do me a kindness by telling me?"

"*Kindness*?" He spat out the word. "How can you speak of kindness when it is surely your *unkindness* that has brought us to this pretty impasse?"

"May I know what unkindness I have done you—done anyone?"

"Madam. We could argue that point all day. You have had years to ruminate on the folly of your wanton actions. Indeed, such wantonness produced the worst possible fruit and now you stand before me heavy with shame and pretend you do not know what you have done? That you had the barefaced audacity to show yourself in decent company in this shameful state; to enter a house of God as if you had the right! It is no small wonder Lady Rutherglen collapsed."

Again Miranda paused and drew a deep breath, the politician's words making little sense; his anger baffling. She did not doubt his sincerity. Yet mention of Lady Rutherglen did elicit a response from her.

"I am sorry Lady Rutherglen suffered distress, but as her ladyship has not given me an ounce of consideration since the day of my birth, indeed would not know me if she stared me in the face, I am under no obligation whatsoever to offer you any words that may be a comfort to her."

"*Obligation*? Dear God, Madam, the woman reared you, put food in your mouth and a decent cloth to your back and you repaid her how? By forgetting your carefully nurtured upbringing, an upbringing afforded you because her ladyship was forced to own to the connection by blood against her better judgment, but did so because of a sense of Christian charity. And how did you repay her? By fornicating with the first fool who offered you a posy of flowers and a wink of consideration!"

They stared at each other across the carpet: Miranda's face bleached white, Sir Charles's cheeks diffuse with blood. One willing the other to own to the accusations; the other wondering how best to refute them without exposing herself and everything she held dear. The only sounds in the room were those coming up off the street below the arch and in through the sash windows over the window seat that had been pushed up to allow fresh air into the parlor: Carriage wheels and the clip-clop of horses hooves over cobbles, the sing-song shouts of a fruit seller, and the low buzzing of a bee…

"By fool, Sir Charles, are you referring to Lord George?"

"You know perfectly well it is to Lord George Stanton I refer, Madam!" he hissed. "As if you can pretend ignorance! As if you care a *fig* if he is a fool or not! Your motives were patently clear from the off. You may have been able to use your malversations on a want-wit like George, that's no great feat, but you were never going to succeed with your designs while living under the watchful eye of Lady Rutherglen and Her Grace of Cleveley. And nor shall you now!"

"What designs were those, Sir Charles?"

Weir stared at her as if she had sprouted a second head, such was his incredulity. She was either incredibly naïve or as wafer-headed as George Stanton; perhaps they had been made for each other after all. He scoffed.

"Come now! Like the rest of your kind, you used all the tricks available in a whore's armory: You ensnared him, opened your legs to him and got yourself with child by him, all in the hopes he would marry you!"

Miranda winced at such crude speech but she did not retreat from the accusation.

"Why must you make a sordid tale of it, Sir Charles? It is just as plausible that Lord George was in love—"

"In love? *In love*? *George*?"

Sir Charles took a step closer, as if he needed to bring Miranda into sharp relief to digest her words. He was now only a stride away from her.

"Why do you find the notion so astonishing, Sir Charles?" she asked steadily, forcing herself to sound calm though she felt anything but. She took a step away, not liking his closeness. "Lord George is capable of such an emotion; I have seen it. He—"

Weir waved his hand about, as if swatting away an insect.

"No. No. No, Madam. What you saw is what you wanted to believe you saw. Are you truly so witless that you could not make the distinction between lust and love? And if that is true, then I am truly sorry for you, but it does not alter the fact that once you found yourself with child by him, you did your utmost to ensnare him into marriage."

"Perhaps I am not the one who has it topsy-turvy?" Miranda countered, a glance at the servant door and then over Weir's shoulder at the door that led out onto the landing, where a hotel servant sat at his post in the passageway waiting and ready to do the bidding of a hotel guest. If she could just get to the door, the servant would surely hear her calls? "Perhaps Lady Rutherglen has persuaded you that there was no love, as she herself is surely devoid of such an emotion and therefore would not know love if it were offered to her on a silver salver? I truly believe Lord George was in love, and if not for the inconsiderate actions of others many years before, tragedy might have been averted, which surely makes it a pitiable state of affairs…"

Sir Charles saw her furtive glance to the servant door, and while she was speaking he stepped across and locked it and slipped the key into the deep embroidered pocket of his frock coat. At his action, Miranda let out a little sigh of defeat, but she did not move from the window seat. The sun was on her back, a breeze coming in through the window tickled her wrist, and the hum of the bumblebee nestled in the bouquet of flowers was growing louder as it was awakened by the warmth of the sun. She hoped Janie would return very soon. But with the servant door now locked what was she to do? A twinge of discomfort made her put a hand to her belly; the other she stole behind her, fingers feeling for the bouquet of flowers. If she could just reach the flowers; throw the bouquet at him; distract him enough to make for the door… But the idea died almost as soon as it entered her consciousness; the flowers were just out of reach.

"Madam, I did not come here to argue with you," Sir Charles said confidently, in control now that he had locked the door and had the key. Besides, the woman was in no state to run from him. "Nor do I care particularly one way or the other about Lord George's pathetic emotions. What I do know is that in the here and now, he wants nothing to do with you or your bastard offspring. That you thought you could blackmail him into owning to being your bastard's father—"

"Blackmail? George? To make him own to being Sophie's papa?"

Miranda looked so confused that Sir Charles almost believed her and for a moment he was tongue-tied. She saw his momentary confusion and had a spark of hope that he might be persuaded from whatever threatening course of action he proposed in coming to her rooms alone and locking the servant door. Her only hope was to remain calm and try to dissuade him with good sense, for she had heard he was not an unreasonable man. At one time he had been a loyal functionary to the Cleveley household; was he not now a politician? Did he not covet his reputation and his standing amongst society? There was only one way to find out.

"What possible reason could I have for exposing George as Sophie's father, Sir Charles? I have not seen or heard from him in five years, which is what I most desired in all the world. I have no wish for George to be known as Sophie's father, for surely in doing so I expose the ignominy of her lineage, and that is something I mean to keep secret, from her and from the world, until the last breath leaves my body."

Miranda grimaced and sat on the window seat, both hands to her round belly, for the twinge had turned into sharp cramp. She took a deep breath, forced herself not to panic, and looked up at Sir Charles. His deepening frown and the confusion registering in his pale eyes were oddly comforting.

"Surely, you can see that it would be my last wish on God's earth to want to expose that little girl to the world's ridicule. She should never know her true parentage. She is the innocent party in all this. I cannot imagine that Lord George wishes it either."

Sir Charles was still frowning but some of the bitter fight went out of him.

"Then if you are not party to the blackmail of Lord George as you claim, then you, too, are being ill-used, Madam. Confiding in the painter was not wise on your part, for in confiding in him you have given him the means to not only blackmail Lord George but to do the very thing you want so desperately to avoid, and that is expose the child to the world."

"The painter?"

"Talgarth Vesey, Madam. It is Lord George's belief that threatening letters were written by the painter on your behalf."

Miranda shook her head.

"No, Sir Charles, that cannot be. I have not confided in Mr. Vesey. I would not, and for the reasons I have just explained to you. He has been a good friend to me and to Sophie, and we enjoy his company for its own sake. His visits have been a welcome change from a daily life living removed from the world. But you must believe me: I have never confided my situation, or Sophie's birth, to anyone save one other. Is Lord George confident these letters came from Mr. Vesey?"

Sir Charles nodded mutely, and then surprised Miranda by flicking out the short skirts of his frock coat and sitting in the window seat uninvited; the bouquet of flowers pressed at his back, disturbing the bumblebee, which buzzed in irritation and lifted its heavy body in flight.

"Was it the Reverend Blackwell in whom you confided?" he asked almost in a whisper, as if fearing to be overheard.

"Mr. Blackwell?" Miranda frowned, nonplussed. "No, Sir Charles. It was he who confided in me."

"He confided in you? But…"

He let the sentence hang, waiting for her to offer an explanation.

Another sharp cramp pulsated through Miranda's body, and she grimaced and took a deep breath before saying candidly to the politician, "Surely you must see that Mr. Blackwell had as much reason as George to ensure Sophie's lineage remained a secret from the world, for if he exposed Sophie to the world's ridicule he exposed George, not only to ridicule and derision but to a far worse fate, given George's greatest wish, indeed he sees it as his God-given right, to be the next Duke of Cleveley."

Sir Charles was so confused by Miranda's assertions that he was still digesting them when he blurted out, for want of something to fill the silence and curb her penetrating regard,

"You are aware the Reverend Blackwell recently suffered a heart attack and died?"

Another painful cramp closed Miranda's eyes tight, robbing Sir Charles of her initial reaction to his news, and when she drew breath and met his open look directly there were tears in her eyes. He was unsure if her tears were from pain or the news of the vicar's demise.

"No. I was not," she confessed, and before he could ask anything further about the dead vicar, said breathlessly, "Sir Charles… I implore you… Unlock the servant door and call for my maid… At once."

"Where is Lord George Stanton's child?" he asked, ignoring her request, something tickling his left ear making him swipe a hand unconsciously in the air near his cheek. "Is she here with you, Madam?"

"Please… The babe will not wait for you or me. The door…"

"Tell me the whereabouts of Sophie Stanton, Madam!"

"Sophie Stanton?" Miranda's eyes opened wide with new knowledge. "So you do not know… George has not confided in you…"

Sir Charles rummaged in a frock coat pocket and pulled out the key to the servant door, and this he held between thumb and forefinger before her eyes.

"Tell me and I will do as you ask."

Again, Miranda closed her eyes on a grimace of pain and willed the cramps to subside, to at least abate until Janie returned. She shuddered in another deep breath and when she opened her eyes it was to find Sir Charles still holding the key aloft (did the man have no idea what was happening to her?) and she knew that if she did not give him a satisfactory response to his question he would not leave her alone or do as she requested, and so she blurted out the first name that popped into her head.

"Lord Halsey. He knows. The door… Sir Charles, *for pity's sake*, I *must* have my maid!"

The name registered with Sir Charles but he continued to hold the key just out of her reach, staring at her, struck not by her beauty, which was self-evident, but by her self-possession, which was striking in one so young and ignorant of the world, even more so given her present predicament; for surely she was going into labor? There was something innately splendid about her; as if she was due his homage as a matter of course. To his utter astonishment he found himself bowing under the weight of noblesse oblige and allowed her words to finally penetrate his skull:

Blackwell had as much reason as George to ensure Sophie's lineage remained a secret from the world, for if he exposed Sophie to the world's ridicule he exposed George...

What did she mean?

Astonishment turned to disquiet and disquiet to doubt.

So you do not know... George has not confided in you...

What did she know that he did not? And what was foolish George keeping from him? Was he being played for a fool? By whom? Stanton? Lady Rutherglen? This whore with the face of an angel? For the first time in a very long while he felt matters were out of his control, and if there was one thing in this life that scared him half to death, it was not being in control. He liked order and predictability, and knowing one's place in the world; only then could he function and be secure. Now, in less than an hour spent in the company of a woman who called herself Mrs. Bourdon, he had the presentiment that his well-ordered existence was about to unravel and fall all to pieces.

His heart began to beat faster and a throb pounded at his temple.

Again his ear was tickled by a humming irritation, and without taking his eyes off Miranda, who was regarding him steadily in the small welcome reprieve from the debilitating contractions, he swiped at the air near the rolled powdered curls of his wig above his right ear.

"You must not swat at it or it will think you mean it harm," Miranda advised, hands gently smoothing over her belly, soothing the baby within, an eye to the bumblebee which, having bestirred itself enough to lift from the dark crimson petals of a fuchsia, buzzed near Sir Charles's ear and then found itself swept and caught in the lace ruffles covering his wrist. "Remain still and the bee will take flight and settle elsewhere, but if you lash out again it will sting you."

But Sir Charles did not hear her advice or notice the bumblebee crawling out of the lace folds covering his hand because the pounding in his head was all consuming; pounding with doubt and an upswell of panic. And with panic came a terrible uneasiness that made his stomach churn, his heart race, and his shaved head bead with sweat under the neat powdered wig. He stared hard at the young woman seated across from him in the window seat, who did not blink an eyelid in fear at his open regard, until her words and her face were cemented into his brain. And it was then that he had a revelation and he knew: They—Lady Rutherglen, Lord George Stanton, and most assuredly he himself—had been duped; they had all been utterly and splendidly duped.

Panic-stricken, he lashed out and grabbed Miranda's wrist and yanked her to him.

"Who are you?" he asked in a terrified, hoarse whisper. "God in heaven, Madam, tell me who you are!"

The bumblebee lifted its abdomen and plunged its sting deep into the soft pad of Sir Charles Weir's thumb.

FIFTEEN

ALEC WAS ENJOYING SOAKING HIS TIRED LIMBS IN THE HOT scented waters of the large copper bath, slipping in and out of consciousness as the aromatics and heat helped to soothe his troubled mind, however temporarily, of unanswered questions regarding the poisoning of a poor old vicar and the murder of a crippled youth far from home.

Into his mind's eye came the crumpled and lifeless body of poor Billy Rumble, whose one wish was to run away to sea for days filled with sea-faring adventure. Instead his young life had been cut short by a stab to the heart; his final moments spent alone in a dark deserted stall. The callous murder of Billy Rumble and the thwarted abduction of little Sophie Bourdon made him frown and lower his wide shoulders into the warm water, as he wondered at the identity of the "London gentleman" who had promised Billy Rumble a few guineas to abduct her. Were the diamond drop earrings, worth a king's ransom to the likes of Annie and Billy Rumble and found in the stables of the George Inn, a further inducement to hand over little Sophie? Now one of those earrings dangled from the ear of his beloved.

He smiled at the vision of Selina, sitting across from him at the inn, fair copper ringlets mussed from travel, the one diamond drop earring dangling from an ear, diamonds winking in the candlelight. She was smiling at him, chin cupped in her fist, black eyes alight with mischief. No doubt by the time she arrived in Bath she would have a pocketful of excuses stored up waiting to present to him as to why she could not see her way clear to becoming his wife, and another pocketful of reasons why it was best she be his mistress.

What was Selina not telling him? And yet she confided in the Duke of Cleveley. As to the revelation she and the Duke had been lovers, that she had miscarried the Duke's child… That was a whole chapter of her life he had no wish to explore. Yet he had a twinge of intuition that her affair with Cleveley and its consequences in some way had a bearing on his future with her.

He would like to wish thoughts of the Duke to perdition, but think of the Duke he must, for he believed the nobleman linked in some way to the death of Blackwell. That the vicar had been poisoned, Alec was in no doubt. But he did not believe the Duke had poisoned Blackwell; he was no coward. But had someone else done it for him? Cleveley was named executor of Blackwell's will, and as such he knew the poor vicar was in truth a wealthy member of the nobility—but did the Duke know that Lord George Stanton was Blackwell's son? Would he have implicated himself irrevocably in Stanton's base behavior and covered up the seduction and subsequent pregnancy of Miranda Bourdon five years ago had he known his stepson's true parentage? Were Cleveley's actions still governed by the misapprehension that Lord George Stanton was his stepson and thus his heir? Or perhaps he had discovered the truth, and yet having no son, continued to champion Lord George as the future heir to the Cleveley dukedom? If so, had Blackwell and the Duke conspired to keep Stanton's true paternity a secret? The codicil would certainly bear this out.

A most astounding document, the codicil only added to the maelstrom of mystery surrounding Blackwell's death.

There were other protagonists who were in some way connected to Blackwell, if not to his death, and these Alec had yet to fully explore, such as Selina's opium-eating brother and the enigmatic Miranda Bourdon. Had Lord George really vandalized Talgarth's portrait of Miranda and her daughter as Weir suggested, or was there a less sinister but no less emotive reason for the portrait's destruction? Alec was confident the painting had been destroyed before it left Milsom Street. If, as Charles Weir suggested, it was George Stanton who had taken knife and paint to the painting, then he must have visited the painter's studio, but when? Talgarth's Italian major-domo never mentioned or described the corpulent young nobleman.

From what Nico had told him, Alec was inclined to discount Stanton as the vandal, and this led him to wonder if a more likely suspect was the furious and knife-wielding Lady Rutherglen, who had lashed out at the prized portrait in a fit of venomous pique. What of the Duke's valet Molyneux and his visits to the painter's studio? What were his reasons for buying up any and all portraits of Miranda Bourdon? That he was doing so on his master's behalf was not in question; the reason for doing so was. Was the Duke again aiding his stepson in having all traces of the girl George Stanton had violated obliterated? To what end? Was the woman herself to be silenced once and for all time? Was that the end intended for Miranda Bourdon?

Miranda Bourdon. The woman remained an enigma. Alec could not wait to finally make her acquaintance and thus have her measure. If he was sure of one thing as he tried to untangle thoughts and the many knots of unanswered questions, it was that Miranda Bourdon was the means by which he would be able to make sense of why Blackwell and Billy Rumble had died. The sooner he was introduced to her the better, he decided, as he slipped into semi-consciousness only to be woken five minutes later by hot water mixing with the warm water at his feet.

It was Jeffries.

He was judiciously pouring hot water from a heavy copper jug into the water near Alec's toes, while silently directing a beefy lackey from the kitchens to deposit the two pails of fresh hot water by the foot of the bath and then take himself off. He put aside the jug to take up two thick bath sheets from the padded seat of a spindle legged chair by the dressing table. These he put carefully on a stool closer the bath. He then disappeared into the bedchamber and returned with a red silk banyan lined with yellow-gold damask, and this he draped neatly over the chair back, and hovered, waiting.

Alec opened an eye and with a toss of his head swept aside a dark heavy curl that had fallen into his eyes, not from having sensed the valet's soft-footed presence, but to an audible and irritating tap-tapping sound. Hands crossed in front of him, the fingers of Jeffries' left hand tapped incessantly on the back of his right, yet his long pale face, with its upturned pinched nostrils and cleft chin, was devoid of his inner thoughts. Mouth set in a thin line, Jeffries gazed at a point on the polished floorboards some two feet in front of his perfectly polished shoes. The slight rise to the thick straight brows and the persistent tapping alerted Alec that someone or something had displeased the normally impassive Hadrian Jeffries.

With a deep breath, Alec slid his shoulders up the side of the bath until he was sitting straight and ran a hand over his damp face and through his wet hair, knowing his internal musings and short respite of solitude were at an end. He asked for the fresh hot water and Jeffries instantly came to life.

Rinsed, dried, his naked body wrapped in the silk banyan, Alec sat on the dressing stool and toweled moisture from his shoulder-length black curls, an eye on Jeffries who hadn't said 'boo'. Alec smiled to himself, knowing the man was bursting to speak but would keep his tongue well and truly between his teeth until given permission to do so; the perfect gentleman's gentleman. But did Alec want perfection? John, who had been his valet before Tam, had been as close to perfection as was possible for a valet to be, but he had also been a complete bore. Was Hadrian Jeffries a bore? He had no idea. In fact, he knew nothing about Hadrian Jeffries other than he had been a footman in his household for two years. When most noblemen could care less than a tester for knowing more than their valet's name and that the servant did his job well, not knowing anything but the man's name disturbed him. No doubt his uncle would have something to say about his lack, or more correctly, his lapse of interest in his household. His uncle always made it his business to know his servants as people, and had instilled the same eccentric habit in his nephew. Alec smiled. His uncle also made it his business to know other people's servants as people too, which meant he would know all there was to know about Mr. Hadrian Jeffries.

Alec tossed the damp towel aside and scraped back his curls, tying them up with a riband he found on the well-ordered dressing table. Well, that was a first! The contents of his traveling toiletries case: Tortoise shell hair brush, clothes brush, ivory comb, sharpened razor, engraved silver etui with its hinged lid slightly ajar should Alec wish to use the implements within the case, a neat coil of black silk ribands, nail file at right angles to the set of brushes, sandalwood cologne from Floris, two pairs of polished shoe buckles, even the engraved silver button belonging to the Cleveley livery Tam had given him (he must have left it in a frock coat pocket)—all were set out neatly, rather too neatly, and in an order known only to Jeffries by the exact positioning of each personal grooming implement.

"So, Jeffries, who is it that requires an urgent word? Or is it something far more entertaining you wish to tell me? Has Mr. Fisher started a fire in the kitchens or Mr. Halsey insulted one of the guests with his apostrophizing on the immorality of Bristol's slave traders?"

Hadrian Jeffries did not move a facial muscle. He did however lower his eyebrows.

"Mr. Barr wishes a word with you at once, my lord. He was most insistent. I told him he must await your lordship's pleasure, and sent him away. Would you care for me to dress you now, my lord?"

Alec saw the quick frowning glance directed at his bare feet and stood, removing his hands from the banyan's pockets. "Very well. I must look my sartorial best for dinner with Mrs. Bourdon or my uncle will never forgive me."

"It was about Mrs. Bourdon that Mr. Barr wished to have words, my lord," Jeffries said, taking the banyan and offering stockings and smalls.

"Have words? That sounds ominous. Was Barr ominous?"

"Yes, my lord. He tried his best, but was in such a state of agitation that he failed to convey his wishes in any meaningful way."

Alec threw a crisp white linen shirt over his head and slipped on a pair of velvet breeches, saying once he had tucked in his billowing shirt and buttoned the falls, "Agitation? With being denied an audience with my esteemed self, or something else?"

"He was already agitated when I answered his incessant rapping on the outer door, my lord. Being denied an audience with your lordship's esteemed self only increased his distress."

Alec mentally rolled his eyes as he stood before the long looking glass and expertly tied the linen stock about his throat. Did the man not recognize irony? *Esteemed self* indeed! Tam would have smiled. Perhaps Jeffries was nervous and he should give him the benefit of the doubt? He allowed Jeffries to shrug him into an oyster silk waistcoat with embroidered pockets and buttons and to fuss for a moment with its fit, then waved him aside to sit on the dressing stool to slip his stockinged feet into a pair of polished black leather shoes, Jeffries securing the plain silver buckles.

"Do you know why Barr was in a state of distress?"

"One of the guests… No it was a visitor to one of the guests. Yes, that was the right of it," the valet explained with satisfaction as he rose up to stand by the dressing table. "A gentleman visiting the guest in the Arch Apartment caused an uproar—"

"The Arch?" Jeffries had Alec's full attention. "Mrs. Bourdon's rooms?"

"Yes, my lord. That was why Mr. Barr insisted he must speak with you. He says you are known to Mrs. Bourdon and—"

"First tell me about Mrs. Bourdon's visitor."

"As I said, my lord, the visitor caused a bit of a fracas amongst the guests. According to the water boy… Apologies, my lord," Jeffries said abruptly, a tinge of color in his cheeks, "I should not repeat what I did not myself see."

"You may if you think the source a reliable one. And, Jeffries, it is 'sir' not 'my lord'. You are my valet."

To Alec's surprise Jeffries blushed, smiled and nodded.

"This visitor…?" Alec said with as much aloofness as he could muster, for he was confident that Mrs. Bourdon's visitor was none other than Sir Charles Weir. "Don't spare the details if you think them pertinent."

"According to the boy who carries the hot water," Jeffries said, bringing his features under control, "one of the lads who was at the base of the stairs helping an elderly dowager with her portmanteaux, witnessed the visitor come charging down the main staircase two steps at a time and without a care for who was coming up them. The visitor rudely bumped the Misses Musgrave, two elderly spinsters who I am told are the aunts of the Baron Stoke and regular habitués of this establishment, and one of the Misses Musgrave fell back against the railing and dropped a hatbox, two hats crushed under the feet of a footman who went to her aid. The lad said the visitor had his left arm folded up across his chest and was clutching his wrist as if he'd broken it, or he'd scalded his flesh with boiling water. But that wasn't the worst of it, my—sir," he said, finally drawing breath. When Alec nodded, he continued. "The visitor had a look upon his face that the lad said could only be described as sheer terror. Like the face of a murderous dog who is about to swing from the end of a Tyburn rope and knows that he is for Hell. It was that sort of face." Jeffries frowned. "One of the footmen, a very irregular fellow who was taken to task the moment he uttered the question, was bold enough to enquire of the terrified gentleman if he had seen a ghost!"

When Jeffries paused for effect, Alec realized it was his cue to ask the obvious.

"And had the visitor seen a ghost?"

The valet nodded, eyes wide. "Yes, sir. That was precisely what he replied. That a ghost had come back to haunt us all!"

"Those were the visitor's exact words? *A ghost had come back to haunt us all?*"

"To the word, sir."

Alec could not hide his surprise; not at the thought of a specter haunting the premises, but that Sir Charles Weir, one of the most self-possessed men he knew, would react in such a melodramatic fashion had he indeed been in the presence of an apparition. Alec was inclined to the opinion that Weir was more likely to coolly question the specter as to whether it was indeed a ghost, rather than show any signs of panic, even if he were convinced he was in the presence of the supernatural. So what had his old school friend seen in this apparent apparition that had so shocked him as to cause a momentary lapse in reason and usual behavior?

"Do you know what the visitor did next, sir?"

Alec had no idea; what he did know now was that Jeffries was partial to the melodramatic and that he expected him to ask the question, so he did:

"What did the visitor do?"

"I am embarrassed to say, sir, but he covered his face with his hands and burst into tears, like a child who had fallen and hurt itself or perhaps been taken to task by its nurse for its bad behavior. It was truly shameful. Sir," Jeffries added in a whisper, a quick furtive glance over his shoulder, "do you think Barr's is haunted?"

Not only partial to the melodramatic, but a believer in ghosts! He was glad to amend his initial impression of Jeffries: Not dull, merely nervous at trying his best to be the perfect gentleman's gentleman. He glanced at the faultless alignment of his personal grooming items and stopped at the razor. Still, the last thing he needed was a valet prone to nerves, in any situation.

"No," Alec replied flatly, "I do not believe Barr's to be haunted. Did the fellow who confided this mention where the visitor saw this specter?"

"The visitor did not mention a specific room, sir, but a person."

"Person?" This did surprise Alec. "He *recognized* the ghost?"

Jeffries nodded vigorously, eyes wide.

"Yes, sir. I suppose that must be the reason Mr. Barr was so insistent he speak with you."

"With me? About a ghost? Why?"

Jeffries moved closer to the dressing stool, as if he did not wish to be overheard by the living or the dead.

"It's the occupant of the Arch Apartment," he said in a loud whisper, gaze darting left and right and then back at Alec. "Mrs. Bourdon: She's the ghost."

PLANTAGENET HALSEY GRIMACED WITH THE PAIN OF

straightening his arthritic knees, but he was determined to stretch to his full height to out-stare eye-to-eye the barrel-chested footman who blocked access to the apartment. The servant was as wide as he was tall and filled the doorframe; stockinged legs with their impressively large calf muscles were splayed and his thick muscular forearms were crossed against his massive chest. He was just the sort of strongman to be found keeping the peace in a local Bristol cathouse when merchant seamen were given their shore leave, except this hulking brute wore livery and the frock coat had silver buttons. What was he doing at Barr's? But the old man did not have the time or the inclination to find out. He just wanted the fellow removed from obstructing access to Mrs. Bourdon's rooms, and he wanted him gone at once. And so he had demanded of the mute bulk and every servant sent to pacify him, until the owner of the respected establishment, Mr. Barr himself, appeared before him, countenance schooled to be as tractable as the old man's was intractable.

"Get that brute out of the way," Plantagenet Halsey ordered, menacing his Malacca-headed cane about, "and open that door!"

Tam and Janie ducked out of the way of the swishing cane, to stand behind the old man as the proprietor threw his head back, the tip of the cane narrowly missing connection with his pointy chin. A couple of footmen standing by the staircase took a few steps forward, eager to bear witness to an altercation between their nose-in-the-air employer and the feisty old guest. With a visitor earlier screaming down the stairs that he had seen a ghost, the day was shaping up to be one worth talking about over a pint at the local.

"I must regrettably inform you, sir, that it is not possible for me to open that door," Mr. Barr said at his most conciliatory, and with a frozen smile reserved for visitors who enquired as to the cost of staying a night at the exclusive lodging house; if one had to ask, one did not stay.

"Not possible? Of course it's possible, damn it!" growled the old man. "Mrs. Bourdon has asked for our presence, and so she shall have it!" He glared at the impassive barrel in the doorway and back at Mr. Barr and swished his cane from the proprietor to the servant. "Tell this oaf to move his large carcass!"

Mr. Barr cupped his hands at his chest and continued to smile yet was aware of the growing crowd in the passageway at the top of the stairs. Joining the two inquisitive footmen, who pretended to be about their duties of standing and waiting in the passageway should a guest require their services but with ears very much open, was one of the Misses Musgrave. Her gloved hand was dug deep in her velvet-lined reticule as if searching for something, and behind her was her maid. And at the old man's back was his young redheaded companion, and for a reason unfathomable to the proprietor, Mrs. Bourdon's wan-faced maid stood beside him.

"My dear sir. Mr. Halsey. My profusely humble apologies that a mute giant obstructs that door, but I am unable to do as you request. I feel it would be for the best to await the arrival of Lord Halsey, whose liberty of conversation is required in this matter."

Mention of his nephew cooled some of the heat from Plantagenet Halsey's tone, but he was no less belligerent.

"*Liberty of conversation*? This isn't a whist party or some dowdy dowager's damn soirée! There isn't time for conversation!"

"There is always time for conversation, dear sir. And I must insist. It is to his lordship that I will most ardently address my concerns."

"*Concerns*?" The old man blustered, a wild-eyed look about at the cluster of onlookers before turning back to the proprietor. Taking a step closer he growled in an under-voice, "Have you any idea what is going on behind that door?"

The proprietor's eyes went wide and his jaw dropped.

"It is not this select establishment's practice, nor will it ever be while I am owner, to have ideas of any kind about what takes place behind the doors and in the rooms occupied by my esteemed guests, Mr. Halsey," he enunciated with a sniff, and loud enough for the cluster of onlookers to overhear. "Barr's caters to the quality—"

"—quality of the gold in the coin we carry if enough of it crosses your greasy palm!"

The snigger and a snort came from one of the footmen eavesdropping, who instantly dropped his chin to his chest and shuffled behind the elderly Miss Musgrave, back up against the wallpaper.

"Sir! Mr. Halsey!" blustered Mr. Barr. "I must tell you that…"

But Plantagenet Halsey had stopped listening. As much as he wanted to beat his cane over the head of the pompous Mr. Barr, such was his angry frustration, instead he turned a shoulder to Tam, who, at the jerk of the old man's grizzled head, came closer.

"Have the girl take you up to Mrs. Bourdon's rooms via the servant stair. If any of the staff give you trouble, you've my permission to knock 'em down. Your paramount duty is the care of Mrs. Bourdon. Understand me?"

Tam nodded grimly and with a signal to Janie, the two turned and disappeared, Janie leading the way through the labyrinth of servant passages down to the kitchens.

Thinking the old man had sent the youth and the maid to fetch Lord Halsey, the proprietor said patronizingly, "I have already requested Lord Halsey's presence, sir. I merely await his pleasure."

"Rightly gave you the brush off, eh?" Plantagenet Halsey again pointed his cane at the servant guarding the door. "What do you expect his lordship can do about Mrs. Bourdon's condition? He ain't an apothecary and he ain't—"

"Yes! Yes! If you please, sir, there is no need for you to state the obvious. Had I known—"

"—a man-midwife."

"—the young woman's *predicament* was so advanced I would have advised her that taking up residence in the Arch Apartment was not the wisest of choices. Barr's is a respectable address for well-bred and genteel clientele. A private residence would have better suited her purpose." He looked over the old man's grizzled hair at the elderly Miss Musgrave, who had finished rummaging in her reticule for nothing in particular and who was now boldly staring at him, and dropped his voice to that of a conspiratorial whisper. "Had I known then what I only discovered this morning, I would not have taken *Mr.* Bourdon's immoral coin, despite him paying handsomely for the exclusive use of the Arch Apartment, and I mean to refund him the balance of his immoral coin as soon as it can be arranged."

"Eh? *Immoral coin*? What are you flabbering on about, Barr? The woman in that room is married and if you are implying anything else, I—"

"So she would have everyone believe," Barr bravely interrupted, his voice a thin whisper. "But, after what was revealed to me this morning, I have serious doubts the marriage ceremony conducted in the Arch Apartment she now occupies was a Christian union under the auspices of Church and state."

The old man ground his teeth.

"I don't care for your insinuations, Barr. Explain yourself!"

Despite his guest's blazing gaze, the proprietor took a step closer.

"Tell me, sir, is it not an odd set of circumstances that less than a twelvemonth ago the young woman was married to Mr. Bourdon in the very rooms she now occupies, not in a house of God as is the usual and proper place, and by the strangest of clerics, a shabby fellow who looked more beggar than vicar, two *servants* acting as witnesses to the union. Naturally I respected Mr. Bourdon's wish for privacy and I did not think it so odd at the time—"

"Bourdon's untied purse strings stopped your brain turning a cog or two, did it, Barr?" Plantagenet Halsey quipped, though his ears had prickled at the description of the clergyman: It had to be Blackwell. He waved his cane. "You said *circumstances*. What else?"

The proprietor smiled a thin, self-satisfied smile of superiority, believing his guest was beginning to incline to his way of thinking.

"The newly-married couple spent a week ensconced in the apartment and then they departed, for where I know not! Mrs. Bourdon has stayed in that very apartment upon three separate occasions since the day of her marriage, arriving alone, without her husband, and in the most improper of circumstances!"

There was a squeaking gasp and then a cough. It came from the elderly Miss Musgrave. In his self-deluded self-confidence that the uncle of Lord Halsey was beginning to show signs of coming round to his way of thinking, Bernard Barr had allowed his voice to rise above a whisper. He now quickly coughed and lowered it again.

"And although I had my suspicions at the time, I am not one to disbelieve my guests, but after what I discovered in the pages of the letter addressed to me by—"

"Improper?" interrupted Plantagenet Halsey, gaze hardened; his question was whisper quiet.

"Would you not call it improper for a female to stay at a lodging house without her maid in tow, and bringing with her a child of an age that anyone who can add two and two would soon realize was not born in the wedlock of her marriage to Mr. Bourdon?"

"Did she receive visitors while she was stayin' here?" the old man asked, conveniently ignoring the proprietor's pertinent question.

Bernard Barr's eyes went very wide. "I beg your pardon? This, Mr. Halsey, is a reputable establishment!"

"So other than the child, Mrs. Bourdon saw no one, no gentlemen callers whatsoever?"

"As to that, sir, my position as proprietor of this most esteemed establishment makes it impossible for me to answer you," Barr replied, face alight with color, thinking of her most recent caller just that very morning; a well-dressed gentleman with a bouquet of flowers, whose exit had been melodramatic to say the least, and had raised many an eyebrow and too many questions.

So Mrs. Bourdon had had visitors, and male visitors at that! That did not mean there was anything improper in the visits, and Plantagenet Halsey refused to believe there had been, whatever Barr's insinuations to the contrary. He would stick with his first impression of Mrs. Bourdon until he was told differently by the woman herself. He sighed. He was beyond being annoyed with this moralizing windbag, and having given Tam what he considered ample time to enter the apartment via the servant stair, his anxiousness for the welfare of Miranda Bourdon returned tenfold. He pointed the tip of his cane at the inert beefy footman, but addressed the proprietor. "It won't be a reputable establishment for much longer if Mrs. Bourdon don't receive the care and consideration she and her unborn babe require and you are the cause of their deaths! Now tell your big oaf to move his elephantine carcass and open that door; and don't give me tripe about needin' my nephew to be present!"

"But, Mr. Halsey, sir, I told you. I—"

"Wait up!" the old man interrupted on a sudden thought, cane swishing from immoveable footman to proprietor. He poked Barr gently in the chest. "What letter?"

Barr's gaze lowered to the cane held to his chest and he quaked.

"Letter?"

"You said you discovered somethin' about Mrs. Bourdon sent to you in a letter. Who sent it? When?"

"Ah! Yes, the letter. A most illuminating piece of script that confirmed my suspicions about the guest in the Arch Apartment and her—"

The old man poked the proprietor's chest.

"Who. When."

Barr laughed nervously and touched his fingers lightly to the end of the cane. It was not removed.

"I received the letter only today, sir. It was delivered by this morning's post, and I happened to be reading its most astonishing contents when the gentleman visitor to this apartment made his hurried exit from the establishment."

"Who."

"Lady Rutherglen."

"*Rutherglen*?"

Barr gave an involuntary yelp, not in response to the old man's thunderous declaration but because the cane jabbed him hard in the sternum.

"Apologies," Plantagenet Halsey muttered and let drop the cane. "You can have that letter fetched. I'm very sure Lord Halsey will be most interested in her ladyship's slanderous discourse! And now," he added with another sigh, his cane swishing up and across to point at the immobile footman guarding the door to the Arch Apartment, "tell that gorilla to move!"

"But, sir, that's what I tried to tell you: I cannot do as you command for two very good reasons."

"Damme! For God's sake, man! What bloody reasons?"

The two footmen, Miss Musgrave, her maid, and three guests—a recently knighted farmer and his wife and young son, who had just joined the eavesdropping party on the landing—all leaned forward, awaiting the response to the old man's explosive question.

"Firstly, the door has been locked from the inside, and secondly—and I presumed it was at Lord Halsey's instigation and thus that is why I wish to speak with him—as your eyes can surely attest, there is indeed a mute footman the size of a gorilla obstructing access to the door. And if he does not belong to Lord Halsey, then I, like you, sir, am just as befuddled by whose order he guards that apartment."

❧

JANIE FOUND THE SPARE KEY TO THE SERVANT DOOR OF THE Arch Apartment hanging on a hook in the housekeeper's pantry, and took it without asking. She did not have the time or the inclination to explain herself. And to do so would surely cause unnecessary gossip about her young mistress; events would soon conspire to do that anyway. The red-haired young man did not seem to mind her theft, in fact his grim smile held a wisp of encouragement as she slipped the key off the hook and pushed it up her sleeve out of sight, holding it in place with her arms folded. She prayed it did not slip and fall with a clatter to the stone floor as they darted amongst the kitchen servants too busy preparing the evening meals to be bothered questioning the trespass of two servants unknown to them, and thus belonging to guests staying upstairs.

When Janie had earlier gone up to the rooms via the narrow servant stairwell carrying a vase for the flowers, she was surprised and alarmed to discover the servant door locked. She had scratched on the paneling and called for her mistress, and receiving no response, had been about to descend the stairs to take the carpeted corridor used by guests to enter via the main door when she had heard a faint calling out. It was Mrs. Bourdon and an involuntary fretful groan alerted her to the possibility that her mistress might have gone into early labor; that the door remained locked heightened Janie's dread. And then Mrs. Bourdon had cried out for her to fetch the friend of Mr. Plantagenet Halsey, the youth with the red hair. He could help her, and Janie was not to send for a physician or a man-midwife, only for the youth with the red hair. And to be quick about it!

Janie had promised but was skeptical, yet reasoned that a woman suffering the pangs of childbirth could have whatever she wished if it lessened her suffering. What the fresh-faced Thomas Fisher could do for her she had no idea. He was not a man-midwife and he was much too young to be a physician. Yet, when she glanced over her shoulder, as he followed her up the circular stone stairwell, she was reassured by his look of grim determination.

The key turned in the lock and opened the door, much to Janie and Tam's relief. Tam let Janie go on ahead, the girl giving him a queer look before she bustled into the bedchamber from the sitting room because he was shrugging out of his frock coat.

From the window seat to the fireplace hearth, where a fire still crackled low, flowers were strewn across the carpet as if flung out violently, the delicate petals of fuchsias, red sage, and dahlias crushed, and stems broken. Everything else in the room—tapestry and damask cushions on the window seat, two wingchairs, a low walnut table, and a basket holding needlework—had, in Tam's quick appraisal, not been disturbed. There being no signs of struggle or distress, other than the wanton destruction of a bouquet of autumn flowers, Tam followed the maid across the room, throwing his frock coat across the back of one of the wingchairs. Yet, on the threshold of the bedchamber he stopped and waited. It would not do to barge in unannounced. Despite the maid saying Mrs. Bourdon had asked for him, he waited to be beckoned within.

He pulled off his plain white ruffles and rolled up the billowy shirtsleeves to the elbow. Six years experience as an apprentice to a Master Apothecary came to the fore and subordinated all considerations and fears of a youth not out of his teens, mind focused on the patient beyond the bedchamber door. He needed his apothecary's traveling cabinet fetched from Mr. Halsey's apartment. He required soap, hot water and bath sheets from below stairs. He presumed there was a washstand in the bedchamber. The porcelain jug would need to be refilled with fresh hot water, the porcelain bowl rinsed out and replenished. A hot brick wrapped in a soft cloth to keep the newborn warm, the maid could fetch from the kitchen when the time came. A pot of brewed tea, too; a cup of the same laced with a strong narcotic to help ease Mrs. Bourdon's pain. There were several drugs to choose from in carefully labeled glass bottles hidden in the secret compartment in the back of the mahogany traveling cabinet, but he must choose the right one and administer the correct dose to ensure the mother was still able to bear down strongly when required to do so by the contractions. What did the pharmacopeia suggest as the correct dosage for…

A cry of distress, then a half groan, half whimper sliced through his pharmaceutical musings, and he flung back the bedchamber door, polite consideration aside, and was two strides from the four poster bed when Janie threw herself in his way.

"I don't know what to do! Tell me what to do for her!"

Tam looked over the distraught maid's head. Miranda Bourdon had her arms wrapped tightly about the carved mahogany bedpost, head slumped forward and was groaning softly. Tam's gaze flickered beyond the dressing gown to her chemise and his heart beat faster at the dark spreading stain. Her waters had broken.

"She needs you to be strong, Miss," he said stridently to Janie. "And you need to do precisely as I say when I say it."

He disengaged himself and held the shaking maid at arm's length to look into her tear-filled eyes and tell her what he needed. He made her repeat his orders and when she nodded and was calmer he let her go and stepped forward, saying firmly but gently to Miranda,

"Ma'am, you asked for me. It's Thomas Fisher. I'm here to help."

Miranda moaned and shuddered as another contraction wracked her body; this one stronger than the last. She took a series of shallow breaths, arms tightening about the bed post, and finally looked up at Tam through a tangle of hair. The terror in her blue eyes was palpable.

Tam swallowed. The self-confidence he had brought into the room, that he was as capable as any man-midwife of delivering a newborn—after all he had helped his master bring more than two dozen babies into the world in Mr. Blackwell's parish of St. Jude's—washed away in the panic of what the terror in her eyes revealed.

The lying-ins where he had assisted his master deliver the babies of London's poorest were all mothers giving birth to their third or fourth baby, sometimes it was the woman's sixth or seventh labor. While all were thrilling events in Tam's limited experience of such matters, they were considered rather pedestrian by his master. There were no complications and only one of the babies had not survived, and that because the little life had pushed its way into the wider world too early.

Despite women dying in childbirth every day, Tam thanked Providence he had been witness to only one such tragic event. It also happened to be his first experience of childbirth, and thus it had etched itself into his memory. His master had been called to St. Jude's for what he deemed an uneventful labor; he had tended the girl for the last two months of her pregnancy, and being a healthy and hearty creature was not likely to have any trouble giving birth. He offered Tam to accompany him and if the opportunity presented itself he would allow him to assist but he was sworn to secrecy; this mother and her child were unlike any other his master had attended upon in St. Jude's, and Tam was to forget all that he saw and heard. Was that understood? To which Tam readily gave his consent and understanding.

And so he had not been surprised to discover that the young mother-to-be was only a girl, not much more than fifteen years of age, but what did surprise him was her fine white hands with nails that were not ragged but manicured, the hands of a lady who had not done an hour, least of all a day's manual labor in her young life, hands that had not known the abject poverty of St. Jude's. Surprise turned to astonishment when he realized there were two young girls: One pregnant, one not; both with dark ringlets and fine features; both exceedingly beautiful.

It was an easy thing to do as his master had asked and forget his attendance at this young mother's lying-in because it was the most traumatic experience of his young life. He had been almost fifteen years of age and although he had seen a great deal of poverty, disease and death in the three years of his apprenticeship thus far, nothing prepared him for the horror of witnessing a baby being ripped from its dying mother's belly.

Tam had sat huddled with the mother's cousin, silent and forgotten in a cold corner of the small dank room pungent with the odor of birth, when the vicar and his master made the decision to save the baby at the expense of the mother. No longer screaming in agony and too exhausted to push, the baby unable to enter the birth canal, the young mother was on the point of death, but not dead.

And then it happened, just like that, and before Tam could take the cousin from the room. There wasn't even time to shield her from the grisly sight. The deed was done and the baby pulled up and out by its little legs. A finger was flicked in its mouth to remove mucus so that it could breathe, and then it screamed, or was it the girl beside him? He could not remember and had tried very hard to forget. The recurring bloody nightmares of the dead mother's belly cut open and the infant extracted took much longer to subside.

Four years on, here he was with a young woman who was about to give birth, no longer the assistant of an experienced apothecary-physician but alone, still an apprentice, but her only help and comfort. She looked as terrified as he felt. With all the mental muscle he could muster he forced himself to focus on the task before him and to put all other considerations aside. He *was* an apothecary. He had surely passed his entrance examination to be admitted to the Worshipful Company of Apothecaries. He was capable of helping this young woman deliver a healthy baby. He kept telling himself this as he quickly went to the bed and flung back the coverlet, smoothed down the sheets and hastily brought the pillows that were against the ornate mahogany headboard halfway down the length of the mattress which would allow him to more easily examine her from the foot of the bed.

The bed made ready and comfortable, Tam took Miranda by the elbow and gently pried her from the bedpost, offering her soothing words of encouragement and comfort as he led her to the head of the bed, all the while thinking that despite not being one for making wagers, he would safely stake all his meager possessions, and everything belonging to his master, Lord Halsey, that Miranda Bourdon was about to give birth to her first child.

"I don't know what to do, Thomas," Miranda pleaded, her words uncannily similar to those spoken by Janie, and confirming Tam's dread. "You do. You can help me."

"I will, ma'am. I will take good care of you and the babe. Here, sit on the edge of the bed a moment. Janie will return soon and then I will be able to give you something to help relieve the pain a little. Don't worry. I won't leave you until a physician—"

She gripped his forearm hard.

"No. No physicians and no midwives. No one else. Just you... You were there... *We* were there... Do you remember, Thomas?

Tam looked up from her blood-covered fingers into her blue eyes. At first he had no idea what she was talking about, and although he suspected pain was addling her brain, she was so very calm and lucid for a young woman in labor. And then her next words sent him hurtling back into the terror of that night he had just been remembering and it made him, too, wonder if in truth Miranda Bourdon was indeed a ghost.

"The shawl, Thomas. What happened to Sophie's shawl?"

SIXTEEN

ALEC WALKED ALONG THE PASSAGEWAY TO THE LANDING outside the Arch Apartment and into a verbal *mêlée*. A crowd four deep had gathered in front of the door, while a knot of curious bystanders hovered on the top steps of the staircase, neither coming up nor going down, yet trying their best to appear as if they were not lingering to eavesdrop.

Miss Musgrave recognized the tall and darkly handsome Lord Halsey, and with a quick tittered whisper near the ear of the person in front of her, the crowd fell apart with the whisper's deliverance down the line, giving Alec easy access to his uncle and the proprietor who had come to an impasse in their argumentative conversation. But it was at the large footman, log-like arms and legs akimbo and filling the doorframe, that Alec's astute gaze lingered, intrigued. His blue eyes flickered across the man's impassive face, then over his well-kept footman's attire, fixing on the silver buttons of his frock coat which caused his left eyebrow to rise a fraction in interest. Without his spectacles he was unable to make out the engraving but he had a hunch as to what was inscribed and it quickened his pulse, though he was able to say smoothly to the proprietor, who was waiting his pleasure with a servile smile,

"You wanted to have speech with me, Barr?"

"That I did, my lord."

Alec turned a shoulder to the onlookers. "Without an audience..."

While the proprietor was busy having the small crowd disperse, Alec said to his uncle in an under-voice, a jerk of his dark head at the Arch door, "Notice the silver buttons, Uncle?"

Plantagenet Halsey had not and he peered keenly at the large servant. His bushy eyebrows shot up, which was enough to convince Alec his gut feeling was proved correct, and he smiled when the old man said in wonderment,

"Well, I'll be damned! Bees!" In the next breath he was grinding his teeth and his pale gaze flashed up at his nephew. "I knew it!" he hissed. "I told you Cleveley was up to his neck in Stanton's dirty dishwater!"

"What has me intrigued is how His Grace knew Mrs. Bourdon would be here at Barr's and not at the farmhouse, and if he knows that, does he know that her daughter is neither at the farmhouse nor here with her mother? And what does he hope to achieve, keeping her prisoner of a lodging house?"

Plantagenet Halsey pointed his cane in the direction of the servant. "Well, it's a damned waste of time guardin' her door because the poor woman has gone into labor, so couldn't flee even if she wished to."

"Labor? She's having her baby, *now*?"

The old man smiled at the panic in his nephew's voice. "Aye. The boy's in with her."

"Tam? *Tam* is delivering her baby?"

"Think of anyone more competent?"

Alec pulled his uncle aside, out of earshot of the proprietor and footman. "Well, yes, if I knew the names of any physicians or man-midwifes in the vicinity! Uncle, you said it yourself: Tam is a boy. I doubt he's seen a woman fully undressed; as for—um—*down there*, I can't imagine a situation requiring him to—"

"Zounds! You do think him ignorant!" the old man said with a smile and a shake of his grizzled hair. "Well, he ain't and hasn't been for years. What do you think he's been doin' with his apothecary skills? Playing dispenser of medicines behind a shop counter and naught else?"

"If I'd had my way, yes. That's what a boy of Tam's age would be engaged in doing," Alec stated with annoyance, a heightened color to his shaven cheeks and a glance back to the proprietor who was making shooing motions at two of his servants to hurry them along. "That others exploited his skill in the past by taking him into unsavory and unsafe places such as St. Jude's, I can do nothing about. But I can and will do something about Tam's present situation—"

"Poor females ain't any different to their rich sisters in their needs for medicinals and salves for all sorts of female complaints," the old man interrupted belligerently. "And there ain't many physicians who will venture into a parish such as St. Jude's to tend to a poor woman when she's in childbirth, when she's in *any* predicament! Blackwell was fortunate to have the services of Dobbs and Thomas—"

"You said it yourself: Dobbs *and* Thomas. Tam no longer has a master. He is alone in that room with a young woman in the pangs of childbirth. What if something goes wrong? Who is he to call on for advice? What if the woman or the child were to die? Tam would be held accountable!"

"You should have more faith in the boy's abilities," Plantagenet Halsey grumbled sheepishly, knowing his nephew was in the right. "I do."

"I have every faith in his abilities, Uncle." Alec said with great patience. "It's the unpredictability of childbirth that sets the hairs up on the back of my neck. Barr!" he ordered, turning to the proprietor who was deep in conversation with a servant, who had dashed up the staircase two steps at a time and was now pointing down the stairs into the foyer. "Barr!"

The proprietor waved the servant away and scurried across to Alec, trying to affect an air of solicitude as he mopped sweat from his brow. He quickly pocketed the damp handkerchief. "Yes, my lord. An altercation in the foyer requires my immed—"

"In a moment. Do you have a regular physician who calls on your guests when they are ill?"

"Yes, my lord. Dr. Ketteridge is most amiable and competent—"

"Send for him at once."

"But, my lord, the guests…"

Alec coolly looked down at the proprietor, instantly closing Barr's mouth, and cocked his head in direction of the gorilla-sized footman.

"There is another way to enter that apartment other than that used by guests. Ketteridge can be admitted via the servant door. Then I want you to place your most burly servant to guard that entrance from unwanted trespass. No one is to enter the Arch Apartment without my permission. I will open the door to the physician."

"A servant to guard the servant door. No one to enter without your permission. Your lordship will greet Dr. Ketteridge at the servant door. Yes, my lord. I will see to it at once. Please now excuse me," the proprietor responded docilely, head bobbing up and down with every sentence uttered.

With a low sweeping bow and slumped shoulders, Barr shuffled away.

He had spent the better part of two decades turning Barr's of Trim Street into an exclusive lodging house, with only the most select clientele. Indeed he had under his roof that very day a marquess, the nieces of a duke, not to mention a widowed viscountess of unimpeachable virtue, and now this: A woman of indeterminate married status had gone into labor and would give birth to her questionable offspring in his establishment, and with Ketteridge called in to attend upon her, he would not be able to keep the event a secret. What member of Polite Society would want to stay at a lodging house that harbored pregnant women of dubious virtue? The situation was enough to send him scurrying for a headache powder, but another circumstance had developed that made the headache powder superfluous. He might as well put a pistol to his head and end his miserable life. He predicted that by nightfall half his guests would have departed. No establishment that he knew of had ever recovered from a resident ghost.

A thud followed by a loud wail that was more from shock than pain drew Alec and his uncle along the corridor after Barr. A footman appeared beside his master, having scampered up the stairs almost on all fours, out of breath and with his hair sticking up above his reddened left ear; it appeared his ear had been boxed.

The proprietor openly sighed and demanded an explanation.

"Lady Rutherglen says she's not interested in your nizy excuses, sir," the footman reported. "Her ladyship demands to be shown the-the *ghost.* She then called you all sorts of names, most of which I forget, but I do remember one: Muckworm. Sir!"

ALEC WATCHED THE PROPRIETOR FLAP HIS HANDS AT THE WIDE-eyed footman who, despite a reddened ear, was more concerned that there was a ghost on the premises than being physically accosted by the reptilian Lady Rutherglen. With Barr out of sight, Alec turned to his uncle, who was looking puzzled, and briefly recounted what Hadrian Jeffries had told him about Sir Charles Weir's melodramatic exit from Barr's.

"And Weir was heard to pronounce that *a ghost had come back to haunt us all,*" the old man repeated, incredulous, "and then he burst into—*into tears*?"

"And not many hours later Lady Rutherglen descends upon Barr's demanding to see this ghost. Fascinating, isn't it?"

"The woman is a menace and Weir a snivellin' coward. I don't know why you're grinnin'!"

"I've never met a ghost before."

"Be serious! I own that that stone-hearted wasp could scare a ghost from its haunt, but it ain't likely she's here to do Barr a service. You heard that servant, she's come to see a ghost. *A ghost*!"

"Yes."

Plantagenet Halsey leaned on his cane, and looked past his nephew's wide shoulder at the immobile footman who filled the Arch doorway and shook his head with a frown. When Alec's grin broadened the old man had a flash of insight. It didn't make sense but he said it anyway.

"She wants to see Mrs. Bourdon?"

"Yes."

"Why?"

"Because she's the ghost."

The old man's voice was explosive.

"Miranda Bourdon is a ghost?"

Alec linked arms with his uncle and they walked along the passageway that led to the servant stairs.

"That she is a ghost answers many questions."

Plantagenet Halsey was about to demand of his nephew if had swallowed bathwater, which would explain his addled thinking. Yet he seemed to be in control of his mental faculties and so he humored him, if only to see where his unexpected thoughts were leading.

"Does it?"

"Yes. But not all. There are some only Mrs. Bourdon can answer."

"Can she?"

They stopped in a dimly-lit alcove outside the servant door.

Alec smiled at his uncle's expression of interested confusion. It was one he remembered from his boyhood, half studious interest, half suppressed incredulity, when he would prattle on at him about the usual things that young boys dream about—being a pirate on the high seas; flying like a bird; what was on the other side of the world if one dug deep enough; where did monsters hide during daylight?

"There is no ghost in any real sense of the word," he replied placidly. "But Miranda Bourdon has risen from the dead of Lord George's past; hence she is a ghost. Though why Weir made a very public declaration that she was a ghost come back to haunt him, when he knows who she is and has accused her of blackmailing Lord George, is not only surprising but exceedingly interesting…"

"Is it?"

"Yes," Alec stated. "A public declaration is the last thing Lord George, Weir and the Duke would want, for it draws attention to the very person they wish to keep firmly below the floorboards. Charles tried to blackmail me into helping him keep the whole mucky business from becoming public. It is that circumstance: Society becoming aware of Lord George's appalling behavior, which he so desperately wanted to avoid. And here he is in a lodging house making melodramatic pronouncements and turning into a blubbering mess, about

Mrs. Bourdon being a ghost!? It does not make sense. Obviously the small matter of dissuading Miranda Bourdon from exposing Lord George's vile behavior has not gone Weir's way, and that whatever carefully-laid plans he had made for his future—and believe me, Uncle, Charles does not leave his house without knowing to the hour what he will be doing for the day. He was the same at school, and—

"Close-mouthed sot!"

"—those plans are now ruined, possibly beyond repair. But that does not explain the very public nature of his disappointment." Alec paused on a thought. "Why Lady Rutherglen has involved herself intrigues me…"

"Does it?" Plantagenet Halsey asked, trying to follow his nephew's complex musings.

"Lady Rutherglen has come hot-foot on Weir's heels to confront the ghost, which means she is well aware of her nephew's sordid past and she too is intent on making certain Miranda Bourdon's blackmail attempt does not become public. But the very nature of her display has also drawn attention to Mrs. Bourdon…"

"If that young woman has blackmailed anyone I'll turn Tory!"

"*Alleged* blackmail, warrant me that," Alec replied with a smile. "I realize Lord George is Lady Rutherglen's nephew, but surely the matter was best left to the Duke to deal with… Though… His Grace may still be at his estate… That one of his liveried servants is guarding the door to Mrs. Bourdon's apartment indicates he knows that she is here, and suggests he means to make an appearance; his servant to ensure she does not—er—*shoot the moon*."

"Think he means to confront her about Stanton?" When his nephew took a moment too long to respond, the old man said emphatically, "I'll not let him touch a hair on her precious head!"

Alec smiled lovingly at his uncle's blatant chivalry. "Olivia assured me Cleveley is not given to bully-boy tactics, so you may put away your knight's armor. His Grace is more circumspect in his approach. Hence, the giant in the doorway."

"So you think Weir went snivellin' cap-in-hand to Lady Rutherglen after his little fright from a specter?" Plantagenet Halsey muttered, feeling foolish at his outburst.

"It would seem so, given Lady Rutherglen is downstairs making demands. Though, like Weir's earlier performance, her being here, and in similar dramatic style, merely advertises the presence of Mrs. Bourdon, and will heighten curiosity amongst Barr's select clientele as to why particular upright members of Polite Society are in a flap about her presence."

"Well, the old hornet's been stirred in her nest, and for a third time in a day."

"Third?"

"She had the bare-cheeked effrontery to send Barr a letter by this mornin's post defamin' Miranda Bourdon's good character and declarin' her unfit to inhabit this establishment. Made all sorts of insinuations about her bein' immoral and havin' gentlemen callers and the like. Salacious rot!" When his nephew remained silent, the old man added, as if reading Alec's thoughts, "I know. You're wonderin' like me why she would do such a reckless thing when, as you say, it draws attention to Miranda Bourdon. By settin' her claims in ink she's linked her name to Mrs. Bourdon's, and with no explanation offered. Of course she ain't goin' to mention why; ain't goin' to air Stanton's shameful dirty laundry, is she?"

"No. The third?" Alec asked, slightly impatient, acutely conscious that the longer he lingered, the longer Tam was alone with a woman in the throes of childbirth.

"While Mrs. Bourdon and I were at the Abbey's eleven o'clock service, Frances Rutherglen had a fit or some sort of turn, and Mrs. Bourdon made the acute observation that Lady Rutherglen had neither a good heart nor a clear conscience. I agreed with her, but didn't think too hard about it. But come to think on it now, not a truer word has been spoken about her ladyship, and by a young woman who, until today, I would not have thought knew Frances Rutherglen from Eve! The poor child had tears in her eyes when she said it, too. Odd."

"Yes," Alec replied calmly, though his uncle's revelations quickened his pulse, for it strengthened his suspicion that the connection between Miranda Bourdon and Lady Rutherglen went deeper than mere acquaintance. "A giant guarding her door will surely prohibit an audience with Mrs. Bourdon, which may be enough to send Lady Rutherglen on her way. For providing a sentry, thanks must go to the Duke. Now you must excuse me, Uncle."

"That don't mean Cleveley ain't up to his eyeballs in muck!"

Alec opened the servant door.

"On the contrary," Alec replied with an enigmatic smile. "What you have just told me makes me even more certain that the Duke is bound up so tightly in this imbroglio that it may just be choking the life out of him."

"Bravo to that! I hope the bindin' cuts off his blood supply, then he might have some notion of what it's like for those poor wretches on board His Majesty's frigates!"

With his uncle's satisfied pronouncement, Alec disappeared into the darkened narrow recesses of the servant corridor, and Plantagenet Halsey returned to the landing outside the Arch Apartment where he intended to encamp until he had news of how Miranda Bourdon was faring. A servant brought him a ribbon-back chair, a side table with lighted candelabra upon it, and the latest newssheet. He ordered his dinner to be brought to him on a tray, and to fetch some food and drink for the mute hulk standing in the doorway. As he was a mountain of a man, the kitchen had best supply a mountain of food to keep him upright, for if he knew one thing about childbirth, which was limited to the birth of his nephew, it was that the process could take anywhere from several hours to a few days. He then opened wide the newssheet and, turning the print to the candlelight, settled behind the pages, a smug smile animating his face when the mute colossus in the doorframe thanked him in a softly spoken voice—a gentle giant after all.

"The shawl, Thomas. I knitted a shawl for the baby," Miranda explained, sitting gingerly on the edge of the mattress, arms stiff and fingers squeezing down tightly into the soft bed covers as another contraction forced her eyes shut and clamped her teeth. When she could breathe easily again she looked at Tam, who was rinsing his hands in the porcelain bowl on the mahogany washing stand. "When Sophie was given to me, she was not wrapped in the shawl. You must remember—"

"Yes. Yes, I remember," Tam answered quietly and went down on his haunches before her. When she nodded, tears in her eyes, he swallowed hard and squeezed her hand. "But I don't remember everything, ma'am. To be honest, I've tried hard to forget that night ever happened."

"So have I," Miranda confessed. "But I never forgot your kindness. You—*we* were not much more than children. No one should bear witness to such horrors. Have you since—"

"No. Never," Tam said quickly. "I've assisted at other lying-ins but nothing so awful as that night." He smiled, hoping to project confidence; inside he was a quaking mass of nerves. "This will be different. It will be as childbirth is: Painful and slow, because this is your first, but you and the baby will come through it. I promise."

He straightened his legs as another contraction caused Miranda to cry out and put one hand to her belly. She moaned and when able to control her breathing said fearfully,

"I want to believe you, Thomas. But the pains are—*unbearable*… I am… I am so scared. So *very* scared."

"Mr. Blackwell took the shawl," Tam said, because it was true and to distract her from her fear.

"Charles Weir told me Mr. Blackwell is dead. Is he?" When Tam nodded, Miranda bowed her head. Tears dropped onto her stained chemise. "He was a good man, Thomas. A *very good* man."

"Yes. Yes, he was, ma'am," Tam replied, tears welling up.

He quickly dashed a hand across his face and sniffed loudly. It would not do to start bawling like a baby! Where would her confidence in him be then? When she made motions to stand he was quick to help her up, an arm about her shoulders.

They shuffled about the room; from the four poster bed to the window seat where Tam had drawn back the curtains and thrown up the sash windows to let in light and air; from the window seat to the wash stand and back to the bed. He could not be certain until he had examined her properly, but from past experience he reckoned the baby would not be born for many hours yet, if at all today.

He waited while she coiled in pain from another contraction, her breathing ragged, and then quieted before he said gently,

"Mr. Blackwell wanted Sophie's ma to be buried with something belonging to the baby. I heard him say so to Mr. Dobbs. You remember Mr. Dobbs?" he prattled on, trying to keep Miranda calm, as much as himself. "He was my master and an apothecary and when called to it, a man-midwife. He delivered many babies in St. Jude's. I went with him many times. Mr. Blackwell said the shawl was something personal that would join mother to child. He didn't want her buried alone. He said she could use the shawl in Heaven. So he took it."

Miranda nodded, satisfied. "I am glad. He loved Miriam in spite of all her waywardness. He was a good father to her."

"Father? Then she wasn't your sister? She was Mr. Blackwell's *daughter*?"

Another contraction and Miranda shuddered and groaned and clung heavily to Tam.

"Apologies, ma'am. It's not my place to ask. It's just… If there is one thing I do remember clearly as if it was yesterday, it's that the two of you were so alike. But if Mr. Blackwell was her father… He was a good man, was Mr. Blackwell…"

"Yes, he was. As was your master—Dobbs? Dobbs found Sophie a wet nurse, assuring me the woman was not a gin-soaked doxy, when I had not the slightest idea at that time what a doxy was, least of that they drank gin." She laughed at the memory and Tam did too. "I had forgotten that until now." She smiled at Tam. "Your master was also a good man, Thomas."

Tam felt tears prick his lids and he cursed himself for acting the girl; some apothecary he would make! He cleared his throat and nodded.

"Yes. Yes, he was. And a fine apothecary. None better."

"Miriam and I grew up together and for the longest time we believed we were natural sisters. We were so similar," Miranda explained, smiling at a memory, "that we could pass for one another, and did upon occasion. So close. So alike. But such different temperaments… We realized in our teens that for us to be sisters meant my father or my mother had had an affair. A singularly foolish thought.

"I know it is disrespectful, and you may be shocked by a daughter's words, Thomas, but my mother is a cold-hearted unloving creature, and my father, if he'd had children out of wedlock, would certainly not have brought them home. And then, one day, Miriam confided in me that her father was Mr. Blackwell! Just like that, she told me. She had no knowledge of her mother, and Mr. Blackwell would not tell her, no matter how many times she pleaded with him. I would like to sit again, Thomas. And you must do what you must."

"Yes, ma'am, I must," Tam apologized, voice steady, though her revelations about Mr. Blackwell sent his mind spinning. "If you would lie down this end of the bed with your head on the pillows where I have them arranged, I will examine you to determine how far along the babe is and when your maid returns with my medicine cabinet I'll give you something for the pain. The physician—"

"*No.* No physician. 'Twas the physician who *killed* Miriam. If he had listened to your master… If Mr. Blackwell had not sent for a-a *painmerchant…*"

"He was obliged to; he thought it was the right thing to do. She was so weak… Even Mr. Dobbs had given up hope… You can't blame him for that. Two days of difficult labor—"

"But to cut into her the way he did… He *hacked* into her. He was bloody and brutal…" She lifted her head from the pillows and tried to look over her rounded belly at Tam. "Promise me, Thomas. No physician."

"I promise. But I will fetch one if your life or the babe's is in danger," Tam stated bluntly. "Not to do so would be a breach of my duty and I will not break the oath I have taken."

"He is not to cut into me. Not unless I am truly dead. *You* must make certain I am dead. Promise me."

"Yes, ma'am. I promise."

Miranda let her head drop back onto the pillow, satisfied, and stared up at the pleated canopy above her head, trying not to think about Tam between her open legs, though she could not stop the blush to her cheeks. But the next contraction, more powerful than the last, dissolved her modesty and she screamed out and cursed long and loud in French.

"That's the way, ma'am," Tam encouraged her. "Scream as loud as you please if it helps."

Miranda managed a half-hearted giggle between pants.

"I am sorry, Thomas. Do you speak French?"

"Well enough to know that what you just said would turn a dowager's ears puce, if that's what you're asking. Lord Halsey is an exceptional linguist and so I've managed to pick up a few choice French phrases."

"Lord Halsey…?"

Tam was quick to see this as an invitation to prattle on about his history and how he came to be Alec's valet, acutely aware how uncomfortable it must be for her with him in such intimate quarters, so he obliged her; anything to take her mind off the indelicacy of their present situation; anything to take his mind off the enormity of the task that was ahead of him.

When Janie came into the bedchamber it was to find Tam between her mistress's wide-open legs. But what made her almost lose her grip on his traveling apothecary case was not the shock of the sight that presented itself to her, which was a shock indeed, it was that her mistress and the young apothecary were on such familiar terms. As if it were the most natural thing in the world and they were conversing over a cup of tea and slices of bread and butter.

When Tam sat back, gently pulled a sheet up over her mistress's bare legs and went to the basin to scrub his hands, Janie deposited the traveling apothecary case, and followed him.

"Is everything as it should be, Mr. Fisher?" she whispered.

"Yes. But she is not far enough along to begin pushing hard. There's a ways to go yet."

Janie nodded, a glance over her shoulder at Miranda who moaned quietly amongst the pillows. She emptied the dirty water into a pail and replenished the porcelain patterned bowl with fresh water to soak a cloth for Miranda's forehead.

"I've had ale and a cold collation brought up for you. It's in the sittin' room. I thought you would prefer it there."

"Thank you, Miss, that was very thoughtful."

"It's Janie. I thought you should know," she said, unable to stop her face flaming, "there's a handsome gentleman sittin' in the window seat. Black hair and looks like one of them statues Mr. Talgarth has in a jotter he showed me once. Do you know him?"

"A Greek statue?" Tam grinned. "Yes. That would be his lordship. Lord Halsey. I'll give Mrs. Bourdon something to ease the pain and then I'll step out and see his lordship for a moment but return directly. Will you be all right left alone with your mistress?"

"A'course! I've had the lookin' after of her since—"

"No. No. I meant no offence, Janie. I just thought in the present circumstances—"

"Make up your potion and then go and eat, Mr. Fisher."

"Thomas. Thomas," Miranda called, thinking Tam about to leave the room when he disappeared from her line of sight. "I have another promise to ask of you..."

From the end of the bed, where he was rummaging in his apothecary cabinet, Tam looked up and nodded at Janie who was mopping Miranda's head with a damp cloth, and said, "He's listenin' to you, ma'am. He's makin' you up a potion to help you with the pain."

Miranda squeezed Janie's hand and smiled at her, thus including her in her request when she said to Tam, "No one is to know the true sex of the child. You must pronounce the baby a girl. It matters not if it is a boy, you must say it is a girl. I beg you. For the sake of the baby. It's what Mr. Bourdon would wish. Promise me, Thomas. Janie?"

Tam and Janie exchanged a worried look before both nodded in mute acceptance of a request both privately thought odd in the extreme. Yet Tam's further verbal acceptance and Janie's quick nod satisfied Miranda and she returned to staring up at the quilted canopy, tense with anticipation as to when the next contraction would seize her, praying the baby would come soon.

"Have you been present at a delivery before, Janie?" Tam asked.

"A'course I have! I was there for two of me Ma's lyin'-ins."

Janie put a tumbler of cordial beside the apothecary case, taking a look over Tam's shoulder, intrigued by its contents which were on display with the two little mahogany doors wide on their polished brass hinges. Two drawers were pulled out, both crammed with what she supposed were various medical instruments: Candles, a small china dish, a folded brass weights-and-measure scale, and several small porcelain ointment pots. Tam removed the false back to the case, revealing a secret compartment lined with small glass bottles of uniform shape and height. Small labels carefully written up and tied with string about the glass stopper of each bottle read Mandrake, Mithridate, Laudanum, and Theriac; but to Janie, who could not read or write, the writing held no meaning. It was at the liquid she stared —some bottles were filled with herbs steeped in liquid, one was of white and blue porcelain, another clear glass; all were marked with a word in big red letters: Poison. She recognized the shape of this word. Aunt Rumble kept a bottle with just such a word on it in the back of the flour cupboard in the pantry.

When Tam selected a particular bottle and carefully droppered a measured dose into the cordial and swilled the tumbler gently so the medicine dissolved, Janie could not contain her curiosity or her trepidation; medicinals made her uneasy.

"What are you mixin' in there, Mr. Fisher?"

"It's called mithridate. It will ease her pain."

Janie tried to sniff the tumbler. There was a mustardy smell about it. "What's in mithri—mithri—What's in it?"

Tam smiled at her tone; he didn't blame her for being wary. "Too many ingredients to list. Opium, myrrh, ginger, cinnamon, and such. It's standard fare for an apothecary to use it to help with pain. So don't worry yourself it will cause your mistress any harm."

Janie took the tumbler when held out to her but did not move from the end of the bed. "It won't make her sick, will it?"

"No. Just more restful," he said calmly, securing the poisons by fixing the false wooden partition back into place on the apothecary case. When Janie still did not move he added in a voice he hoped held a note of sternness,

"If you want to help me help your mistress through this labor, Janie, you must do as I tell you." And as if on cue, Miranda let out a great cry filled with pain and anguish and it sent Janie scurrying to her aid. *For God knows*, he said to himself as he closed the cabinet's mahogany doors, *I need all the help I can get.*

SEVENTEEN

JANIE WAS BUSY SCURRYING TO AND FRO BETWEEN BEDCHAMBER and kitchen, fulfilling errands for Tam. At one stage, two wide-eyed but head-down maids followed her carrying a large copper pot and fresh sheets. She worried about her mistress and the progress of her labor, and yet she was conscious of Lord Halsey watching her from the window seat. She even dared to steal a long sideways glance at him when he turned to the window at the noisy arrival of a carriage-and-six, its occupants alighting in the cobblestoned street below. He was the handsomest man she had ever seen, with his black wavy hair, olive skin and angular profile. Resplendent in velvet and lace, he was even more handsome than Mr. Talgarth, who left her tongue-tied and giddy when he came calling on her mistress.

Under the present trying circumstances, and because she knew she would blush rosily if his lordship dared to address her, she decided to get on with her errands as if the nobleman was not in the room. This tactic worked well until his lordship's valet materialized in the servant doorway. She was looking at her feet and not straight ahead and so collided with Mr. Hadrian Jeffries, upsetting not only the tray he was carrying but creasing the front of his immaculate frock coat.

Watching the maid and his valet jostle each other, the girl mumbling profuse apologies while an outraged but contained Jeffries brushed the creases from his frock coat, provided Alec with some much needed relief from the couple of fraught hours spent sitting still and silent in the window seat, listening to the cries and moans of a woman in the throes of childbirth emanating from the next room. He had hoped the physician would arrive soon. By the reckoning of his gold pocket watch, it was at least two hours, possibly longer, since Ketteridge had sent a message apologizing for being delayed; a small child with burns and an elderly patient who had slipped and broken his femur at the King's Bath.

Not many minutes after Ketteridge's message, a surprising note from Lady Rutherglen, delivered by one of the lodging's footmen, demanded of Alec that he give her immediate access to the Arch Apartment or she would have the local militia storm the rooms. Why she needed access was not stated; that she demanded access Alec found of great interest. His refusal of her demands, coupled with the continued presence of the bearlike footman at the entrance to the apartment, must have sent her ladyship on her way because he heard nothing further from her until Jeffries appeared in the servant doorway.

Jeffries repositioned a spindle-legged writing desk and matching ladder-back chair closer to the window seat and into the path of the fading afternoon light. He then produced paper, quill and ink, and a pair of Alec's gold-rimmed eyeglasses, which he arranged with exacting straight-line precision on the small escritoire. He lit a candelabra, set this on the desktop and with a bow to Alec, who watched all this with polite interest but said nothing, he left the sitting room to return not many minutes later with two kitchen boys at his heels, one carrying a tray laden with silver-domed dishes and the other with a silver coffee pot and service.

"Dinner, my lord," Jeffries intoned, not a facial muscle movement in recognition of the wails and moans of childbirth in the adjoining room.

Alec was silently impressed and a little unnerved. The fellow could very well have been in a stately dining room, such was his haughty demeanor.

"I took the liberty of bringing you your writing implements, my lord," Jeffries added needlessly when Alec glanced over at the arrangement of desk and chair. He handed Alec two sealed letters. "So that you might reply to these at your leisure. I thought, perhaps, you may have the time…"

Ah, so Jeffries had some idea of what was going on in the next room; he wasn't completely devoid of sentiment!

Alec recognized the handwriting and seal on one of the letters; it was from his godmother, the Dowager Duchess of Romney-St. Neots. The other was from Lady Rutherglen. His godmother's letter could wait. He slipped this into a frock coat pocket and broke the seal on the second and held it out until the script came into focus. Blotches of ink dotted the sentences, as if the note had been written in great haste, or great agitation. Alec was inclined to the latter explanation because of her ladyship's emotive prose; phrases such as *make a mockery of justice*, *cunning trickery*, and *outrageous abuse of trust* leapt out of the page, along with the predictable demand that Alec give her access to the apartment, and that he had no right to deny her entry to see *the creature for herself.*

An interesting choice of moniker, *creature*, for a young woman whom his uncle was convinced beyond doubt, and would defend to the hilt, was all sweetness and light, Alec pondered as he ate tidily of the slices of lamb set before him. Lady Rutherglen's ink dripped from an ill-tempered spleen, but there was an undercurrent of something else… fear? Yes, that was it. She *feared* the woman in the next room who, at that moment, let out such a wail that Jeffries gave a little jump on the spot.

Alec pondered if the nervous anticipation he felt at the impending birth was what men about to become fathers experienced when their wives were in labor. Would he ever have that opportunity with Selina? Were they ever destined to marry and have a family? He had not thought too deeply about that aspect of their marriage: Children. He was so set on getting the woman he loved to the altar and made his wife that all other considerations were secondary. Now, rather curiously, as an unwilling eavesdropper on a woman suffering the pains of labor to deliver up a new little life, he realized that he did want children of his own, very much.

He wished Tam would emerge from the bedchamber, if only to satisfy himself the boy was indeed bearing up under the demands of being responsible for the lives of a mother and her unborn. Too much responsibility for one so young, in Alec's opinion, regardless of the experience Tam had gathered as an apothecary's apprentice. He was still that, an apprentice, and yet to attain the dizzying heights of being admitted to the Worshipful Company of Apothecaries. Whatever his uncle's staunch belief in the boy's ability to handle himself in dangerous and emotionally draining affairs, particularly deadly affairs of which childbirth most definitely was one, Alec had no wish to see Tam's career over before it had started should the birth not produce a happy outcome.

"Sir? My lord?"

It was Tam. He closed the bedchamber door but did not shut it, and wiped his flushed face and then his hands with a damp towel which he then tossed aside. He was disheveled, damp red curls stuck to his scalp, crumpled white shirt pushed up over his elbows and wet with perspiration. He licked his dry lips and sighed, looking about the room, as if for something in particular. His eyes widened at the tray on the sideboard holding a jug and tankard, and it was Alec up off the sofa, and not Jeffries, who stepped forward and poured him out an ale and handed it to him. But before either could speak, the valet said, in answer to Alec's earlier comment,

"If you have finished, my lord, shall I clear away the dinner things? And I do assure your lordship that I prefer to remain, should you need my assistance in the event anything untoward occurs. I am of more use to your lordship here than elsewhere."

The stress on the word *untoward* did not go unnoticed by Alec or Tam, but as Tam was the only one facing the valet, he was the one to see Jeffries' eyebrows raise and his mouth pull down to add further emphasis to the insinuation Tam was not wholly competent in the situation in which he now found himself. But Tam was too tired and too involved in the event unfolding in the next room to be bothered with a petty squabble with, when all was said and done, a footman elevated temporarily above his station. Still, he could not let Jeffries get away with such boldness so he threw Hadrian mightier-than-thou

Jeffries a look of complete disdain, a look Alec caught and also chose to ignore, saying over his shoulder to Jeffries,

"Be good enough to clear away my plate, pour me out a coffee, and take yourself off for half an hour or so while I speak with Mr. Fisher in private. Kick your heels with Mr. Halsey. I would like to know how he is faring and if he has anything to report from the other side of that door. Now, Tam," he said, taking from Jeffries a coffee cup on its saucer, "Mrs. Bourdon's maid has left you a cold collation. I assume that's who she is, though she seemed to go out of her way to avoid looking at me, as if I had two heads and would frighten her. Are you all right? Is there anything I can do for you?"

Tam shook his head. "No, sir. That is, I am all right. There is nothing anyone can do. Nature will take its course and so we wait. By my reckoning it won't be long now."

Alec noted with concern the tiredness in the boy's eyes and the grim line to his mouth.

"I am sorry the physician hasn't come sooner to relieve you."

"As to that, sir, I—"

He stopped abruptly, realizing Jeffries was still in the room, so drank down his ale, suddenly very thirsty indeed, an eye on his replacement who, in his opinion, lingered far too long over stacking the remnants of his master's dinner onto a tray, before fussing unnecessarily with the coffee pot on its little stand, picking it up and setting it down as if it were necessary to do so to see if the candle in the warmer remained alight.

As Jeffries finally closed the door, Tam lifted the domed silver cover off the plate, a glance at Alec who waved at him to eat, and peered at the arrangement of slices of cold roast beef, carrots and potato, a fist of bread and the wedge of cheese, and his empty stomach growled in response. Yet inexplicably, he did not feel the need to eat. Still, he knew he had to fortify himself for a labor that could go on all night. He forked a slice of roast beef.

"Mrs. Bourdon will not have a physician, sir. She made me promise. But I had her agree that if things got bad, if complications arose, if her life or the babe's were in any danger, then I would fetch a physician in to help her. I can't break my promise."

"Of course not, but she's placed a tremendous burden on you."

"She's scared out of her wits, sir. And rightly so. She witnessed her cousin die in childbirth in the most horrific of circumstances; we both did. The physician hacked the baby from her belly; it saved the child but killed the mother. The thing of it is, sir, the girl wasn't dead, near death but not dead, when he butchered her."

Alec blanched. "Good God. How horrifying… But… Surely Mrs. Bourdon should be reassured that won't happen to her, given this is her second lying-in?"

Tam swallowed hard, wanting badly to confess all to his master yet hesitating to do so because it would be a breach of trust. But he needed to confide in his lordship; he could think of no one else who would be more understanding to his plight and to hers, except perhaps Mr. Halsey. And what if something did go wrong with the birth? It had been her cousin Miriam's first child and it had killed her; it could happen to Miranda Bourdon. But he would not let anyone do to her what had been done to her cousin, under any circumstances. He needed Alec to realize that, to support her decision and his.

One look into Alec's eyes full of worried concern and the accompanying understanding smile and everything came tumbling forth: Cousin Miriam's difficult labor—all thirty exhausting hours, with Dobbs unable to turn the baby from the breech position; that she was only fifteen years old, as was Miranda; the girls so alike in countenance that it was uncanny. They were runaways and Mr. Blackwell had given them sanctuary; the heartbreaking decision the old vicar had been forced to make to choose between dying mother and child; that a physician had cut open the dying girl in the hopes of saving the baby; that he had never witnessed anything so horrifying in his life and never hoped to again; how he had wondered and worried what had happened to Miranda and the baby, and to save his sanity Mr. Dobbs had told him he must put the whole episode out of his mind as if it had never happened. And then Mrs. Bourdon had been thrust back into his life, and revealed to him that her cousin Miriam was the Reverend Blackwell's natural daughter.

"...So you see, sir, it's no wonder Mrs. Bourdon is scared out of her wits, this being her first babe."

Alec did not answer immediately. He could not. He was still trying to absorb everything Tam had told him. It was as if he had just woken from a nightmare, and in a mental fog was recalling details of the bad dream without really wanting to. He picked up his coffee cup, drinking down the last of the coffee without realizing it was cold and nodded distractedly, a glance over Tam's shoulder at the bedchamber door.

"The poor woman has every reason to be terrified... Her cousin, she confided, was Blackwell's *natural* daughter? And Mrs. Bourdon and her cousin—Miriam? Mrs. Bourdon and Miriam were so similar in appearance they could be mistaken one for the other?"

"Yes, sir. Mrs. Bourdon said that when they were growing up, sometimes Miriam would pretend to be her, just to make mischief." He smiled crookedly. "Sounds as if Miriam was a right wild thing."

"An understatement. The girl was pregnant at fourteen."

"Mr. Fisher! Mr. *Fisher*!"

It was Janie, calling from the bedchamber. She appeared at the door in a rush, hands bunched in her petticoats, but seeing Alec, she dropped into a curtsy and lowered her eyes. "Beggin' your lordship's pardon." She glanced up at Tam. "I think the babe's almost here. She's askin' for ye. You'd best come quickly." And disappeared back into the room on Tam's nod.

"Sir," said Tam, immediately on his feet but staying his ground. "Mrs. Bourdon made one last request concerning the babe. She wants me to say it's a girl, whatever its sex."

"How curious... But if it makes her comfortable and less fearful, there can be no harm in it. She could very well give birth to a daughter. Now go. Mr. Halsey and I, and indeed Mrs. Bourdon, we have every faith in your abilities." He smiled. "I know you'll do splendidly."

Tam returned Alec's smile, feeling more confident about the task ahead of him, made a quaint little bow and was gone into the bedchamber just as Hadrian Jeffries re-entered the sitting room.

Alec wrote three short notes of invitation, one each to Sir Charles

Weir, Lord George Stanton, and Lady Rutherglen, requesting the pleasure of their company in the drawing room of Barr's of Trim Street at their earliest convenience, promising them they would have the opportunity to meet a ghost.

"Which should see them here with all speed," he said with satisfaction as he folded in half a fourth sheet of paper and ran his thumbnail along the fold to give it a clean crisp line, much to the approval and admiration of Jeffries.

He handed his valet three notes and kept the fourth back; it was addressed to Talgarth Vesey.

"See these are delivered at once. Then inform Barr I shall require exclusive use of his drawing room. I want my uncle to be present also..." When the valet stood riveted, listening in pale-faced terror to the screams and grunts and loud encouraging chants of *push* coming from the bedchamber, Alec dared to grin and slap the young man's rigid back. "Terrifying, isn't it? But necessary to bring a baby into this world."

"Necessary? Are you certain? It sounds positively frightening!"

The pronouncement came, not from Hadrian Jeffries, but from the servant door, and it broke the spell on the valet who could not leave the sitting room fast enough, though his exit was temporarily blocked. He caught a fleeting glimpse of a halo of mussed apricot-colored curls and the glint from a swinging diamond drop earring before the servant door was thrown wide, and he could make good his escape without a glance at the majestic woman who swept into the room on the pronouncement.

Selina took one look at Alec by the fireplace and her dark eyes softened.

The two hours of torment, of being bumped about on a wet and rutted country road, confined in a carriage with her somnambulist-like brother, her long-suffering lady's maid, and a precocious chattering child of four who hardly drew breath and never sat still, was forgotten. As was her resolve to be strong-willed enough to resist her need of him. One welcoming smile and she melted.

She stripped off her kid gloves and tossed them on the window seat, a curious glance at the bunch of wilted flowers, and did her best to appear unruffled. "You stand there as if it's the most natural thing in the world."

This made Alec laugh, and he drew her to him. "Well, childbirth is natural, is it not? I am very pleased to see you safe here, if a little tired from your ordeal?"

She returned his kiss and pouted. "Childbirth is natural, yes. But I meant you, you here in this room listening to that and remaining composed. And yes, it was an ordeal, but I had you to look forward to."

He kissed her again and touched his forehead to hers. "Oh, I won't be so cool and I'll be far from composed when it's you having our child, rest assured. And it's a façade. Inside I am as wobbly as a frumenty. What is it?" he asked when she pulled out of his arms, a knot of pain between her brows.

"When your uncle told me it was Miranda giving birth, you could have knocked me over with a feather!" she said, ignoring the restriction in her throat at his gentle pronouncement.

She had so wanted to have his child, and to confide in him she had miscarried their baby in Paris. But she did not know with absolute certainty the child was his, because just before he had shot himself in the head, her violent husband, George Jamison-Lewis, a favored member of Polite Society and nephew of a duke, had raped her, as he had done throughout their six year marriage. And so she had not mourned the loss of her unformed child, as she had not mourned the time she had fallen pregnant by Cleveley only to miscarry that baby too. But the miscarriage in Paris had affected her deeply, because the baby might have belonged to Alec, and because it was the opinion of the Parisian physician who attended her that the miscarriage had left her barren.

And so the cries of a woman in the throes of childbirth coming from the other side of the bedchamber door only served to underscore the heartbreaking reality of her predicament. The Duke of Cleveley had rightly pointed out, gently but no less bluntly, that if there was no hope of her providing the Marquess Halsey with a son and heir, then she did not have the right to give him false hope by marrying him.

"There's a veritable crowd gathered on the other side of that door," she told him calmly, stopping herself from falling into a pit of despair and pointing to the entrance door where the mountainous footman stood guard in the passageway. Talking was better than ruminating on what might have been. "Barr has given up on trying to get them to disperse. Footmen are now bringing old ladies chairs and cups of tea and gentlemen tankards of ale. Of course your uncle remains master of ceremonies. He and his walking stick are in charge and he is enjoying himself hugely! I remarked that wielding such control must surely conflict with his republican principles, to which he replied *begone, witch*! And so here I am—having run the gauntlet of the kitchen staff—scullery maids, cook, and a startled pot-scrubber, who has possibly never before seen a lady in a kitchen or scuttling up the servant stairs." She smiled with self-satisfaction. "And as I've never been in a lodging house kitchen, that makes two of us. Such a novel experience!" When Alec grinned and shook his head, she smiled. "Your irascible republican relative has also become fast friends with Bear Brown—"

"Bear Brown?"

"You can't have failed to notice the bear-sized footman in the doorway?" she replied rhetorically. "Bear because he is the size of a bear and Brown because that's his surname. Quaint. He's been in Cleveley's household ever since I can remember. If memory serves me correctly, the Duke rescued him from a traveling circus when he was but a child, but a very oversized child."

"I hope Bear Brown told my uncle so. It may soften his intractable opinion of the Duke."

"Does it soften yours?" she asked too quickly, and instantly bit down on her lower lip, coloring up at her impetuousness.

"Selina... *Dear heart*..."

A frightful wail, much louder than previous cries of painful childbirth exertion made them both look to the bedchamber door in expectation, but when the door remained firmly closed and there was a period of quiet with only the sound of voices in conversation, Selina blurted out,

"It's not Talgarth's!"

"I know that."

"Oh? Then you know who the father is?"

"I believe I may, but I am not at liberty to say. Miranda must tell us that herself."

"Miranda? So you have met her?"

Alec grinned at her note of feminine jealousy and the unfathomable fact that even beautiful women suffered from uncertainty. He gently pulled her into his embrace. "I do love you, despite your foolishness. No. I have not met Mrs. Bourdon. That delight still awaits me. Tell me about your journey from Philip St. Norton. Did everyone behave as they ought, or were you sorely tried by the company and the carriage ride?"

"Both, and I was sorely tried *because* everyone behaved as they ought."

Alec drew her to sit in the window seat with him, her hand in his, and she told him about the journey to Bath; he was at pains to look grave and be sympathetic of her loathing for cavorting about the countryside in a carriage.

"Did you reunite Talgarth and Nico?"

"If you mean did I set my brother down in Milsom Street before coming here? No. I ordered him to remain in the drawing room downstairs to keep an eye on Sophie while Evans dealt with bags, rooms, and a lodging house whose servants seem incapable of functioning because upstairs a woman is in labor! I need him here until Sophie can be returned to her mother. Aside from Evans, Tal is the only one capable of keeping that child occupied. And he does so with such languid ease that it makes me feel completely ineffectual. I don't see what there is to laugh at in that!" she said squeezing his hand a little too tightly when he chuckled. "Five minutes cooped up with an overactive child is five minutes too long in my reckoning book; and I had *two hours* of her restlessness and chatter. If I did not know her for human, I would say she is a mechanical clock fashioned as a doll, with her springs wound so tight she ticks along at time-and-a-half!" She shook her fair red hair at his cluck of sympathy, saying on a sigh, "So very different to her mother, who is the most biddable, sweet creature living."

"Selina, there is something I want to ask you about Sophie..."

"My lady! The baby! She's been snatched away by a-a *monster*."

Alec and Selina were instantly up off the window seat, Selina glancing at the bedchamber door, but as that remained closed, the moans, cries and words of encouragement ongoing, she turned to the servant door where Evans swayed on the threshold as if glued to the floorboards, one thin hand twisted up in her plain linen petticoats, the other holding fast to the door jab; her face white and fearful.

"Evans? *Monster*? Don't be absurd!" Selina said dismissively, and more harshly than she intended because she was tired and anxious about mother and child in the bedchamber. "The journey has worn you thin. I shall come and keep Mr. Vesey company and you will lie down for a few moments and feel better directly."

"No! No, my lady! I cannot. Miss Sophie! Miss Sophie's been snatched away by a pockfretten *devil*."

"Snatched? What can you mean, Mary?" Selina demanded, alarmed. "Who snatched her? Where is she?"

Evans stared at Selina, stricken. "I thought Mr. Vesey was keeping watch over her..."

"He's in the drawing room where I left him, isn't he?" Selina asked.

Evans nodded. "Yes, my lady. Asleep."

"How like Tal!" Selina stated, annoyed. "Sophie probably wandered off to find someone else to play with. I'm sure the hotel servants will find her—"

"Oh no, my lady," Evans replied with uncharacteristic firmness. "They won't be able to do that."

"Why ever not?"

"Because she's been taken."

"First I am told by a Miss Musgrave there is a ghost in this establishment and now, you, Evans, the most sensible woman I have ever known, declare there is a monster—or is he a devil? Which is it? Perhaps this creature is both? Poor Mr. Barr. Soon he will have no clientele to bow and scrape to!"

Evans burst into tears and covered her face.

"Don't be so harsh on her. She's had a shock," Alec murmured at

Selina's ear, which sent color flooding into her cheeks because he had misinterpreted cajolery for criticism, and after all, Evans was *her* lady's maid.

"Come in, Evans," Alec said calmly. "Mrs. Jamison-Lewis was just seeing to tea, and you will tell me in your own good time what happened to Miss Sophie."

He had picked up on the maid's use of the word *pockfretten* and his pulse slowed, for he had a fair notion who had taken the little girl. What he needed to ascertain was the manner in which she had been taken, though he was confident his intuition would not fail him.

Thus he was calmer than Selina would have supposed at Evans' pronouncement. And so when he beckoned her lady's maid forward and expected her to fetch the tea, Selina just stood there, mouth agape. First he had insulted her as to her conduct with her own maid and now he expected her to disappear to the kitchen. Yet, when Alec smiled at her, she could not refuse him. She swept out of the room and down the stairs in her silk mules, cursing handsome men in general, one in particular, and muttering to herself that the noise, heat and smells of a kitchen were preferable to listening to the painful exertions of a woman in labor. At least she would be spared such a fate, she thought with satisfaction. But satisfaction turned to self-pity and misery soon followed.

Alec had Evans sit on a wingchair and pressed his clean linen handkerchief into her stiff hands.

"Thank you, my lord."

"Tell me what happened to Sophie and then I will be able to help."

"Shouldn't—Shouldn't someone go after him, my lord? Find out where's he's taken her?"

"Yes. We will do that. But first tell me what happened."

Evans nodded, feeling less apprehensive at Alec's quiet but firm tone.

"Yes, my lord. I was away from the room for just on a quarter of an hour," she explained, twisting the handkerchief between her fingers. "One of the chambermaids had offered to fetch a fresh chemise, gown, and stockings, and if she was able, a woolen cloak, for

Miss Sophie; her sister has a little girl the same age and is a maid in a house one street across. And so I left the little one… I left her… Apologies, my lord, I am… The shock of seeing that man in her company…"

"You said he is pockfretten. Is that why you called him a monster? Because his face is ravaged with smallpox scars?"

Evans nodded. She looked up at Alec with remorse. "I should not have called him a monster or a devil. That was uncharitable. But he is a frightening sight."

"Perhaps you were shocked more by his appearance than seeing Sophie in his company…?"

Evans pondered this a moment and her eyes widened, and she was even more repentant. "Yes… Yes! That is true, my lord. For when I came into the drawing room, Miss Sophie and he were seated on the carpet before the fireplace, chattering away together in French as if it was the most natural thing in the world!" She shuddered. "He is so hideously scarred that it is a wonder a grown person would talk to him, least of all a little girl."

"*Molyneux*!" Selina declared from the doorway. At the bottom of the stairs she had encountered a maidservant, ordered her to fetch tea and fled back up to the room, intent on not missing a word of Alec's interrogation. "Molyneux has Sophie! It has to be him because who else has—"

"Yes, Robert Molyneux, the Duke of Cleveley's valet. Thank you, Mrs. Jamison-Lewis," Alec interrupted her with a knowing wink and then turned to Evans and said, "That Sophie was prattling on with Molyneux, and they were easy in each other's company, would suggest she was not at all frightened of him, would you not agree?"

"Yes, my lord," Evans said with a sigh of relief. She glanced at her mistress and then back at Alec, feeling foolish for her earlier outburst. "Mrs. Jamison-Lewis is in the right. I am worn thin. I did not think… Miss Sophie was not frightened of him; of his appearance or his behavior."

"Please think carefully, Evans, and then answer me this: Was Sophie taken by Molyneux or did she go with him willingly? There is a difference…"

"To be perfectly truthful, my lord, I thought this Mr. Molyneux was acting a bit too familiar with the child, trying to win her trust so he could snatch her. Thinking back on it, and now that I know that you both know who he is and that he is in the employ of the Duke of Cleveley, it does seem the little one and Mr. Molyneux were known to one another."

"That's nonsense, Evans!" Selina said from the window seat. "First you accuse poor Molyneux of being a monster, then too familiar with the child, and now you think he is the child's best friend. Which is it? Truly, Mary, you do need a good night's sleep."

"And she not the only one," Alec murmured, and said audibly, "My dear Mrs. Jamison-Lewis—"

"Oh do stop calling me by that hateful name, Alec!" Selina complained with a tired sigh. "Evans is my lady's maid, not my mother!" She met his steady gaze openly. "Truth be told, Evans knows everything there is to know about me, and more than is good for her about *us*."

"It only takes a special license, a vicar and you, my love, for me to expunge that name," Alec said quietly, and mentally sighed when Selina would not hold his gaze, the only signs of her inner turmoil, her stubbornly clenched jaw and the way in which she gently tugged on the diamond drop earring.

"How could they be known to one another?" Selina demanded, curiosity overcoming stubbornness. "Molyneux is valet to a Duke and Sophie is a four-year-old child who has lived her entire life on a farm in the depths of the country."

"It is not only plausible but highly probable if you substitute the Duke for his valet in the equation," Alec explained. "Molyneux as valet to Cleveley is an extension of his master. And thus all he does, he does in the Duke's name."

"By that logic, it is the Duke who took Sophie from the drawing room. It is the Duke who knows Sophie and she is known to him?"

"Yes."

"But… No! That is not possible!"

"It is very possible. You said yourself Sophie has lived her entire life on a farm. Who owns that farm?" Alec argued. "And you told me that the Duke's pile of country stone is atop a hill, and that from one of the windows where he keeps a telescope, the farm, of which he made you tenant for life, is perfectly visible."

Selina's mouth dropped open with incredulity. Were the sounds emanating from the next room affecting good sense? "Are you suggesting Cleveley spent his time *spying* on the farm?"

"Not spying as such, but he certainly kept a watchful eye."

"Why?"

"Why position the telescope where he has the perfect view of the farm if not to watch?"

"I should not have told you!"

Alec frowned, not understanding her meaning until he happened to glance at Evans, whose face had ignited with color, and who was regarding Selina with sympathetic understanding. She had told her lady's maid everything, Alec thought with a wry smile.

"This has nothing to do with His Grace's interest in you," he said gently, adding with an apologetic smile, "It was not you he was watching over. Though I am very sure he was pleased to have you there."

"Are you saying Cleveley's interest is in *Sophie*?"

Alec was about to reply when Evans filled the mutinous pause between the couple, "Yes, my lady, because, now I think on it, there can only be one explanation: The Duke is that little girl's father."

The quiet exploded with Selina's laugh of incredulity. She so far forget herself as to fall back amongst the cushions of the window seat, but clamped a hand to her mouth to stop a fit of the giggles: It was one thing to laugh at the statement itself, but to laugh in company at a servant was insupportable.

"Please continue, Evans," Alec said smoothly.

Evans sat up taller at Alec's polite enquiry and explained herself.

"At the time I disregarded Miss Sophie's prattle because she is only four years old. She told me on more than one occasion she would soon see Papa Bumblebee. I presumed he was her imaginary playfellow as only children are wont to have. She told me when I bathed her at the inn, again in the carriage, and when I set her down before the fire in the drawing room downstairs." She glanced at the now silent Selina, but said to Alec, "When Mr. Molyneux took her away in his arms, I followed him into the foyer, pleading with him to leave her be, but in a mild-mannered way because I did not want to cause the child distress. But she was far from upset! She waved at me and declared happily that she was off to see Papa Bumblebee. My French is reasonable but not exacting, my lord, and I know you to be an exceptional linguist so you can tell me if I have translated correctly *Père Bourdon*—that is Papa Bumblebee in English, is it not?"

"*Père Bourdon*?" Selina remained incredulous. "Evans? How could you possibly deduce that the Duke is this Papa Bumblebee from such a circumstance? Just because the child's name is Bourdon? It is a mere coincidence that the French word for bumblebee is Bourdon, and that Miranda and her daughter bear that surname."

"I think not."

Selina blinked at Alec's statement, and with tongue firmly planted in cheek replied,

"So you believe Miranda Bourdon, a young woman of no family and connections, who has a bastard child whose father may or may not be George Stanton, and who is yet to turn twenty is Mother Bumblebee, while Cleveley, this country's premier statesman, a direct descendant of William the Conqueror, oh! and a duke, not to mention being twice Miranda's age, is this Papa Bumblebee; and that little Sophie, whom the Duke has accepted as his child… She is their little bumblebee?" Selina squirmed on the window seat and squared her shoulders. "Fanciful nonsense!"

"And so it will remain if you continue to view the matter emotively and with the prejudice of your social standing, and not with the objectivity it deserves," Alec counseled, and was not surprised when Selina's face flushed with heat and she put up her chin to be so criticized. He pulled at the lace at his wrists and said matter-of-factly, "My uncle suffers from the same prejudice and lack of objectivity where the Duke is concerned, but for very different reasons. He, like you, views the Duke's character as one does a shadow puppet—flat and black. There are no shades of gray and certainly no dimension to his being. To you he is this elder statesman upon a pedestal, and you are a little in awe of him. He can do no wrong in your eyes. Oh, his armor is chinked because he once over-stepped the boundaries of propriety with you, but you forgive him that because deep down you know him to be a good and decent man."

When Selina made no comment, but her shoulders eased, he continued.

"My uncle, however, is a humanist, and believes that not everything should be left to the will of God. And because Cleveley is a duke and a descendant of kings, he thinks he should get down off his pedestal and use his social position and political power for the good of mankind; to make this world in which we live a better place. It is precisely because the Duke puts his country's welfare and its standing in the world first and foremost, all other personal and social considerations aside, that my uncle has branded Cleveley a heartless, conscienceless politician of the worst kind."

"And you? How do you see His Grace of Cleveley?"

Alec smiled crookedly. "A sennight ago I would have agreed with my uncle. I am not in accord with many of the Duke's tenets, but as a diplomat I understand why he has doggedly pursued his policies to ensure the security and prosperity of the kingdom. His conduct towards you should surely have cemented my low opinion of his character…"

"So is the Duke your uncle's black or my white?"

Alec laughed and shook his head. "Darling, he is neither, and that is what I am trying to tell you, as Olivia tried to tell me at the opera. Cleveley is defined by his class and status, but he is also a man, and like all men, he has shades of gray. He possibly did not know this himself for many years, and then something happened that changed him, or at least opened his eyes to the possibility that his life could be very different from the one he was then leading. And thus we have arrived at where we are on this day of all days."

Selina frowned. "What happened? What opened his eyes? Not the murder of that poor vicar? Do you still believe he had any part in that?"

"No. That is, the death of the Reverend Blackwell was not the catalyst that changed Cleveley's life, but," Alec added with an enigmatic smile, "the good vicar did help the Duke on his present path. It was you. You opened his eyes to possibility."

"Me?" Selina was nonplussed. "How so?"

There was no hiding the note of sadness in his deep voice.

"He told you so himself. And then you told me. You gave him *hope...*"

There was a long silence between them. So long that Evans felt an intruder and bowed her head to look at her hands, for she knew precisely to what Alec was alluding. So did Selina, but she was not strong enough to nudge that old wound, for that would lead to real pain and heartache and so she said with a frown,

"But there is more to this than you're telling me, particularly about the death of Reverend Blackwell."

"Yes. I have not told you everything," Alec said without apology. "I intend to offer a full explanation, and be able to reveal who was responsible for Blackwell's murder once I have had a word with Mrs. Bourdon, and the *Dramatis Personae* have assembled in Barr's drawing room. I am confident that my notes of invitation have been accepted and they are gathering as we speak."

The prospect of a reveal was enough to divert Selina from her dark thoughts and her eyes shone as she hopped off the window seat and shook out her crumpled petticoats. "How marvelous! I trust your uncle and I have seats at this select gathering, or are only those accused permitted entry to the drawing room?"

Alec made her a sweeping bow. "You shall have a front row seat, my lady."

"Wonderful! But you have not convinced me that Cleveley, of all the noblemen in this kingdom, would ever allow himself to be called by such a ludicrous pet name as Papa Bumblebee!"

"Won't I?" Alec replied, rising to her challenge. "You may not have noticed—Why would you—but I am sure Evans has done so, and it is something servants in great households pride themselves on, and that is their livery. The Cleveley livery has the unusually extravagant and quite unique addition to its frock coat of an engraved bumblebee on its silver buttons. Nor is it fanciful for persons to hide behind a *nom de guerre* if they do not wish to be found, or," he added with a rueful smile, "use a pet name as a term of endearment with a loved one."

Selina's dark eyes widened with new knowledge, but then she frowned and said bluntly, "But the Duke cannot be Sophie's father! It is a mathematical impossibility. The timing is all wrong because if you calculate the date of conception plus the four years since her birth and the fact that Cleveley and I were—"

"Damn your mathematical mind, my darling," Alec interrupted and drew her to him to kiss her forehead. "Have you noticed how quiet it is of a sudden…?"

And then, as if on cue, the quiet was shattered by the welcoming and joyous sound of a baby's first wail: A loud, long and strong protest at being violently pushed forth into the world from the warmth and security of its mother's womb. It set Alec's heart racing and he looked to the bedchamber door in expectation, as did Selina who stood beside him and took hold of his hand. Alec caught up their entwined fingers and kissed the back of her hand. The baby's hearty cries drew Evans to stand behind her mistress, gaze riveted to the door, all three with smiles of expectation and celebration.

The loud and lusty cries of a healthy newborn continued, and so did the waiting. And just as all three occupants of the sitting room began to lose their smiles and feel the beats of their hearts increase with anxiety, the bedchamber door flung open to bang against the wallpapered wall.

It was Tam on the threshold, exhausted and utterly relieved that both mother and baby had survived the ordeal of childbirth. He was full of pride that he had delivered a healthy newborn alone, without the need of a physician, and he beamed from ear to ear. He eagerly took the hand of congratulation Alec held out to him.

"Sir! It's a healthy—"

EIGHTEEN

"I APOLOGIZE FOR HER ILL-TEMPER," ALEC SAID TO TAM AS HE was ushered into the bedchamber. "Her disappointment at being denied access to Mrs. Bourdon is understandable. But threatening to have you drawn and quartered..." He chuckled and let the sentence hang.

"It's fine, sir," Tam said good-naturedly, for nothing could spoil this of all days. "I'm surprised Mrs. Jamison-Lewis would be eager to see a newborn. Most females in her sad predicament convince themselves for a time they don't care for 'em, and usually avoid mothers and infants, particularly new mothers with newborns. I guess anger's her way of dealin' with the loss."

Alec pulled up. "I beg your pardon? Loss?"

Tam mentally cursed himself for his free and easy tongue, pretended deafness and continued across the room to the foot of the four-poster bed. He blamed a combination of tiredness and exhilaration for letting down his guard. The frown of incomprehension on his master's face was enough to tell him that Mrs. Jamison-Lewis had not confided in his lordship about her miscarriage in Paris. Tam had found out from a loose-tongued apothecary's lackey who had delivered a tonic to her apartment on the Rue St. Honoré at the same hour Tam was delivering his master a set of new clothes.

"If you don't need me, Mr. Fisher, I'll fetch up some tea and slices of bread and butter for the mistress," Janie said brightly, a curtsy to both but eyes remaining on Tam, for whom she had newfound respect and admiration after watching him deliver Mrs. Bourdon's healthy baby. "And I'll have a hot brick fetched for the bed. Will you be wantin' some tea, too?"

"Thank you, Janie," said Tam, grateful for the interruption. "Coffee for his lordship—"

"—and brandy," Alec said, come to stand beside Tam at the undraped end of the four-poster bed, the curtain drawn along the left side to stop the draft from the open window.

He found the bedchamber surprisingly airy, given the cloistered drama of previous hours. The curtains were tied back on the night sky and a window pushed up to allow in fresh air. A fire crackled in the grate, and whatever the detritus of birth, it had been removed, possibly to the small adjoining servant bedchamber. A candelabra on the bedside table cast a warm yellow glow across the bedcovers and illuminated mother and newborn, who were tucked up amongst down pillows.

"You have done a wondrous thing today, Mr. Fisher," Alec said quietly, inexplicably filled with pride as he gazed upon mother and newborn.

"Thank you, my lord." Tam beamed, eyes bright with a film of happy tears. He stood at Alec's shoulder and he too was looking down the bed at Miranda and her baby. "He's a fine little man."

"A boy? How splendid! His father will be doubly pleased with your efforts, and hers. It may get you a knighthood…"

"Lord Halsey?"

It was Miranda and she forced herself awake from a contented doze. She was utterly exhausted, and like Tam, could not help her smile. Her cheeks were flushed and her long black hair fell about her shoulders in messy disarray. Still, despite her painful and hard-fought exertions, she was radiant, and quite possibly the loveliest female Alec had ever seen. It was a limpid beauty and when she smiled, he saw that it also came from within. Not surprising then that his uncle was her fierce champion and Talgarth felt compelled to immortalize her in paints. Yet, for all her beauty, Alec was not so enamored, for he preferred females—one female in particular—with more fire and ice, and there was something about the love of his life's pale golden-red hair that warmed his blood… What did Tam mean by *loss*? What loss?

Alec bowed to Miranda, face suitably blank of his thoughts. "Congratulations on the birth of a son, Your Grace."

"Is he not the most perfect baby in all creation?"

"His father will certainly agree with you," Alec replied with a smile at a mother's singular adoration. He drew up a chair but did not sit upon it. He had seen Tam sway at his salutation and look at him with wide eyes of dismay, and so he gently pushed the chair under the boy's legs and with a hand to his shoulder pressed him down. "Sit before you pass out, my boy."

Tired he might be, but it wasn't that which had Tam reeling. He was in shock. He wondered if exhaustion had affected his hearing because he was sure his master had greeted Mrs. Bourdon with a salutation reserved for those of ducal rank. He stared up at Alec, who winked at him, and then at Miranda, who was smiling upon her sleeping infant, oblivious to all. He gripped the padded seat hard. "Sir, is she—"

"—a duchess? Yes. You have successfully delivered the Duchess a son, heir to the Cleveley dukedom."

"*Oh my God.*"

Alec grinned. "I don't believe even His Grace thinks of himself as God, despite my uncle's low opinion of the Duke's overbearing hubris. Enjoy the moment. You have certainly earned it. Have you thought of names for his little lordship?" he enquired politely of Miranda.

"I was in two minds for a very long while. Had he been a girl she was to be named after Mr. Bourdon's Grandmamma, but being a boy…" She sighed contentedly and was suddenly distracted when her infant son turned ever so slightly toward the warmth of her skin. She played with his tiny fingers. "But I have settled on two names I like very well indeed. Mr. Bourdon may care to choose a third and fourth, if it is necessary for such a little one to have a string."

"Mr. Bourdon...?" Alec enquired letting the sentence hang, knowing full well she was referring to the Duke of Cleveley, and to test the theory he had explained to his doubting Selina.

"Oh, my husband and I have never stood on ceremony with each other," Miranda replied, understanding Alec's inference. "Even before we were married not quite a twelvemonth ago, I called him Mr. Bourdon. It was a schoolroom name that stuck. There is a beehive on the Cleveley coat of arms," she explained, "and a bumblebee on the livery buttons. Mr. Bourdon says bees are a symbol of industry and perseverance, which suits him very well, don't you agree?"

"Yes. *Aut viam inveniam aut faciam*: I will either find a way or make one," Alec stated, adding, because Miranda was looking at him with polite enquiry, "The motto on the Cleveley coat of arms, Your Grace. And if I may be so bold, very apt for the Duke where you are concerned."

Miranda tilted her head, not fully comprehending his meaning and politely said, "Years ago, Mr. Bourdon gave me a bumblebee button as a token of his perseverance that we would one day marry."

"On one of his visits to hear you play the pianoforte perhaps? He turned the pages of music for you."

"Yes. Yes, he did! Thomas told me how clever you are." A sudden thought made her brows contract, but only for a moment and instinctively she held her baby son a little closer. "Miriam laughed when I confided in her my feelings for my M'sieur Bumblebee. I suspect she told George, too; she confided everything in George. She said Mr. Bourdon's only interest in me was to-to lift my-my petticoats..." Miranda swallowed and was suddenly bashful at such revelations. "He was never like that. Not once while I was in the schoolroom did he-he make an improper suggestion or-or remark. Why! Our first kiss was on our wedding day."

"I can readily believe that, Your Grace," Alec agreed, adding with a touch of irony, thinking of Selina, "As a husband I am sure he has been the very model of noble rectitude."

"He is. Thank you. I knew you would understand. Lord Halsey, the reason I wished to speak to you is to ask a favor." When Alec inclined his head, Miranda said, "I would very much like you to be my son's godparent. Please," she added quickly when his smile faded, "please give the offer serious consideration, because I can think of no better protector for my son should anything happen to his parents."

"Your Grace, I am honored, truly honored, but… You do not know me," Alec said, flustered by such a grand gesture. "You must consult with the Duke, who will surely have his own ideas as to who would make a suitable godparent for his son and—"

"But I do know you," Miranda interrupted, a smile at Tam. "Thomas told me all about you and unless you argue otherwise, I believe him to be truthful and trustworthy. Mr. Bourdon may choose a second godparent, as is his right; but you are my choice."

Alec did not know what to say. How could he refuse her? How could he refuse the new little life nestled in the crook of her arm his protection if required? He bowed his head in acceptance, a sideways glance and raise of his black brows at Tam as if to ask *what have you been saying about me*? "Then how can I refuse you? I would be honored to accept… Is there anything else I may do to make your stay comfortable until His Grace arrives?"

For the first time since Alec had entered the bedchamber, Miranda became flustered.

"I do not know what is keeping him from me… It was arranged that I would have my lying-in at Bratton Dene, and then his letter came telling me to come here and wait for him. And I have waited and he has not come…"

"He will be here very soon, Your Grace," Alec assured her, though he was not sure of that at all. He was confident the Duke was in Bath, the mountainous footman at her door and Molyneux's presence in taking Sophie to the Duke told him that. But as to why he remained distant from Miranda, and at such an auspicious time baffled him. "You and your baby are safe here. That I promise you. No one can cross the threshold with the impassable Bear Brown and my uncle both guarding the outer door; Bear Brown with his entire being, and my uncle armed with his Malacca cane are a formidable team. There was a crowd gathered to hear news of the birth, but it would have dispersed by now, Mrs. Jamison-Lewis giving them the good news that you were safely delivered of a girl."

"Thank you," Miranda said with a sigh of relief. She smiled at her sleeping infant. "His father should be the one to tell the world he has a son… My precious darling will be safe now…"

"Why, Your Grace?" Alec asked bluntly. Knowing the answer, her response did not disappoint, but it did surprise him.

"Cousin George will not be happy. Indeed he may be very angry. I have no way of knowing until I speak with him. And I would rather be the one to tell him his father now has a son of his own. The birth of my son considerably alters his prospects. Though… I have always wondered if, in his heart, George truly wants to be Duke. Whenever he spoke of it to us, to Miriam and to me, it was always what other people wanted of him, but he never once said it was what *he* wanted. He certainly never wanted to marry me, as his mother and mine were demanding should happen. He loved me as a cousin but not in *that* way. He was in love with Miriam. He told me he was going to marry her; that he cared not a penny what my mother and his thought of the match. Nor did he care that she was base-born. Miriam's pregnancy changed everything…"

A small domestic interruption halted their conversation. Janie entered with a tray of tea things, and following her was a wide-eyed maidservant carrying a hot brick. Alec took the brandy offered him, suddenly tired. He was acutely aware that Miranda must be in need of sleep, for soon her infant son would be demanding her breast, and that Tam and the maid were also limp from exhaustion. Yet if he were to front the persons now assembled in the drawing room, and to whom he had sent Selina to keep entertained until his arrival, he needed to make certain he had all his facts correct to be able to level an accusation of murder.

He waited for Miranda to take her tea, the baby given up reluctantly to Janie to hold and who cooed and clucked over his little lordship from the safety of a wingchair in the corner of the bedchamber.

"Earlier today, Sir Charles Weir left here greatly agitated. In fact, he declared he had seen a ghost."

"Yes. He had. I have spent the past four years of my life, if not being someone else, then not being myself," Miranda confessed matter-of-factly, sitting her teacup on its saucer. "I am sorry I frightened him, but he has only himself to blame believing me to be Miriam. It was not unreasonable he would think so, because I died four years ago, but when he threatened me, accused me of blackmailing George… I didn't know what else to do to convince him otherwise! I still do not understand why he would think I would want to harm George?"

"Was your death from pneumonia the Duke's idea?"

Miranda nodded.

"And Miriam's body in the casket?"

"Yes. It is a relief that you know. I only hope Mrs. Jamison-Lewis will forgive me—*forgive us*—our deception, but Mr. Bourdon was adamant I remain in my grave until we were safely married. That could not happen until after the Duchess's death. She was very ill; we thought it only a matter of months, but she lingered."

"Three years is a very long time to wait when two people are in love," Alec remarked, thinking of his own predicament. "Legally there was no reason for you to do so. After all, the Duke and Duchess were in truth never legally married, though they lived as husband and wife for twenty years."

"Oh? So you know that too? You *are* clever! We could not—I *would not* marry—while his wife was alive. And she *was* his wife, despite her earlier marriage to Mr. Blackwell—a sorry affair. Mr. Bourdon confided he had known for many years that the Duchess was in truth another man's wife, but that he had no motivation to change his way of life until—until—"

"—until he fell in love with you," Alec said, wanting to add, but did not: *Because Selina fell pregnant with his child, which gave him hope he could have children of his own.*

"Yes. We fell in love. And I made him wait. Even after we were married, I remained at the farm while Mr. Bourdon spent the twelvemonth in public mourning for the death of the Duchess. It was not important that the Duchess had lived in a state of bigamy with Mr. Bourdon. She was to me, to my mother, to Miriam and to George, indeed to Mr. Bourdon and to all Society, the Duchess of Cleveley."

"Do you think Lady Rutherglen has any idea of her sister's previous marriage—that she was the wife of Mr. Blackwell before she was ever the wife of the Duke of Stanton and then the Duke of Cleveley?"

Miranda's face flushed with embarrassment. She glanced at Janie, but she was preoccupied with the baby, and then looked for Tam, but he had excused himself and gone into the small servant bedchamber with the maid who had delivered the hot brick, to see to the removal of soiled sheets and ensure the copper containing the afterbirth was left for the physician to examine.

"I would like to tell you my mother had no notion, that she believed her sister legally married to the Duke of Cleveley, but that would be a lie. She knew. She knew, too, that the Duchess was pregnant by Mr. Blackwell before her marriage to the Duke of Stanton, and that George was Mr. Blackwell's son, not Stanton's. She knew also when the Duchess and Mr. Blackwell were briefly reunited on his return from the West Indies, and that nine months after that bittersweet reunion Miriam was born, in the country and in secret. And knowing this, she still did nothing to stop George bedding Miriam."

"Pardon, Your Grace, but how did you discover the truth? Did His Grace—"

Miranda shook her head.

"No. I overheard my mother and the Duchess in heated argument." She looked steadily at Alec. "It is not easy for me to say this, but it is a truth I have known since a little girl: Lady Rutherglen—my mother—is a nasty, mean-spirited woman capable of great cruelty. I was not the boy she so desperately wanted, and so I was considered of no value and was locked away, as one puts to the back of a dusty cupboard an ornament one is given but considers worthless. She spent years encouraging my cousin George's worst traits, seeking his approval and lavishing what love she possessed on his welfare, much to the detriment and sadness of my aunt, who could not persuade George away from Lady Rutherglen's corruptive influence. And then, when Lady Rutherglen realized George was interested in Miriam, she gave my natural cousin to him as one gives a boy a puppy; Miriam was to be George's plaything. What Lady Rutherglen could not understand and never comprehended was that George fell in love with Miriam; he truly loved her.

"Naturally my poor aunt was horrified to learn George was bedding Miriam; she was even more appalled when Lady Rutherglen laughed at her. Yes, my lord, she laughed most cruelly when the Duchess begged her to spirit Miriam away before more damage was done. And what did my mother say? She said it was God's punishment for her sister's wickedness in marrying a penniless nobody and yet she paraded about society as a duchess, to which she had no right. What did my mother do? She encouraged George and Miriam, giving them every opportunity for the calamitous outcome that was to come. I believe Lady Rutherglen hated Miriam all the more because George loved her. My poor aunt's health deteriorated rapidly after that. She became bedridden and never recovered.

"My lord," Miranda added, blinking back tears, "it has always been my fervent wish that George never discover the true nature of his connection to Miriam…"

Alec voiced what Miranda could not and never would.

"That he and Miriam are in truth brother and sister, and Sophie their child?"

"Mr. Bourdon and I will never allow Sophie to know the hideous truth. She is inked in St. Jude's parish register as my daughter; Mr. Blackwell saw to that. Sophie will never suffer from lack of love and will know every advantage we can provide her. But George must never know…"

"I fear there is more certainty in keeping him ignorant of Sophie's paternity, Your Grace," Alec said with a small smile, "than there is in knowing what his reaction will be to the news his father has remarried, and that you, his cousin, have delivered the dukedom a legitimate heir."

"Oi! You can't go bargin' in there as if you own the place, just because you think you're His Grace Lord-Bloody-God-Almighty! Have some manners! Give the woman her peace! She's just given birth…"

It was Plantagenet Halsey, and Alec had bowed to take his leave of Miranda when his uncle's shouts penetrated from the sitting room and he turned to the door in expectation of the old man storming in brandishing his cane. The other occupants continued on with their duties, the two maids, under Janie's direction, were clearing the servant bedchamber of clutter, Tam was rummaging in his apothecary's cabinet for a salve or some such medicinal balm for the new mother, while Miranda catered to his little lordship's immediate demands for nourishment.

Into the bedchamber strode His Grace the Duke of Cleveley, and on his heels was the old man holding his cane aloft and repeating his threat. The Duke was as one deaf and blind to all else, his attention wholly on the four-poster bed. Disheveled, in woollen frock coat and dusty jockey boots, thick brown hair streaked with gray cut short above the ears and in wild disarray, he came to an abrupt halt at the undraped foot of the bed. Alec blinked, as if to assure himself that this panic-stricken countrified gent was indeed one and the same as the self-possessed nobleman in velvet and powdered wig magnificence he had studied at the opera.

Cozily propped up amongst down pillows, Miranda looked up from watching her newborn son suckle at her breast and her blue eyes brightened. She smiled and said as if it were a most commonplace thing,

"Mr. Bourdon! You are here at last. Come and meet your son Thomas."

The Duke swayed and slumped against the bedpost, Alec at his back in two strides lest he faint. It was Plantagenet Halsey's turn to blink, and his jaw fell open in amazement, not only at the change that came over his political nemesis, but at the discovery that this most despised of noblemen, *the great man*, a man whose politics he reviled, was none other than the husband of sweet-tempered Miranda Bourdon. It made no sense to him. He must have misheard. He retreated to the window seat and sat there, leaning on the handle of his Malacca walking stick as if the wind had been knocked out of him.

"I've been halfway to London and back in search of you and Sophie," the Duke finally said, as he gingerly inched his way up the bed, a leg pressed to the mattress as if needing support to remain upright. "Robert's been at his wits' end, riding the length and breadth of Somerset, as well as losing shoe leather up and down Bath's streets. Why is Sophie not at the farm? I thought we had agreed—But none of that is important. You're both safe and so is—so is our son. A son! Oh, Mimi! My precious, darling dear…"

"Please—Mr. Bourdon—*Ninian*—you must not upset yourself," Miranda chided playfully, her free hand extended across the coverlet for him to take. "We are both safe and very well indeed, thanks to the efforts and care of Thomas, Janie and Lord Halsey. Oh! And Mr. Halsey, whose fine name I have also saddled on our son. And we will add your name too. Thomas Plantagenet Justinian Beaumaris. It is such a mouthful for one so tiny." She glanced down at her now milk-drunk sleeping son and then smiled up at her husband. "But not for a duke. Until then, shall we call him Thomas Bourdon?"

"As you wish… Thomas… A fine name…"

It was all the Duke could utter as he stared down at his wife and newborn son. And then emotion took hold and would not let go. The reality that the woman he loved beyond reason and their son—he had a son!—were alive and well, safe and unharmed, hit him in the chest, and so hard that he was utterly undone. He shuddered in a great breath, crumpled to his knees and sobbed into the coverlet.

Plantagenet Halsey thought he had seen it all until now. If he was struck speechless to discover that the Duke of Cleveley was the elusive Mr. Bourdon, he was now shocked rigid to see a man he thought devoid of sentiment and possessing the temperament of a cold cod reduced to quaking emotional wreckage. He did what any decent gentleman would do in such a circumstance: He offered the nobleman his clean white handkerchief, and with a perfunctory pat to the stooped shaking shoulders, his hearty congratulations, before making Miranda a bow befitting her station as Her Grace, the Most Noble Duchess of Cleveley. He then turned to his nephew, and taking his arm, walked with him out into the sitting room, still in a daze of new knowledge and much subdued.

"I'm not entirely certain I believe what's goin' on in there, and if you told me to pinch m'self and I'd wake up, I'd do it! But I can see by that grin that you are perfectly reconciled to it. I need a brandy.

There's one to be had in the drawing room, where you won't be surprised to discover an assortment of interestin' individuals. And kickin' their boot heels in the servant corridor and awaitin' your instructions are a handful of militia under direction of a pompous git named Rawlinson, who tells Barr he's the local magistrate." He glanced over his shoulder just as Janie closed the bedchamber door and caught a glimpse of the Duke sitting on the edge of the bed, cradling his newborn son. "Oh, and this here," he added, joining his nephew in the passageway, a nod to Bear Brown who still stood at his post, pointing his cane at a stout little man in dark cloth and brown bob wig who waddled up to them, round cheeks diffuse with blood, "is the painmerchant Ketteridge, with his black bag and bottle of leeches. I've told him he's not wanted but he won't go away."

"Sir! My lord! I must be permitted access to the woman in that room. If she has indeed given birth to a live child, then it is the law that she, the baby and the afterbirth, be examined…"

Plantagenet Halsey stopped listening to the physician on the word *afterbirth*, leaving him in his nephew's capable hands. But as he slowly descended the stairs with the aid of his Malacca cane he heard the physician list off his qualifications, experience and the letter of the law, and shook his grizzled head in sympathy for his nephew. He hoped Alec would soon join him in the drawing room so there could be a swift resolution and application of justice. He had had enough excitement to last him out the month. And after what he had witnessed upstairs he wasn't up to any more surprises. He was to be disappointed.

NINETEEN

ALEC SLID INTO THE CHINESE DRAWING ROOM OF BARR'S OF Trim Street and into a conflagration of argument. The room was so designated because of the crane and lotus blossom wallpaper, elaborate chinoiserie black-lacquered sideboard, and the *toile du jouy* covered sofas depicting the French ideal of a Chinese landscape with pagodas, lanterns and bamboo bridges. The effect would have been charming in a room four times the size, but in its present space, occupied by half a dozen fractious individuals Alec wasn't at all surprised by their irritability. He immediately wanted to push up the window sash for fresh air, to clear his head and to gather his thoughts for he was about to reveal a murderer, but it being a cold night and with a fire in the grate, he curbed the desire and went straight to the sideboard, poured himself a brandy and surveyed the occupants.

Lady Rutherglen and Sir Charles Weir sat side-by-side on a sofa, both straight-backed and each nursing a half-glass of spirits. Talgarth Vesey was sprawled out in a wingchair, thin long legs crossed at the ankles, head leaning on his fist and eyes closed. Selina held his other hand, propped on the chair's rounded arm, and was fanning herself with an ivory and blond lace fan while deep in low conversation with his uncle. No need to guess their topic of discussion: Both were united by mutual incredulity and affront at the Duke of Cleveley's clandestine marriage. The final occupant but one, who, Alec was relieved, had accepted his invitation, was also sprawled out in a wingchair by the fireplace. Lord George Stanton had his chin in his stock and a hand deep in the pocket of his silver-threaded velvet waistcoat. He was swirling brandy in a glass, brooding gaze on the little leaping flames amongst the burning logs in the grate.

It was at Lord George that Hadrian Jeffries, the only other occupant of the room, directed a significant sidelong glance when Alec came up to the sideboard. He continued to pour drinks for the guests and deliver them on a silver salver with a suitably blank face but, Alec suspected, very much with ears wide open. Alec savored his brandy and casually directed his attention to Lord George, wondering what there was about the brooding corpulent nobleman that warranted his valet's particular look of alarm, and then he noticed his lordship was still wearing his sword.

"Halsey! Attend! Why are we here?"

It was Lady Rutherglen, and to add emphasis to her pronouncement, she rapped the side of her glass with the closed ivory sticks of her fan.

"Did you not come to see a ghost, my lady?"

"Ghost? Fanciful rot!" Lady Rutherglen sniffed. "I do not believe in specters."

"And yet, when Sir Charles told you there was a ghost here at Barr's, you could not get here soon enough. In fact you demanded of Barr to be shown the ghost."

"In actuality I did not tell her ladyship that there was a ghost," Sir Charles corrected, "but that I had seen the dead."

"Caught your reflection in a looking glass, more belike, Charlie," Lord George grumbled, not taking his eyes off the crackling fire.

"Seeing the dead or seeing a ghost. Surely an exercise in semantics?" Selina teased. "Though I think her ladyship and Sir Charles saw neither."

Lady Rutherglen and Sir Charles opened their mouths to refute this when Lord George suddenly sat up and rounded on Selina with a sneer.

"Don't pretend you know what's bloody well going on here, *Mrs.* J-L, because you don't!"

"Oi! Watch your language, Stanton!" Plantagenet Halsey growled, Malacca-headed cane up and pointing menacingly.

"Ghosts and specters and the dead! Ha! You and your opiate-soaked brother are so bloody smug! You don't know the half of it," Stanton ranted as if the old man had not spoken. "And you can take out that earring! Only the Duchess of Cleveley has the right, *the right* to wear the Beaumaris diamonds." He sat back in his chair and waved a lace-covered wrist at Alec. "Just get on with it, Halsey. The militia are waiting and you look fit to burst with smugness at wanting to show us all up as frauds, fiends and fopdoodles. Go on, get on with being so damned bloody clever!"

There was an embarrassed silence and no one dared speak. All eyes were on Alec, who drained his glass and set it aside.

Lady Rutherglen sat forward and put out a hand to her nephew.

"George. No more spirits—"

"No! Don't! I'm beyond saving *now*; it's *all* beyond saving, *now*."

"But, George—"

"My lady, may I counsel that we hear what Lord Halsey has to say," Sir Charles advised. "We may all know then why we are being held captive against our will."

Lord George let out a series of animal sorts. "Act it out, Charlie! Don't think the pretence will save *your* neck any better than it will mine! Halsey? Get on with it!"

Alec inclined his head to Lord George, and with a brief glance at Selina and his uncle, said flatly, "I have gathered you here because you are all connected in some way to the death of the Reverend Kenneth Blackwell."

"Hoo-bloody-rah!" Lord George exclaimed with a pig-like snort. "That's to the point right enough!"

"*What*? *All* of us?"

The second outburst came from Selina.

"Yes."

"M'dear, he said *connected*, not guilty," the old man pointed out quietly, adding with a look about the room, "But I dare say the murderer is here in this room or the militia wouldn't be kickin' their heels in the corridor."

"First, I wish to revisit the mutilation of Talgarth's portrait of a young woman and her daughter."

"For God's sake, Halsey, must we?" Lord George whined and was unsuccessful in stifling a belch. "I didn't care for that exhibition at the time, why would I want to now? Certainly the painter don't want to. He's got his eyes shut tight, doped to the eyelids!"

"You know who did it, my lord," Sir Charles said to Alec. "I told you. George did. He did it in a drunken rage."

"Yes you told me, Charles, but that is not what happened," Alec countered. "And before you say so, you may well have believed Lord George to have done so, but my guess is Lady Rutherglen told you that was the case when in fact it was you, my lady, who defaced the portrait, and in a rage, though you do not have the excuse of being drunk at the time."

"I have never been drunk a day in my life!" her ladyship announced, though she did not deny the accusation.

"You received a letter of demand for payment for a portrait of yourself and your husband, which you had commissioned Talgarth Vesey to paint. You had not paid him because you did not approve of the portrait. To point out fact, it was to the life and thus unflattering. You ordered he repaint the portrait to your satisfaction and when you went to his studio to see how the work was progressing you were met by Mr. Vesey's Italian major domo Nico, the author of the demand for payment."

Alec paused to see if Talgarth was listening and had the satisfaction that the painter had opened one eye. He continued.

"What you got was a momentous shock, for amongst the canvases and charcoal sketches there was one in particular that caught your attention. It was a portrait of Miriam, or so you thought. Yet, how could that be? She had died in childbirth five years before. You had it from Nico that the woman in the portrait was his master's lover. He knew differently, but it never hurts to give a painter a reputation with women, and Nico assumed such a reputation would help with commissions. It usually does. Your ladyship quickly presumed that you had been lied to about Miriam's death, and that the girl had spent the past five years living on her wits and was most definitely the painter's whore—"

"Painter's whore! Ha! Auntie said as much; but his whore?" Lord George spat out, half out his chair, glaring at Talgarth "I'd sooner believe that for a lie!" and only sank back down when Alec agreed with him.

"Yes, it is a lie. But we will get to that in a moment. To continue with Lady Rutherglen's visit to Mr. Vesey's studio. You, my lady, believing the lie and believing Miriam had escaped just punishment for her libidinous past, went into a rage. Nico told me you brandished a knife at him. You were intent on doing harm, if only to extinguish your immediate fury, and so you vented your spleen on the portrait in oils of Miriam that was intended for the exhibition."

"No!" It was Selina and she had gasped the word. She looked swiftly at Alec and then at Talgarth, who had not moved, before staring at Lady Rutherglen who made no attempt to deny the accusation. "How could you destroy something so beautifully wrought?"

"Was it Miriam—" Lord George asked and was interrupted.

"Of course it's her!" Lady Rutherglen countered. "Who else could it be? Don't be an ass, George! She duped you—us—and ran away."

"No, Auntie, I don't believe she would—"

"Let his lordship get on with it," Plantagenet Halsey growled, "and you two can scrap about it on the carpet later!"

"As Lady Rutherglen does not deny taking a knife to Mr. Vesey's portrait, let us move on to its further destruction and complete obliteration of the person in the portrait with the application of red paint. Having vented her spleen, her ladyship left the studio. Nico would have been beside himself as to what to do. If he told his master he risked having to tell him about the threatening letters he had written in his name, as well as trying to explain Lady Rutherglen's particular anger at the pronouncement that the woman in the portrait was the painter's mistress. And as it was his letter which had brought Lady

Rutherglen to the studio in the first place, he blamed himself for the portrait's destruction.

"He panicked and did the only thing he could think of. He had the portrait uploaded onto the cart and covered in black cloth, telling his master to leave the cloth in place until the portrait's unveiling at the gallery. I dare say Nico hoped that a mishap might befall the portrait between Bath and London that would negate him ever having to confess. It arrived safely in London, and the rest you know."

"So it was Nico's idea to drape the portrait in black cloth?" Selina asked her brother.

Talgarth shrugged. "It is of no consequence, Lina. None of it." He opened an eye to stare at Lady Rutherglen who was fanning herself languidly. "It's not as if he had a hope in Hades of defending the painting against a dog-ugly dowager brandishing a dagger."

"The red paint…?" Plantagenet Halsey prompted.

"When Tam and I left the Milsom Street studio after talking with Nico I noticed the property next door was under renovation. Scaffolding still covered the façade. The door was newly painted—a vibrant red. I can only assume that Molyneux found a pot of paint by the freshly-painted door. He splashed the paint over the portrait, using his hands to smear the paint in well and truly. Leaving the canvas ripped would still have allowed anyone viewing the destruction to identify the sitter."

"Molyneux? *Robert Molyneux*? His Grace of Cleveley's *valet*?"

Alec inclined his head to Sir Charles who had voiced the rest of the room's incredulity.

"Yes. Nico told me that a man with severe smallpox scarring had visited the studio upon several occasions and offered to buy up all the likenesses of the woman in the destroyed portrait. And that he spotted Molyneux across the road from the studio on the day of Lady Rutherglen's visit. He might not have witnessed her take a knife to the portrait, but he would have seen the men put the destroyed canvas on the cart under Nico's direction, and Nico cover it with black cloth. Molyneux would have known at once that Lady Rutherglen had stabbed the woman in the portrait, and he would have known why. He did the only thing possible to protect not only his master, but the woman and the little girl in the portrait. He made certain no one would recognize them, and then he reported everything he saw and knew to the Duke. Molyneux is very astute. He is also fiercely loyal, and beneath the cold exterior," Alec added with a small smile, "at heart, he is a romantic."

"What? Molyneux a-a *romantic*?" Lord George blustered. "What tripe! The man's a *valet*, for God's sake. He does what he's told. He's not in service to have *feelings*. You're not making sense, Halsey. And if you would all just listen to me—"

"Shut up, George!" Lady Rutherglen snapped, fan waving in agitation. "Of course you cannot prove any of this," she said to Alec with a haughty sniff. "No one will believe the word of a little foreign monkey and his drug-addicted organ grinder over mine."

"Oh, I would not treat the intelligence of others so shabbily, my lady. I am confident everyone in this room believes you capable of taking a knife to a canvas in a fit of parental fury." When no one disagreed, Alec said, "Once you had spent your anger on the portrait, you decided to exact your revenge. To do so you needed to discover Miriam's whereabouts and so you struck upon the idea of blackmail. Nico's letter of demand gave you that idea. You told your nephew George and Sir Charles about the portrait, and that you had made the startling discovery that Miriam was alive. You had proof. Miriam's current lover, the painter Talgarth Vesey, was demanding money or Lord George would be exposed to the world as a rapist. Naturally, Sir Charles offered his help. Being the consummate politician, he did so not for altruistic reasons—

Plantagenet Halsey huffed. "How surprisin'!"

"—but to ensure Lord George, the future Duke of Cleveley, was in his debt. The rumor circulating Westminster halls and drawing rooms is that the present Duke of Cleveley is to resign from office and relinquish his posts. No one knows why, but everyone assumes it was because the death of his Duchess the year before has taken its toll on his health. As *the great man* has made no comment either way, the rumor has strengthened into belief." Alec looked at Sir

Charles; his smile was grim. "You knew for a fact Cleveley was on the brink of resignation; you had this information from the Duke's political rival Lord Russell, whose friendship and patronage you had been cultivating for some time, and who you hoped would make you his son-in-law by allowing you to marry his daughter Lady Henrietta—"

Lord George burst into incredulous laughter.

"*What? Hatty Russell* and *you*, Charlie? Come now! You can't be serious! Hatty's prospects of a great match are slim to none at best, but even Russell wouldn't stoop so low as to marry off his daughter to a lowly secretary turned MP, however damaged her goods!"

Sir Charles was up off the sofa, fists and teeth clenched.

"Retract those remarks, my lord! Retract or I'll—or I'll—"

"Retract what? That you're a lowly secretary or that Hatty is damaged goods?" Lord George asked with a shrug. He drained his glass of brandy and held the tumbler up for Hadrian Jeffries to replenish. "No, Charlie, I won't, cause they're both true."

Lady Rutherglen caught at the skirts of Sir Charles's frock coat and pulled him backwards before he had taken two steps forward. "Sit and be quiet!"

"My lady, I cannot allow Lord George to besmirch the name of the woman I—"

"Shut up!" Lady Rutherglen hissed. "Shut up if you know what is good for you!"

Lord George laughed at the antics of his aunt and the secretary while Selina, the old man, and her brother were baffled by them. Alec understood and thus was not surprised when Lord George said matter-of-factly,

"For God's sake, secretary, you must be the only man in London who has not a jot of an inkling that it was I who tupped Hatty behind the firescreen at the Cavendish Fireworks. Nice plump thighs, has Hatty, and a bit of a giggler," he added with a smile of recollection, taking the tumbler of brandy from the silver tray offered him by Hadrian Jeffries, who almost overset the lot at his lordship's self-satisfied pronouncement. "Likes her men big-thighed as well. Suppose that's why she came back for seconds at the Devonshire turn-out…"

He grinned at Sir Charles. "Bet you're slim in every department, hey Charlie? Wouldn't satisfy Hatty one bit; not one bit."

Sir Charles made a lunge for a smugly laughing Lord George and Hadrian Jeffries stuck out his foot. It was an instinctive movement and once done could not be undone. So when Sir Charles tripped and fell flat on his face, not only did Selina gasp but so did Hadrian Jeffries. Lord George laughed louder and pointed a fat finger of accusation at the valet, who stood as stone. With a hard jerk of his head, Alec sent Jeffries scurrying to the sideboard, face aglow. Alec helped his old school friend to his feet, marched him across the carpet to the sofa and pushed him onto the seat.

"Stay there. Say nothing," Alec ordered, and rounded on Lord George. "You will also hold your tongue until I'm done. No one is interested in your crude conduct except Lord Russell and your father, the meaning behind their very public meeting at the opera now patently obvious!"

It was not so obvious to the others in the drawing room, who were still fathoming it out when Plantagenet Halsey said quietly,

"You were sayin' 'bout the secretary's part in helpin' Lady Rutherglen with the blackmail of Stanton…"

"Yes. Thank you, Uncle. Lady Rutherglen was determined to discover where Miriam was hiding and needed a way of flushing her out into the open," Alec continued. "Blackmail was the device and I the means. Charles enlisted my help, his old school friend, thinking me gullible enough to swallow their story of blackmail and knowing I would always help an old friend." He met Selina's unblinking gaze and when she smiled, he smiled back. "My connection to the Vesey family, in particular my attachment to Mrs. Jamison-Lewis, and her love for her brother, was used to persuade me to cooperate; Sir Charles was confident that Talgarth Vesey was the blackmailer. This plan went ahead in spite of the death of the Reverend Blackwell. I say in spite of because everything changed when I happened to sit beside the Reverend Blackwell at dinner and the good vicar died at my feet."

"Huzzah! 'bout time we got to the shabby vicar!" Lord George announced with a smack of his lips as he drained another glass free of brandy. He immediately shut his mouth at a glare from Alec and pouted like a naughty schoolboy.

"Why do you say *happened*?" Selina asked, exchanging a frown with Plantagenet Halsey. "As if the vicar died without warning when you suspected he was murdered? Was he murdered?"

"Yes."

"Poisoned as Tam suspected?" asked the old man.

"Yes."

"I do not see at all," Lady Rutherglen stated with a sniff, "what this scruffy non-entity has to do with that whore Mir—"

"Stop calling her that!"

"Can you not, my lady?" Alec stated coldly, ignoring Lord George's emotional outburst. "Yes, you do see. You know full well that the Reverend Blackwell was in truth Kenneth Dempsey-Weir, second son of a Viscount, and the only man your sister Ellen truly loved. And if you wish to preserve her memory and thus your family's reputation, as well as your nephew's sanity, do not tempt me to reveal all that I know. And when I state I know everything about your sister and Blackwell, you can believe me."

Lady Rutherglen stopped fluttering her fan at mention of her sister and took a quick furtive look about the room at the other occupants before returning her gaze to Alec's blue eyes. She glared at him with controlled anger, but just under the surface there bristled loathing, resentment and hatred. Alec saw that she yearned to take the stage to vent her feelings about her sister and the shabby vicar and most of all about Miriam, but Alec's threat of revelation and family ruination was enough to make her pause in thought. He saw this when she glanced away to Lord George, possibly the only person in whom she had ever invested any feelings akin to real love, before again meeting his gaze. There was a moment of indecision and then she reluctantly closed her mouth, set her jaw, and resumed fanning herself. Ellen, Duchess of Cleveley and the Reverend Kenneth Blackwell, their secret marriage and their offspring were to be left to rest in peace.

"Blackwell wasn't the intended victim," Alec said with a note of sadness, addressing his uncle. "He just happened to have in his possession a snuffbox identical to the one carried by the Duke of Cleveley. Perhaps given him by the same gift bearer, I do not know."

"Good God, the poor man," Selina murmured, a hand to her white throat. "The poison was intended for *Cleveley*?"

"That is my belief."

"But who? And how?" Selina demanded. "And *why*?"

"After dinner, when the gentlemen were sitting over their port, Lord George and Charles moved away to a locked cabinet containing jars of snuff," Alec explained. "Several gentlemen had their boxes refilled. At first I presumed this to be the moment when the snuff-boxes were switched, or when the poison was introduced to the Duke's snuffbox. But neither the Duke nor the vicar handed up their snuffboxes to be refilled. The Duke was rather possessive of his, and the vicar took his out to take a pinch while Charles and Lord George were standing at the cabinet. Therefore the snuffboxes must have been inadvertently switched before the Duke and the vicar arrived for dinner. Perhaps when the two men were ensconced in the Duke's library alone earlier that day, as Lord George complained about at the dinner.

"The Duke's death was not meant to take place at such a public occasion. It was supposed to be a quiet affair, made to look like he had had a heart attack, which is how it appeared when Blackwell was poisoned. The poison was successful in its application just not in its execution. Had Cleveley died at his residence, no one would have questioned a physician's diagnosis that he had suffered a fatal heart attack. For the murderer, this would have been a neater solution and an easier, unquestioned transition for the heir to become Duke."

"Stanton! I knew it!" the old man announced with satisfaction. "You murdering cur!"

"Wh-what? I didn't kill Father!" Lord George whined in falsetto. "Why would I do such a thing? He's my father, for God's sake! I had no reason to want him dead! I wouldn't even know where to get poison. God, I don't know what poison causes a heart attack. What do you take me for, a damned apothecary? That's Halsey's ilk! He knows more about that hocus-pocus than anyone! Auntie! Charlie! Tell them! Tell Halsey I couldn't kill a beetle! Tell them, Auntie!"

"Hangman's noose for you, Stanton," Plantagenet Halsey goaded him, a sad shake of his grizzled locks though he looked anything but sad. He winked at his nephew and said cheerfully, "Time to call the militia so we can go to our beds. A satisfactory end to the evenin', wouldn't you say so?"

When Lady Rutherglen and Sir Charles continued to sit as silent and unmoved as did the rest of the occupants, Lord George's bottom lip began to quiver, tears to fill his eyes and his nose to run. Panic set in and his bloodshot eyes widened in terror.

"No, I wouldn't say so!" Lord George retorted. "Halsey! You're a Trusty Trojan! Always said so. You don't seriously believe I meant to kill my father and killed a shabby vicar by mistake, do you? Do you?"

"Oh, for pity's sake, my lord, put him out of his misery!" Selina demanded, provoked beyond tolerance by Lord George's pathetic runny-nosed pleas.

"No, I do not. Nor did I say you did," Alec stated.

"Eh? You don't and-and you didn't?" Lord George repeated and unconsciously wiped his nose free of snot with a swipe of his sleeve. "Then who is the murderer?"

"Charles."

There was a short silence and then Lord George, having instantly regained his bravado on Alec's one-name pronouncement, thumped the padded arms of the wingchair and stamped his feet with undisguised relish.

"I knew it! I *knew* it was you, Charlie! I knew! I said to Auntie that Charlie was a snake and a-a black dog and not to be trusted. And he is! He is!"

"Be very certain of what you accuse me, my lord," Sir Charles stated very low, gaze never wavering from Alec's face. "I challenge you to produce evidence of any kind that will stand up in a court of law. It will not."

"Let's hear what his lordship has to say in any event," the old man said cheerfully.

When Sir Charles shrugged and the others nodded, Alec said matter-of-factly,

"You needed the Duke out of the way. You feared he was at the point of altering his will, of disinheriting Lord George because of what Kenneth Blackwell had confided in him. If he disinherited George all your hard work spent pandering to a nobleman whom you considered a parasitic waste to humankind, but whom you could influence to do as you wished—he would certainly continue your sinecures—would be wasted. You were not prepared to allow that to happen. You certainly did not want the Duke walking away from his posts—that would leave you very little if any income, no influence, and there was no certainty of Lord Russell offering you a post, least of all his daughter's hand in marriage. Thus for you to continue, you needed Lord George to inherit the title.

"What you did not calculate or foresee was that the Duke had known the truth about the Duchess and the Reverend Blackwell for years. When Blackwell and the Duke came together recently you were more than ever convinced the Duke was about to resign. And then you had intelligence, possibly from Lord Russell himself, of a late night clandestine meeting between the Duke and Lord Russell. You tried to intervene before there could be any announcement, but the vicar died instead of your mentor, and the very public truce at the opera between Cleveley and Russell went ahead as planned. You and everyone else presumed this truce meant the Duke was about to remarry; that Lord Russell had accepted an offer for Lady Henrietta's hand in marriage. Russell had, but not for the father but for the son, Lord George—"

Lord George was half out of his chair. "*What*? Father is having me leg-shackled to *Hatty Russell*? Auntie—"

"Shut up, George! She's your social equal in every respect. You could do much worse. I applaud Cleveley's astuteness. Go on, Halsey."

Alec inclined his head in agreement to Lady Rutherglen's clipped statement, and as no one disagreed with her, Lord George sank back down in his chair with a pout and grumbled into his stock, a wave at Alec to continue.

"Thus, Charles, you misinterpreted why these men had come together, and why the Duke had set about putting his affairs in order for a future that you could not possibly imagine him contemplating, least of all living... But I digress and the militia await... The good vicar up and dying at your dinner party and the Duke very much alive was the worst possible outcome for you, Charles. You had not only killed the wrong man, but the Duke was alerted to the very real possibility that he was the one meant to inhale the poisonous snuff. He realized this soon after Blackwell's demise, when the attending physician was asking me questions. Cleveley went to take a pinch of snuff. He flicked open his snuffbox, but one look inside, possibly at an inscription inside the lid, and he went white. He dropped the snuffbox and its contents all over your dining room floorboards. He knew then he was the intended victim, not Blackwell, and he stormed from the room."

Sir Charles waved a hand in dismissal. But Alec saw the trickle of sweat at his temple. "All conjecture and unsubstantiated. Tell him, my lady. Surely you don't believe this nonsense?"

Lady Rutherglen shrugged a shoulder with indifference and said blithely, "Why ask me, Sir Charles? I am merely an ignorant old woman who knows nothing of politics."

Sir Charles blinked at this public betrayal; he was now very much on his own. Still, he managed to say with a veneer of confidence, "You won't convince a jury, Halsey! None of this muck will stick to me. None of it!"

"He's convinced me!" Plantagenet Halsey stated jovially. "What about you, ma'am?"

Selina smiled behind her fan but kept the laughter from her voice. "Lord Halsey's argument is very persuasive, sir."

Alec ignored them both. He withdrew his spectacles and the Duchess of Romney-St. Neots' sealed letter from a frock coat pocket, perched the eyeglasses on the end of his long bony nose, and then held up the letter.

"How perceptive of Lord George to point out that I do know quite a bit about the hocus-pocury of the apothecary. Thanks to Thomas Fisher, who was, until quite recently, my valet and who is in the final year of his apprenticeship, discreet enquiries were made into the recent purchases of poisons, a register of which is kept by every apothecary. This letter I have here—Jeffries!" he shouted. "Your foot to it!"

Before Alec had time to utter the name of his correspondent, Sir Charles Weir was up off the sofa. He made a dash for the door. There was a general outcry. Lady Rutherglen leapt to her heels, fan and reticule falling to the floor. Plantagenet Halsey and Selina Jamison-Lewis did likewise, though they remained where they stood. Talgarth Vesey opened an eye, saw Sir Charles making a run for it, saw Alec's valet in pursuit and closed his eye again, a satisfied grin splitting his face.

Balancing a tray of clinking empty glass tumblers and a bottle of brandy, Hadrian Jeffries took three long strides across the room and stuck out his right foot. His polished black leather shoe with its plain silver buckle connected with Sir Charles's stockinged shin, which instantly tripped him up just as he was lunging for the door handle. The fugitive was in the air for a matter of moments and then fell flat on his face, this time his chin hitting the floor hard before the rest of his stocky person came crashing down. He yelped in pain as his jaw jarred shut and his teeth ground against each other. He yelped some more when he was hit on the head by a heavy glass tumbler. Three glass tumblers had slid off Jeffries' drink tray. One hit Sir Charles, another smashed on the floorboards; the third was caught in mid-air.

"Well done, Jeffries!" Alec complimented, catching the third tumbler and replacing it on the tray as half a dozen militia, their captain at the helm burst through the door, all brandishing swords.

"And you, my lord," Jeffries replied as he scooped up off the carpet Alec's eyeglasses and handed them to him, all admiration for his master's quickness of eye and hand coordination. "A masterful cricket catch, if ever I saw one!"

"Thank you, Jeffries," Alec grinned, pocketing his eyeglasses and the Duchess of Romney-St. Neots' letter; a ruse, but one, he was relieved, had worked to his advantage.

"This is not over, Halsey!" Sir Charles growled as he was roughly hoisted up by two of the militia, arms whipped behind his back, and marched from the room. "I'll tell all and sundry what I know! Lady Rutherglen! Stanton! I'll let them all know what I know! And they'll listen! No one cares about a shabby vicar! But they care very much about..."

"And I thought the evening was going to be wretched," Lord George exclaimed with a self-satisfied smile, fat fingers splayed to the warmth of the fire as Alec followed the militia out of the room and Hadrian Jeffries closed the door. "Charlie's for Newgate and I'm for bed. Coming, Auntie?"

"The evenin' ain't over yet, Stanton," Plantagenet Halsey pointed out. "Some questions still need answers and you may very well be the person who can answer 'em!"

"Me? What would I know?' Lord George snorted. "Charlie was the bright one. Fat lot of good his brains did him in the end!"

"I'd like to know who had me bopped over the skull by a couple of thugs in Cleveley livery," said Plantagenet Halsey, eyes narrowing at Lord George. He jerked his head at Hadrian Jeffries, who was quick on the uptake and moved to stand in front of the door. He smiled at the valet before saying to the room, "Left their calling card—a Cleveley livery button. Wanted me to think your father was after me. Me and a young lawyer in canary yellow were both accosted. Know anythin' about that, Stanton?"

"Me?" Lord George looked startled. "Not a needle! Dare say Charlie put the footmen onto you. And for that I don't blame him. Father don't like you one drop. You're a damned republican and a public nuisance. Come on, Auntie! Let me help you up."

"And what I would like to know, dear sir, is who killed poor Billy Rumble," Selina said to Plantagenet Halsey, "and why. His sisters and aunt are entitled to an explanation. Such a waste of a young life..."

"Sit down, George," Lady Rutherglen ordered, and flicked open her fan. "We will remain until I've seen with my own eyes that thieving kneeling-whore upstairs."

The door opened and Alec stepped back into the room, having seen the magistrate, the militia and their struggling prisoner off the premises, to hear Lady Rutherglen's proclamation and witness Lord George's explosive response. There was an almost imperceptible swish through the air of a blade, and the loose flabby flesh under Lady Rutherglen's chin was tickled by a sword point before anyone in the room realized Lord George had unsheathed his sword from its ornate scabbard.

"My lord, please put away the sword," Selina asked quietly, a terrified glance at Alec who trod slowly across the room. "Lady Rutherglen doesn't deserve—"

"You've no idea what Auntie deserves!" Lord George spat out. He stared down at his aunt. "Retract! Retract what you said, Auntie, or I swear to God, I'll stick you!"

Lady Rutherglen did not flinch.

"I cannot retract the truth, George," Lady Rutherglen replied in a patronizing tone one uses on a small child. "Miriam was a thief and a liar and a slut. She stole your mother's jewelry and ran away. Mrs. Jamison-Lewis has one of the earrings. See. And you recovered the other pieces yourself from that thieving farm boy. Isn't that proof enough of her deceit?"

"Dear God, Stanton, *you* killed Billy Rumble?" Selina demanded, "For what? A few *trinkets*? He was just a boy!"

"They're the Cleveley diamonds," Lady Rutherglen stated, affronted. "They're worth a king's ransom and that *boy* stole them from Miriam, who had stolen them from my sister. Thus, he was in possession of stolen goods. He deserved what he got."

"He was promised a few guineas to do the deed. How is it then that he is deserving of being cut down and left to die all alone?" Selina argued. "Your nephew murdered that poor boy in cold blood!"

"Murdered?" Lord George exclaimed, a blink at his aunt before addressing Alec, the one person in the room who had not accused him of murder. The sword point remained at his aunt's neck. "I didn't murder anyone! God! Why would I kill a wastrel farm boy? Why go to the effort? Halsey! You believe me, don't you?"

"Come, George, tell the truth," Lady Rutherglen purred coaxingly. "Charles told me everything and I don't blame you one penny for cutting down a filthy fleshmonger. The cripple tried to sell you a child, so he deserved what he got." She looked at Alec. "I challenge anyone to find a magistrate who'll say differently."

"He didn't deserve to die! No child deserves to die!"

Lady Rutherglen smiled thinly at Selina's emotive outburst.

Mindful of her nephew's sword point, she looked straight at her and said, "My dear, you are the last person who has a right to cast stones. The cripple was put out of his misery, for surely he would have been strung up for his crime, and be remembered forever more by family and his parish as a thief and a kidnapper. In the eyes of society George merely did the law's job. You, however, have no reason for your despicable actions towards your unborn children, and the law certainly would not side with you!"

"I didn't kill anyone!" Lord George whined in the heavy silence.

Selina swayed and gripped the back of the wingchair. She dared not look at Alec. "I suffered a-a miscarriage… I lost—I lost the baby…"

"In Paris? That was for the best. Miscarriage is preferable to bringing such ill-gotten progeny into the world for others to deal with. But your actions while you were married were quite deliberate, were they not?" Lady Rutherglen added silkily. "Caroline Cobham told me in the strictest of confidences that you cunningly used methods to prevent conception, thus denying your husband his right to an heir."

"Egad, but you're a cold-hearted serpent!" Plantagenet Halsey uttered, eyes riveted to Lady Rutherglen. He took Selina by the elbow and helped her to a wingchair. He, too, dared not look at Alec as his nephew came across the room to stand beside Lord George Stanton, not a glance at Selina.

"Come, sir!" Lady Rutherglen argued. "You know as well as I that Mrs. Jamison-Lewis's actions are unlawful. They quite possibly are a hanging offence. Thus she, of all the persons in this room, cannot point a finger at my nephew." She put up her chin at Alec. "I suggest we forget all about the death of one insignificant farm boy, and I shall conveniently disremember what Lady Cobham told me about Mrs. Jamison-Lewis. What say you, my lord?"

There was a long silence, so long Selina dared to glance at Alec and wished she had not. He was regarding her with a knot of pain between his brows, and when she looked up into his blue eyes he quickly glanced away and addressed Lord George Stanton, a whisper of the emotional turmoil he was experiencing sounded in his voice.

"Stanton. Be a good fellow and put away your sword… It has been a long night and I think we can all agree that this episode is best ended here."

"I didn't kill anyone!" Lord George whined again, and sheathed his sword as requested. "You believe me, Halsey, don't you?"

"That is not important, George," Lady Rutherglen said with satisfaction, shaking out her velvet and quilted cotton under petticoats. "What is important is taking Auntie upstairs to confront that whore once and for all time."

Lord George stared at Lady Rutherglen and took a step away from her. "So you think me a murderer of children, Auntie? You think I could kill a cripple? Zounds, but the old man is right! You are a cold-hearted serpent!" He went for his sword again, but before his hand as much as touched the jeweled hilt Alec said calmly,

"I do believe you, my lord. And I have every confidence that the truth of what happened to Billy Rumble will come out during Charles's interrogation." He glanced at Lady Rutherglen. "And just how the Cleveley jewelry happened to come into the possession of your aunt."

George glared at his aunt. "I told you! I told you it was Charlie!"

"What I want to know is who thwacked me over the head and set thugs, dressed in the Cleveley livery, on poor Fanshawe?" Plantagenet Halsey demanded loudly, a significant glare at Lord George.

"And made sure to leave silver buttons as calling-cards?" added Alec, a smile at Lord George's response, which was to let his mouth drop open with incredulity that accusations continued to be cast in his direction. "I am confidant further questioning of Charles will quickly reveal he used Cleveley livery and buttons to reinforce the notion it was the Duke or Lord George who wanted to get their hands on Blackwell's will—"

"What would I want with a vicar's—"

"—but in truth, it was Charles who wanted Blackwell's will—" began Alec, cutting off Lord George's bewildered outburst, only to be cut off himself.

"—because with Blackwell's will destroyed, nobody would know the truth contained within it and Stanton here could succeed to the dukedom, no one else the wiser?" Plantagenet Halsey stated and smiled with satisfaction at Alec's nod. "The cunning fox!"

"Look here, old man!" Lord George demanded. "I don't know what you're on about but no one has ever asked me what I want! *Ever*. And what I want is to go to m'bed and sleep for a week! Tonight's mishmash has given me a damned headache."

There was a general grumble of assent and movement of leave-taking in the drawing room, but Lord George Stanton, for all his bravado, did not move. He beckoned Alec over.

"Halsey. You're a Trusty Trojan. Always said so," he said in a low voice. "Tell me the truth. Is it Miriam or Miranda upstairs? I must know. *I must.*"

"It is your cousin Miranda, and that is the truth."

"Come now, my lord!" Lady Rutherglen scoffed, taking her nephew's arm. "You cannot produce compelling evidence to make me believe that the woman upstairs is my dead daughter. Mimi died five years ago of pneumonia after being led astray by her wicked cousin. It is Miriam upstairs. I have seen the portrait. I saw her in the Abbey. That was a shock I admit, but nonetheless, I would know my own daughter. You do not know her, nor have you ever seen her. George and I both know it is Miriam upstairs. The whore has hoodwinked you right royally."

Lord George shrugged her off.

"If Miriam was a whore it was because I made her one! Just as I did Hatty. But Miriam and me… I-I… Just shut *your* mouth, Auntie!"

"She's certainly not my whore," Talgarth Vesey offered, as he languidly stretched himself out of the wingchair. "Mrs. Bourdon is as white as the day I met her."

"Mrs. Bourdon indeed! She can't wallpaper over her past! Whatever she calls herself, she is still Miriam, *not* Miranda."

Lord George ignored her and stared at Alec.

"I must know, Halsey," he pleaded, a pathetic catch to his voice. "She ran away from me. I didn't know why. I think I do now. It was because I got her with child, isn't it? Aye, Halsey, that's the truth of it! But she didn't tell me. I didn't know! No one told me! Constant inebriation keeps her from my thoughts, but if I could just know the truth… I beg of you…"

Alec regarded the obese unkempt and thoroughly repugnant nobleman and wondered if there was any hope of rehabilitation for such an ugly specimen of humankind, one who was pathetically immature in thought and deed and, if Alec had his way, would be sent out to earn a living at some meaningful trade to know the value of honest work. But he begrudgingly had to admit that for all his social ineptitude and worthless preoccupations, Lord George was as much a victim of his milieu as anything else. His mother, his adoptive father, and most certainly Lady Rutherglen had all pandered and catered to his lordship's every whim. What stood before him was a bloodshot, inebriated, whining idler, but for all that, innocent of any crime save falling in love with his sister unknowingly. Perhaps Lord George Stanton's life could be made to mean something; at the very least be steered away from the insidious influence of his aunt and people such as the self-serving Sir Charles Weir. The Duke had started him on some sort of path to rehabilitation by arranging an engagement to Lord Russell's daughter. Perhaps if he could be kept on such a path there was hope for him yet. He knew just the person to aid in this endeavor.

"George! Dearest George, how I've missed you! Come in! Come in and meet your baby brother."

Lord George Stanton continued to hover on the threshold of the bedchamber, all agog. Bear Brown shifted from foot to foot, holding the door wide. It was the Duke who stepped forward and beckoned his stepson into the room where Miranda sat propped up in the four-poster bed cradling her newborn son.

Alec nodded to the mountain-sized servant as he stepped back into the sitting room of the Arch Apartment, smiling as the door closed on the family reunion. He was not smiling when ten minutes later he encountered Selina on the arm of his uncle coming up the main stairs.

"My lord! Alec! I—we need to talk—I want to explain—"

"No! No," he said softly, yet there was no disguising the aloofness in his tone. "Not yet." From his frock coat pocket he took out his godmother's letter. "Tomorrow. Perhaps. I need some time—alone. Goodnight, Mrs. Jamison-Lewis. Uncle."

Selina and the old man watched Alec ascend the stairs and disappear along the passageway to his suite of rooms.

EPILOGUE

Alone in the peace and quiet and sitting before a new fire, a silk banyan thrown over his nightshirt, Alec broke the seal and spread out the single sheet of parchment from his godmother and read.

Dearest Alec

You must come to London at once. I cannot stress enough the urgency of my need for you. Civil war has broken out in Midanich. The Margrave holds firm in the north, while his brother Prince Vicktor has, with the help of French troops, taken control of the south. No family has been spared bloodshed. There are reports of thousands dead and of thousands fleeing to the border. But all borders are closed. No one gets in or out of the principality.

Why am I writing about a minor European principality to you? I can see your frown! What does this old woman care how many Midnachians are killed in their beds? Now you are laughing at me! In truth, I am so distraught I am shaking all over and my hand can barely form the words on the page to tell you. Emily's life is in peril. She is in Midanich. She and Cosmo are prisoners of this Viktor. There is a demand for money and jewels… A lock of my darling girl's hair was sent me as proof. If we do not act on their demands I am told her finger will next be severed to prove their intent.

Dearest boy, come to London at once. I need you…

A.H.

Alec Halsey's adventure continues in...

ALEC HALSEY MYSTERIES, BOOK 3

WINTER 1763. Alec, Lord Halsey is sent on a diplomatic mission to Midanich, imperial outpost of the Holy Roman Empire, to bargain for the freedom of imprisoned friends. Midanich is a place of great danger and dark secrets; a country at civil war; ruled by a family with madness in its veins. For Alec it is a place of unspeakable memories from which he barely escaped and vowed never to return. But return he must, if he is to save the lives of Emily St. Neots and Sir Cosmo Mahon. Awaiting him at his destination is the Margrave and his sister, demanding nothing less than Alec's head on a pike.

CASTLE HERZFELD, PRINCIPALITY OF MIDANICH, (EAST FRISIA), LATE AUTUMN 1763

THE BEDCHAMBER was dark and airless. The odor of stale urine, bloody phlegm, and medicinal, pervasive. Only one branch of candles cast a yellowed haze across the heavily embroidered coverlet from the bedside table. The wicks needed trimming but no one had bothered to call a servant. Focus was on the occupant of the big state bed with its enormous carved headboard—where all Margraves of Midanich came to die.

Leopold Maxim Herzfeld was breathing his last. Shrunken and

weak, he was propped up on soft feather pillows. A white linen night-shirt with fine lace at wrists and collar covered wasted flesh, the collapsed veins in both arms hidden from view. He had been bled so often the fat-bodied leeches could suck their fill no more. In and out of consciousness, he rasped and gurgled, head thrown back and mouth wide, straining to draw breath down a tinder-dry throat to watery lungs.

A devoted servant had removed his master's silk nightcap and in its place had arranged a magnificent wig, the flowing locks pomaded, powdered and curled, as befitted its royal wearer. In life, such an artifice to fashion complemented Margrave Leopold's strong fleshy features. In his dying hours, the wig was a gross conceit. It served to underscore the state to which his health had deteriorated since returning to Castle Herzfeld six months ago, and why the whisperings about poison remained persistent.

A thousand candles illuminated the castle's chapel, where prayers were said around the clock. Devout members of the court came and went, filling up the pews. Some stayed for hours, on their stockinged knees, praying for a miracle—that Margrave Leopold would recover. If he did not, civil war was likely, and this on the heels of a decade of war that had seen the country occupied first by an enemy and then by an ally, both wreaking havoc on the countryside and its people.

Other members of the court, who were not willing to leave the future in God's hands, thought it politically prudent to loiter in the magnificent gilt and marble anteroom off the state apartments. They huddled in their court factions, arguing in fierce whispers, deciding if they would support one prince or the other, or remain neutral when civil war came. None could afford to leave the anteroom, for not only did they fear being betrayed in their absence by their friends, their movements were being carefully monitored by the household guard who lined the walls of the long room, and stood to attention at the doors to the state bedchamber.

Many a nervous courtier bedded down on a makeshift cot, sent lackeys to and fro for food and drink and to empty chamber pots. They scrawled updates to wives, mistresses, and daughters alike, who paced in their apartments within the castle complex, ready to flee with their belongings to their country estate at a moment's notice. Some had decided to take the drastic step of crossing the border into Hanover—the only option left to them if they wished to keep their heads.

Foreign dignitaries and bureaucrats, too, shuffled in and out of the state anteroom, wanting news. No one could tell them anything, so they went away again, and sent their subordinates to rub shoulders with the bewigged throng while they wrote reports home to their masters for instructions—support Prince Ernst, make overtures to Prince Viktor, or get the hell out of there while the country's borders and ports remained open.

Death of the Margrave was a foregone conclusion. So, too, should have been his successor. Son followed father, and had done for thirteen generations. Prince Ernst was the Margrave's eldest son. Yet there were those who favored the more charismatic Prince Viktor taking his father's place. But the younger half brother of Prince Ernst was barred from the succession by virtue of his common birth. The Margrave's second marriage had been a morganatic one.

The Seven Years' War changed everything.

Midanich was overrun by the French and then occupied by the English. Everywhere was chaos, battle and bloodshed. The end of war brought relief from battle, but not from hardship for the Margrave's subjects. And further afield, across borders, political and economic alliances were being redefined and rewritten, and not to Midanich's benefit. Many at court wanted a complete break with the old order, to which Prince Ernst belonged, and staked their lives on change. From his palace in the south of the country, Margrave Leopold had listened to these voices for change, and also to those courtiers who recommended the *status quo*. He had then journeyed north to Castle Herzfeld where Prince Ernst was stationed as head of the Midanich army, crossing the drawbridge and entering the main square with his entourage to the rousing cheers of his war-weary people, the obsequious bows of his courtiers, and the welcoming open arms of his eldest son.

Prince Ernst, who had fought bravely in the war, was honored in a public ceremony with the country's highest military tribute, the

Midanich Minotaur, a star and garter rarely bestowed. It was the last occasion the Margrave was seen in public. He never set foot outside the castle's fortified walls again. Within months, the seventeenth Herzfeld to rule in an unbroken line from father to son lay dying.

The head physician had no idea what had caused the Margrave's illness, but he was certain it was fatal. Yet the Margrave clung obstinately to life, his intermittent terror-stricken outbursts indication his mind was grappling with an inner conflict known only to himself. His physician said he was delirious. His priest said he was purging his soul of guilt. His son agreed with both of them. But no one knew what tormented him.

When the Captain of the Household Guard reported the castle's inhabitants were becoming increasingly restless for news of their ruler, whispers of poison growing daily more confident, Prince Ernst ordered a second detachment of troops deployed throughout the castle. What happened beyond the thick walls of Castle Herzfeld was of no interest—for now.

The court chamberlain appealed to Prince Ernst to have a proclamation of some sort read out, at the very least to the courtiers in the anteroom, if only to quell disquiet amongst their number. Prince Ernst said the court could wait; death would come soon enough.

When the head physician declared death to be imminent, the prince had the bedchamber cleared of its occupants. The Margrave would spend his last earthly moments with only family present.

At the double doors the chamberlain glanced over his shoulder for one last look at the Margrave, whom he had faithfully served for three decades. What he saw made him turn and pause. It was not that his master was unrecognizable in his skeletal form covered in a thin jaundiced skin. It was that the Margrave Leopold had used what strength was left to him to lift an arm off the bedcovers and point a finger in his direction. Alarmed, the chamberlain scuttled back into the dim light, only for the Captain to hiss,

"Leave him, Herr Baron. He's not in his right mind."

The chamberlain ignored him. He went to the end of the bed, the Captain on his heels. The Margrave struggled to lift his head off the pillows, stare fixed, as if willing his faithful servant to read his thoughts. The chamberlain moved up the bed, even closer.

"I beg you…" the Margrave whimpered, looking past his son who had taken hold of his hand, to the chamberlain. "Don't—leave—me… Not—*with her.*"

"Your Highness, of course I will stay if that is your wish."

"He's delirious, Haderslev. He doesn't know what he's saying," Prince Ernst said wearily, then addressed the captain of the guard. "Westover! Get him out of here. He's only upsetting him."

"Of course, Highness," Captain Westover replied and clapped a hand to Baron Haderslev's shoulder. "Herr Baron, it is time to leave."

"His Highness wants me to stay," the chamberlain complained, and shrugged the Captain off to step closer. "So I will stay!"

"Do not worry, Papa. She's not here," was Prince Ernst's whispered reassurance to his father.

"I don't—" the Margrave muttered, agitated, and fell back amongst his pillows. "Ernst. Don't—let her…"

"I made you a promise."

The Margrave closed his eyes, but he was no less agitated. "That—won't stop—*her*… She—she *hates*—me. Hates Viktor—*all of us.*"

Prince Ernst sensed the chamberlain and the Captain hovered at his back and he swiftly glanced around. "My stepmother," he stated, as if they had asked the question. He looked at Captain Westover. "Countess Rosine is under house arrest, yes?"

"As you ordered, Highness," the Captain assured him. "She is not to have visitors, and no one gets in or out without your permission."

Prince Ernst nodded. "And my brother?"

Before the Captain could answer, the Margrave opened his eyes and turned his head on the pillow to stare wide-eyed at his son, and burst out,

"Control her, Ernst. Do not allow *her* to—to—rule *you.*" He let out a frustrated groan of pain and shut tight his eyes again. "Oh God, let this torment end!"

"Be still, Papa," the Prince replied, giving his father's hand a squeeze. He again looked to the Captain and the chamberlain. There were tears in his eyes. "For pity's sake. Allow us these last few moments alone!"

Both men blanched white and bowed low. With a nod they backed away into the shadows to the double doors. The room was so dark it was only with the click of the latch that Prince Ernst knew both courtiers were gone. He also knew his twin sister was there, lurking in the blackness, biding her time, waiting for the others to leave before showing herself, showing who was the stronger of the two. Prince Ernst, the great military leader, fearless in combat, victorious in battle, was weak against the wiles of Johanna.

Princess Johanna appeared out of the blackness to peer down at the father who had banished her from court, banished her from society, and had kept her a virtual prisoner in this fortress for over a decade. She watched him tossing and turning in the big bed under the haze of yellowed candlelight and gently patted his thin hand.

"Papa, I'm here," she whispered, kissing his brow then running a cool hand across his damp hot forehead. "It's Johanna, Papa. Your darling little bird has flown her cage to save you. Papa…?"

The Margrave's eyes blinked wide and he looked for his son. But it was Johanna who stared down at him with a loving smile. He was so overcome he began to cry. And when Johanna kissed his forehead again, murmuring soothing sounds, his thin frail body shook all over with great aching sobs that omitted no sound. She went about tucking his arms back beneath the covers, and then gently removed one of the pillows out from under his head, making sure not to disturb the elaborate full-bottomed wig, and so his head lay flat in the bed.

"It's time, Papa," she said.

The Margrave shook his head back and forth, but he was so weak and with his body now constrained under the bedclothes, he was powerless. What fight for life he had managed to muster in his plea to the chamberlain had vanished. Yet, he still had his voice, thin as it was.

"Ernst!" he pleaded, looking for his son in the shadows. "Are you there?" But when his son did not respond he appealed to his daughter, though he knew this to be futile. But he had to try to reach into her mind—to what was left of it. "Johanna. Listen to Pa—"

"I don't do this for myself, but for Ernst, dearest Papa," Princess Johanna said calmly, covering the Margrave's face with the pillow and holding it firmly in place until her father was utterly still. "You understand that, don't you, Papa? For Ernst."

It was Prince Ernst who gingerly removed the pillow, to the sight of his father, small and frail in the big bed, mouth open, and the magnificent powdered wig askew and covering one eye. He gasped in shock, disbelieving his father was no longer breathing. He put his ear to his mouth, touched his cheek and then his forehead. But he knew, he knew as soon as he had looked at him that he was dead.

The Margrave Leopold Maxim Herzfeld, who had ruled the small principality of Midanich for thirty-five years, was dead. Murdered in his final hour. Prince Ernst, the decorated military hero of the last war, governor of Herzfeld Castle, and Leopold Maxim's eldest son, would now succeed as Margrave and rule Midanich.

And his sister, the Princess Johanna, would rule him.

He burst into tears.

BEHIND-THE-SCENES

Explore the places, objects, and history in
Deadly Affair on Pinterest.

www. pinterest.com/lucindabrant

CPSIA information can be obtained
at www.ICGtesting.com
Printed in the USA
BVHW031920300620
582692BV00001B/117